WALKING

K

WES

DeMOTT

ADMIRAL HOUSE PUBLISHING, Box 8176, Naples, FL 34101
AdmHouse@aol.com

The Library of Congress has catalogued this hardcover edition as:

DeMott, Wes.
Walking K / Wes DeMott. — 1st ed.

   p. cm.
ISBN 0-9659602-6-9 (hardcover)

97-74742

ADMIRAL HOUSE second hardcover printing February, 1998

10 9 8 7 6 5 4 3 2 1

Printed in the U.S.A.

Dedicated to my father,
Arthur L. DeMott,
and all warriors,
throughout history,
who answered
their country's
call-to-arms.

Many first chapters are written on inspiration, but most last chapters require the faith and encouragement of friends and family. Without those precious people, few authors would suffer the process through completion. In my case it was my daughters, Stacy and Kelsey, and their mother, Vicki, who kept me writing — never wavering in their strong support. Thank you, girls.

Thanks also to Sterling Watson, a great writer, teacher, and friend who guided me all the way down the road;

Kathryn Byler Clark, Donna Ceglia, and Gary Byler, who helped me over the finish line;

Robin and Michael Mueller for the use of their sailboat, *Pairdaeza*, where much of this novel was written;

Dr. Bill Aughton, for his unshakable confidence in this story;

and Kevin Casey, for the inspiration and breezes of his oceanfront porch.

"Speaking for myself, I interpret the evidence as saying that P.O.W.s and M.I.A. have been alive, or were alive, up through 1989. I stand on that."—*Senator Robert C. Smith, Vice-Chairman, U.S. Senate Select Committee on POW/MIA Affairs.*

Senator John Kerry:	"Now, with respect to the K up there, it has been referred to occasionally as a walking K. Without getting into great details about walking, does that appear to be a walking K?"
Mr. Erickson, JSSA:	"To me, it does."
Senator John Kerry:	"It does?"
Mr. Erickson, JSSA:	"Yes, it does."
Senator John Kerry:	"And it has the walking appearance, whatever that extra—I don't want to get into any classified area. Do you believe it's distinctly a K?"
Mr. Dussault, JSSA:	"It to me looks like a K, and that's how I think we ought to consider it . . ."

—1992 sworn testimony from members of the Joint Services SERE (Survival, Evasion, Resistance, & Escape) Agency

"Yes, it is possible even as these countries (the United States & Vietnam) become more and more open that a prisoner or prisoners could be held deep within a jungle or behind some locked door under conditions of the greatest security. That possibility argues for a live-sighting follow-up capability that is alert, aggressive and predicated on the assumption that a U.S. prisoner or prisoners continue to be held."—*1993 Report of the United States Senate Select Committee on POW/MIA Affairs*

1

Jacob Slaughter paced to the bed and turned. He made another slow lap of his hotel room as he waited for Lu Kham Phong. His lean, six-foot frame crowded the small spaces, his blue eyes checked his watch, and his mind wrestled with the delay.

He tried to avoid the mirrors, but they seemed to be everywhere, reflecting back the image he had never wanted to see again. It was the frightened face of his own youth, eroded by time to match his forty-six-year-old body. Even now, his fear of this country crawled down his neck like the warm breath of a predatory animal.

The deep cut through his nose was only a shadowy scar and his right cheek had healed from the gouging until it was only slightly more sunken than the left. Laura often told him he was good-looking. But his wide, questioning eyes and raised brows made the mirror's product intolerable to him. He understood the look too well, knew exactly what it said about him. Slaughter was sure of himself where fear was concerned.

Lu Kham Phong had been insistent, demanding, for such a quiet little man. Wait there, he had said. Stay off the streets of Hanoi. Anything could happen here, even now, and the trade agreement between their two governments was much too important to risk an unnecessary setback.

So Slaughter waited in Hanoi's best hotel, taking inventory of all the differences between this room and the last one Vietnam had provided him. And he worried, too, because he knew Secretary of State Walter Mills was worried about his skills as a foreign service officer, and concerned about how much those abilities would be encumbered by his past – reasons Slaughter understood completely. But the Vietnamese Foreign Minister had personally insisted on Slaughter, giving Secretary Mills no option but to send him.

Slaughter stepped to the open window and took in the smells and noises of Hanoi from three stories up. They were less threatening now, more innocent than when he'd been here as a pimpled teenager, a bottle of Clearasil as necessary as his M16A1. He closed his eyes and breathed deep, concentrated on the sounds, discovered that most of them were the noises of any big city. But the rattle of broken-down bicycles set Hanoi apart. Always had, and probably always would.

He stayed at the window with his eyes closed, the vivid memories terrorizing him until they were spooked off by someone pounding on his door. He jumped straight up, then bent, midair, into a crouch. He realized in that same piece of a second exactly how hard this would be for him. Maybe impossible. But he forced himself to the door and opened it. Saw the small men.

The one who'd pummeled the door was stepping back into line with a bitter twist on his little face. Slaughter's stomach knotted and his vision sharpened. He curled his mouth into a smile and stiffened himself against the fear the uniforms unleashed.

He forced his attention from the uniforms to the three men wearing suits. The negotiators. Lu Kham Phong, who had picked him up at Noi Bai Airport, stood in front of the other two like the tip of the spear. He was an intelligent man, American-educated, about thirty-five years old. He was pleasant looking, with tight, smooth skin. Handsome in that dark, precise, Asian way. Slaughter liked him.

Spread along a line behind the negotiators were six armed men wearing the Socialist Republic of Vietnam's current military uniform, along with odd bits and pieces of the old wartime one. Like military men everywhere, they hardened their faces to match the severity of their clothes. As a group, and individually, they looked unpleasant. Some managed the look better than others. Slaughter's smile began to feel stupid, and he wanted to let it fade away. But he didn't. He kept smiling and stepped into the hallway, passed each soldier in slow review, inspected them very closely. Then he stopped in front of Lu Kham Phong. He did not bow.

"Mr. Phong, are these soldiers here to protect me or suppress me?"

Phong did not bow either. He took one step forward and extended his hand. "Hello, Mr. Slaughter," he said in exact English. "They are for your protection, of course. Are you ready?"

Slaughter returned the handshake, watched the soldiers carefully. The oldest, a scarred warrior about Slaughter's own age, stared back, his pistol worn high at the waist in an odd, cross-draw fashion. Several small war decorations hung from his brown uniform.

The five other soldiers were much younger and carried automatic weapons. Chinese AK-47s. They carelessly poked their gun barrels around the hall and into Slaughter's room, their eyes watching for trouble.

Slaughter pulled his focus away from the guns and looked back at Phong. "Yes, I suppose I am, although I still don't understand what this is about. Let me grab my attaché; I'll be right with you."

3

Slaughter turned into his room and headed toward the small desk where his briefcase had sat for a week. He barely heard the noise behind him, but it was enough to spin him around and put him on defense.

The lead soldier, the one with the cross-draw pistol, had shoved his way past the negotiators and rushed into the room. He was five feet away, the weapon already pulled part way out of the holster, almost ready if Slaughter drew a gun from some hidden place.

Deafening panic alarms went off in Slaughter's head, as if the last twenty-five years of freedom had never happened. He was cornered, but not yet trapped. He rushed at the soldier, ready to explode as he raced against the man's reflexes.

But Lu Kham Phong beat Slaughter to the soldier, jammed himself between them, wedged his face into the soldier's and hurled urgent Vietnamese at him. Phong ordered the man to back down, then shouted the order again. Finally, the soldier moved out of the room with four quick, military, backsteps. Phong followed him out, then turned back to Slaughter.

"Mr. Slaughter, I am very, very sorry. Even though a soldier always needs to be on guard for an attack, this officer's actions are unpardonable. I cannot possibly offer enough apologies for them. If you wish, I will see to it that he is severely disciplined."

Slaughter stared at the soldiers in the hall, hands on their weapons, fingers pulsing the triggers. The lead soldier was staring back, looking wholly unrepentant. "No, Mr. Phong, don't bother. Let's just get on with our business."

Phong turned and looked at the soldier again, then spun back around with a narrow smile on his thin lips. "As you wish, Mr. Slaughter. Now, if you are ready, we should go. The others will be waiting, and nothing can be gained by our delay."

Slaughter picked up his attaché and walked into the hallway, stared down into the lead soldier's eyes as he passed. The soldier broke out of the eye-lock and charged down the hall, shoving other guests violently and forcing them back into their rooms at gunpoint.   Slaughter and Phong raced after him, stomping through the lobby and into the sunny street where three vehicles waited. Slaughter and the three negotiators rode together. The soldiers split up and took the front and rear cars.

After almost an hour, the cars slowed in front of a rotting building several kilometers from the other government offices. Slaughter did not know the building, had never been here before. It was big and very old, certainly pre-dating the war. There were few windows in the thick exterior walls. Civilians, crowding along the opposite side of the street, did not look at the building nor venture near it. It seemed to be isolated, quarantined. Although Slaughter had no idea where he was, he felt a scary sense of familiarity. He looked at Phong, who turned away.

Their car stopped and the soldiers jerked the doors open. The older soldier took a position about four meters from the curb, facing the building, waiting for everyone to line up behind him. They did.

Slaughter marched with them through a gate guarded by Army regulars, then continued without slowing, deeper and deeper into the disquieting old structure. Finally, they stopped at a large wooden door. It must have weighed thousands of pounds and hung from four, heavy, wrought iron hinges. The wood was blotched by decades of ugly stains. Lu Kham Phong opened it with a clunky antique key, then led all of them into a dark room. The echoes of their footsteps bounced off far-away walls.

There were no windows. The air tasted like it had been used and reused until it was hardly worth breathing. Four bare bulbs dangled, like ghosts, from the twenty-foot ceiling. Slaughter's eyes had trouble adjusting. When they did, he saw that an eight-foot table had been set up near the center of the room, with four folding chairs on his side. Directly across the room, maybe thirty feet from the table, was another door exactly like the one they had passed through. There was nothing else in the room except filth.

Again, Slaughter looked at Phong. But the handsome young negotiator turned and led his team to the chairs, where they waited, silently, for Slaughter to join them. The soldiers stayed back, all of them waiting for Slaughter. Once he'd taken a seat, they spread out in a line behind him. He set his attaché on the dusty table, then folded his hands into his lap.

And then they waited. Minutes passed in silence, and the silence bred questions. Slaughter's question was, Why? Why were they here? What did this place have to do with America's trade status with Vietnam? He thought about standing and demanding some answers. After all, this matter was supposed to be urgent. He had a right to know why they were wasting precious time.

But he held back, not really sure why. The time would pass. It always had. He could be patient, too.

But the longer he sat there, the harder it was to push back the jangle of panic that had rattled around in him since February 6, 1969 – the day of his last battle in the long-ago war that had spawned today's meeting. He had just made corporal, humping along on a Zippo squad with the 3d Battalion, 3d Marine Division. Although he'd forgotten much of what had happened on that day, the years that followed were burned into his mind with a hot, steel rod.

He shifted in his chair and closed his eyes. The dungeon was getting to him, hitting his senses harder now, throwing his mind back into the dirty concrete cell he'd called home for four years, one month, and one day. Was it the smell? The stench of urine puddles and rotting cabbage – the putrid, signature scents of Far East Prison? His mouth began to taste the stale rice, and his closed eyes replayed the images of fearless rats gnawing at his wounds during his last five hours in the Nam. Those final few hours of captivity had almost destroyed him. Three hundred minutes that had ruined much of his life.

Slaughter's head was banging. His hands were sweating and his guts were trembling. He glanced at the negotiators sitting beside him, looked at their nice suits and carefully combed hair.

6

Did they hear his brain screaming? Had they noticed how heavily he'd begun to sweat?

Suddenly, the heavy door across the room banged, then creaked, then swung open. An emaciated prisoner – a black man wearing pajama pants – shuffled into the huge room under soldiers' guard, his American eyes staring at the distant wall and giving Slaughter nothing of his thoughts. His ancient body baby-stepped slowly, as though his bones and muscles were tangled, the essence of motion forgotten altogether. He had big hands – heavy weights that belonged on the arms of a much taller person. Years in squatty, bamboo tiger cages had hunched his back into an ellipse.

But the man's head stayed level. Proud. Belligerent. Slaughter's eyes swelled with water. He could not take them off the prisoner. He felt his legs moving as the dying specter shuffled toward him. And then, without quite realizing it, he was standing, trying to keep his mouth closed as he lifted a salute to the ragged man.

Slaughter stood there, erect, respectful, waiting for whatever would happen next, unable to hide his shock at the sight of an American prisoner of war. Then, more soldiers began to file in behind the prisoner. And that's when he heard the laughter.

Slaughter's spine squeezed tight underneath his suit coat, and he wanted, more than ever before, to run. Run without thinking. Grab the shabby prisoner and run hard and fast. Carry the man, drag him, whatever. But run until they made it out or were killed trying.

But he stood like a board, didn't flinch an eyebrow, fought to keep his trembling locked inside. Slowly, he lowered his salute and stood firm, clenching himself against the sound of his old enemy. He was back now, the cover of his business suit and diplomatic status lost in the indiscriminate landscape of terror.

Vu Van Vinh slid out from behind his soldiers and took in the room like a toastmaster. He squinted queerly at Slaughter for a few seconds, then threw his head back and gave a wicked laugh of noisy recognition. His flat, stumpy face and jug ears had changed little since he'd been Slaughter's captor, back when Vinh had first imprisoned himself in order to enjoy power over Americans.

Slaughter caught the light in Vinh's eyes, knew he was going to show that power again. Vinh smiled, waited until he had the attention of everyone in the room. Then quickly, in the room's thick silence, he whipped his baton through the air. It buzzed with the warning of pain, then struck the American prisoner across the back of the legs. The old man crumbled onto the concrete floor, his knobby knees breaking the fall with an unsettling snap. But his head stayed erect, and his mouth stayed closed. He gave no sign of pain. Long ago, Slaughter figured, he'd forgotten that it was possible to live without it.

The blow had come too quickly; Slaughter'd had no time to interfere. But he watched Vinh now, leaned in his old guard's direction, his hands on the table and ready to fly over it, dive into the impact zone if more was coming. He was not trembling anymore.

Vinh straightened his simple uniform and grinned as he made polite introductions. "This is your American Captain Charles Wooten. He is guilty of crimes against our people, having used the weapons of your nation to attack civilians in the Phuol Long Province. He is the senior officer of the twenty-three men we still have here."

Slaughter snapped his eyes to the prisoner, tightened him into the sharpest possible focus. My God, could it really be Chuck Wooten? He looked harder at the man, at the pale brown skin and broken teeth. Long, gangly arms with huge, bony hands hanging helpless at the ends.

"Chuck? Captain Wooten? It's me, Jacob Slaughter."

Wooten did not look at him. Instead, he wobbled his head around toward Vinh, who slowly nodded his approval to speak. Wooten's mouth began to move, very slowly, as if he couldn't quite remember how to use it. Everyone in the room waited. And waited. Slaughter leaned closer.

Finally a noise came out. Almost a word, but not quite. And then Wooten quit, lowered his head and watched his own hand scratch a crude letter K in the dust. A tear formed, then dropped, from the blind left eye that wandered.

Vinh started laughing, and kept laughing as he rested the cauliflower stump of his left hand on Wooten's shoulder. Then, quickly, he struck Wooten across his back, hard enough to knock Wooten face down onto the dirty floor. Slaughter lunged, going over the table to protect Wooten. The negotiators scattered at his explosion of power, their briefcases spilling secret contents onto the floor. Metal chairs banged against the concrete floor as Slaughter blasted out of his little piece of the room and headed toward Vinh like a missile.

But it was pointless. The old soldier who'd escorted Slaughter had kept his men close. They grabbed Slaughter's legs and shoulders, dragged him out of the air. Vu Van Vinh's soldiers moved, too, and quickly closed ranks around their prized prisoner.

Slaughter struggled with the restraining hands, shouted at Vinh for the first time, an experience he'd never even considered possible. It would have meant torture, or death, at any of their previous meetings. But he was shouting now and getting louder with each word. "All right, damn you, forget it! I don't need to hear him, I believe it's Captain Wooten. You don't have to beat the poor man, you son-of-a-bitch."

Vinh stopped laughing and charged toward Slaughter. But he stopped just as quickly, distracted by what the prisoner was doing. Wooten was struggling to rise. They all watched as he scraped his crippled hands along the concrete, tucked them underneath his chest, them pushed against the floor with useless determination.

Slaughter gagged and bent over. The bitter contents of his stomach exploded into his mouth. His nightmare and his vision had finally met each other. This quiet pile of noble American flesh proved that Wooten had not died, and his imprisonment

had not ended. He stared at Wooten, then at Vinh, then at
Phong.

This time Phong did not look away. His face seemed
apologetic, and he started to speak. But Vinh's voice burst out,
stopping everyone as the short, terse command echoed off the
black, stone walls. Slaughter stared hard as Vinh came stiffly
toward him, hate pouring from his eyes, his nostrils flaring. He
came all the way to the edge of Slaughter's table, watching
Slaughter's eyes as if looking for the old signs.

Slaughter knew Vinh wanted his fear. He wanted to see it
up close, just like when they'd first met. Slaughter would never
forget the terror he'd known that day. He knew Vinh still
wanted to see it.

Slaughter shoved himself across the table until his breath
collided with Vinh's. And he waited, keeping an eye on Vinh's
right hand, which revolved the baton by squeezing it, then
relaxing, then squeezing again. Keeping his muscles loose and
fluid. Ready. It had only taken a few minutes, but Vinh had
him back now. Back in a place of torture and tap codes, silence
and pain. And Slaughter was standing firm and scared to death.
Again.

Vinh glanced over his shoulder, ordered his soldiers to pick
Wooten off the floor. Then he grinned at Slaughter and ordered
Wooten's food withheld for three full days – almost a death
sentence.

Slaughter struck out, grabbed Vinh's neck and plunged his
thumb and forefinger far behind Vinh's Adam's apple. Instantly,
soldiers began beating Slaughter's back, hammering his skull.
But he endured, would not let go. He was finally killing Vinh,
his fingers closing down on the windpipe like it was a handle.
Slaughter knew he was smiling, rapt with the exhilaration of
vengeance. He was racing his conscience, trying to kill Vinh
before his personal vow ticker-taped across his eyes, his solemn
promise never to kill anyone again. If he hurried, he would
make it. Vinh would die here.

But in the silence of this dream-come-true, where Vinh's gurgling was soundless and the soldier's attacks carried no pain, he suddenly heard Captain Wooten's voice, strange and weak like a death cry. He had to stop. He had to hear it.

Wooten sputtered again, much louder than before. "Khong! Khong!" And then he found his English. "No. Jacob, please, no!"

Slaughter held Vinh's throat for a few more seconds, understanding the plea, realizing that it would fall upon Wooten to pay for Vinh's death, damning himself for his temper. He loosened his grip and pushed Vinh away. Vinh dropped to the floor, his head up and returning Slaughter's hateful stare while his body folded over double. He tried to straighten, but failed – finally staggered out of the room behind the men who had dragged Wooten away.

Slaughter shook off Phong's soldiers, shoved them away from him. His head was leaking blood into his eyes, but he smeared it away and watched the door close behind Wooten. Then Phong touched his shoulder, gently, bringing him back to their business.

"I am very sorry for that, Mr. Slaughter. Although I remember the war from my youth, I am too young to really understand this hatred. Vu Van Vinh is . . . how shall I say it . . . still at war with your nation."

Slaughter stared at the door, listening with very little interest. Once the door was shut and locked, he straightened his clothes, pushed back the bloody mats of his hair and struggled for diplomacy. "You people are bastards, Phong. And Vinh isn't doing this alone."

Phong spoke carefully. "No. There are others like Vinh."

"I'll just bet there are. And you know what, Phong? There are some Americans that haven't stopped hating either. You think they should start torturing Vietnamese? Maybe cruise the streets of Hometown, U.S.A. with baseball bats and Vinh's sense of humor?"

"No, Mr. Slaughter. Of course not. But –"

"You son-of-a-bitch! What you people are doing here is unforgivable. An abomination."

Phong lowered his head. The other negotiators did the same. The guards did not move at all. "Yes," Phong said. "It is."

Phong kept his head down as he held out a thick file for Slaughter. "Sir, I have copies for you of everything we know about the twenty-three men still in prison here. Their names, ranks, serial numbers, places of capture, squadrons or units – everything we've learned from them. It is not very much information, I'm afraid. Apparently they were very good at keeping silent."

Slaughter studied the folder, thought about all the torture the prisoners had endured for the little bits of knowledge it contained. He did not reach for it. Phong held it out until his arm started to droop, finally set it on the table in front of Slaughter.

"What about the rest, Phong? There are over two thousand Americans still missing from the war. You only have twenty-three? Bullshit!"

Phong lifted his head now, looked genuinely surprised. "I do not know what to say, Mr. Slaughter. But since the first release we haven't held anywhere near that many prisoners. Several of the names your country has submitted over the years were never even recorded by our army. Their bodies may have been dumped in battlefield graves or swept out to sea by our rivers. They may have escaped altogether. I honestly do not know. But these twenty-three men we do have. They are the last."

Slaughter opened the expandable folio and flipped through the contents while Phong watched. Duplicate photographs of each tattered prisoner tore at his nerves, but he hid his shock from Phong, or at least tried to. When he could not stand it any longer, he closed the file. "I will take this back to my government, Phong. I hope we'll be able to work through this, but, by God, I'm holding you responsible for these men, regardless of what happens with your trade request."

Phong and the other negotiators bowed now, but held it too long. Slaughter stared at the top of their heads, frustrated, knowing the long bow was an advance apology for more bad news. Finally, Phong and the others raised their heads.

"As you know, Mr. Slaughter, we are a patient people. But the suffering inflicted on my country by the Trade Embargo of 1964 has been severe, and we desperately need to be granted a Most Favored Nation trade status in order to begin putting all the damage behind us."

Slaughter gave Phong's words some time, used the extra minute to calm down a little. "Sure it's been hard for your country, Phong! Hell, that's the purpose of an embargo. That's why we did it! But we restored trade ties in '94 and normalized relations in '95. For a despicable little country that's still holding our men prisoners, I think we've covered more than our share of the distance."

Phong remained silent, his head up but his eyes down. Slaughter turned back to the heavy door, tried to see through it. "But nevertheless, my government will find these circumstances compelling. Disgusting and outrageous – but compelling."

"Thank you, Mr. Slaughter. I am very glad we agree in principle, because the foreign minister has respectfully requested a resolution within thirty days."

There it was, Slaughter thought, just what the long bow had promised. He studied Phong for any weakness to work on.

"Thirty days? Come on, Phong. You know what a delicate issue this is in my country. A thirty-day deadline is ridiculous."

Phong didn't hesitate. "Again, I am sorry, Mr. Slaughter. I can only tell you the instructions I have been given. Thirty days. That is all I have been authorized to offer."

Slaughter turned back to the door which had closed behind Chuck Wooten. He locked the scene into his memory. The sickly skin stretched over frail, old bones. The glazed eyes, the knots, bruises, and scars of torture. His rigid fingers, fused by repeated breakage until they were, simply, claws.

13

"President Simons is sympathetic to your problems. We will do the best we can. That's all I can promise."

Phong bowed again. "I am pleased to have your help with this situation, Mr. Slaughter. My personal hope is that this effort will help my country become an ally to America."

Slaughter did not return the bow. He held the portfolio close enough to feel the pain of its contents. "Phong, I don't give a damn about your country. Or your hopes. I'm doing this for Wooten, and twenty-two other men. Don't you dare misunderstand my motives."

2

The Air Force 727 was somewhere over the Pacific, heading back to the World. But Slaughter's mind was still in-country, thinking: How in the hell could this be happening? After twenty years of bitter denials, why had the Vietnamese suddenly paraded Chuck Wooten out?

Wooten was supposed to be dead. Slaughter had been on the fact-finding mission that had recovered the piece of jaw two years ago. Vietnam's documentation had been convincing, and the pathologist's report was conclusive. Everyone had been absolutely positive that the jaw belonged to Captain Wooten. How could he go back to Washington now and tell Wooten's daughter, Sarah, that it had all been a mistake? Could he ever tell her? What were the odds that those prisoners would actually be released?

He leaned back and closed his eyes, tried to delay worrying about Sarah. He took a deep breath and let his thoughts wander. The plane's engines were whining in a soothing drone, and the humming noise relaxed him a little.

His last flight out of Vietnam was still a fresh memory, as though it was a movie he'd just seen yesterday. All the P.O.W.s were given fresh uniforms on the plane, and they'd helped each other remember how to wear them. There were new shoes, still in the box. And socks. Underwear that felt strange after so many years without it. The Air Force had even sent along a barber to cut their hair and shave their faces. They would look good when they walked down the ramp and touched American soil in front of thousands of spectators. They were going to be heroes, for no other reason than they'd failed at doing their jobs. They had been captured, had been the losers instead of the winners.

But that didn't seem to matter, didn't dampen their exuberance during the plane trip to their homecoming celebration. America needed heroes. President Nixon was going to have them come to the White House for a formal reception. They would be the center of America's attention, even though Slaughter had feared it would overwhelm him.

Six hours after leaving the White House reception, blessed with the country's gratitude and a shiny medal, he'd boarded a Delta jet headed for Houston International Airport, just another Marine in uniform. Nothing too different about him. A soldier going home to his parents, and his old life.

His friends had swarmed over him as soon as he landed, fussed over him like they might a movie star. They shook his hand and bought him beers, organized homecoming parties and had a small parade.

But Slaughter didn't see himself as a hero, or a celebrity, or a novelty of any kind. He was just another man home from the war, looking for the busted pieces of his life. He cut the homecoming short. He had the chance to live a life now, and he didn't want to waste any of it telling tales in bars or accepting honors at ceremonies. The stories weren't worth telling, and he hadn't done anything to earn the honors.

He just wanted to find work. Hard work. But he had never done anything other than the Corps and had never gone to college. The war was over and his education was thin. He knew jobs were scarce.

Surprisingly, several of Houston's business leaders offered him some great options. But they'd only done it out of national pride, or obligation. They felt he was a hero, and they wanted to reward him. But other veterans weren't given the same options, and Slaughter had found it impossible for him to leave them behind.

He finally found his own job, working on an oil rig. He labored on that platform in the Gulf of Mexico for almost a year. It was hot, sweaty work that put big muscles on his lanky frame and confidence back in his mind. He used his free time to write letters to the national chapter of the P.O.W./M.I.A. organization, trying to help the P.O.W.s that were left behind. What could he do to help? What direction could they give him?

A year later – just because he was a former P.O.W. who sincerely believed there were still prisoners there – the National Organization of P.O.W./M.I.A. families plucked him from his oil rig and arranged for him to testify at a morning session of a Congressional hearing. He had been forceful with the Congressmen. Convincing. His testimony brought a lot of attention to the issue of P.O.W.s and to him.

Slaughter never went back to Houston after that. He joined the fight for the P.O.W.s and M.I.A.s full time. Although he was intimidated by the enormity of the United States government, he took it on with zeal and determination.

But it was a formidable foe, a leviathan of red tape. Every request for information or assistance was handled a dozen times, then rejected. It was confusing, frustrating work, but he was committed to it.

Gradually, he realized that he could not work The System without understanding it, so he used his G.I. Bill to pay for night classes at Georgetown University. He graduated five and a half years later and immediately took the State Department exam for foreign service officer. He had lots of contacts in Washington now, and they all seemed anxious to help him get the job.   Secretary of State Walter Mills had personally approved his appointment, burying the record of Slaughter's brief stay in a V.A. mental hospital so deep that it would never turn up.   It was not pertinent information, Mills had relayed to Slaughter.   Some things were better left undisclosed.

Somewhere along the line, not long after his return to Washington, he had met Chuck Wooten's wife and his daughter, Sarah.   As painful as it was, he had told Mrs. Wooten that he did not know what had happened to her husband during those last, hectic days before he was released.   But Captain Wooten had served honorably, he'd said.   And nobly.   She could be very proud of him.

He started visiting Mrs. Wooten regularly after that.   They traded stories about Chuck Wooten and talked about how great it would be if he was alive, waiting for something to happen that would return him to the States.

Slaughter also developed a wonderful relationship with Chuck Wooten's daughter, Sarah, and he had the great pleasure of watching her grow up.   She was a cute girl, with a striking face and chestnut brown skin.   She liked his jokes and his company, and they became great friends.   He never missed any of her birthdays or graduations.   He had given her away when she married Benjamin, and he was there with Mrs. Wooten when both of Sarah and Ben's kids were born.   He was their kids' godfather, and he loved them just as if they were his own. He baby-sat for them every chance he got, rolled and played with them until they were exhausted from laughter.   They were his family.   He loved them that much.

Two years ago, Slaughter had brought home Wooten's remains, and Mrs. Wooten had finally accepted her husband's death.   She closed herself off from Slaughter, another broken victim of a terribly costly war.

Sarah, however, never gave up on her father, even when they laid the proud memory of Captain Wooten to rest at Arlington National Cemetery.   Slaughter had walked with her from the grave site, silent, waiting for her grief to pour out.   But it hadn't come. Instead, she'd stopped at the car, stood on her toes, and hugged him. Then she squeezed his hand. "Don't feel so bad, Jacob," she had said. "That wasn't my daddy we just buried. His last letter promised that he would come home to us. And I believe he will, Jacob. I'll never stop believing that he will."

And now it looked as though she might be right.

The jet shook in some heavy turbulence. Slaughter opened his eyes, leaned over and looked down at the vast Pacific Ocean – beautiful, desolate, and empty. It was hard to believe that millions of animals lived below the surface, hidden by the reflective, blue screen that protected them.

He kept staring down, fascinated with the thought that when he'd been given this assignment, his briefing had mentioned that the Vietnamese were ready to contribute some new evidence on the P.O.W./M.I.A. issue. It was, of course, their standard procedure when they wanted something. They had done the same thing dozens of times since the war ended - promise the United States more help in searching for remains, exchange their promise for a shift away from economic sanctions.

But there had been nothing concrete about this most recent offer, nothing in it was extraordinary. No one at the State Department had even thought to consider that there might actually be prisoners still alive over there. Korea, sure. Everyone knew a handful of American prisoners remained there. But not Vietnam. America had pushed too hard, looked every place imaginable. They were all gone. Lost. The P.O.W. families, and Slaughter himself, had mostly given up, consigned themselves to sad hopes of a wedding ring, maybe, or a femur. Something tangible to bury. Anything.

But he had just seen Wooten with his own eyes. Seen the usefulness of his life gone, vanished, like the pieces of teeth that had been smashed out of his mouth. He thought about Chuck Wooten, knowing that he'd long ago stopped counting the days, weeks, years, and decades. That poor man had managed to survive in that awful place, probably cursing America for abandoning him yet still praying that someday his country would come for him.

A lieutenant walked down the plane's aisle toward him, his khaki uniform pressed crisp, his thin, little face too sweet to have ever seen war. He was the only other person on the plane except for the cockpit crew.

"Excuse me, Mr. Slaughter.   Secretary of State Mills is calling for you."

Slaughter took the phone, pushed it to his chest. "Lieutenant, how secure is this line?"

"Very secure, sir.   The same signal-scrambling as the president's plane."   The lieutenant smiled when he said "president," obviously impressed with himself.

Slaughter nodded. "Thanks."

"Yes, sir."

After the lieutenant turned back toward the cockpit, Slaughter took the call off hold.   "Hello, Mr. Mills.   This is Slaughter."

"How are you, Slaughter?"   Secretary Mills' voice was thin and tinny, a nervous balance of power and intelligence.

"I'm fine, Mr. Mills."

"Call me Walter, okay? Your star seems to be rising so you might as well start dropping some of the formality around me."

"Fine with me, Walter."

"Good.   So tell me, how did it go over there?   Did the Vietnamese bring anything new to the table, or did they just give more lip-service to healing old wounds?"

Captain Charles Wooten shuffled into Slaughter's vision with that long-dead look in his good right eye.

"Sir, you might say they brought something very interesting to the table."

"Is that right? What was it?"

"I'm really not comfortable with this communication link. Can we wait until I get back to Washington?"

"I think, Slaughter, that you can feel confident with the security of your circumstances."

"Maybe so, Walter. But I'd rather wait."

"Well, I'd rather know now! What did they say?"

The line was silent. Maybe a minute, maybe five. Slaughter didn't know, and didn't really care. Time was relative. Its value depended on where you were. And right now, Slaughter's mind was in prison, a place where time was almost meaningless.

"Slaughter, damn it, what did they say?"

"I'll be in my office first thing tomorrow. I'd really prefer to talk then."

"You'd better not be screwing around with me!"

"I'm not. I'm sure you'll understand when we meet."

Mills muttered something, banged things around on his desk. But then he quieted down, began talking like a professional. "Okay, Slaughter, I can't force you to talk. You want to do it in the morning, we'll do it in the morning. I have a meeting with President Simons at seven o'clock. You will be here by five-thirty a.m. Sharp. I don't care if you have to come straight from the airport. Do you understand?"

Slaughter brushed at his jacket, still trying to dust the prison filth from his clothes. "Yes, sir."

"Good! Have your brief ready so that I can pass it along to the president. He's very interested in what you've found out."

"Really? Why? If this was just a routine trade meeting, why is Simons so interested?"

"He just is. All foreign policy matters are a priority with this administration. You know that."

"No, I guess I didn't."

"Well, you know it now. Five-thirty. Got it?"

"I'll be ready. I've started on my brief already and will be working throughout the flight home."

"You'd better. Good-bye."

Slaughter held the phone long after it went dead. Mills was angry, but it didn't really matter. Slaughter's report could generate all kinds of activities, from political concessions to trade agreements to military strikes – whatever it took to get those twenty-three men home. He would not risk an accidental disclosure. If Mills was angry, tough.

He rolled around Mills' statement that had bothered him instantly – why was President Simons suddenly so interested? When Slaughter had left Washington, he'd been given vague instructions, no fanfare, and extremely low expectations of anything significant happening on this trade mission. So why the great interest now? What did Simons know? What did Mills know? What didn't he know?

His decision was instinctive. For now, he would not disclose any information about the other prisoners. Just as Mills had taught him, some information just didn't need to be disclosed. He would show them Wooten's picture and run that information up as a trial balloon. Then wait and see what happened. He could tell the rest of the story anytime after that. It didn't really matter what the consequences might be. By God, he was going to save Chuck Wooten. If he compromised his career a little, who cared? Getting Wooten and the others back was all that mattered. They were his responsibility now, just like he'd once been Wooten's. He would do as good a job getting them out as Wooten had done keeping him alive. Better, even, if that was possible. But he doubted it.

He closed his eyes again, tried to get comfortable with the deceit. Captain Wooten was alive on the back of his eyelids. Alive and big and strong, and coming out of his parachute harness, his pistol in his hand as Slaughter's squad cleared the tree line, going to get the pilot they'd seen eject from his disabled F-4 Phantom. It was a fool's mission, just like every other one in that hot, shitty landscape.

But the V.C. were coming, too. Across the clearing Slaughter could hear their shouts – short little pops of a strange language. Slaughter understood them clearly. Not the words, maybe. Not back then. But the meaning was clear in any language. Adrenaline, aggression, fear. War.

Slaughter forced his eyes open. His tie was too tight, so he loosened it, then reached up to adjust the air flow. He picked up the phone and dialed.

"Hello. Dr. Warner's office."

"This is Jacob Slaughter for Laura Warner."

"Yes, Mr. Slaughter, hold on, please."

He took three quick breaths, then a deep one that he held as long as he could. "Jacob?" Laura's voice was sincere, sensitive. She was like that with everyone, but much more so with him.

He pushed the air out. "Laura. Hello. How's your morning going?"

"Good. Where are you?"

"I'm on my way home."

"Great. I've really, really missed you. How did it go over there?"

"Fine." He looked down and saw that his hand was caressing Phong's portfolio.

"Really?"

"Pretty good."

She was quiet for a few seconds. "What's wrong?"

He pulled his hand away from the portfolio, dabbed at the minor gashes Phong's soldiers had made on his skull, struggled to think of something other than the prisoners. "Nothing, I'm just hungry, that's all."

"You're sure?"

"I'm sure."

The dialogue stopped. She had one of the finest psychiatric minds in Washington. Right now she was using everything she'd learned in twenty years of counseling vets for the V.A. and running his words and tone through that processor. He knew what she was doing. He appreciated it.

When she spoke again it was soft, understanding. "It was just as hard as you feared, wasn't it?"

No, not true. It had been much harder. Worse than the memory, worse than the nightmares. Worse than all of that. "Yes."

"I was afraid it would be. Do you want to talk?"

He stood and paced a tight circle in the plane's narrow aisle. "No. Not right now."

"Have you spoken to Walter?"

"Walter? I assume you mean Secretary of State Mills?"

"Don't act like that, Jacob. It makes me wish I'd never told you about him and never introduced you two. You know I love you, so please, just stop it. Okay?"

He pinched himself for saying it. "I'm sorry, Laura. It's just awkward, now that I'm working closely with him. But you're right; I'm being foolish. To answer your question, yes, I've talked to him. Just hung up with him."

"Good. That's good. When will you be back in Washington?"

"About eleven o'clock your time."

"I'll come to Andrews Air Force Base and pick you up."

"You don't have to do that."

"I know."

"You're sure you don't mind?"

"I'm sure. It's not a problem."

She was silent. He was, too. It was time to hang up, and all of their good-byes included silence. The last sentence, a few seconds of awkward silence, then good-bye.

"Good-bye, Jacob."

Slaughter cut the connection, dropped his head, and closed his eyes. He hoped that eventually he'd get used to seeing Chuck Wooten there again.

3

One nightmare, one terrible scene had haunted Slaughter's sleep for twenty years. He had managed to escape it once, had been a free man for the last two years, ever since he returned home with Wooten's body. It had taken lots of secret counseling and a lifetime of work for the P.O.W.s. But he had earned his release from guilt. Every night at bedtime he prayed that it would never come back.

It was back now, though. He was forced to watch Chuck Wooten shuffle through his mind in prisoner's shackles – an endless, painful parade with his cell-mate coming around again, and again, and again.

But Wooten understood what Slaughter had done, knew there had been no choice but to follow orders. You could see in the grim ghost's sad eyes that he didn't hate Slaughter for it. Slaughter was sure that Wooten would have said so as he filed past, said something brave and understanding. Except that he would have been too severely punished by the guards.

Some fingers touched Slaughter's arm, snapped his mind out of the Vietnamese prison. He twitched violently, hurled himself out of his sleep and onto his feet. His eyes popped open, and he searched for a target among the empty seats of the 727.

The young lieutenant leaped back, six feet down the aisle, not a trace of confidence remaining on his sweet, young face.

"I'm sorry, sir," he said. "Sorry. Really. I didn't mean to startle you."

Slaughter tried to disarm himself. He dropped his hands and eased his stance, took two deep pulls of cabin air. "It's all right." He took another breath, held it, exhaled slowly. "What do you want?"

The lieutenant was trying to look brave. But his shoulders were up around his ears and his face was pinched into sharp attention. He looked like a mouse at the first sound of footsteps.

"It's a little after twenty-three hundred hours, sir. We'll be landing at Andrews shortly. I thought you might want a few minutes to get squared away."

Slaughter searched the young man's face, but found they had nothing in common. The lieutenant had not seen war yet, and therefore had no basis for understanding.

"Thank you."

"You're welcome, sir." The lieutenant backed to the cockpit and fumbled behind him for the door handle. He never took his eyes off Slaughter.

There was a warm Coke by his seat, and Slaughter rinsed some of it through his mouth. It had been a long, long flight. Lots of time had been lost in the battle to save Wooten. Laura would be waiting for him and he looked like shit. Time to get it together.

He walked back to the head and washed up, scrubbed his finger across his teeth and brushed his hair over the scabs from his short beating. He carried the portfolio with him the whole time, held it tight with one hand, the corner jabbing at his ribs, the pain feeling natural and necessary.

He returned to his seat, opened the flap and stared into the portfolio until he gathered enough courage to drag out the pictures. They were bad. Awful photos of brave American fighting men – beaten, and shamed, and degraded. And forgotten. The world had gone on without them, had left them behind and stopped caring.

He stared at each man for a few seconds, then flipped to the next picture. The photos hurt a lot, but he deserved the pain. When the wheels touched down he closed his eyes, made sure he remembered every one of the prisoner's faces, then forced the photographs back into the file.

Laura's car was parked just beyond the Transient Aircraft Line. He stood at the open door of the jet until the steps were wheeled over and secured. Then he climbed down, hurried over to her car, and slid in.

Laura leaned over to kiss him. The courtesy light cast a shadow that made her brown hair and dark features a little hard to distinguish. But then, just before their lips touched, he made a wonderful connection with her soft brown eyes, and he knew he was home. Back where he belonged.

She was wearing faded jeans. Business suits to work; jeans just about everywhere else. A light cardigan sweater over a dark blue T-shirt. White Reeboks. No make-up. Her hair was pulled back in a ponytail, which chased around behind her each time she moved her head.

She wore the comfortable smile of intelligence – the educated woman who held all the secrets, knew everything about him. She kissed him again, slipped her hand around his arm. "I'm happy to see you, Jacob."

It was a big welcome from her. Laura loved him deeply, he was sure, but she wasn't a woman who displayed much emotion. She seldom attempted a passionate phrase or a sensual display of affection. Too many years dealing with other people's lives, he figured, had put a heavy lock on the door to her own feelings. But he knew those feelings were there, was absolutely sure that she loved him.

He smiled and pulled his door closed. "I've missed you a lot."

She glanced at his head, noticed the small scabs as she watched him with those big, sympathetic eyes. It was clear that she understood – could see that his nightmare was back. Her fingers wrapped around his forearm and squeezed hard. "It was bad, wasn't it?"

His eyes went to the floor.

"Jacob, I can help you with this. We've worked through it before and we can do it again. This is just a setback, unless you decide to let it become a failure."

"Yes, I know. I appreciate your help, and I'll definitely take you up on it. But right now, I have to keep this to myself."

She squeezed his arm again, then released it, shifted around and started the car. "I understand. But, eventually, you'll need to talk about it if you want to continue getting better. You know that. I'll be here when you're ready. I'll always be here to help you. No matter what."

"I know. Thanks."

They rode in silence. Slaughter was too tired to be sharp, suspected that Laura was too busy interpreting the silence to interrupt it.

Slaughter was trying to put Chuck Wooten out of his mind until five-thirty tomorrow morning. He had worked most of the flight and hammered out a report and a trade agreement he hoped would provide both sides with acceptable terms. He'd worked on it until even the Navy coffee couldn't keep him awake. Now he needed some rest. A couple of hours, maybe, if he was lucky. This assignment already had the potential to become impossible. Without a few hours sleep he would not stand a chance.

Laura parked at the brownstone they'd bought together last year, a major step in their slow-moving relationship. It was one of the nicest homes on the block, remodeled just before they bought it, and already worth much more than they had paid. She jumped out, quickly, gracefully, then turned and waited for him.

He stepped out onto the curb and looked around at the city. Even at this late hour, cars were rushing through signals, people walked along the street, and the glow of a million lights declared that this city was still open for business. His senses made the identification – freedom – and he savored it. He had not taken it for granted since his return in 1973.

She took his hand, slowly, and looked up into his eyes, watched him look around, probably knew what he was thinking. Then she hooked her arm through his. "Ready?"

"Yes."

"Let's go then. I have some wine chilled. How about a glass before bed?"

"That would be great."

They entered the brownstone and Slaughter set his suitcase and attaché by the door. His mail was stacked on a small hall table, but he resisted the urge to look at it. Instead, he gently put his hands on Laura's shoulders and turned her around. Pulled her close. Wrapped her up in his arms. Held her tight and long and quietly, his face pressed into her soft hair, her subtle perfume washing the stench of prison from his nostrils.

She held him, too, her body pressed into his, her head nestled underneath his chin. She ran her hands up and down his back, scraping her nails against his shirt. Her touch was sincere, loving, in an easy, unquestioning way. It felt wonderful, and would have felt even better at some other time. But tonight, with Wooten's ravaged body so fresh in his head, this would be as far as they would go. He was sure she would understand. She always did.

She slipped away after a few minutes, went to the kitchen to pour them both a glass of Chardonnay. He took off his shoes, then followed her. They sipped the wine over a gentle conversation of little consequence.

An hour later, they were in bed. She wore one of his soft, old T-shirts, and he rubbed her back until she fell asleep. He kept rubbing after she'd drifted off, hoping that his turn for sleep was not far away. But another three hours passed, lonely and

29

silent, filled with worry about Chuck Wooten and the other men. Finally, exhaustion caught up with him and he dozed off.

His lieutenant was shouting into the PRICK 25 handset, racing his radioman to the clearing. "Roger, that, Sandy. Fly in from the east, lay down some Willy Pete at the southern edge of that tree line. We're gonna try to get the downed pilot, then meet the parajumpers at the LZ in about twelve minutes. Have 'em ready to extract, buddy, 'cause we'll sure as hell be under heavy fire! You got it?"

Slaughter ran along with them, the pressurized fuel tanks bouncing up and down on his back, the straps digging at his collarbone. He exchanged eye flashes with the radioman, sent him a signal of empathy. They were both tall men, and therefore, soul mates. Both of them were assigned heavy-ass pieces of gear to hump through this hot-as-hell section of Earth. Sometimes they laughed about their burdens, especially when Slaughter swore he was going to run naked into his C.O.'s tent and show him how skinny he really was. Tall, sure. But skinny.

But they were not laughing now. It was unimaginable. The weight of the equipment oppressed them like the heat. Fear made their loads unbearable. Slaughter had to fight it, and humor was his weapon.

"Damn, Louis, you see that pilot. Look man, it's Bill Cosby."

The radioman looked up at the parachute, then shook off the joke. "Don't start up with your shit, Slaughter. I'm way too puckered here."

"No shit, man. Bill Cosby falling out of the sky, right on top of a V.C. patrol. Don't that beat all. Hell, that U.S.O. is doing all right by us."

"Knock it off, Slaughter. Man, your dumb-ass jokes are going to get you killed someday."

Slaughter tried to laugh as they ran, but the lieutenant interrupted, shouted to the M-60 machine gunner and his assistant. "Soulful, Big-Time – you guys set up at the edge of the clearing. Get The Pig ready to rock 'n roll. Little Brother, you stay back, too. Give us lots of suppressive fire. The rest of you guys come with me, keep your eyes peeled. Going out into the open like this is going to suck!"

Slaughter angled off, looked back and winked at the radioman who was hooked to the lieutenant by the coaxial umbilical cord. The other men moved farther apart too, running in that weird way that only happens when you're hurrying your ass toward some very serious trouble. They were still protected by the trees now, trip wires and toe-poppers their biggest worry. But in a few seconds they would be in the clearing, a hundred yards of open rice field with Bill Cosby landing in the middle of it.

Slaughter ran to the edge of the shadows, forced himself to charge into the sunny clearing. It was like diving into treacherous waters. Sudden, bracing, frightening. All senses on alert and popping their messages back to his brain. His pistol was still in its holster, his hands were filled with the flame-thrower nozzle as the rest of his equipment swung from web belts in a rhythmic jangle.

And by God, how he could run, covering ground like a sprinter, even with all his bulky gear. He was the first one there, overran the fighter pilot just as he climbed away from his tangled parachute with his pistol at the ready. So far, so good – no shots fired. Slaughter ran past the pilot, set up in front of him and the lieutenant, adjusted the nozzle and prepared to lay out a long stream of flame that would burn the flesh off anyone who dared approach the opposite tree line. They would be here soon. He could hear them coming, chattering and breaking branches as they raced for the prize from the other side of the clearing.

But then, the world suddenly fell silent, like the moment before an opera begins. Slaughter shifted his position, cursed the mud that sucked at his boot and filled his ears with worthless sound waves.

And that was when hell busted wide open. Viet Cong and N.V.A., moving up to the clearing and hiding among the trees, began laying down heavy fire. Slaughter heard his lieutenant scream. He turned and saw him blasted backward in a crimson shower, his helmet ripped from the chin strap by the bullet that entered it, front, dead center.

All of Slaughter's squad was firing back now, full auto, their terrified young fingers strangling the grips and triggers of their weapons. The gunfire was deafening and constant in both directions. Where were the white phosphorous bombs? Where were the gunships? Damn it, Sandy, get down here and give us some smoke!

Two V.C. ran along the edge of the clearing and Slaughter opened up on them, incinerating them with a long tongue of high octane. Then he dug deeper into the mud, ready for the down side. He kept his eyes wide open, searching, knowing that his hundred-yard ribbon of flame had centered their attention on him. He had to be ready.

And he was ready, but nothing moved. His flame thrower seemed to have incinerated every sound of battle. An insect buzzed near his ear, just before the bullet struck and the world winked out.

"Name?"

An English word, certainly, but the Vietnamese accent made it hard for his aching head to understand. He didn't answer, lay quietly where he'd been dumped on the dirt floor of the bamboo hut.

"Name?" The short man in the Communist uniform stood over Slaughter and twisted a wooden baton in his right hand. His entire left hand was missing, a raw, wart-like stump at the wrist. His voice was angry, his face red and shaking. Sweat covered most of his uniform.

The baton went up over Slaughter's ribs, aimed at a spot just above his badly bandaged bullet wound. It vibrated in the air, gave him one last chance to answer. Slaughter tightened his muscles, but they spasmed, moved the broken rib in his back where the bullet had exited. He held back his scream and waited, too hurt and scared to think or answer. He watched the tip of the baton, wondered how it was going to feel when it smashed into him. What part of his body would the man attack after smashing his ribs? His head? His groin? His legs? There were no good choices; it was all too terrible to think about. The soldier could do whatever he wanted; no one would stop him.

Slaughter tried to remember a prayer, a good prayer that might help him. Something that would impress God with its sincerity. But nothing came except childhood verses. He closed his eyes and began, silently. Now I lay me down to sleep, I pray dear Lord my soul –

Suddenly, a voice came from behind him. An American voice that was as calm and peaceful as a Sunday picnic. A powerful voice that said, "Hey, hold on there a minute, mister."

The baton cut the air in a fast arc over Slaughter, diverted away from his ribs at the last possible second. The interrogator's head snapped up and onto another prisoner as his neck and shoulders absorbed the explosive power of his arm.

An American – the black pilot they'd gone out to get – sauntered into view above Slaughter's face, reached down and picked the chain of tags off his neck.

"His name is Slaughter, Jacob V., Corporal, United States Marine Corps. Service number 2122700." The pilot set the tags back on Slaughter's chest, smiled like a father as he touched him on the shoulder, then stepped away.

The interrogator had listened to this brief performance with a stunned look on his flat face, his upper body twitching like he'd been electrocuted. He kicked Slaughter in the head, then ran at the pilot, who was stepping back to line up with the other men. The interrogator's mouth opened wide as his eyelids peeled back. He leaped at the pilot, shrieking insane Vietnamese as he smashed his baton against the pilot's collarbone. Slaughter squeezed his eyes closed, heard the pilot's skin rip and his bone break. Heard absolutely nothing from the pilot.

The interrogator was screaming now, jumping up and down into the pilot's face. "What is your name?"

The pilot's voice still sounded calm, but intense. Burdened with pain. "Wooten, Charles R., Captain, United States Marine Corp. O135680. Semper Fi, you asshole."

Slaughter had to open his eyes and look. He couldn't believe what his ears were hearing. Muffled laughter came from the other American soldiers. Nothing big, certainly. In fact, it was hardly louder than a whisper. But it was laughter all the same. The insolent kind that runs in close partnership with unspeakable fear. Slaughter couldn't see very well from where he was lying, but it sounded like five or six Americans. He heard the pilot laughing, too, although not very convincingly.

But they all stopped when the interrogator cocked his baton again. Slaughter ignored the pain in his head, rolled back on his neck until he could see them all clearly. Six men, including Wooten, stood in line, none of them laughing now. Wooten stood solid, waiting, watching as the baton made a big, speedy arc toward him. The interrogator smashed Wooten in the face, just below the nose. The crackle of shattering bone and splintering wood tortured Slaughter's ears.

"Noooooo," Slaughter screamed. He tried to get up and go help Wooten. But someone began to shake him violently.

"No, you son of a bitch!"

He shot his hands out, desperate to punish someone, anyone. He was shoved again, and this time his hands caught hold of a neck. He held on, squeezing and shaking it like a savage animal, trying to kill one enemy, then hoping for another, and then another.

"Jacob, wake up! Oh, God, please wake up. It's a nightmare, Jacob! Jacob! It's your nightmare!"

He opened his eyes and found himself on his knees with Laura pinned in his grip. He stopped shaking her. Moved off of her body. Stared at his hand like it was possessed.

Laura jumped up and ran to the corner of the room, clutching her throat and watching him, terrified. Angry. Hurt. All of her pain and fear pouring out of her eyes as she stood there, trembling. He tried to look at her, but he was too ashamed. He didn't know what to say. Finally, he sat down on the edge of the bed, staring at his hand and hating himself for the return of the dream, damning himself for hurting Laura.

"I'm so sorry, Laura. I'm so very sorry. Are you all right?"

She eased away from the corner, just a little, catching her breath, still holding her neck. But he could see she was settling down, going slowly from victim to psychiatrist, her love for him beating back her fear of him.

She sat down beside him, slowly, then stretched her arm around his shoulders and pulled him close. Pushed his head into her lap and stroked it, gently touching the scabs with her fingers. "It's all right, Jacob. It's all right. I'm okay. Shhh, now, everything will be okay."

He twisted his head and raised his eyes to hers. He dug in deep, desperately searching her mind for the switch that would turn off the nightmare. It was in there, someplace. She'd gotten him through this before, had almost cured him completely. But now he was back at the beginning, back where he'd been when he had first gone to her.

And for what? Was anything going to be different this time? Hell, no. He knew the truth, understood that this was another fool's mission. The Vietnamese were never going to release those prisoners. After all these years, and all his work, he would still not be able to help Chuck Wooten. But he would suffer the nightmare all over again. For nothing.

Finally, he took a deep, slow, shaky breath. Then another. She did the same. And then she was crying, softly. Rocking him gently in her arms.

He closed his eyes and waited for daylight, silently reciting the only prayer he'd ever known to work.

4

The Vietnam Memorial was only a short walk from Slaughter's parking place at the State Department. Fifteen minutes, even if you were moving slowly. He had more than enough time. Shame, embarrassment, and frustration had driven him out of Laura's caring arms, and he'd had no other place to go but State.

It was four-thirty a.m. when he climbed out of his car and locked the doors. Washington was dark and, for the most part, quiet as he walked down the hill toward The Wall, passing through the shadows created by the Lincoln Memorial's lights.

He was completely alone when he stepped up to the statue of three soldiers on patrol. He stayed there, staring up at their faces, understanding the pensive look of "Hey, listen! Did you hear something over there?" in their eyes. It was one of three looks for soldiers on patrol, almost like the facial expressions were government issue. One of four looks if you counted how people looked when they were dead. Some guys counted it; some guys didn't.

He watched the soldiers for a few minutes, couldn't help but look where their stone eyes were looking, and listening for what they'd heard. Then he walked down the sloping sidewalk beside The Wall.

It was as if he was wading into a deep stream. The names of the dead rose up beside him, piled on top of each other like a mass grave. Thousands of names, etched neatly into the shiny stone as if they should be proud to be there.

Like always, he found his lieutenant's name first, eighth row from the bottom, fourth name from the left. Not far away was the name of the radioman, Louis. And then, one by one, he found the names of the five other Marines that had died in that muddy field on February sixth, nineteen sixty-nine.

He did not touch the names with his fingers anymore. He had stopped doing that years ago, hadn't done it for thirty visits, at least. But he still cried for them. The tears would not stop coming when he was here. He would resist, sure, but it was impossible. He could walk down the slope without too much trouble and make it all the way to the bottom, where the names of the dead loomed highest over him. But when he stopped at the names of his friends and thought about them, he would always cry. He didn't expect that to change. He wished like hell it would.

He was still staring at the wall and crying softly when a man in well-worn camouflage clothing stepped out of the shadows and walked up to him. He looked like he'd just woken up. Craggy lines were etched into one side of a terrible face that was partially hidden behind a dirty gray beard. His brown eyes looked to be glazed over by alcohol. A Ranger patch rode his sleeve. In any other place on the planet, Slaughter would have guarded himself against the man, turned to keep an eye on him, or walked away. But here, in D.C.'s criminal darkness, Slaughter was not afraid.

The man stood silent, a quiet, powerful presence that seemed ready to help, if help was needed. He never said a word, just stood shoulder to shoulder with Slaughter and stared at the wall with him.

After fifteen minutes, Slaughter started to leave. The man moved for the first time, swiveled his head around to face Slaughter. Then he nodded, slowly. His eyes, too, were wet with fresh tears. Slaughter nodded back. Then he walked away. At the top of the monument Slaughter looked again. The soldier was still standing at sloppy attention, staring at The Wall, five o'clock in the morning.

Slaughter stepped into Secretary of State Mills' office at five twenty-five a.m., his first full day back in Washington. In the great tradition of statesmanship, he immediately looked Mills over while he searched his own mind for common ground.

Today it was easy; they had three basic things in common. They were both forty-six, they both looked like shit, and they both loved Laura. He would have been a lot more comfortable with only the first two things.

Mills' green eyes were traced by red veins. His short, thin, frame seemed weaker than usual, as if he'd been in a fight last night and lost. His pleasant, narrow face had aged significantly in the week and a half Slaughter had been gone. Dark circles and sagging eyelids seemed like tarnished settings for his emerald eyes. He sat in a droopy position, hiding his pointed jaw and thin lips behind a Captain Kirk Star Trek coffee cup—one that was never, ever seen on his desk after eight a.m.

Mills was peeking over Captain Kirk's head, watching Slaughter cross the room, studying him, too, and examining his steps as if they were going to tell a secret. It was the way men like Mills and Slaughter made their living. Pick up all the non-verbal clues they could, then season their meaning into the words about to be spoken. Mills stood up, still watching Slaughter, and waved him over.

Slaughter crossed the large office, his suit coat over one arm, his briefcase containing Phong's portfolio in the other. He stepped up against the huge oak desk and held out his hand. "Good morning, Walter."

"Have a seat, Slaughter. There's coffee on the bar."

Slaughter sat down, tossed his coat onto another chair. "No, thanks. I've still got the jumps from the gallon I drank on the flight back."

Mills focused closely on Slaughter's face, gave him a steady stare, looked harder for signals now that the dialogue was going. "Hell of a long trip, huh?"

"You bet. When you think about it, it's amazing how much attention America focused on that distant chunk of ground. All of the ships, planes, men, and equipment we sent over there for something we thought, at the time, was absolutely necessary. Like the threat was in our own backyard. Now, hell, it's just like you said – nothing but a long, long trip."

"I know what you mean."

Slaughter broke the stare. Nodded. "Yeah." He leaned back in his seat and rubbed his burning eyes again. Waited.

Silence seeped in from the other offices, all of them empty this early in the morning. No phones were ringing, no feet moved down the hall. Soon, this building would be jumping, but right now it was quiet. Too damn quiet. Slaughter waited some more, tried to guess what Mills was thinking, wondered how badly the photograph of Captain Wooten was going to shock him.

Mills sat down and cleared his throat.

"So, Slaughter, you said that they brought something interesting to the table. What was it this time? An offer to ease restrictions on American business? An old set of dog tags?"

Slaughter's lack of sleep made him a little nervous. "Walter, can I ask you something before I get into this?"

Mills tilted Captain Kirk back, spoke into the cup just before he drank. "Shoot."

"Thanks. When I was given this assignment, there was a tremendous sense of urgency. Specifically, two other projects– important projects–were shelved so that I could jump to this and work out an improved trade status with the Vietnamese."

"That's right. What's your point?"

"I'm wondering why there was this sudden push for normalization."

Mills shifted, started to spin his chair a little to the side. Slaughter tried to interpret the signal. Was Mills nervous, or hesitant, or relieved? Or was it something else? He watched for it again, but Mills caught himself and went back to his training, straightened in his chair.

"Well, Slaughter, I think the answer is simple. President Simons wants some lasting successes in foreign affairs before his administration ends. Vietnam is developing rapidly, and has the potential to become a major trade partner. We both know the president is planning to normalize trade tariffs. I think he sees your mission as the next logical step. It's as simple as that."

Slaughter nodded, intentionally put some wrinkles in his forehead. "I suppose that makes sense."

Mills put his wristwatch in front of his eyes. "Good."

Slaughter opened his attaché. His hand began to shake as he pulled out a photograph of Captain Charles Wooten. He held it gently, searching Wooten's eyes for the man he'd known a quarter of a century ago. He didn't quite find him. Almost. But not quite.

He stepped up to Mills' desk and dropped the photo, centered, so that Wooten's face was perfectly oriented, the hand-scrawled nameplate easily readable.

Mills jumped out of his chair so fast that it rolled across the carpet and slammed into the window. "Where in hell did you get this?"

"The Vietnamese gave it to me."

Slowly, Mills crept back to his desk, carefully picked up the picture, handled it like a sacred object. "Do you think it's genuine? Or could it be fake – maybe generated by a computer, or trick photography?"

Slaughter couldn't help but stare at the photo with Mills. "It's genuine."

"Sure?"

"Sure."

"Any idea how old it is?"

"Not very."

Mills turned it over and checked the back. "How do you know? There's nothing to prove it, at least nothing I can see. No way this can even be considered proof."

Slaughter's eyes tried to jump up and grab hold of Mills', dig around in those burned-out bulbs until he got an idea of what was going on. Something, certainly. Probably not a good thing.

But he held control, kept staring at the photo, relaxed his voice until he had most of the shock out of it. "Proof, Walter? What are you talking about?"

Mills put the photo on his desk, angled his little body toward the windows behind him. "Well, I just mean this is tremendous news. Very exciting. Very encouraging. But, if badly handled, it could be too shocking. It could give the president a black eye. It could damage his image without helping this P.O.W. You see what I mean, don't you?"

"No, I don't. We're talking about a prisoner of war here, Walter, left behind to rot in Vietnam. A man who's still alive and deserves the highest level of attention. Under these circumstances, it's a little difficult for me to worry about President Simons' image."

"That's a narrow perspective, Slaughter. Simons is our president, and he's our primary responsibility. Certainly, this man – if he really is alive – will be a high priority. But it will be dealt with in the context of Simons' –"

Slaughter snatched up the photo, held it high above his head. "You're kidding, right? Look at this man, Walter. Look at his eyes? Can you see the misery there? Well, I have. I saw him beaten like a bad dog, just twenty-eight hours ago. It was sickening. So don't ask me to worry about the president's image because I don't care. I just want to get this man home."

41

Mills' mouth dropped open, his words seemed to tumble out. "What did you say? You actually saw him? They let you see him? Really?"

"Yes. I saw him."

Mills ran over and grabbed Slaughter's wrist, pulled the picture close enough to check the name plate. "And you're sure it's Captain Wooten? Hell, I don't even think he's on the list anymore. His remains . . ." Mills let go, flung open a file drawer and grabbed a list of names, four pages long. He scrolled down it with his fingertips. "Wooten's remains were identified two years ago. Returned by the Vietnamese government during Vice-President Cuthbert's fact-finding mission. I've got a summary of the incident here someplace. You were on that trip, weren't you?"

"I was. But guess what?"

"Damn, you really saw him?"

"Yes."

"Then I can guess what you're feeling. It doesn't take a genius to understand your anguish. And I can promise you that every step will be made, every action will be taken to get Captain Wooten home. And any other prisoners that might still be there."

"It's about time, don't you think?"

Mills slowed down, dropped the list on his desk. "Don't get snotty with me, Slaughter. It's not my fault Wooten's still over there."

"Maybe not. But you'll have to share the blame if we don't get him home now. I'll see to it that you get your share."

Mills sat down, perfectly erect, his hands folded in his lap. "Are you threatening me?"

Slaughter leaned on Mills' desk. "No. I'm just telling you this: I know this man, and I want him home. It's personal with me."

Mills swung his right hand to his chin, propped up his head with it. "That's a good point. An excellent point. In fact, maybe it's a little too personal with you. I'm sure you're aware that you were hand-picked for this mission by the Vietnamese government. Well, now you know why. Hell, Slaughter, they knew how you'd respond when you saw Wooten. You'd do anything to get him home. Anything at all. I understand that, and so do they. That's why you were selected. But I can't have you working on this if your judgment is impaired."

"Don't even think about assigning this to someone else."

"Then convince me I shouldn't. You're way too close here. You say you don't care about the president, but that's the President of the United States we're talking about. You'd better start caring about him or your ass is out of here. I will not allow your personal issues to cloud the objectives of this administration. Do I make myself clear?"

Slaughter closed his eyes. Kept quiet. Shut down. Endured. It was what he had to do it if he was ever going to help Wooten. "Yes. I understand." He reached across for the photo.

"Leave that there! I want to show it to President Simons. What else did they give you?"

"Nothing."

"Nothing? You sure? No information on other P.O.W.s?"

"No."

Mills smiled, very slightly. "Slaughter, I truly believe you could do some great work here. And Lord knows the United States could use it. The president could, too. And I'm sure Captain Wooten wouldn't mind the help, either. But I need to be absolutely sure you're up for this job. Too much is riding on this. It can't be botched by misguided emotions."

"You're right."

"Can you do it? There'd be no shame if you couldn't. Those people put you through hell, and I understand what you're feeling, believe me I do. But you have to be able to distance yourself from your past, use the skills you've learned here and do your very best."

"I can do it."

"Are you sure?"

43

"Yes. Absolutely."

"All right, then. There's no more time to waste. Give me your brief and your situation analysis. I've got to get moving or I'll be late. And Slaughter, I'm sure I don't need to remind you that anything short of absolute secrecy will put Wooten's life in jeopardy."

"It already is."

Mills pressed his lips together and shook his head sideways. "Don't fight me on this, Slaughter. You know damn well what I mean."

"Yes, I do."

"Good. Stick close today. I'm sure you'll be called to a meeting at the White House."

"I'll be ready."

Slaughter picked up his attaché, moved toward the door. He stopped there and hesitated.

"Is there something else, Slaughter?"

He had one hand on the door. His other held the attaché containing photos and files of twenty-two other military prisoners. Was it really in their best interest to keep quiet? How could it be? What good would it do them if he didn't let people know they still existed.

He let go of the door, turned to face Mills. "Walter, what if there were more men over there? More than just Wooten?"

Mills shoved the position papers into his briefcase, stuck Captain Kirk in a lower drawer. He didn't look up. "I doubt there could be, Slaughter. Think how many years it's been. It's a miracle Wooten is still alive. But to give your question an answer, President Simons would demand the immediate release of all prisoners of war detained by the Vietnamese. Absolutely. Why? Do you have some reason to suspect there are others?"

Mills' answer didn't convince him. Maybe it was too much like the tired promises that had allowed Wooten to suffer so long already. Slaughter had heard thousands and thousands of those empty words during his years working with the P.O.W./M.I.A. families. To those suffering relatives they were

44

fighting words – the government's standard, dishonest pledge of good faith.

"No. I was just wondering. That's all."

Mills opened the door and aimed Slaughter out. "Go to work, Slaughter. Let's get Wooten home as soon as possible."

"Good idea."

*   *   *   *   *

Mills closed the door and leaned against it, thought about the problem Slaughter had just tossed on his desk. So, the Vietnamese had actually shown Wooten to Slaughter.

It was stupid of them, and he couldn't understand why they'd done it. Surely President Simons had already given them enough assurances that the trade agreement would be signed. Couldn't they see he was giving them what they wanted? Hadn't it dawned on them that Slaughter could ruin the deal now?

But they'd shown others over the years, too, and Mills had diffused those situations without much trouble. It was the one thing in the world he could do with exceptional ability. Diffuse situations. When people argued or nations fought, he could always find a way to work through it with them. Get them to strike a deal. Find a way to hold onto the peace.

He was thirteen when he'd discovered his talent for it. It was late on a school night, and his father was arguing with his mother. It was the only argument he ever heard them have, a terrible, noisy clash that lasted for almost an hour. Ugly words were said by both of them, and Walter could feel the pain it caused his parents, just as if the words were an attack on his own heart. He stood in the hall outside their bedroom, listened to them yell, understood what both of them said. What both of them wanted. Even though he was such a young boy, he understood their positions, and their needs, better than either of them. Much better.

The yelling stopped abruptly. Then he heard his father drag the big suitcase out from under the bed and pack it with noisy carelessness. He heard it slammed shut, then listened as his father stomped for the door.

Walter backed down the hall, hurried to neutral ground by the front door, got there just as his father stepped into the hallway. Although Walter was frightened by the enormous strides of the grown man with the big suitcase, he stood his ground and waited for him to get closer.

Somehow, he knew to speak quietly, almost too low to hear. He'd never learned that anywhere; he just knew it was true. Knew it intuitively. Talk softly. Whisper. People will try hard to hear you.

"Dad."

His father stopped marching toward the door, looked down at his little boy from five feet away, his anguished face showing he was unsure that anything had actually been said. He waited there, glanced back toward the bedroom, then waited some more. Half a minute passed. His dad's breathing slowed down. His eyes softened a little. He set the big Samsonite on the floor.

"Dad," Walter said again, completely stupid about what he would say next.

"Yes, son."

"Dad, I know you're unhappy with mom tonight. I can hear it. I can also hear she's plenty sore at you, too. I see your suitcase, and it looks to me like you're leaving."

His father lowered his head, put a hand on Walter's shoulder. "I'm sorry, son. That's right."

"Have you ever left her before, dad?"

His dad held his answer in for a little bit. "No, son, I haven't."

"Will she be all right without you?"

46

His father stared down at him, his lean face softening, moving to the loving face of a man who'd spent years working hard for his family, and doing it gladly.

"What do you think, son? You're a smart boy. Will you two be all right without me?"

Walter sat down on the edge of his father's suitcase, pinned it to the floor. He looked up at his father, then at the other side of the big piece of luggage. Walter was close to his answer when his father made a slight glance down the hall. Walter saw it, saw his dad's eye caught by the sight of his mother stepping into their bedroom doorway and leaning against the jamb. Listening.

His dad sat down with him, put his arm around his shoulder. "Walter, I asked you what you thought. Will you two be okay?"

Walter nodded, easily, but careful not to be too convincing. "Oh, sure, Dad. I think we can get along okay without you. We always could, I think. But we'll sure miss you a lot. That's what I think, anyway. We'll get along fine. But we'll miss you. You're a good dad. Mom and I love you."

His father pulled him close, then looked down the hall again. This time he didn't sneak his look. He stood up and took a small step.

"How about you, Doris? You think you'd miss me?"

Walter's mother stepped clear of the doorway, out into the bright light of the hallway. Then she stepped once more, swiveled her hips so that her Donna Reed skirt swirled around her knees. She was smiling a little now, absolutely the most beautiful woman in the world.

"Well, I don't really know. You can't cook at all, you know. You snore. And your driving makes me downright queasy."

Walter jumped up from the suitcase, ready to slap on another bandage. They were talking adult again, and he was having difficulty with the dialect. He was ready, but waited before he spoke.

His father chuckled. "I thought you liked my driving."

47

His mother was spinning that skirt like she was trying to take off, the hem rustling against her legs, her hips picking up an easy rhythm. "It isn't your driving I like, honey. It's the places you take me that I'd miss. You understand?"

She leaned back now, a little too far, stretching for the wall with her shoulders but not hitting it until a little worry jumped into her eyes. But once she was solidly against the wall, she smiled like that was what she'd intended, tilted her head to the side, closed her eyes slowly.

Walter's father pushed on his shoulders. "You go on to bed, son."

His father was moving down the hall. Walter knew there was something special and mysterious in what he was watching. He didn't understand it, but he knew right then that a deal had been struck that would keep his folks together, at least for another night. And, amazingly, he'd played a part in it. It was the most exciting few seconds of his youth.

If he'd had more time, he would have read Slaughter's situation analysis to learn the specifics. But he was running late. President Simons would be waiting. They'd go over them in detail together. He would use these few minutes for a phone call. Keep his checks and balances in order.

He dialed direct on a secure line. After one ring, a crisp, smooth, fully awake voice on the other end said, "Hello."

"It's Mills."

"Good morning, Walter. Did you have your meeting with Slaughter already?"

"I did."

"And? How did it go? Does he know anything?"

"He thinks he saw a P.O.W." The words tried to stick in his throat, but he managed to force them out before they lodged there.

"Hmmm, is that right?"

"Yes."

"That's not good."

"I know."

"Well, Walter, what's he saying? What was his reaction?"

"Shock, mostly. He just left a minute ago. Seemed pretty shaken up. Of course, he wants to get the prisoner out. Obviously, that's very important to him."

"Well, sure it is. Which is exactly why they demanded that he represent the United States in these negotiations. They knew he'd put the release of prisoners at the very top of his list; do whatever they wanted in order to get a P.O.W. out."

"That's right."

"Pretty shrewd of them"

"Yes. Very smart."

"Well, Walter, keep a close rein on Slaughter. Make sure he stays on the team. He has a heavy load of bad news, and we don't want it getting out. If the American people hear his story, there will be hell to pay. And I can damn sure guarantee you that we'll get caught in the cross fire. I don't need that problem. None of us do. Do you understand?"

"I understand. No problem."

"Good. Stay on it. Keep me posted. Good-bye."

5

Slaughter ate his lunch in the car as he drove to the suburbs near Dulles Airport. It had been a good morning; he'd done a lot to help Chuck Wooten. But he could have done more if Sarah Wooten wasn't on his mind. He'd had a stack of messages on his desk when he'd gone to his office and the majority of them involved Sarah. She was in trouble, or damn close to it. He would make time to see her, hoping like hell the president wouldn't call until he got back.

Slaughter turned off the main highway and wound his way into Sarah's neighborhood. Everything looked new out here. The roads, the stores, the homes. Schools and office buildings. Everything. This was the growth area of Washington, the newest benefactor of urban sprawl. Herndon, Virginia. All the comforts of suburbia with a short commute to Washington.

Sarah and Benjamin had bought their home three years ago. It was a big step for them, moving from city life to a two-story fantasy with hardwood floors and a big backyard. Sarah's mother had helped them with the down payment, and Slaughter had bought them new furniture for the entire first floor.

He was proud of himself for that, for the fact that they had adamantly refused but he had done it anyway. It went against his nature to be impulsive, but he'd loved the feeling it gave him. He tried to make himself do things like that more often.

He parked in the two-car driveway and walked up to the front door. He was only halfway there when it was flung open by Sarah's son, Samual, a ten-year-old, four-foot-tall version of Chuck Wooten who came charging down the sidewalk toward him, his little brown face stretched out in a huge smile.

Samual ran up to Slaughter like he was going to jump into his arms, the way he'd done when he was younger. But then he screeched to a stop. "Hey, Uncle Jacob! Our volcano got an honorable mention at the science fair last week! Look at the ribbon I won."

Slaughter took the ribbon and admired it. "No kidding? Good for you, Samual. I'm really proud of you. Did the lava flow out of the top like it was supposed to?"

"Boy, it sure did. It was so cool. Just as the judges walked by I turned the switch. Wow, you should have seen it."

"I'm sorry I wasn't there. But I had to be out of town. You understand, don't you?"

"Sure I do."

"Thanks. Is your mom home?"

Samual took back the ribbon, admired it a little more himself. "Sure is. She's on the back porch. I've got to run down to my friends for a minute, but I'll be right back. Are you staying for dinner? Can we play ball later?"

Slaughter was already edging toward the side yard, feeling his time slipping away. "No, sorry, Samual. I've just got a few minutes, then I have to get back to work."

"Shoot."

"Maybe this weekend, though. I'll see if your mom has plans. If not, Laura and I might come over, bring some things for a cookout."

"That would be cool."

Slaughter laughed. "Yeah. Cool. You bet."

A little boy three houses down called Samual's name, and he ran off. Slaughter walked around to the backyard of the house.

Sarah Wooten was sitting in a porch swing, talking on a portable phone. Her hair was long for a black woman. Not too curly. Her skin was the color of honey. She was sitting with her legs up under a sundress that looked great on her small body.

She smiled as Slaughter sat down beside her in the swing, still talking on the phone.

"Well, Anne," she said, "you won't believe who just walked up and sat down beside me."

Slaughter leaned over and whispered, "Is that Mrs. Kinsey?"

Sarah nodded that it was, kept talking to the phone. "You guessed right, Anne. And no, I don't know what he's doing here. Probably came by to raid my refrigerator." She turned to face him, talking loud. "Jacob, did you drive all the way out here just to see what I've got in my refrigerator?"

Slaughter stuck his hands up in protest. "No, of course not." Then he took the phone and spoke into it. "Hello, Mrs. Kinsey."

Sarah pulled the phone away with a smirk, listened, then laughed. "She says hello, Jacob. Says you should stop by her office and see her sometime."

"Tell her I will."

Sarah rolled her eyes. "He says he will, Anne. I guess we'll have to wait and see. Anyway, I'd better go now. Can't wait to find out what this tired old man wants. I'll call you if he tells me anything the organization should know. Bye."

Sarah set the phone down and shifted around to face him. "Well, go on. What's brought you all the way out here?"

She was always direct like that; always caught him off guard. "Not much, really. I just wanted to talk for a few minutes."

"Uh-oh, Jacob. I know that sound in your voice. Are you talking that way around Laura, too?"

"What way?"

"That 'Oh, have I got a problem' way."

Slaughter watched himself digging into the ground with his toes. "Is it that obvious?"

She reached over and shook his leg. "Probably not. Least-wise not to anyone who doesn't know you like Laura and I do. So, what is it?"

"It's about you, Sarah. And your job. And your dad."

"Good. I've been thinking a lot about my dad, especially since hearing the rumor."

"What rumor?"

"*The* rumor. You haven't heard it yet?"

"No."

"You're kidding!"

He wasn't kidding, and he was too short of time to keep waiting to hear what she was talking about. He gave her a look that showed that; hoped it wasn't too severe.

"Well, it goes like this. Seems that some time after the Soviet Union collapsed, a bunch of highly classified documents became available that prove the Vietnamese intentionally underreported the number of American P.O.W.s to us. They gave the Soviets accurate numbers."

"Really?"

"Yup. At first, the Pentagon just speculated that the Vietnamese had been trying to make themselves look good to the Soviets by impressing them with their stats. But the names checked out, the dates and places of capture. Everything."

"If this is true, how come I haven't read it in the papers or heard it at work?"

"Well, the G.R.U. files were just recently discovered, and the reporter from Hungary who has read the documents called our headquarters for a comment. He's writing an article on it now, hoping for worldwide publication. Isn't that exciting? It means that those men have never been accounted for. There's seven hundred of them. Seven hundred new names. I'm sure we've lost most of the men, Jacob, but a few of those families might still see their sons and fathers come home."

"Is that why you're in trouble at work?"

"Oh, you've heard. Well, I suppose it is. Since my employer does government contract work, he doesn't like the attention I attract when I'm testifying and protesting. He's planning on firing me. Right now I'm on paid leave, at least until next week. But really, I don't care. If it costs my job to get my father home, then that's the price. I'll pay it. Hell, I'd pay it a thousand times over."

"I know you would."

"My boss doesn't have a dad who's stuck over there. If he did, he'd – "

"I think you should back off a little, Sarah."

"You what? Jacob, don't you tell me to back off. I won't do it. I can't believe you'd even ask."

"You need that job, worked too hard to get it. Can't you just tone it down a little? Compromise with him? Work for your dad but still keep your job?"

Sarah stopped swinging. She sat still and glared. Said nothing.

Slaughter eased off. "You've never given up, have you? Even after the funeral service –"

"Hold on a minute, Jacob. I appreciate all you've done to help daddy, I really do. But you can't expect me to believe those little pieces of bone were my father. I've told you that before."

"You have. I understand you have doubts."

"I don't have doubts. I have faith, Jacob. And love. And a daddy who loves me right back."

Slaughter smiled a little. What a treasure to have a daughter like Sarah. He knew how proud Wooten would be; couldn't wait for them to be together.

"My daddy will come home someday. I still have the letter he wrote when I was four. You've read it. What did it say?"

"He promised he'd come home."

"That's right. My daddy promised me he'd come home. He doesn't break promises, Jacob. From what my mom tells me, he's not that type of man."

"She's right. He isn't."

Sarah started pushing the swing again. Back and forth.

"Sarah, you know I did everything possible to help your father, don't you? You know how hard I worked to bring him home."

"I certainly do. I appreciate it. You know that."

"I've spent half my life working to get him home."

"I know that, too. Everybody knows that. Why are you telling me this? What's bothering you?"

"It's nothing, Sarah. I just wanted to make sure you knew."

"When daddy comes home, I'll tell him, too. You've been a great friend to him."

Slaughter hung his head. Shook it. Bit his lip.

Sarah put her hand on his arm. "Tell me what's bothering you. Please."

He leaned back and closed his eyes. "Dreams, Sarah. That's all. Your good dream, my bad dream."

"Hey, we all have dreams."

"True enough. Yours might even come true. I hope so. Will you trust me to do everything possible with this news report from Hungary? If I take it on, will you quiet down and go back to work?"

"You're that worried about my job?"

"I just don't want you to lose it unnecessarily. It's a good job. Without it, you'll have to move. Samual will have to change schools. Besides, I'm working on something, and I don't need the attention either."

Sarah jumped up in front of him. "Damn! You know something, Jacob Slaughter! What is it?"

"It's just what you said and nothing more. A news piece from Hungary."

"Bullshit."

"Do we have a deal? Will you quiet down and go back to work?"

"I want to know what you know!"

"What I know is that you need that job."

55

"You won't tell me?"

"Nothing to tell."

"Bullshit, again." She paced around the yard, then sat back down in the swing. "But, if you say you'll run with the ball, that's good enough for me. I'll quiet down a little."

"Good. Now, how's your mom? How's she holding up?

"Mom?"

"Yes. Has she been doing okay? I haven't seen her in a couple of years. Not since –"

"Not since the funeral. I know."

"Has she been getting along all right? I feel bad that I haven't done a better job keeping in touch with her."

"Hell, Jacob, she's alone. Like she never wanted to be and always feared she would be. It nearly killed her when you brought back those remains. Then, something about the funeral service destroyed what little energy she had left. You remember? You had a long talk with her right after the service."

"I remember. It was a bad day for all of us."

"A very bad day. Giving up was hard on her."

He thought about how she'd looked, all dressed in black, standing beside a full-sized casket with a tiny piece of bone in it, holding back tears as the Honor Guard handed her the folded flag, little Samual holding her hand and looking up at his grandmother.

"Listen, Sarah, do you think she'd mind if I called her someday? Not today, but . . . someday?"

"She'd love to hear from you. To be honest, Jacob, I thought you two would stay better friends. After all those years working together, it's sad to see you guys so far apart."

Slaughter nodded. "You're right, it's a shame. But really, I was only involved in the organization for your father. When I brought his remains home, I sort of lost contact with the organization."

"Those weren't his remains."

"Sure. I understand. Anyway, I should call her."

"That would be nice. I'm sure she'd like it."

She stood up when he did, walked with him through the green summer grass. He climbed into his car and drove away.

He drove too fast returning to his office. When he got there, the message Mills had predicted was on his desk, right on top and in the middle. His secretary had written it on a whole sheet of paper to make sure he saw it.

But the meeting at the White House would have to wait. He wanted to call Lu Kham Phong first. It was almost midnight in Hanoi, yesterday, but Phong had promised to stay available.

"Mr. Phong? It's Jacob Slaughter."

"Yes, Mr. Slaughter."

"I've been called to the White House, Mr. Phong. I think this might be good news for your country."

"I am very pleased to hear that, Mr. Slaughter."

Slaughter heard the crackle of anticipation on the line. Phong was waiting, expecting more information.

"Was there anything else?"

"Well, yes. I just wanted to emphasize how awkward this situation is for the United States and remind you again how extremely important those P.O.W.s are to your treaty's success."

"I understand what you're saying, Mr. Slaughter. Rest assured, sir, that nothing will change from our earlier meeting. I give you my word, their situation will not deteriorate."

"I'll take you at your word, Mr. Phong. Because you know how crucial your end of this deal is."

"I do. I understand completely."

"Mr. Phong?"

"Yes?"

"When the time comes, you will let the prisoners go, right? No more tricks? Our countries have been down this road several times before, you know."

"Yes. I know. But I promise you, Mr. Slaughter, on my honor, that a Most Favored Nation trade status with the United

States will bring your men home. We have held them much too long already."

"Good. I'm glad I can count on you."

Slaughter hung up, tightened his tie, picked up his coat, and headed for the exit. He walked northeast, away from the Vietnam Memorial, toward the White House.

The presidential aide was about thirty-five years old, small, and weak-looking. He escorted Slaughter through the White House in silence, five steps ahead of him. Slaughter had only been here once before, but he felt like it had just happened the other day: the joy of coming home, his passion and respect for this country, Nixon's wonderful handshake, the public reception, and the brief flash of attention that had followed his return from captivity. It was exciting to be back now. This was the seat of authority, the one place in the world where there was enough power to get Wooten home.

"Will President Simons be at this meeting?" he asked the aide as they turned a corner.

The aide didn't break stride when he turned and smiled, his pinched lips stuck together by years of blue-suit protocol. His tiny eyes aimed along his sharp nose and looked Slaughter up and down. "No, I'm afraid not. He was briefed on the situation this morning, and is very, very interested. But his agenda is completely full today. He didn't want to lose time waiting for his schedule to clear, so he's asked Vice-President Cuthbert to take his place." He turned back around, slowly, still walking at a brisk pace. It seemed as if he could navigate this building with a blindfold.

"Who else will be there?"

"Besides the vice-president, only a couple of cabinet members. A small group, really. But, of course, operating with the full force of the presidency."

"Of course."

The aide stopped at a set of large wooden doors. "Here you are, sir." He opened them and stepped inside with Slaughter.

There was a long table in the room. Mills and two other men sat at it. All their eyes settled on Slaughter.

"Gentlemen," the aide said. "May I introduce Mr. Jacob Slaughter, a foreign service officer assigned to Southeast Asia." Then the aide spun around to face Slaughter, shook his hand, then backed out of the room. He closed the doors as he left.

Slaughter stopped just inside the room and waited. The other men went back to their conversation, a low, unhappy dialogue. About a minute later, Mills stood up and walked over to him, shook his hand, and led him to the others. "Slaughter, I think you know everyone here," he said, a little too cheerfully.

"I do."

The other two men bobbed their heads. One of them mumbled a "Hey." Then they went back to their copies of his report. Slaughter watched and wondered how much they knew? What would they ask him? How quickly could they get those prisoners home?

Secretary of Defense Tanner headed the table. He was short and stout, with beefy pockets of flesh encroaching on his little black mouse eyes. Small, broken blood vessels spider-webbed his nose and cheeks. His thinning hair was black, too dark to be his natural color. Three long greasy strips of it swept across his head like skid marks.

Vice-President Andrew Cuthbert sat to his immediate left, savoring the smoke of his small cigar. Cuthbert was a handsome contrast to Tanner. He was tanned and tall and angular, with a nicely trimmed head of graying hair. He wore a gray suit with a light blue dress shirt. Red and blue rep tie. All of the colors set off his blue eyes, and drew Slaughter's attention to them. He was the perfect presidential poster boy.

Mills sat down and motioned Slaughter into a chair. Then Secretary of Defense Tanner looked up from his papers, shoved them away, leaned way back into his seat and cupped his hands behind his head. "Mr. Slaughter," he said in a Georgia gentleman's accent. "I understand that you just returned last night with this picture." He reached forward, picked up a blow-up of Wooten's photograph and waved it around with his hand.

"Yes. That's correct."

"Uh-huh. And am I correct in believing that you actually *saw* this man while you were over there in Vietnam." He said Vietnam like a redneck, putting heavy emphasis on the middle syllable.

"Yes, sir. That's right."

"Well, now, Mr. Slaughter. Did those nice folks in Vietnam ever bother to tell you *why* they were showing you this poor old man?"

Slaughter's muscles tightened, already starting to hate Tanner. Wooten wasn't some poor old man. He was a United States Marine, shot down, captured, and left behind.

"Proof, sir. Their motive was to offer proof."

Tanner grinned a little, picked at his ear. Then he shook his head, kindly, as if amazed by a small child's innocence. "I see. I see. Okay, well, maybe I can accept that. They wanted to prove to you that they still have this fella . . . uh, what's his name? Wooten? They wanted to be sure you knew he was still alive, huh? Do I have the right idea here?"

"I believe your assumption is accurate, Mr. Tanner."

Tanner stopped fidgeting with his ear. His head stopped moving and the smile disappeared. He leaned forward with a nasty look on his swollen face. "Well, sir, I guess you feel pretty sure of yourself then, having seen this man with your own two eyes and all."

Slaughter leaned in Tanner's direction. "You bet I do."

Tanner looked around, stopped at each of the other faces as though he was looking for something. Slaughter followed his eyes, saw what he saw: Cuthbert, staring back, his little cigar pinched between two fingers, the soggy stub resting on his lip. Mills, looking down at the table.

Tanner and Slaughter's eyes snapped back together. "Hmmph. Well, I'm gonna tell you something, Mr. Slaughter. You ready?"

Slaughter didn't answer.

"I think you're a damn fool."

"Is that right?"

"Yes. That's right. P.O.W.s left over from the war? Why, the whole idea is ridiculous."

"You don't believe my report?"

"No, damn it, I do *not* believe your report. And I don't believe *them*, either! I don't believe they have any prisoners still alive over there. And I don't believe, not for one moonlight second, that you actually saw one. You understand what I'm saying to you?"

Slaughter lost all vision of Cuthbert and Mills, gave Tanner his total concentration. "If you don't believe me, Mr. Tanner, why am I here?"

Tanner looked at Cuthbert and they both chuckled. Then he turned to Slaughter. "You're here, Slaughter, because you need to be aware of some fundamental truths, and I guess I'm the one's gonna tell 'em to you. Ever since you turned this photo in this morning, we've had top photographic experts analyzing it."

"Top experts. Uh-huh."

"The best in their field, Slaughter. A whole lot smarter than you and me about these things. And they do not believe, in fact, they are absolutely positive that this man isn't Wooten. Maybe a very close resemblance, probably an American, but sure as hell not Wooten. I think you've been shown a reasonable facsimile, Mr. Slaughter, and you've accepted him as the genuine article." Tanner scratched his chest and sat there with a smug look.

"Mr. Tanner, are any of these experts the same ones who said the last remains we brought back were Wooten's?"

Tanner leaned a forearm on the table, pushed off with it and drove himself closer to Slaughter. "Yes they are. So what's that to you?"

"And you think they're right and I'm wrong? You think I wouldn't recognize the man I knew in prison, the man who risked his life for me, the man who got me through that horrible ordeal? Wouldn't know him if I saw him? But these 'experts'

61

can make an accurate determination by comparing this picture with an old service photo? Is that what you're saying?"

"Yup! Sure am. Nice summation."

Slaughter pointed his finger at Tanner, knowing it crossed the line. "And you think *I'm* a damn fool."

Mills snapped his head up, ready to take responsibility for his employee, hold onto the peace. But Tanner raised a hand up, held the palm toward Mills as if to hold him back. "Hell, Slaughter, I can see how you could make a mistake without knowing it. My God, it's been more'n twenty years. I, myself, have looked at Wooten's service picture and I can't even see a resemblance, much less enough similarity to positively identify him. But those Army men are very highly trained. They know what they're doing. Yes, sir, those Vietnamese bastards are just serving us another dose of bullshit communist propaganda, plain and simple."

Slaughter looked at Mills, then at Cuthbert. "And the rest of you? Do you agree with Mr. Tanner? Do you think I was duped?"

Mills' head went back down while Cuthbert puffed his cigar. The room was completely quiet. But then, slowly, Mills took up the call, raising his head, then standing. "It's not a question of picking sides here. It isn't us against you or anything like that. But the Army has examined the photograph and pronounced – without question I might add – that the man is definitely not Captain Wooten."

"And you don't think they could be wrong?"

"No, not exactly. I could concede that they could make a mistake. But I've talked to the Army pathologists, too, and they still have a high level of confidence that the remains you and Vice-President Cuthbert brought back in 1996 were accurately identified as Captain Wooten's. Combined, it makes for pretty strong evidence. I believe we've drawn the only logical conclusion."

Could it be possible? Slaughter stood and walked to the windows, wanted to go out onto the balcony and get some of that fresh, warm air into his lungs. But he stayed inside, arms folded across his chest, and replayed his meeting in the Vietnamese prison. Was there a chance that Tanner was right, that the Vietnamese had decided to try such an elaborate hoax, knowing full well that the United States would find out as soon as the prisoners were released?

But so what? By then, they would have their Most Favored Trading Nation status, and no one would dare go back and try to disassemble it. There would be too much embarrassment; the politicians would have to keep silent.

"What if you gentlemen are right? How does that affect their trade status?"

Tanner wound himself up, looked like he was going to blast Slaughter, tell him it wasn't any of his damned business. But Mills took to the floor a half second ahead of Tanner, worked the room like he'd been trained to do.

"Slaughter . . . oh, excuse me, Mr. Tanner." Mills didn't sit down. He kept looking at Tanner, waiting for him to yield.

Tanner screwed up his lips and scowled. "No, hell, Walter. You go on ahead."

"Thank you, Mr. Tanner. I was just going to mention to Slaughter that, regardless of the identity of the man he met in prison, we have every intention of granting Vietnam's request. After all, it's been more than thirty years since the trade embargo began. I think we all, as a country, feel enough is enough."

Slaughter took Mills' words, rolled them around to get every possible interpretation. "So, then, if I understand what you're saying, the Vietnamese will get what they want and the prisoner, regardless of who he is, will be released."

"Yes," Mills said. "That's exactly right."

Cuthbert and Tanner shot their eyes to Mills.

"Then I assume, gentlemen, that I am authorized to finish preparing the terms of the trade agreement."

"Absolutely," said Mills.

"It will include the terms and conditions for the release of this prisoner," Slaughter said. "I also think it would be prudent to use the term 'all prisoners,' just in case there might be others."

"I don't see a problem with that."

"What about the thirty-day deadline?"

Mills looked at Tanner, then they both looked at the vice-president. He had been completely quiet during the meeting, his thick, gray hair cut perfectly around his thin, stony face. He seemed reluctant to speak now, his bright blue eyes popping around the room until he decided on an answer. Then he trained those eyes, like twin-.50's, on Slaughter. "If there's a time crunch, I'll take care of it. But Slaughter, I want you to be a little obtuse in the way you phrase the issue of returning prisoners. Make it sound like a safety measure – a 'just-in-case' kind of clause. I don't want it to get a lot of attention. If we're not careful, it could be the only part of the agreement the press reads." He smiled.

Now Tanner started grinning, rubbing his hands together. "There, Slaughter. That should put things right. Keep us posted on your progress. And don't worry. The president will be ready as soon as you are." Tanner stood, then Mills, and finally, Vice-President Cuthbert.

Slaughter picked up his attaché and headed toward the door. He stopped before leaving and looked back. They were smiling at him, projecting some hybrid strain of team spirit.

"Good-day, gentlemen."

Mills called out to him. "Let's meet this evening, Slaughter. About seven. My office."

"I'll be there."

Tanner raised his hand and waved. "Good-bye, Mr. Slaughter. Good luck."

*   *   *   *   *

Mills watched the door close, listened to it latch – a loud little noise in the big quiet room. Cuthbert and Tanner were shuffling toward the wall, over near a corner, whispering. Mills wanted to join them but he kept looking at the door, thinking about the personal agendas of all the players and wondering how in the world he would keep them working together.

Slaughter worried him most. His motivation was absolutely pure, the easiest kind to understand. And the hardest to control. Or predict. He knew Slaughter didn't care about the trade agreement, even knew he would sacrifice his career, if necessary, to get Wooten home. He was going to be difficult. Most people had a wide variety of desires, and each one of them was a tool for Mills to work with. But Slaughter had only one. Nothing else mattered. Mills would have to make Slaughter's singularity of purpose his top concern, if he was going to pull this off without getting anyone hurt.

"Walter," Tanner called. "How 'bout joining us over here."

He moved to the wall and huddled with the others. Cuthbert was leaning against the wall, his arms across his chest, glaring at nothing as he spoke to Tanner.

"Do you think he's convinced?"

Tanner scratched his chest with a stubby hand, his short-sleeved shirt riding up with each stroke, pulling the shirt tails farther out of his pants. "How would I know, sir? We're talking about a man who thinks he saw a real live P.O.W. How convinced would you be?"

Cuthbert tilted his head. "I don't know. I thought your presentation of the facts was persuasive."

"So did I," Mills added as he joined them.

Tanner dragged his hand away from his chest and poked at the air in front of Mills. "Well, you didn't just see a ghost. If the

65

boogie man had just popped out of the ground and scared the bejesus out of you, could anyone convince you he didn't exist."

Mills pushed Tanner's annoying finger away. "Probably not. But nevertheless, your position was sound, your evidence seemed firm. It created a nice breeding ground for plausible denial."

Tanner smiled, looked a little shocked. "Well, thank you, Walter. It did do that, didn't it?"

"Yes, it did. I hope we won't need it."

Vice-President Cuthbert closed his eyes, put his right hand over them. "All right, gentlemen, that's enough of that. I don't want to hear any more talk of denials or cover-ups. There is absolutely no way I'm going to let the issue of P.O.W.s infect this Administration. Go ahead and give the Vietnamese what they want, Walter. That's what President Simons wants us to do. It'll get them off his back and make happy voters out of all those irritating businessmen who are pestering him. But never, and I repeat, never bring up P.O.W.s again. And don't let one show up at our front door either. Cover all the bases. Are you completely clear on that? No P.O.W.s will come home from Vietnam. Period!"

Tanner straightened up, although he was still a short, stumpy man. "Yes, sir, Mr. Cuthbert. You can count on me. I'll make sure – "

"Mills," Cuthbert said. "I want to know exactly where you stand. Can President Simons count on you to carry your end?"

Mills spoke slowly, wanted to phrase it well. "Yes, Andrew. I believe we can accomplish everything you've requested without much trouble. I do have some concerns about Slaughter, though. As Tanner just said, he may have trouble doubting his own senses, especially when you consider the emotional attachment he has to this situation."

Cuthbert stepped close to Mills, cut Tanner out of range, growled in low tones. "Then assign someone else. Move Slaughter over to some other job."

Mills lowered his voice, too. This exchange was just going to be between them, although Tanner was weaving around behind Cuthbert, trying to see what was happening. "That would be difficult, Andrew. The Vietnamese foreign minister requested Slaughter. As you know, he personally asked the president for him. I tried like hell to convince them he wasn't up to the job, but they refused to budge. Slaughter is respected over there, I guess, because he was gracious in the way his book presented them. If we change F.S.O.s now, it will upset them a lot. They'll think something's up, and of course, they'll be right. We'll be back on square one. The thirty-day time frame will run out, and then what? I don't want to risk this fellow, Wooten, or whoever he is, showing up here in prison pajamas. Do you?"

Cuthbert sucked his upper lip down and bit it hard. "It was stupid of them to show Wooten to Slaughter. What's even more idiotic is that we allowed Slaughter to go in the first place."

"It was a terrible choice. But we had no idea they'd show him a prisoner. Not this close to a final resolution. No one could have predicted it."

"Then why'd they do it? What do you think their reasons were?"

Mills shrugged his shoulders. "I guess, really, it's just the same as always, the same disaster President Simons and the rest of us have been dealing with all along. Although, I think they see Slaughter as insurance. They know he won't keep quiet. They know how strong he is. He's their ally, now, because of what they've just done. And, I'll tell you my opinion; he's a dangerous man for them to have in their corner."

Cuthbert turned a little, looked at Tanner for just a second. Tanner's face perked up like a dog about to get a biscuit. "You mean he's a bad man to have against us," Cuthbert said.

Mills saw their exchange of looks; wished it hadn't happened. "You could put it that way, I guess. Although I don't think it's come to that. Not even close."

Cuthbert glanced back and forth between Tanner and Mills. But his words were meant for Mills alone. "Slaughter needs to be a player on *our* team. That's all there is to it. Or he needs to be pushed so far out of the way that he's forgotten."

Mills started to nod, like Tanner was doing. It seemed an obvious solution. But he couldn't quite do it. "I'm sorry, Andrew, but could you please be a little more specific? Do you mean reassigned? Or fired? Or –"

"Out of the way, I said! He needs to be pushed out of the way!" Cuthbert was yelling, but in a well-heeled way.

Tanner hurried over, enthusiastically pushed himself in front of Cuthbert. "I understand, sir. I know just what you mean. I will see to the problem personally, if and when it becomes necessary."

Cuthbert looked at Tanner for a few seconds, then shifted away from him. He squinted sharply at Mills as he talked to Tanner. "Thank you, Tanner. It's good to know you're ready to handle my concerns so capably."

Mills and Cuthbert were locked up with each other's eyes. Tanner stood beside Cuthbert at a right angle. Tanner sounded content to be there when he said, "You're welcome, sir," to the side of Cuthbert's head.

6

Slaughter ran all the way back to his office building, wove his way through sidewalks crowded with summer tourists and streets jammed with cars from everywhere. Probably none of them were actually from Washington. Not the tourist nor the people who worked here. D.C. was a huge geographical waystation, a nexus of sorts. Mecca. Eventually, every American would make a pilgrimage and pass through Washington. But they would never stay. They would come for a relatively short time to visit or to work. Then they'd leave. He didn't know a single person who called this place home.

He was sweaty when he rushed into his office, grabbed a fresh boxed shirt out of a drawer, then went to the men's room. He toweled off quickly and changed, then went back and picked up his frantic pace. Mentally, he kept looking over his shoulder. He had understood Tanner's message, probably much more clearly than Tanner had intended. *Expect some surprises, Slaughter. We have some reasons for our actions that you don't understand.*

But so far, things were working out well. He had made every call that would help speed up the signing of the trade agreement. Every objection raised by either side had been resolved. His friends and allies at State had all pitched in and done a lot of the legwork. They were excited, enthusiastic about being a part of history. They were breaking down a huge barrier, doing their part to remove the last vestige of enmity over a ridiculous war.

The world, it seemed, was ready to welcome Vietnam back. There was an amazing shortage of setbacks. Without even mentioning the P.O.W.s, Slaughter had people lining up behind him, ready to help get the deal done.

But word was leaking out, and that worried him. He couldn't identify the source of the leak, but he knew it existed. A few businessmen started to call him. One was the C.E.O. of the largest corporation in America. He just couldn't help himself, the man had said. He'd called to offer his support, tell Slaughter what a great thing he was doing, paint the trade agreement in red, white, and blue. And, of course, green.

Slaughter still kept Phong's portfolio close to him, carried it to every meeting, wherever he went. Even the men's room. He didn't plan to show the pictures of the other prisoners to anyone, but he was protecting them. Guarding those men with his life while he worked like a maniac to get Wooten out. And really, wasn't that the same as working to get the others out? Certainly they would all come out together. Why muddy the waters, as Mills might say.

But the truth was something else, and he knew it. Something made him squirm inside, a queasy feeling that ordered him to keep the other prisoners secret, warned him that he could put their lives in jeopardy if he wasn't careful. Besides, no good was going to come from exposure. Even Mills had said that. And damn if Slaughter didn't believe him, especially after his meeting with Tanner.

By six-thirty p.m. he'd completed the last, most delicate wording of the treaty. Both sides had settled on the terms long ago, so it had been pretty easy. He just needed to massage the sentences so that no one was offended. Make it as simple as possible while leaving no room for eleventh-hour maneuvers. At a few minutes before seven he entered Mills' office, carrying the stack of work he'd done.

Mills was almost buried alive in paper. Slaughter knew he'd caused a lot of it. Everything he'd asked someone to do had resulted in authorization requests from F.S.O.s to their supervisors, who'd advised the deputy assistants to the secretary, who'd advised the assistant to the secretary, who'd advised the chief assistant to the secretary, who, of course, had advised Mills. Everyone made sure that their enthusiasm hadn't allowed them to leave their own asses hanging out. The protection was paper, and Slaughter found it funny.

"Hello, Walter. Damn, what happened? It looks like the file room exploded."

Mills glanced up quickly, then went back to work. "Come on in, Slaughter. You've obviously been busy. I've probably been copied ten times on everything you've done."

"Maybe more. This place is a mess."

"Yeah, I've got a ton of problems to deal with. You're just one of them. I haven't even started to prepare for the press conference in the morning."

"I'm a problem?"

Mills signed his name on something, then threw the pen down and stood up. Stretched.

"No, of course not. Or, maybe so. My standard is simple: if it's on my desk –"

"It's a problem," Slaughter joined in. "The great motto of the State Department."

Mills laughed. "I thought I was the only one who said that."

"Uhm, I don't think so. Not unless you're the one who wrote it on the men's room wall. That's where I got it my first day here."

"Damn. So hard to be original."

"You bet. Now, what was that about a press conference tomorrow?"

Mills walked away from his desk, eyed it suspiciously, as if it might follow him around the room. "Oh, sorry, I assumed you knew about it. President Simons wants me to make some televised comments about Vietnam – about how many years have passed since we were enemies, how cooperative they've been recently, things like that. I'll be laying down the groundwork, getting the public ready for improving relations."

"Really?"

"Really. Apparently you've been doing a first-rate job. I'm not sure exactly *what* you've been doing, but President Simons' phone has been ringing like crazy. Mine, too. Simons has pushed Vietnam's request for Most Favored Trading status to the top of his priority list. Things will really happen now. You'll see. Are you finished with your end of the deal?"

"Yes. I think I've got all of the concerns covered. The language is simple and clear but not too generous in its wording. The issue of P.O.W.s, as Cuthbert wanted, is couched under the heading 'Repatriation of any detained American citizens and/or their remains.' "

"That's not bad, but I think the White House is going to want something even less provocative where any detainees are concerned. Make it sound like a logistical, transportation question instead of a release or return issue."

"Sure. I can do that."

"I know you can."

Mills watched him closely. It wasn't one of those "I'm going to look right through you" stares. Rather, he seemed to be searching Slaughter's face for understanding. He stepped up to him, stood close and spoke gently. "Slaughter, I want to ask you something."

Slaughter stood his ground, defied the instinct to step back. "Shoot."

"How did you feel today when Tanner said that man wasn't Wooten?"

72

"Honestly?"

"Sure."

"All right. I felt that he failed to allow any margin for error. He never doubted the photo experts' analysis, not for one second. Frankly, I expected him to be a little more cerebral than that. A little more thoughtful."

"Oh? Why should he be?"

"Well, for starters, because he's paid to act intelligently. Do you think he'd have accepted their report so quickly if we'd been talking about his son?"

Mills seemed to ponder this for a few seconds. "Hmm. I see what you mean. And, you're probably right. In fact, I'm sure you're right. He would have a lot of trouble being objective if there was one chance in a million that the man in the photograph might be his son. I see what you're saying." He paused and turned away, then snapped right back. "That was your point, wasn't it?"

Slaughter knew he'd stepped into Mills' trap, but still, there was only one answer. "Yes."

"Good. I'm glad I understood correctly, because frankly, I'm concerned that you might be having the same trouble."

"Is that right?"

"Yes, it is. Listen, no one could blame you for wanting that man to be Captain Wooten. I've read your personnel file and your service jacket. I know what he meant to you. And I'm aware you have a very close relationship with his family – his daughter, Sarah, her husband and kids. You couldn't be any closer if they were your own family."

"So?"

"Don't you see? It creates a huge problem in your work. You have a very difficult job to do, and you need to be objective to do it. Do you understand what I'm saying? You have to accept the facts, Slaughter, just like Tanner said, whether you like them or not. Think about it. The facts are all you can rely on to show you the truth."

Slaughter closed his mind, didn't want to think about what Tanner had said. It didn't matter, had no relevance. Slaughter wasn't having a problem being objective. For crying out loud, he *had* seen Chuck Wooten. Talked to him, seen him get beaten. The man who'd been so strong, so brave, so many years ago.

And even if it wasn't Wooten, so what? He'd bring him home anyway. Let Tanner prove him wrong here in Washington. There was no way he was going to leave the man behind. Not Wooten. Not the man who'd helped Slaughter survive, kept him believing, risked torture to teach him the code. Slaughter wanted to stop right now, hold up everything until he could send Wooten another message. Send it right now. Tap it out, that's the way it was done. Let's see, could he remember? Five rows of letters, five letters each. C used for K to make it even. First tap gives the row, second tap gives the letter. Come on, Slaughter, tap away.

"Slaughter, I have to know if you understand, if you can be objective?"

Can you hear me, Captain Wooten?

"Slaughter?"

Mills' voice wormed into his brain, shoved Wooten back into his filthy cell. And it *was* Wooten. Slaughter would not doubt it again. He'd seen him, just a few days ago. Captain Charles R. Wooten, in the flesh. He would not allow a nice office and a few thousand miles to change that. But with Mills, he knew better than to deal in direct answers.

"Walter, I have a question for you, too."

Mills seemed to appreciate the evasion. "Okay, Slaughter, go ahead. We'll come back to mine."

"What was all that crap Tanner said about communist propaganda. Where in the hell did that come from?"

"What do you mean?"

Slaughter smiled, looked down, shook his head. "Come on. What's he afraid of? What's he getting ready to hide from?"

Mills hunched his shoulders, just a little. "Be careful, Slaughter. You're on thin ice."

"I don't think so. You ask me, I think Tanner is the one on thin ice. Personally, I don't really care. But I just want to make sure that Chuck Wooten doesn't die when it cracks."

Mills' hands were on his hips now. "I have no idea what you're talking about."

"Don't kid with me, Walter. I have too much respect for your intelligence. You know he's hiding something. My guess is that you know exactly what it is, otherwise you would have called him on it at the White House."

Mills puckered, as if a foul taste had filled his mouth. But he said nothing.

Slaughter stopped talking and waited for some kind of response. Prepared to wait a long, long time. Waiting was something he knew how to do.

Finally, Mills walked past Slaughter, touched his arm as he headed for his desk. "Why do I feel I'm on trial here?"

"Oh? You feel you're on trial?"

Mills stacked some papers. "No, Slaughter, I don't. It's just a figure of speech."

"I'm sorry. I never intended to put you on the spot, Walter."

"I don't feel like I'm on the spot."

"You haven't answered the question."

"You haven't answered mine."

Slaughter knew he needed to slow down, would rather back off than force Mills into withdrawal. "You're right, I haven't. So here's your answer: I do understand why I need to be objective. I realize it is fundamental to the work we do."

"Excellent."

"And Tanner's bit about propaganda?"

"That's easy to understand, Slaughter. You just need to keep in mind that Tanner is the Secretary of Defense. He's not a negotiator, never has been. His job is to be ready – and I mean right down to the muzzle flash – when people like you and I fail. If you'd made the ridiculous statement he made, I would have fired you. If I'd said it, President Simons would have asked for my resignation. But Tanner's on the other side of the fence. He doesn't give two dots and a dash if he offends people. In truth, he'd probably prefer it if he did. Then at least he'd have a clearly defined enemy. And clearly defined enemies, as we all know, are in rather scarce supply these days."

Slaughter shook his head, tried to laugh. "And so Mr. Tanner – Secretary of Defense of the most powerful country on earth – is simply . . . what? Bashing the Vietnamese? Calling our future trade partners liars? Race baiting?"

"I don't think I would put it like that."

"No, I'm sure you wouldn't, Walter. But if the press ever picks it up, I'd like to hear Tanner explain his comments to them, see how the columnists would interpret his statement."

"I don't think you'd really want that to happen."

"Maybe not. But I'm telling you, Mills, that Tanner is wrong. The man I saw in prison wasn't an actor, and he wasn't some unlucky American tourist, and he sure as hell wasn't Ho Chi Minh. He was Charles R. Wooten, Captain, United States Marine Corps."

Mills jumped to his feet, looked almost astonished that he'd done it. "Damn it, Slaughter, do you really believe that? Believe that a country, *any* country, is going to maintain war prisoners for decades, just so they can hand them back someday? Is that really what you think?"

"Yes."

"Come on, don't be so naive. It doesn't happen that way."

"No?"

"No!"

Slaughter moved in close. "Well it sure did this time."

Mills lurched around behind his desk, but he didn't say anything. Slaughter tapped his papers into a neat stack and walked out.

*   *   *   *   *

Mills propped his hands on his narrow hips, stood there smelling the air, the odor of trouble that was coming his way. He was stuck in that spot for most of a minute, as if it were dangerous to move. Then he breathed deeply, lowered his hands, spoke toward the speakerphone.

"Why don't you come in now?"

Mills heard no answer. Damn frustrating, too. He didn't like dealing with this guy and certainly didn't like his manners. But he would be stuck with him until this ended, so he would keep quiet about it.

A side door to the office opened. A short, thin Mexican stepped in, dressed much like a business executive but not quite managing to pull it off. Something about his face ruined the disguise. The coldness in the eyes, maybe. Nothing flickering away behind them except, possibly, hatred. But Mills couldn't even be sure of that; it was just a guess. Truth was, he didn't understand anything about this man. Never had. Hoped he never would.

The man was about 5'8". Lean, in a strong, stringy way. His face was pocked by old acne scars and, when Mills had looked close once, he'd noticed that the top of his right ear was missing, as if it had been bitten off. Just the top edge was gone though, nothing really dramatic. But it made the man look a little out of balance. His teeth, however, were absolutely perfect, and he seemed to show them constantly.

"Mr. Cortez, could you hear everything over the speaker?"

The man walked to the desk without answering, flipped off the speaker button, looked at Mills as though he'd been careless. Then he walked straight to him and stood six inches inside Mills' personal space. "Yes. I heard. It sounded to me like Slaughter is going to make trouble for us."

Mills stepped back, gave up the ground gladly. "No, he's just upset. Any of us would be. Let me talk to him again in the morning; see if I can't bring him around. He's been through an awful lot, but he'll be okay."

Cortez picked some papers off Mills' desk and rifled through them with little interest. "Mr. Duncan had hoped that you'd have him in line by now. But we both just heard him, Mills. I wouldn't call that being in line."

Mills decided to give Cortez the lead. It was always easier to change someone else's argument than defend your own.

"All right. Since that's your opinion, Mr. Cortez, what do you suggest we do?"

Cortez leafed through the classified documents, read some of them closely.

"Mills, my instructions are crystal clear. My company was given this responsibility a long, long time ago. We have been working closely with everyone involved, through several administrations, to make this thing happen. "

Mills started to nod. Agree with the obvious, divide the distance between them in half. But he didn't. He waited, more than a little surprised at himself.

Cortez continued. "And I have no options when it comes to setbacks. My instructions leave me absolutely no latitude. I have no trouble understanding my orders or following them. I will not let Slaughter do anything to screw this up for us. Far too much is riding on it."

Mills turned, gladly releasing the man from his focus. He reached for his coffee, cold remains in the bottom of his workday cup. He tried to create a useful distraction while he spoke, something that would make him look relaxed, even though his insides were grinding.

"Mr. Cortez, I don't believe there is any need, at least not yet, to do anything meaningful."

Cortez picked a photo of Mills' parents off a shelf, fondled the frame, then pressed his thumbs on the glass until it shattered. "That's not your call, Mills."

Mills stared at the broken glass, but didn't reach to take it away. "It could set back the treaty process."

Cortez tossed the frame on the desk, picked the classified documents up again. "He could ruin it altogether."

Mills eased over and picked up the photo, held it close to his chest. "He could ruin it regardless of your actions. He may have already told someone. Someone we might not be able to control."

Cortez smiled. "Who are you thinking about? His girlfriend? Personally, I don't believe so. But, maybe I should go see her. Ask her. Maybe she has some things she'd like to tell me." All of his teeth were showing now, something about this new idea lighting up his perfect smile.

"I didn't mean Laura. Hell, I don't think he's even had time to see her since he got back."

"He went home to her last night."

"Oh?"

"Yes."

"But I didn't mean her. I just thought that Slaughter might have spoken to someone, or several other people, here at State. They may have the same knowledge he does. Surely you can't silence all of them."

The challenge seemed to catch Cortez off guard. But he recovered quickly, went right to plain language. "You listen to me, Mills. I am not going to disappoint Mr. Duncan. If I have to kill Slaughter, I will. If I have to kill his girlfriend, I will. If I have to start right here in this office and kill every swinging dick that works in this building, believe me, I will."

Cortez had moved, like an animal, to within striking range. Mills backed up, bumped into a chair. Cortez's eyes were no longer empty, but what filled them was too ugly to look at. Mills wanted to stare into them, search for something good to work with. But he had to turn away. He let his own eyes fall on the floor.

"All right, Mr. Cortez. I think I'm clear on your position."

Mills saw the flash of brilliant teeth. Cortez was smiling again, a man happy in his work. "I'm glad you are, Mills. It makes it so much more of a pleasure to work with you."

Cortez laughed, and kept laughing as he turned and headed to the door.

"I'll give you until tomorrow, Mills. Turn Slaughter around or I will. Understand?"

Mills forced his eyes onto Cortez, but oh, how they ached for the floor. "I understand, Mr. Cortez."

"Good, Mills. Good for you."

Cortez raised the classified documents high, then threw them into the air, laughed as they floated down to the floor. "I'm glad we've had this talk, Mills. Don't make it necessary to speak again. This kind of thing tends to piss me off." He smiled big, those perfect white teeth an aberration to his ugly face. Then he left.

Mills stood there while the papers fluttered down, despising what he was feeling. The humiliation of being bullied. He'd known it all his life, especially as a puny kid in a tough neighborhood – back where he'd first discovered that his skills at negotiations could help him survive. He had learned those lessons well, eventually making a pretty good career out of them. But every now and then, whether it was behind the high school gym or at peace talks in Geneva, someone would come along who just could not be dealt with. Someone who was going to bully you into submission, no matter what you did. Damn them. Damn them to hell.

Mills shuffled slowly to the loose documents, knelt to collect them. Some of them had drifted around the room, so he crawled across the carpet to get them. His bottom lip began to quiver, but he bit it until it stopped. The pain gave rise to tears.

7

It was a little after ten p.m. when Slaughter returned home, went to the kitchen for some wine. It had been a long, long day. A month seemed to have passed since he'd seen Wooten. But at least he'd finished the agreement. After leaving Mills' office, he'd gone back and made the last few changes, specifically, the wording regarding the release of prisoners.

Laura wasn't home. She'd called him at the office, told him she was working late again, helping someone else fight life's demons. He had no idea how she did it, listening to people express terrible pain all day but still staying happy herself. Maybe it was the payback for bringing those poor souls back to normal, or at least a little farther in that direction. Was that what kept her going?

Slaughter wondered about it, knowing that whatever the benefits of her job, it would have made him unbelievably depressed. There were already too many devils in his own life. They left him no room to take on others' burdens.

But she was a fantastic psychiatrist, had been the one who conquered his nightmare. Of course, the bad dream was back

81

now. He could expect it to wake him several times every night, allowing him the barest essence of sleep. He knew it would continue for the rest of his life if he didn't work on his cancerous guilt – the terrible secret he had shared with Laura. Only Laura. After years of building a relationship of trust, he'd told her the truth. And then, about two years ago, the same time he'd returned with Wooten's body, she'd cured him.

He poured some wine and sat at the kitchen table. He remembered how calm Laura had been when he first met her. She wasn't aloof or clinical like the other psychiatrists. Laura was nothing like that. Rather, she was peaceful. Confident and secure, satisfied with her life. He saw her happiness and wanted exactly the same thing for himself. He was even willing to talk to her to get it, talk like he had never talked to the other psychiatrists at the V.A. hospital. Describe the horrors that had taken root in his brain and grown into a sinister forest of guilt.

When the front door opened, he jumped up and went to meet her. She had two bags of groceries – probably nothing that required cooking – and a newspaper, The Post. As usual, she had changed clothes at her office, replaced her expensive suit with jeans and a T-shirt. Her small body bounced down the hall on little sneakered feet, her brown hair swinging in its ponytail.

He couldn't keep from grinning at the way she padded through the house. Although she was not beautiful in the tall, classical sense, he adored her and found her irresistible. She guarded her smile and her emotions, which made some people think she was distant. But she wasn't. The smile and emotions were both there. You just had to earn them. He loved the challenge of bringing them out. Loved her more than he knew how to show.

"Hey," she said as she hurried toward him.

He took the groceries and leaned into her kiss, a passing glance off his cheek. "Hi, sweetheart. How are you?"

"Fine. Really good. You feel like going out? If we hurry we can still catch a late movie."

He set one bag of groceries on a counter near her, rested the other on his hip. "No, sorry, Laura. I'm still bushed from the trip. Sounds like fun, though. Maybe next week?"

"Sure, that's okay. Just an idea. So, how did it go with you today? Did you make some progress on the trade agreement with Vietnam?"

The bag of groceries slipped off his hip, but he grabbed it before it hit the floor. "What are you talking about? I didn't tell you I was working on a trade agreement with Vietnam."

She stopped putting away groceries, watched him with a curious look. "No, you didn't. I read it in the paper."

He shoved the groceries aside and reached for the paper. "You're kidding. It's supposed to be a secret."

"Not much of one. Here's the article."

She held out the paper. He took it and read the article slowly. It detailed Vietnam's push for an improved trading status and suggested that the chances of success were high.

"Is that a problem for you, Jacob?"

He didn't look up until he'd read it again. "I sure hope not. Man, I can't imagine who would have tipped off the press, or why."

"Will it make your job more difficult?"

"I don't know. I suppose it could inspire people to protest the improved trade relations. Of course, it might encourage them to endorse it, too. Either way, it could generate a thousand reasons to delay my mission. I've been given a thirty-day time frame. I can't exceed it."

She sat down and looked up at him as he leaned against the counter. "Why? What happens in thirty days?"

"I don't want to find out. Don't even want to talk about it."

"Where have I heard that before?"

"Come on, Laura. My job is challenging enough without me talking about things I can't change."

She stopped watching him. Found an interesting mark on the table to rub. "I see. Kind of the same way that you don't want to talk about the nightmare you had last night?"

His eyes jumped to her neck and searched for bruises while he prayed he wouldn't find any. "It's not the same thing, Laura."

Her eyebrows went up, but she didn't turn from the table. "It isn't, Jacob? Are you sure?"

"Okay, so maybe there is some overlap, but –"

Now she stood and walked over to him, picked up his hands, squeezed them. "We both know you can't do this. You have to talk through these things. If you keep them inside they'll destroy you. You've only been better for two years now. That's not the same as being cured. And things are going good for us. Please, don't slip backwards."

"Laura, I won't."

Her voice went low. Factual. "This is how it starts, though. It's textbook."

He pulled his hands away and paced the room. "I know, I know. And I appreciate that you worry about us, Laura. Really. I promise, if I move any farther in that direction, we'll talk. Okay?"

"Sure. I guess."

He stood there for a few minutes with nothing to say. She watched him. "Are you ready for bed? I'm want to try catching up on my sleep. I'm dead tired."

"No, you go ahead, Jacob. I'll finish here, be up in a little while."

"Okay, then. Good-night." He headed for the stairs.

"Jacob."

He stopped and turned around. She was standing in the middle of the kitchen, right under the light, her hands empty and low. Shadows were cast down over her eyes, obscuring them. Her voice carried a sound of pleading, and it hurt.

"Yes?"

She took one step toward him. Now he could see that her eyes were closed. "When this is over . . . that is, when you finally finish with Vietnam, let's take a vacation. Okay? A little time for ourselves, away from Washington. What do you think?"

He walked back to her, put his arms around her, pulled her close. "That's a good idea, Laura. Maybe the Cape?"

"The Cape," she repeated, like it was an eroding dream. "Exactly what I had in mind."

Slaughter couldn't sleep. The nightmare of Chuck Wooten kept waking him over and over again. At a few minutes after four a.m. he gave up, rolled out of bed and headed to the kitchen. He put on some coffee and sat down, starting doodling in the margin of the newspaper.

Laura wobbled in without speaking and he pulled down another cup. She sat down at the table and hid behind her hands.

"I knew you wouldn't stay asleep," she said through her barrier of fingers.

"You were right."

"Don't give up, though, Jacob. We conquered those dreams once before. We can do it again."

"Sure we can."

She moved her hands, looked at the letter he'd been drawing, a K with little feet, the rescue signal for downed pilots in Vietnam. Then she looked straight into his eyes. "I'd really like to know what's on your mind. Will you please tell me?"

"It's a government secret," he said, half-smiling. "Like they say, I could tell you, but then I'd have to –"

"So what? I hear government secrets all day. You know you can trust me."

"Yes. I know I can."

"So? What?"

He poured the coffee, sat down with her.

"Laura, I know you remember me talking about Chuck Wooten?"

She sipped at her coffee. It was too hot, so she blew across the top of the cup. "Of course. How could I forget?"

"I saw him the other day, in Vietnam."

She almost spilled her coffee. Her hand shook as she lowered it to the table. "What? He's dead."

"No. He's alive. I saw him, talked to him a little. He's still in prison over there. That's why he's haunting me again."

"It can't be, Jacob. You told me yourself he was dead. You brought back his remains, and they were positively identified."

"Yes, I know. And I believed that to be the truth, too. Only problem is, the Army was wrong in their identification."

"What do you mean? How can that happen?"

"I don't know how. Carelessness, maybe? A simple mistake? I'm not really sure. But those doctors have a tough job. The Army gives them a few pieces of bone, maybe a crash site location, and then expects a positive identification. It's probably a bad career move for the docs to come up empty, so maybe they just wing it sometimes."

She narrowed one eye, tilted her head. "You think they wing it? You can't be serious. Families are suffering over here for some news of their son or husband or father, and you think these guys just decide to wing it?"

"No. At least, no, I don't think they decide to wing it. I just think that . . . well, hell, they have to come up with some kind of answer. They can make mistakes."

"Those are pretty big mistakes."

"You're right, they are. Of course, Secretary of Defense Tanner is backing their original decision. Mills and Cuthbert, too. I'm climbing uphill on this, and I'm already on their shit list. It will take a lot of luck to get him home. Vietnam always plays a tough hand and, with our government giving me static, it's going to be close."

"Why?

"Like I said. They say it isn't Wooten."

"How sure are you that it is?"

He sipped his coffee, held his answer for ten seconds. "Pretty sure. He looked like hell, though. I had a little trouble making out the face. But I honestly believe it was Chuck."

"You're just pretty sure? If you're going to risk your career over this, shouldn't you be positive?"

He jumped up. He hadn't wanted to; it just happened. "I'm sure enough, Laura! Okay? For crying out loud, do you think I'd be going down this road if I wasn't? You, more than anyone else, know how hard it was to put all that behind me. Absolutely the last thing I want to do now is take another trip down memory lane."

She jumped up, too. "Then don't! Don't do it. Forget about this man. It can't be Wooten."

"I don't believe you just said that."

"Jacob, I love you. I don't want to see you suffer, especially if you could be wrong. Haven't you ever considered that Vietnam might be tricking you? The man they showed you could have been anyone. Don't destroy yourself without being positive."

He stopped and thought it through. "It's not that simple. There's something else. There are other men still in prison over there, too. Wooten, and twenty-two others. All of them still waiting for someone to get them out."

She eased herself back into her chair, seemed to go off the attack. "I . . . I can hardly believe it, Jacob."

"Neither could I."

"Wow, I've seen the black flags flying and watched the determination of the P.O.W. wives. But I always figured that those women operated out of fear. Fear of giving up, of not doing enough. Nobody ever wants to quit on a loved one unless they're sure they've been beaten."

He sat down, too, looked at the spot on the table she'd been rubbing earlier. "I know. I quit on Wooten."

"No, you did not. You didn't quit. You were beaten. It's not the same thing. Don't torture yourself over that again, Jacob. You did everything you could. Everything possible."

"I didn't get him home."

"It was impossible."

"Yeah. That's what I thought, too. But it's not impossible now. I'm going to do it this time."

"You don't sound too confident."

"Jeez, I wish I could be, but something weird's going on. Like I said, Tanner is doing some kind of an end run on me. I can feel it. He's trying too hard to convince me that Wooten is dead. He didn't accept the photo as proof."

"My God, Jacob. You had a photo?"

"Yes." He opened his attaché case, took out the duplicate copy of the full color tragedy.

Her face tightened while her hand went to her throat. "Oh, God, this is horrible."

"It is. And it gets worse. I've got files and photos of all the men still there. Many of them are in much worse shape."

"Worse shape than this?" She turned the photo over and handed it back, closed her eyes and covered her mouth.

"Yes."

"What did Mills say when you showed those photos to him."

"He had pretty much the same reaction to Wooten as you did. I didn't show him the rest."

"You didn't? Jacob, why not? The Army can't say that *none* of the men in the photos are P.O.W.s, can they? Wouldn't those photos prove Tanner wrong?"

"It might. I've thought the same thing. But if it doesn't work, I'll have nothing left."

"What do you mean?"

"I mean that if Tanner, by whatever means, can concoct some kind of believable proof that all the photos are fraudulent, where will I be?"

"Come on, Jacob. You think Tanner would do that? It would be criminal."

He put the photo away, tucked the attaché behind his calves, where he could protect it. "I know."

"So, you haven't told Cuthbert, either? No one but me?"

"That's right. I know it might be wrong, but I won't risk those twenty-three men still in prison over there. Until I know how the teams are divided, I'm holding this information back."

"Jacob, do you realize you're accusing the Secretary of Defense of criminal misconduct. If you're right, the P.O.W.s in Vietnam will be just one of your problems. Everyone knows what a mean little bastard Tanner is. If you make an allegation against him, you can expect a very ugly backlash."

"I already do."

She rose up so fast her legs pushed the table, slopped some coffee out of the cups. "Well, that's just great! What if you end up arrested over this? Suppose Tanner trumps up some allegations against you in retaliation? That's what he does, you know. He's the Secretary of Defense; that's his job. Retaliation! How do you like the sound of spending the next twenty years in some Federal prison?"

"Laura, I –"

She spun around, turned from him just as she started to cry. First a whimper, then, suddenly, an explosion of tears. He had never seen so much emotion pour out of her. Not even close. He hurried over to hug her, but she jerked herself away, crying harder than before. Her eyes seemed sad, but her voice was almost completely given over to anger. Maybe a little fear mixed in.

"I tell you how I like it, Jacob. It stinks. You have to back off. I insist. Damn it, I demand that you go to work tomorrow and tell them everything. Get the facts out, then let the government do their job. If you don't, we could both suffer. Do it for me, please. This could destroy our relationship, Jacob, and I love you too much for that to happen."

He turned, walked away, stopped at the doorway. "I'm sorry, Laura. I can't do that."

She threw her arms up. "Oh, well, thanks a lot, Jacob. I'm glad I know where it stands with us. Maybe you don't mind the idea of going to prison, but I do. I won't wait for you, Jacob. Damn you, I won't wait."

He hung his head. "I don't trust them, Laura. I won't tell them."

"Damn you, Jacob. Damn you for doing this to us."

"I'm sorry, Laura. Really."

He waited for two or three minutes, standing silently in the doorway, waiting for her to say something else. Then he left her there, went to his study and called Phong's office, just to make sure he was still standing by and ready.

*   *   *   *   *

Laura threw herself into a kitchen chair, calmed herself down by wondering how different she would be if she had been the one tortured? How different would anyone be? Experiences like that were life-changing.

But through all of Jacob's pain she loved him, even if things weren't perfect between them. She didn't make excuses for him, but she understood his problem. Commitment was a bad thing to him, an obligation that he might not be able to fulfill. He wanted the relationship, she was sure. Wanted the bond of marriage. Wanted, more than any of that, the children.

She had seen him countless times with Sarah Wooten's kids, chasing them around and playing like he was still a kid himself. She loved to see him like that; they were his very best times. And, of course, his worst times, too. They were the days that made Slaughter suffer, ashamed of himself for enjoying precious times with Wooten's grandchildren, doing things Wooten should be doing. If only she and Jacob could have their own children, it would be so much better.

She knew she would wait for Jacob. After all, he was her miracle man, one of the few soldiers who had passed through her Emotional Trauma Facility with most of his humanity still intact. He was not like any of her other patients. He was not cold or indifferent or angry. He didn't hate his former enemies, didn't despise them for their treatment of him. It had happened. He had endured. He would go forward, usually with a smile and a joke. He was, maybe in some respects, even a better man for it. Rock solid. A good man, nothing like the other veteran she was now spending a lot of time thinking about, the man who had attacked her at the hospital. Robert Abbey. True, Abbey and Slaughter had shared many similar experiences, even if Abbey had not been captured by the Vietnamese. But, like thousands of others, they had both gone over there and killed people, never really certain why, but pretty sure they had no right to do it.

Both of them had killed women in Vietnam. Abbey had even killed a small child, a little boy about six years old. It was the way they did things there, both men had said that to her at different points in their therapy. Kids could have bombs lashed to their bodies; widowed women would destroy themselves in a group of G.I.s for revenge. As grunts, they'd both said, you couldn't allow age or gender to influence your target selection. It could cost you your life, and maybe the lives of those around you. If you felt the threat, you eliminated the threat. One, two, three. The simple by-product of good training. Don't think about it. Just get the job down. Popping caps.

The bomber pilots, they'd told her, never seemed to worry about it. They dropped their loads on targets so populated that any reasonable person would know, absolutely, that innocents would get killed. But hell, then they would fly away, back to their base, maybe to celebrate with a drink. From the ground, it all seemed cavalier, as if they'd been spraying for mosquitoes.

Be like the bomber pilots, both men had prayed over there. Yeah, be like those pilots. Don't think about what you've done, or what you're about to do. Don't remember the wailing mother from the last village, cradling the bloody remains of the little boy who'd had a happy smile, a sweet tooth, and exceptionally bad timing. A thin, cute, village boy who'd rushed Abbey in hopes of a Hersey bar but got a full clip in the head as an answer.

Laura knew Abbey had a problem she couldn't help him with, understood intuitively that he would be better off dead. It was one of the hardest things she'd ever had to accept, that some people were just too far out of reach. He secluded himself in her psychiatric wing, spent all day writing long letters to the dead little boy. The letters were apologies, mostly. Sad, tormented pleas for forgiveness.

Too curious to leave them alone, she read some of them when he fell asleep, his papers dropped on the floor or wrapped in the folds of his sheets. Sometimes a letter, written on a sunny day of temporary relief, would tell the boy of baseball, of the complexities of the game, how the Reds were doing, and why.

But mostly they were dark and morose – long, meandering sentences in which Abbey placed the blame for the senseless death on everyone but himself: the politicians who'd supported the war, the draft board that had refused to defer him from it, the R.E.M.F.s who had sent him to that region, and, finally, placed the harshest blame on the little boy himself. How could that cute little guy have been so stupid? Why hadn't he known better than to run up to a G.I. who was taking his first, cautious steps into a new village?

Late one night she was making last rounds in her ward. In the uneasy quiet, she stopped and read one of those letters in the minimal lighting, tried to shift through the pages of blame and find something to work with, some tool to help heal the man's mind. It was several pages long, written in an angry scrawl that almost defied decoding. But as she struggled with it, she was shocked to read of the hatred the soldier now had for the little boy. He was a demon, the letter said, who would not leave him alone.

Abbey had started off pitifully, begging the boy to go away. But then he had turned to threats. He would do it all over again, Abbey warned. Come near me again and I'll splatter pieces of your skull all over your family, just like before. You know better than to come at me. I'll kill you!

She heard the soldier shift a little in his bed, probably searching for a dry spot on the sheets. She would check him in a minute, take his pulse, check his eye movement, wake him if he was having a nightmare, tuck him under his sheet if it was just restless sleep. As soon as she finished the letter. Only two paragraphs to go now.

He slipped his hand over her mouth with deft precision, a move he must surely have practiced over and over again. His palm kept her from screaming, while the top edge of his hand plugged her nostrils. She tried to suck in some air but choked on the vacuum created in her windpipe. He held her right arm with his other hand; her left was pinned against his chest.

His face came up from behind, barely visible as his whiskers bristled against her face. "What 'cha doing, Doc? You're not reading my mail, are you?"

She shook herself in his grip, tried to wiggle away. But he was too strong. She could not move.

"I figured I might catch you spying on me, Doc. Why? Why you spying on me?"

She shook her head, or tried to. Tried to move it from side to side. Tried to say that, no, she wasn't spying on him. A lie would be as good as the truth if it got her away.

But there was no chance of her getting free. He held her too tightly. There was nothing she could do. He would kill her here. Her time was short, her oxygen almost gone. She was going down, slipping into unconsciousness. Then she caught a glimpse of Edgar Jennings running from the other end of the ward, tried to hold on while he covered the length of the long room, his black skin lost in the dark depths of the building.

Edgar was the ward's resident simpleton, a man in hiding, too ashamed of himself to go back home to Ocala, Florida. He was an idiot, true enough, but still smart enough to know they'd never understand him back there. He had joined the Army to fit in. Uniforms, formation marching, clear and simple orders: they would keep him from standing out.

But all the Army had done was make him more freakish, given him a killer's experiences. A big, stupid man who'd gone overseas and killed people, and done it very well. Too well. No second thoughts muddling his simple mind or delaying his big hands as they moved for the enemy.

Edgar was just marking time until the good Lord came for him, as he was fond of saying, making small children's toys with thread and clothespins. He stomped up to Laura and her attacker.

"Hey! You need a hand there, Doctor Warden?"

Abbey backed away a half step, kept Laura between them. "Get away from here, you idiot. Go back to your stupid dolls."

Edgar stood in front of Laura, looking brighter than she'd ever seen before, like he was about to involve himself in something that actually made sense. Confident that this was something he could do pretty damn well.

"Doctor Warden?"

Abbey had his nose pressed into her cheek. He didn't even bother to look at Edgar again. "I told you to go away, creep. Now beat it!"

Edgar stood there another minute, his big hands rubbing up and down on his pajama legs like a kid before batting practice.

"Ooooo, I think I'll get him off you, Doctor Warden. You want I should get him off you?"

She tried to shake her head yes, strained against Abbey's grip, slipped out of it enough to scream. But she had no air to power it. All she could do was gasp in a quick breath before he covered her mouth again.

Edgar looked worried for her, his wide face drawing into a knot at the center. "Okay, soldier, that's enough. Let go of her."

Abbey cracked her head to the side. Her eyes felt like they popped out of her head.

"She's not going anywhere, creep."

Edgar moved around Laura, shouldered his way close to the man. His voice came out slow, but clear, strong and direct. Impressive. "Let . . . go . . . of . . . her."

"You go to hell."

Edgar swung his big arm at Laura with the speed of a springing trap. His giant hand slipped right behind her head and struck Abbey's neck, forced him back and away from her. Smashed Abbey's head down against the metal headrail. Edgar pinned him there, like a big grizzly with a fresh-caught salmon.

Laura scrambled a few feet away, gasped for the air she'd been denied. Then she saw that Edgar had her attacker's neck in a tight grip, had total control of him. Neither man made a sound as one of their lives slipped to the very edge.

Edgar kept the man pinned with an outstretched arm, his giant hands wrapped most of the way around the man's neck, his fingers squeezing the thick carotid arteries. Edgar looked calmly at the soldier's bulging eyes, leaned in close and examined them like they were interesting bugs.

"What you want me to do with him, Doctor Warden?"

She was gasping, still panicked.

"You want me to kill him, Doctor Warden? You say the word, I can kill him for you. He's a bad man, Doctor Warden. You want I should kill him?"

The offer was so simple. Regular or decaf? Chips or fries? Life or death? What do you want? Just say the word.

She choked on her struggle as she watched the silent drama a few feet away, seeing up-close the narrow slice of civility that separated the warriors from the war.

"No."

Edgar twisted around with a big question on his face. "You sure, Miss Warden? It ain't no problem for me."

She wanted Abbey dead. She really did. And it would have been much easier for her to let Edgar kill him if she didn't realize how natural that emotion was. But she was a psychiatrist; she wouldn't give in to her own feelings.

"No, Edgar. Don't kill him. I'm sure. You go back to your bed now. And thanks." She forced herself to get close to them as Edgar rose away from the man. Tried to piece together a truce. "Thanks a lot, Edgar."

Abbey glared at them while he massaged his neck. Then, suddenly, he apologized to them both. Edgar produced a huge, childish smile, held out his giant hand and waited until Abbey shook it.

The next morning the orderlies found Edgar dead, suffocated in his sleep.

8

Seven thirty-seven a.m., his second day back. Slaughter was rushing to get ready for work, half-listening to *Good Morning America* while he flicked his razor around his face in hurried strokes. He stopped shaving when he heard the distinctive thump of M-79 grenade launchers, went into the bedroom to look at the news.

The screen was filled with combat battle scenes – file footage from the network archives of U.S. forces engaging the Viet Cong at Khe Sanh. The voice-over was about P.O.W.s and M.I.A.s – the men of that war who'd been left behind. Then the screen switched to a State Department feed, where three women sat in solid unity in the front row of a press conference. Secretary of State Mills was at the podium. One of the women was Sarah Wooten.

"Shit," Slaughter said. "Laura, you'll want to see this."

Laura came in from the bathroom, buttoning her blouse with one hand while holding her skirt together with the other. "What is it?"

"Mrs. Kinsey, Sarah, and another P.O.W. wife. They look like they're about to jump on Mills. Damn, I asked her to cool down."

Laura sat down on the edge of the bed and listened.

Mills began. He was charming, in his element, paving the way for better relations with Vietnam, making it sound like angels would sing at the signing. He did a masterful job of setting the stage. Magnificent.

Slaughter was dazzled, truly impressed by Mills' charisma on camera. When Mills stopped, Slaughter was disappointed that he was done. But Mills had timed it perfectly – left his audience wanting to hear more. Certainly, now, the world would be anxious to endorse the trade agreement. Who could argue with such an eloquent speech?

Mills stayed at the podium after he finished, offered to field questions from the audience, most of whom were reporters. One of the three women in the front row jumped up just as a reporter began to ask a question. "Mr. Mills," she said. "We are very concerned about this increased push for improved trade relations with the Socialist Republic of Vietnam. There has never been an accurate accounting of the soldiers missing there, and President Simons has promised us that we would have definite answers before any additional trade barriers fell."

Mills didn't miss a beat, smiled as if he was her best friend. "And, Mrs. Kinsey, this administration fully understands and agrees with your concerns. Nothing has changed." He widened his smile, gave her nothing to argue about.

Mrs. Kinsey raised her voice, interrupted a second reporter whom Mills had called on. "But we've all read in the paper that further improvement is imminent. Some papers have even speculated that President Simons might be planning to give them a Most Favored Nation status. Is that true?"

Mills looked a little less perfect now, but Slaughter was sure he could handle Mrs. Kinsey. She was out-matched. He felt sorry for her, would have wanted her to win in any other venue.

But this was too important. He didn't need a protest on national television.

"Mrs. Kinsey, you know I cannot discuss any current or future foreign policy plans with you." He smiled, "Especially in front of all these cameras." He waited for the chuckle to roll through the audience, then slipped back down to serious. "But you have my word, Mrs. Kinsey, as you have already gotten the president's, that this issue, which is near to the hearts of all Americans, will not be forgotten." He hastily pointed to another reporter, cupped his ear as if straining to hear the question.

Mrs. Kinsey came back again, standing up and taking three steps toward the podium. Television crews stuck cameras and mikes in her face as she advanced on him. Sarah Wooten went with her, held her by the arm. "Mr. Mills, damn you, don't you dare brush me off! I want to know where my husband is!"

Mills was clearly frustrated now, the pain of confrontation showing on his face. "Mrs. Kinsey, I, and the entire country, grieve with you for the loss of your husband. And I would be willing, even happy, to let you harass me all day if it could possibly bring a single man home. But the facts have been proven. They've been borne out again and again and again. There are absolutely *no* P.O.W.s left in Vietnam. Every single human remain found in that country has been turned over and examined. I'm sorry, Mrs. Kinsey. I really am. But there are no more reasons to penalize the Vietnamese. They've done everything reasonable. Absolutely everything we've requested of them." He looked at her, pity and sorrow and frustration in his eyes. He didn't turn away from her pain.

The screen changed to Mrs. Kinsey, who had stood strong a moment ago. But now she staggered back, her hand wandering for her seat like a blind person's while Sarah helped her sit down.

Slaughter snapped off the television and wandered to the kitchen, understanding that Laura would gaze at the blank screen for another minute or two and think about what had been said. When he came back she looked at him, but didn't speak. He held out a photo and she took it. Winced when she saw it.

"Kinsey?" She asked.

He nodded, grabbed his suit coat and turned toward the door. Stopped. Said it low. "Yes. Kinsey."

Slaughter didn't get to his office much before nine, but he'd worked most of the night on phase two of his assignment, guessing what objections might come up first, and from which nation – figuring the most expedient, logical times to coordinate the signing, and planning the transportation to bring the prisoners home. And all the while trying to plan for the unimaginable setback, remembering that decades ago Vietnam had wasted months in Paris arguing about the kind of table they should use for the peace talks.

Mill's announcement had the entire state department buzzing. Slaughter was ready to get into the thick of it and start butting heads. He would begin with Mills.

His access to the Secretary of State had improved immensely, and he was going to use it. One more useful tool for prying Wooten out of prison. He marched in unannounced, cornered Mills at his desk.

"I saw you on television this morning, Walter."

"I'm sure you did. Judging from the angry messages I've received so far this morning, the whole country saw me. Damn, I hated talking to her like that. "

"I should think so. How could you get up there and promise that there are no P.O.W.s over there, when you know you're going to be proven wrong in just a few short weeks? What in the world were you thinking?"

"I had no choice, Slaughter. It's as simple as that. If, and when, the time comes that I look foolish, I'll confess my mistake and go on." He looked up and smiled. "Sometimes, Slaughter, it's nice to be a political appointee. I don't have to worry a whole lot about things like reelection. Now, did you want something?"

"Yes, you're damn right I want something! I want to know what's going on. First Tanner's denying the truth, and now you are. I want to know what you guys are so afraid of? I have a right to know."

Mills picked up another stack of messages, flipped through them slowly. "We're not afraid of anything, Slaughter. And I don't appreciate your making such outlandish accusations. It shows bad judgment."

"Is that right? Well, I'll tell you what bad judgment is, Mills. Bad judgment is lying to the American people, going on national television and telling them something you know is a lie."

Mills threw down the messages like he was going to fly out of his chair. But he didn't. Started to, but didn't. "Damn you, Slaughter, I was not lying. What I said may turn out to be false, but it definitely wasn't a lie when I said it."

"What the hell are you talking about? I've shown you a picture –"

"Bullshit! You showed me a picture of an old guy who's had the crap beaten out of him. It could have been anyone. Tanner says it isn't Wooten, you say it is, and I don't know. That uncertainty is precisely what allows me to say that there are no live American prisoners remaining in Vietnam. As far as I know, they have all been returned, therefore I did not lie."

"And you think that makes it all right? Not lying is the same as telling the truth? What you should have said is that there *might* be prisoners over there, and if so, they will definitely be released before or in conjunction with any future trade concessions."

Mills shook his head quickly, side to side. "I couldn't say that. And don't you ever say that again."

"Why not? It's the truth."

"It doesn't matter. The United States of America can't do anything that appears to be a vacillation. We have to take a firm position on every issue. We can't –"

"Who the hell cares about positions. There are . . ."

101

Slaughter stopped himself so quickly that he almost fell forward. His vision had snapped into a new focus, suddenly, as if by a miracle, going all the way to 20/20 and shocking him with the evil it saw.

Positions. It was as simple as that. Wooten, Kinsey, and the others weren't prisoners of the Vietnamese. They were prisoners of positions.

"I've got it, Mills, and shame on you. I know what's going on now."

Mills was rising with a new look, one he'd never shown Slaughter before, something like . . . what was that old word, beseeching? That was it. Beseeching. Begging. It was bright and luminous on Mills' face as he headed toward Slaughter with his arms straight out.

"Now hold on, Slaughter. Don't go jumping to conclusions that might prove difficult to confirm. I mean it, Slaughter. They'll have your job. You want that? You want to ruin your career over some old bag of bones that might not even be American? You can't do it. Damn it, I won't let you do it!"

Slaughter was backing toward the door with Mills shadowing him. "I know," he said again. "I know why you're afraid. And you want to know something else? I'm going to stop you."

"You're not stopping anything, Slaughter. I'll fire you."

"Go ahead. It doesn't matter."

Mills brought his hands up around his face. "Please don't do this. Trust me, okay."

"Sorry. Nothing doing."

"Okay, then, you're fired. I mean it, Slaughter. That's it, that's your career."

"Then you're going down with me, Mills. Tanner, too. And anybody else who gets in my way." He slammed the door and walked out.

* * * * *

Mills let him go. For all the trappings in this historic office, he was powerless to stop Slaughter. The walls of his office were lined with great portraits of former Secretaries of State, and he wanted to apologize to them. Christopher, Baker, Shultz, Haig, Muskie, Vance, and Kissinger. He was failing with their legacy. He shrunk back to his desk, feeling ashamed. But it passed quickly, replaced just as fast by anger.

Well, then, let them come down off the wall and try to stop Slaughter, find out for themselves what it was like trying to hold back a man like him. Hell, destroying him might not even do it. But if you were going to stop Slaughter, that would be about your only chance. Destruction. Did any one of them feel up for the challenge? Haig? You were always spoiling for a fight. You want to take Slaughter on? Baker, you think you can outfox him; tell him a convincing lie?

Mills stood back up, marched over to the portraits, passed them in review. He felt better, at least until the sadness of his situation started to move inside of him. But he worked to keep it, as he did most emotions, from showing up on his face. They were all useless. Old relics, misplaced somewhere deep inside him, their individual purposes forgotten altogether.

But somehow, they continued to survive. Down where his heart pumped and ulcers formed and ambition was fed like a wild dog. Down where his most human quality, compassion, had reclused itself from the unprincipled realities of political life.

Now, pragmatism had to rule Mills' actions. Expedience. Damage control. Reelection. Those were his masters. And compassion was in hiding.

But still, he didn't want to make the call. Didn't want to do this to Slaughter, even though he knew it was necessary. He stared at his desk from across the room, leaning under a portrait of Jefferson, watching the phone like it might suddenly learn to dance.

He knew he had no choice. He walked over and picked it up. Dialed. Waited for the voice. Closed his eyes. Said the words. The words that would end the problem and get things back to the way they were supposed to be. The way they had always been. "Slaughter has turned into a problem I cannot handle."

There wasn't any answer, and Mills was glad for that. The less said the better. It was done. Now he could start forgetting about it. Have a drink, even this early in the morning. Wash Slaughter's words from his ears, his disillusioned look from his vision. It was over, truly, or at least it soon would be.

* * * * *

The high-rise office building was just outside the beltway in northern Virginia. It probably had a million miles of wire, and lots of it had to be phone lines. But Roger Duncan knew the complete history of the one that had made his phone ring. It started at the basement terminal block and ran directly to his desk, one unbroken thread of two-strand phone line. There were no splices in the line. Never had been. His security system monitored it continuously.

Like every other time, Duncan had been the one to take Mills' call. He was always the one. He'd been taking calls like it for two decades and intended to continue taking them until this thing was over. He had given too much of his life to trust anyone else with the responsibility.

He eased back into his chair before he made the final decision, rolled the loose flesh on his neck between his fingers. The fat was a product of gross overeating, and he didn't pretend otherwise, although he preferred to think of his rich diet as a symbol of wealth. Immense wealth. If only he had more hair and fewer years, he was sure he could impress some of the beautiful women of Washington.

So, Slaughter was turning into a problem. Big deal. Lots of others had been problems, too. Many of them more powerful than a low-ranking foreign service officer. How much of a problem could a guy like that be? Maybe a little noise before it was over, maybe some bad press after he was gone. But nothing significant.

Duncan moved his fingers to his eyelids, stroked the corpulent flesh back toward the side of his big head and brought reality into focus. And the frightening reality was that Slaughter had a very real chance of ruining this entire deal. He might actually make it impossible. They'd been painfully close several times over the last dozen years and were extremely close now. But this man Slaughter could screw it up forever.

He drank his ulcer medicine before he made the call, even though it was too soon after his heart medication. He looked forward to the day when all this would end, when he could take the time to relax and use some of his fortune to nurse himself back to good health.

105

9

Slaughter went straight to his office after leaving Mills. The promise of his termination was still ringing in his ears, his awareness of Mills' sin still crystallizing in his mind.

His office was small and tightly furnished. He'd never cared much for it before and cared even less now that this would be his last day there. Mills was probably arranging Slaughter's firing right now, building a framework that would support whatever reasons he gave for the termination. Slaughter had to use this time wisely, do the things that he couldn't do anywhere else on the planet.

He called Vietnam and tried to reach Lu Kham Phong, ignoring again that there were thirteen time zones between them. But for the first time, Phong wasn't there. He left messages everywhere – Where the hell was he? – then worked at a feverish pitch to get everyone ready to sign. He wanted their foreign minister to agree today, make an irrevocable commitment. Phong could help with that, would be thrilled it had been done in two days instead of thirty. And with

Vietnam's foreign minister on board, he might be able to put enough pressure on Mills and Tanner to overcome the fears they faced. Get the deal signed. Bring the men home.

There was a clock ticking somewhere. Any minute the door would open, the security staff would walk in, and he would be forced to leave the building. He'd expected them right after he left Mills' office. He was amazed when he made it through an hour and was apprehensive by noon. Why hadn't they come? Where were they?

Then the phone rang and he grabbed it. "Yes? Hello."

"Mr. Slaughter?" The voice's perfect English, the careful enunciation, was much too clear for an American."

"Yes."

"Will you please hold for Mr. Phong of the Socialist Republic of Vietnam?"

"Yes, yes, certainly. I'll hold."

Phong was on the line immediately. "Good morning, Mr. Slaughter. Or, I guess I should say good afternoon to you. How are you?"

"Doing okay, Mr. Phong. You?"

"Very well, thank you."

"I appreciate you calling me back so promptly, Mr. Phong. I'm sorry if I'm testing your patience."

"Not at all. Quite the contrary. We have heard of your progress, and are very impressed with your diligence. You are a hard worker. Tireless. And since your message said it was very urgent, this is my first call today. Actually, I was contacted at home, came in early to call you. So, what is it I can do for you?"

Slaughter thought about Phong. He remembered the shame the man had shown at Wooten's beating, and his apologies which had sounded true and straight from the heart. Certainly, Phong had gained a clear understanding of Americans while attending college here. Those would be Slaughter's tools.

"Mr. Phong, as you probably know by now, my country is very interested in succeeding with your petition for Most Favored Nation trade status."

"I am happy to hear that. You must have been excellent at expressing our needs to your government. Thank you."

"You're welcome. But, as with any piece of important legislation, there are several potential pitfalls we have to avoid in order for it to succeed."

"Of course, Mr. Slaughter. Can you help me understand what those pitfalls might be?"

"Well, Mr. Phong . . ." he started, then added quickly, "and please keep in mind that I'm speaking personally here."

"Certainly. I understand."

"Mr. Phong, my greatest fear is, simply, that the return of the prisoners might fail. Maybe not your fault, maybe no one's fault. But somehow, the men in your custody just don't ever make it back. That would be a death sentence for your trade request."

Phong began slowly. "I see. Well, I can assure you that there is no need to worry, Mr. Slaughter. Nothing will happen to them."

Slaughter wanted Wooten out of harm's way, but it had to be Phong's idea. Otherwise, he would owe Phong for the favor, and he was in no position to rack up debts. Phong was a smart man, though. Slaughter hoped he would pick up the message.

"Oh? What makes you so confident they'll come home safe?"

"Mr. Slaughter, we have kept these men alive for decades. Frankly, I am as anxious to get rid of them as you are to have them. We would not –"

"Oh, no, Mr. Phong. Of course not. I'm not suggesting that you would. At least not intentionally. But I am concerned about the devastating results if something did happen. Suppose . . . well, let's just suppose that Vu Van Vinh did not want to give up his power over men he'd devoted his life to controlling. What could he do?"

"Don't worry, Mr. Slaughter. He could do nothing. Despite his ugly display at our last meeting, Vinh has very little power. Our country has great respect for him because of his sacrifices and has allowed him to keep his position of authority. But you have my word, he will not threaten our agreement."

"You know him that well?"

"No. Actually, I hardly know him at all. But he would not do anything to put his country in jeopardy. I know of his patriotism."

Slaughter clicked his tongue off the roof of his mouth, abandoned his diplomatic training. "Hey, if you're willing to bet the economic future of your country on your faith in this man, then he must be a great guy. Sorry I doubted him."

"You're trying to manipulate me, Mr. Slaughter. Vu Van Vinh is an honored member of our society. As such, he deserves the benefit of doubt in any question regarding him. I believe that."

"Fine. I just – "

"But, I'm also sure that his great service to Vietnam has taught him that, from time to time, things may need to be done that might seem unjust, or unfair, to him."

Slaughter knew he was winning, backed off a little. "Those things can happen."

Phong was all business now, tired of the game. "Mr. Slaughter, I do not share any of your fears regarding the well-being of the American prisoners. I have every belief that they will be kept alive and returned in due course. However, I'm also sure that my country will take your concerns into account, and will make every possible effort to assuage them, even to the point of separating your men from Vu Van Vinh."

Slaughter counted the seconds as they crawled past. He wanted to jump on Phong's offer right away, before his mind changed, shout out that yes, he wanted them separated from Vinh. But he had to give Phong a chance to reconsider. If he'd just overstepped his authority, it would be better to know now.

But Phong said nothing. A half-minute passed. More than enough time. Slaughter started to breathe again.

"Thank you, Mr. Phong. I would appreciate it. I can only believe that it's better for us both to use great caution."

"I suppose that's true. Then I think that the best thing is to cover all bases, as you might say. I see no reason to expose our agreement to any danger if it is not necessary."

"I see your point."

"I will have the prisoners transferred immediately from Vinh's custody. They will be under my direct control."

"Thank you, Mr. Phong." Slaughter felt the relief hit him, felt his insides slump into a heap, suddenly noticed that he'd wound the entire phone cord around his left hand. Wooten would be away from Vinh for the first time in almost thirty years.

"You are very welcome, Mr. Slaughter. However, you must understand that my responsibility for the prisoners ends once your soldiers arrive."

Slaughter's guts snapped back to attention. "What? What soldiers?"

Phong picked up the same tone. "What do you mean, 'what soldiers'? We received Vice-President Cuthbert's promise during the night – two o'clock this morning, our time. He gave his personal guarantee that our treaty request would be granted. Subsequently, we received the call from Secretary of Defense Tanner saying your soldiers were coming for the prisoners. Certainly that is why you called."

"My God, Phong. What do you mean?"

"Just what I said. The same thing we . . . "

The phone went deadly silent. Slaughter pushed it so hard against his ear it hurt. "Phong?"

"Excuse me for being blunt, Mr. Slaughter, but weren't you included in this decision?" Phong spoke his words carefully, but his tone said it all.

110

"I . . . it's been pretty hectic here, Mr. Phong. Your request is being handled on several levels. No one knows everything. There's, well . . . there's lots of –"

"Excuse me, Mr. Slaughter, but I've just been handed something that needs my immediate attention. I hope you understand that I must go now."

"No! Don't go, Phong. I have to know where it stands with us. Will the prisoners be under your protection? At least until our soldiers arrive? Come on Phong, give me your personal guarantee."

"Mr. Slaughter, I really have to go." Phong was struggling to get away, but Slaughter wouldn't give him the slack, wouldn't make it easy.

"Your word, Phong. I want your word! You owe those men that much. Give me your word or I swear I'll kill your petition."

"All right. I said I will put them under my control. I'll keep that promise. But only until your soldiers come. Good-bye."

10

Secretary of Defense Tanner waited in the hall of Dynet International's twenty-third floor until two twenty-five p.m., smoking a cigarette and praying that the elevator doors would open and Mills would step out. He hated him for dumping this in his lap. Mills was supposedly too busy working on damage control to break away, but whatever his excuse, it wasn't good enough. This was Mills' line of work, and Tanner hated standing in for him.

In truth, he probably owed Mills the favor. But it just didn't matter anymore. Mills' blue flame was burning out, and Tanner wouldn't be able to use him anymore. When President Simons' term expired at the end of the year, Mills would leave town with him. Tanner could just picture it, Mills going back to his elite little country club and his high-dollar lifestyle. Back home where he could brag about never taking any crap from that cracker Secretary of Defense, Tanner. Mills had done his bit, and it seemed to be enough for him. He was going home with another check in the box – Secretary of State of the United States.

Tanner was sure that Mills could have played his cards better and still have his job after Vice-President Cuthbert ascended to the pinnacle. Cuthbert didn't have anything against him, not really. Certainly nothing Mills couldn't have overcome with a few sincere gestures of respect. Like it would kill Mills to show Cuthbert how highly he thought of him.

But Mills had never gotten along with Cuthbert, had never put much into the effort. When the presidency changes hands early next year, Tanner thought, Mills will pay the price for his ego. Tanner would never pay that price for his own self-respect, but it didn't seem to bother Mills. He'd known the cost all along, so he didn't deserve any of Tanner's pity.

The good news was Tanner would keep his job. Not much else mattered. Cuthbert had already told him, as much as promised that he'd get to run the armed forces of the United States for another four years. Maybe eight. Life couldn't get much better.

How had he been so lucky? All his life he'd managed to be around people when gold lightning struck them. And all his life they'd pulled him along with them. He hadn't asked them for help, no sir. He was a genuine Southern gentleman, and gentlemen didn't ask for help. That would be too close to begging. But somehow those rising stars just seemed to understand that he wanted to ascend with them, would settle for a good job just a few steps below them. It was miraculous how they knew. Were they all psychic?

President Simons had been the most amazing, though. All Tanner had done was run his campaign in Georgia, maybe garnered a few extra precincts in Alabama. But Simons had remembered that after his election. He'd called Tanner to the White House – the very first person he'd called – just like he'd promised he would do during that dinner they'd shared on the campaign trail, the night the two of them had spoken in private and had come to an understanding.

Simons had appointed him secretary of defense at that White House meeting. And Tanner hardly knowing the man, really. But Simons had seen the same thing others had. Seen that Tanner was a good guy to have on your side.

He took another hit from his cigarette. Two men nodded to him as they walked by, heading for the conference room. How many were in there now? Fifteen? Twenty? He figured them all to be Ivy Leaguers. Harvard snots, probably. He imagined them spending their college days rowing those ridiculous, skinny boats up and down the Charles River, instead of working in the cafeteria of State College. They would probably look down on him the second he opened his mouth and came across with his Georgia twang.

He looked down at his shoes, rubbed the brown toes along the backs of his gray suit pants, just like his father had always done before an important meeting at a bank or loan company. There was a window at the far end of the hall, and he wandered down to look out of it. He waved cigarette smoke out of his eyes and leaned forward, looked all the way down to the street below. He felt sick, turned around and stared down the hall as two more businessmen stepped out of the elevator. They hesitated at the conference room door and looked Tanner over. One of them whispered something and the other one laughed. Then they went into the conference room. Tanner ground his cigarette out on the marble floor, took a deep breath and went in to join them.

He picked up a Seven and Seven at the bar, then rambled around the room for a few minutes, playing Vice-President Cuthbert's words back through his head and watching the businessmen ignore him. If he moved toward a group of them, they would scatter, like deer. He got a second drink and went over to the wall. Drank alone.

After fifteen minutes everyone turned in Tanner's direction, on cue, as though there'd been a secret signal. The sudden flush of attention made him want to climb behind the drapes. But he yanked up his belt and walked quickly to the head of the table.

"Gentlemen," he began. "As you can see, Secretary of State Mills could not join you tonight. I know you're accustomed to his presence in these matters, but I hope I can be an adequate replacement."

There was a little murmuring, which Tanner wanted to hear. He stopped talking and turned his best ear toward it. But he couldn't make it out, and some of them began to chuckle. One man put his head down and shook it from side to side. Another got up noisily, stepped back to the service bar for a drink.

Tanner had to get moving, had to get it over with. This was just too much like public speaking. Hell, it *was* public speaking. And from where he'd come from, public speaking ranked somewhere between a bad sermon and a good haircut.

"As you all know, we've got a little hitch in our plans regarding Vietnam."

The man next to him – a foreigner, European – rolled his eyes, and right there and then Tanner made a vow to stop saying 'Nam' like 'Ma'am'.

"Anyway," he continued, "I don't rightly know what we can do about it. The F.S.O. who's screwing things up, Jacob Slaughter, is certainly an embarrassment. But honestly, ain't a whole lot *we* can do. We're firing the man and kicking him out of his office. But what I understand of Slaughter, that isn't going to stop him. And the last thing any of us need is an angry former P.O.W. running around with a sharp ax and a national secret."

One of the businessmen tilted his head back, subtly, like he was making a bid at Sotheby's.

Tanner pointed his big, fat finger right at the man. "Mr. Duncan, you've got something to say? How does all that strike you?" Tanner felt himself smile for the first time. This diplomacy thing wasn't so hard once you got the hang of it.

Duncan looked away and shook his head. Maybe Tanner hadn't done so well after all. But then Duncan rose and began, so maybe things were all right after all. It was pretty hard to tell. Damn this was frustrating business.

"Mr. Secretary." Duncan's voice surprised Tanner with its volume, made him straighten his stubby frame. He was listening.

Duncan swept his hand through the air. "Dynet's client companies, represented by these distinguished men here, have always pushed for the fall of trade barriers between the United States and Vietnam. And, sir, I know you understand completely how much we want the volume of business that is waiting to be transacted. Vietnam is a country with absolutely nothing, with the potential to become a superpower. This is a chance for American business to fund the start of an industrial giant, like Japan."

Tanner's head started bobbing up and down. He had trouble making it stop. "This administration has no misunderstandings about that, Mr. Duncan."

"Then you understand that we cannot, will not, let Slaughter stand in the way of our objective?"

Ah-ha! Now Duncan was speaking Tanner's language. Blunt. Clear. Threatening. "No question. I understand. I'm sure the president does, too."

"Well, then, do you have the time problem covered, the thirty-day limit? Have you handled your end of things?"

Tanner was grinning now. This wasn't going to be hard at all. "We sure do. Vice-President Cuthbert called over to Vietnam earlier. Gave them his word that they would get the trade deal if they'd be a little flexible. They're going to give us the time we need to cover our asses."

Duncan paced a little, then stopped behind an ugly little man in a solid black suit, rested his hands on the man's shoulders. "Good. Gentlemen, I think most of you know Mr. Cortez."

Several people murmured. Tanner heard himself say, "Yeah. Hey."

Cortez had been staring at Tanner since he'd come in, and he didn't look away now. Tanner locked up with him, but Cortez's black little eyes dug into Tanner's until it began to hurt.

Duncan looked back and forth between them for about ten seconds, Cortez to Tanner, Tanner to Cortez. Then he patted Cortez on the back. "I guess you're ready then, Mr. Cortez. Do whatever you need to do." Duncan stared at Tanner as he spoke, made him a party to it by giving the order in front of him. Tanner only recognized it after it happened, knew Mills, even with all his weaknesses, would have been quicker.

Cortez smiled and rose, whispered something in Duncan's ear. This time, Tanner was glad to be out of hearing range. "Good," said Duncan, smiling, too. "Yes, that will be excellent."

* * * * *

Thirty minutes later, Angelo Cortez was prowling Duncan's office in silence, giving Duncan time to worry. Finally, he stopped behind Duncan, knowing his boss would hate having him there. He looked down on Northern Virginia from the thirtieth floor of Dynet International. "You should not have drawn so much attention to me," said Cortez. "It wasn't smart. I didn't appreciate it."

Duncan was not the same man now that they were alone. He showed no confidence, had none of the audacity he'd shown in the lower floor conference room. "You're right, Mr. Cortez. It wasn't the smartest thing I've ever done. I'm sorry."

Cortez grinned. Checked his face in the glass's reflection, noticed a small scab and picked at the blemish.

That would do it, he decided. He'd just wanted to hear the apology. The little sound of the big corporate leader groveling to Cortez. It sounded wonderful. Words of respect. He absolutely loved the feeling they gave him. Every time he felt it he silently thanked that bastard Rijos.

In Angelo Cortez's slum *barrio* in Mexico City, Rijos had been a well-built eighteen year old who reigned supreme. He ruled the filthy streets and the starry nights and everything trapped in between them. Only four years older than Angelo, he lived a totally different life, a life of alcohol and young girls and an occasional stolen car.

Rijos frightened Angelo, as he did everyone. On Angelo's way to his job at the corrugated box company and on his way home he would have to pass Rijos and his gang as they lingered around their command post — a narrow alley that no one ever entered without being invited, or dragged. Angelo would always pass quickly, as far across the narrow street as he could, holding his breath and praying Rijos' sentries didn't notice him.

Early on a sweltering Thursday morning, Angelo's converting machine quit, and the company sent him home until they could repair it. As he passed Rijos' alley, he was a little surprised that none of the blue-jeaned sentries were guarding it. He stopped at the entrance but heard nothing. He took a few steps. Still heard nothing. Walked a little farther into the shadows.

At the back, Rijos sat on top of a wooden crate, alone. His eyes were fixed, staring at Angelo with an unpredictable look. Rijos was a fairly big kid with strong shoulders and long black hair that swayed around him when his head turned. His face was badly scarred from the knife fight that had made him a legend, and his nose was badly bent, almost smashed flat. Angelo had heard that Rijos' father had done it to him when he was a kid. Several times. His father was dead now.

"Hey," said Rijos, sounding more bored than angry. "What are you doing back here?"

Angelo was embarrassed by the reason, knew Rijos could never relate to the desperation of a boy in love. But he'd never expected this day to come, a time when it was just him and Rijos. He wouldn't waste it. "I want to talk to your sister, Bernadette. I wanted to tell you first, so there wouldn't be a problem."

118

Rijos glanced up at a window. Angelo looked, too. Bernadette was looking down on them from two floors up, her pretty dark skin and dark eyes more beautiful than anything else in his world.

"Do you think my sister wants to talk to you, Little Man?"

Little Man? Was that a compliment? Angelo felt like a man, that was for sure. He did a man's job and shouldered a man's responsibility – caring for the family of his long-gone father.

"I think she likes me some," he said. "I've seen her on the street, and we've said hello. The rest is up to the future."

Rijos seemed to find this funny, like maybe the future was so close at hand he could sit right where he was and watch it all go by. "You're filthy," Rijos said, and Angelo knew it was true. "Get cleaned up and come back tomorrow, this time. You've got courage, Little Man. I'll introduce you to my sister." Then Rijos jumped off the box quickly, as if to startle him. But Angelo didn't even twitch, wondered why Rijos had done it.

"I'll be back tomorrow, then. This time."

Rijos shrugged, walked to a side wall and pissed as Angelo walked away.

As usual, Angelo was up before dawn the next morning. He'd counted his money the night before, heaped three years' savings into one pile, counted the secret fortune so many times he could recognize most of the paper bills at a glance. His mother needed the money, he knew that. Needed it desperately for the rent and the groceries and a dozen other things, none of which they'd ever been able to afford. But there would be more years to work, more money to make. The rent bill would still be there. Today would only come today.

When the store opened, he was the first one in. He knew just what he would buy, had admired the outfit so many times that the store owner had finally asked him to stop coming in to look. But today he had money. Today he would buy the shirt and the matching trousers. Long pants that weren't denim and weren't his uncle's hand-me-downs. They were beautiful. Pure, clean, white.

Angelo had bathed last night, too, and he was spotless. He went to the dressing room and shed his own rags, stood naked in the small room as he touched the shiny fabric, caressed it, fondled it. As the clothes touched his body they changed him, made him better than he'd been a minute before. Made him attractive. Respectable. He didn't live in the slums anymore. He lived in a clean, white house with Bernadette. She loved him completely, and their future would unfold together.

He wore the clothes out of the store, leaving his rags behind. His life would make a wonderful change today. He strolled around the neighborhood until it was time to meet Rijos.

Today, the sentries were at their positions, eyeing the street, abusing everyone on it. But they let him pass. He strutted through the alley without slowing down. Like a tunnel, there was light at the entrance, then it was dark in the middle. Then it grew light again at the other end – where a collection of garbage cans and wooden crates served as makeshift seating for Rijos and his followers. All the seats were filled. Several boys were standing, watching Angelo approach, knowing something he couldn't quite comprehend. Bernadette was there, too, wearing a pretty, floral print dress. She was beautiful, standing beside Rijos, waiting for Angelo to take her hand and lead her away. He got close enough to do it but didn't speak until he'd given Rijos a chance to swallow the beer he'd been drinking.

"Hey! Little Man!" Rijos' was different today. Angelo could hear in his voice why he terrified people. He felt the fear himself.

"Why are you here, Little Man? I didn't order any ice cream." Rijos jumped off his crate again. This time Angelo flinched.

"I'm here to meet your sister, Bernadette. Like we agreed."

Most of the boys laughed. Rijos laughed. It was loud and getting louder. "Hey," Rijos called out to the crowd, "anyone order ice cream from the ice cream man here?" He flipped up the collar of Angelo's shirt, smudged it with his dirty fingers. All the boys laughed some more.

But Bernadette didn't laugh. Angelo was watching her, trying to ignore the boys, concentrating only on her. She was smiling, but her smile was for him. She was trying to show that she liked him. He could endure this for her.

"Go away, Ice Cream Man. My sister don't want to date nobody who looks ridiculous. Take your silly clothes and go away." Rijos raised his beer over Angelo's head. Angelo didn't move, kept watching Bernadette. She still hadn't laughed.

Rijos tilted the bottle. The beer spilled out, all over Angelo's face and across the front of his new shirt. The boys were laughing so hard now that some of them fell down. But Angelo stood still, watched Bernadette. Her smile started to change, and he started to hurt.

Then it happened. She started laughing along with them. Her beautiful smile turned into an ugly black hole. Her eyes shriveled and died behind her wrinkled eyelids. Someone handed Rijos another beer, and he danced around Angelo with it, sloshing the brown liquid on his ice cream clothes, stopping in front and laughing at him from two feet away.

Then Angelo felt something he'd never felt before, something that scared him more than anything else in his life. Deep inside, down where he'd always been afraid to look, something broke. Probably nothing he needed anymore, but something, certainly. He wondered what it was as he stepped up to Rijos, so close that the toes of their tennis shoes touched.

"I'm going to kill you, Rijos." It wasn't his voice that came out. The words had certainly come out of his mouth, but it wasn't his voice. It frightened him. Frightened Rijos.

Rijos leaned back a little. Just an inch, maybe, but a retreat. Angelo moved with him. No one was laughing anymore. No one made any noise at all. Angelo noticed some music from a faraway radio.

Rijos started to talk, probably lay down his own challenge, live up to the reputation he'd built for himself. But Angelo didn't wait to hear it. From that same cavity inside him, maybe hell, a devil's power raged through his body and settled in his hands. He struck up at Rijos with his right hand, so quickly that Rijos never saw it, struck his throat so hard and deep that he could have closed his fingers around the back of Rijos' neck.

Rijos gagged, then choked. Shock and terror bugged out his eyes. But Angelo wouldn't stop. Couldn't stop. It wasn't enough. He had shown respect; he deserved it back. Not laughter. Respect!

He closed his hand around Rijos' windpipe. Squeezed it. Crushed it, just like that. Kept squeezing. The flesh of Rijos' neck ripped and the crowd scattered, but Angelo didn't let go. It seemed to him that Rijos was dangling overhead in his grip, his blood running down Angelo's arm and all over his ice cream suit.

He kept shoving Rijos away, then jerking him back. Away and back, over and over and over. The flesh was completely torn open now, his fingers dug into Rijos' throat and overlapped behind his windpipe. It felt strange, like squeezing a thick snake.

Rijos' eyes closed. Angelo felt the extra weight as he died. But he didn't drop him. Didn't need the strength of his left arm to hold him up, either. He walked around the back of the alley with Rijos' body, hauling it around to anyone who was still there, the blood soaking the right side of his body, all the way to his shoes.

Bernadette was hysterical, but he no longer cared. He dumped Rijos there, at her feet, then turned and walked back down the alley, past the panicked followers, through the dark tunnel, and out beyond the sentries.

"I said, I'm sorry," Duncan repeated, the delay putting a little extra worry in his voice.

Cortez flashed his smile. They could put it behind them now. He would even get them started on the right path. "Has Mills had Slaughter thrown out of his office yet?"

"It's in the works right now," Duncan said. "Slaughter will have no government access after tonight."

Cortez wandered away from the window. "He's a very interesting man, you know."

"Who? Mills?"

"No. Slaughter. Have you read his book?"

Duncan looked surprised, like maybe he didn't know Cortez could read. Cortez buried the insult for some other time.

"I haven't. I heard he wrote a book after his release, though."

"You should read it sometime. It's quite interesting."

"Maybe you could just tell me about it?"

"You should read it yourself, Mr. Duncan. It would help you understand your enemy."

Duncan waved his hand, as if to sweep away the idea of reading Slaughter's book. "He's not really my enemy, Mr. Cortez. Your relationship to him may be different. But for me, and Dynet, he is simply a –"

"Mr. Duncan, if Slaughter upsets your plans and the plans of your clients, causes all of you to lose billions of dollars, won't he be your enemy then?"

"Yes. I suppose so."

"Then he is your enemy now. You're foolish to believe otherwise. He's your enemy, and you should know him."

Duncan looked at his watch, very slowly, as though it were a secret, then stroked his forehead. "All right, Mr. Cortez. What did Slaughter's book say?"

Cortez flashed his white teeth. "Oh, not much, really. Only that he is an honorable man."

Duncan suddenly looked surprised. Interested. "Slaughter said that in the book?"

"No. Of course not. A man like Slaughter would never say that. In fact, the book was written with grace and humility."

Duncan poured some wine from a decanter. He didn't offer any to Cortez. "So, what did he say?"

"He said that he's often been asked how he held out in prison, never gave in to any of the Vietnamese demands, even after they tortured him horribly, once for twenty-one days straight. Do you know what he said?"

Duncan raised his glass to his lips, although Cortez didn't see him drink. As he moved it away he asked, "What? What did Slaughter say? What was his answer?"

"Slaughter said that he would have told them anything they wanted, done absolutely anything they wanted him to do, except – here's the amazing thing – it never crossed his mind. Can you believe that? The man didn't say a word to them for four years because he had decided, day one, that he wouldn't. Never gave a second's thought to changing his mind."

"That's crazy. All those years to sit and think? Impossible."

Duncan was fascinated. Cortez didn't even have to check. He could hear it in his voice.

"No," Cortez said softly. "I don't think so. I believe that my enemy – our enemy – is a man who deals in absolutes when he's afraid. Absolute silence. Absolute honesty. Absolute loyalty. Loyalty to America and the P.O.W.s. Loyalty to Charles Wooten."

"Maybe we can use that as a weapon? Is there a chance we could convince him that his actions run counter to the best interests of his country. It might be worth a try, you know. It might save us the difficulties involved in killing him."

Cortez let the laugh come out, a perfect chance to show his teeth. "You're not listening, Mr. Duncan. Slaughter isn't some kind of bureaucratic follower. He makes up his own mind, is governed by his own sense of right and wrong. In his mind, anything that might delay the prisoners' release would be absolutely wrong."

Duncan set his drink on the desk. "Well, damn, Cortez. If we don't have any other options, why are we wasting time talking about it? You'll have to kill him. Why does that seem to bother you?"

"Because, Duncan, I believe he is the genuine article. One of very few I've ever come across. Strong, tough, intelligent. Honorable. It is a tremendous shame to destroy him."

"I don't see an option."

Cortez looked at Duncan as though he'd just spoken in tongues. "Oh, no, you're right. Make no mistake about it, there are no other options. I will destroy him. Certainly." He moved to the door and opened it, heard Duncan breathe for the first time in a while. "It's a shame, though. That's all I was saying."

"A shame," Duncan said. "Yes. Absolutely. A damn shame. But since it has to be done, do it quickly. Decisively. Send as many men as you need. Ten men. A hundred. Spend whatever. I don't even care how you do it, just get it done, soon."

Cortez didn't bother responding. He just walked out.

He stood at the elevator and waited for the express, almost too excited to hold still. This was the job for which he'd been born. The opportunity of a lifetime. Duncan had given him the nod in front of everyone. And – his protest to Duncan aside – he'd loved the attention in the conference room. Absolutely loved it. All those rich, smart, college boys nodding with pleasure. And why? Because Cortez was going to help them. He had their confidence. They were depending on him; they had no choice but to depend on him. And wouldn't their respect for him increase with their dependence? Surely it would be impossible for them to need him so desperately without holding him in higher regard. If they were drowning, wouldn't they worship the man who saved them? Of course they would. And Dynet's clients *were* drowning, could sink in rough economic seas if Slaughter showed the world what they were doing. Slaughter had to be stopped. Cortez was the one who would do it.

He would make it look like he did this job alone. Why share the glory? Slaughter stood between Duncan's clients and billions of dollars. The man who stopped him would be a god. And that sounded pretty good.

He had already put his cover story and alibi in place, chosen the best method, and selected the man he would use. His was a business of little details and it was hard, time-consuming work.

He had to be careful. He could kill him however he wanted, but it could not be tied to Dynet, or the White House, or Vietnam, or the treaty. And any evidence Slaughter had with him needed to be collected or destroyed. Nothing could be left to chance.

These were the kinds of circumstances that made Cortez better, and he relished them. When weaker men began to fail and fumble from exhaustion, Cortez would tap the devil-power inside him, the power that had lifted Rijos off the ground. The power to keep going. Never turn back, never yield an inch. Never, ever fail. Just keep on hitting, attacking with increasing ferocity, harder and harder and harder.

The elevator doors opened and he climbed in, couldn't wait to get to the street and start hunting.

11

Slaughter was pushing the limits, trying to do more than time allowed. It was nearly four p.m., a lot longer than he'd expected to last after Mills' threat this morning. But his time was almost up. Two days. That's all he'd had to work with.

He had Phong's file in his briefcase, ready to go out the door. Just one last call. He hoped to get it done before the guards came for him. His friends had passed along the rumors all day, and the messages reminded him of times in his prison cell. Now, like then, he felt completely alone and isolated. Yet, then and now, the communication network had operated efficiently. Today's messages had been delivered by cool office innuendo instead of code words and tapping, but it was still urgent information. Only the method of encryption had changed.

You'll be gone before tonight, the rumor had said. *Get ready, prepare yourself in whatever way you can. The guards are coming.*

He picked up the phone and called Phong one last time, still unable to believe what he was going to demand of him. It was too much of an abomination.

"Hello, Mr. Slaughter. I'm . . . a little surprised to hear from you."

"I bet. You've been talking to Mills?"

Phong turned defiant; it came through loud and clear. "Yes. Your secretary of state has contacted me."

Slaughter heard men's voices outside his door.

"You'll have to listen carefully, Mr. Phong. I've only got time to say this once."

"I'm listening."

"Your country's future and the prisoners' lives depend on you trusting me and doing what I ask."

"You have dealt honorably with me, Mr. Slaughter. I will try to do the same, as far as possible."

"You might have to go farther than that."

"I don't understand."

"Makes two of us, Mr. Phong. I can't believe what I'm going to ask you to do, but here goes. I want you to guard those prisoners very carefully."

"I already have them under my protection, they will –"

"No! That's not what I mean. I want them taken back to Vinh, or anyplace else where we can't get to them. I want them under the tightest possible security. Don't let them go; don't release them to anyone."

"You can't be serious. You've been working so hard –"

"You'd be foolish to trust our government, Phong. Don't trust Vice-President Cuthbert. Political winds are shifting, and our agreement is too fragile. If you release the prisoners, you'll have nothing left to deal with. Under no circumstances should you turn them over to the American soldiers. Wait until you have a signed copy of the presidential order and, even then, talk to me first. Insist on having that right."

"I'm not sure I can comply, Mr. Slaughter. The position you're putting me in is a difficult one."

Slaughter's office door swung open. Three uniformed Secret Service agents stepped in, hurried toward the desk.

"Make up your own mind, Phong, but I'm telling you what you need to know. Do the smart thing with the information I've given you. You can trust me, you know you can."

The lead agent, a large, ordinary-looking man about fifty-years old, ran up beside Slaughter and snatched the phone from his hand, slammed it down. The other two agents stopped in front of the desk.

The agent stood there, his height looming over Slaughter, his severe face glaring down at him, his hand still on the phone. "You'll have to leave these premises now, Mr. Slaughter."

"Really? On whose orders?"

"Mr. Mills, sir."

"Wilbur Mills? Walter Mills? General Mills?"

The agent looked bored, unamused. "Don't be a funny guy, okay. It just makes my job harder."

Slaughter stood up, rose into the agent, made him back up. "Well, I wouldn't want to do that. I'm sure your job is already hard enough, what with standing at the door and taking names all day."

"Let's go, sir."

Slaughter reached for his day planner. "Sure. Just let me pack. Clean out the desk. Spruce the place up for the next person."

"No, sir. You leave everything here."

Slaughter put his hands on his hips. "That seems a little rude."

"Sorry, sir. Let's go."

"Okay. I'll make it easy on you boys –"

"Don't you worry about us." The lead agent grinned, as if this could turn into a fun thing if Slaughter would offer some resistance

"I wasn't really, big fellow. Just a figure of speech." He picked up his briefcase with Phong's photos. "Ready," he said.

The lead agent grabbed the briefcase with his left hand, tried to wrench it away.

"Sorry, Mr. Slaughter. You leave empty-handed."

Slaughter jerked back on it, hard enough to pull the agent off balance. "That's my personal briefcase. It doesn't belong to the State Department."

The agent yanked it back. "I'll have it returned to you, sir. I'll even deliver it personally."

Slaughter stopped pulling but didn't let go. "Well, I guess that seems fair enough. Then let's . . ."

Slaughter grabbed the agent's left wrist, just above the briefcase handle. He pushed it down, then pinned it to his desk. He used his other hand to jam the agent's elbow over until the shoulder popped – just like the Vietnamese guards had done to him. The agent screamed, loud in his ear, but not loud enough to drown out the sound of the youngest agent's holster being unsnapped. Suddenly, a gun was coming up, raising the ante. The lead agent screamed again as the other two agents lunged at Slaughter. But, just as quickly, Slaughter had the lead agent's small frame revolver out of its holster and in their faces. He felt like a lion tamer with a chair, the agents leaning back and forth, looking for their chance.

"Easy, fellows. Let's all keep our heads here." Slaughter kept aiming at the young agent as he let go of his leader, who collapsed into Slaughter's chair, his left hand hanging almost to the floor. The young agent's gun was still low, but threatening. Both of the other agents twitched like cats ready to pounce while Slaughter picked up his briefcase and backed up about ten feet.

The young agent's arm made a sudden twitch. It was just an accident, or a muscle spasm, or, maybe, just plain inexperience. But it made his gun move a little and all of them gasped. Slaughter aimed the revolver at the tip of his nose, ready to fire.

"Okay, kid, slow down! Gentlemen, put your guns on the desk. First you." He kept aiming at the forehead of the young agent. "Easy now, real slow. Go at your granny's pace. I don't want to kill you, but I'm not going to get killed, either. So, go slow and we can all live through this."

The young man looked at the lead agent, who held his right hand to his shoulder. He nodded. The young agent was suddenly full of cooperation, rushed to put his gun on the desk, very gently.

"Nice work. Very nice –"

The other agent snatched out his weapon. He was fast, his hand at his side and his pistol coming out in a blur. Slaughter whipped his gun toward the man. It was very, very close, but Slaughter got there first, aimed right into one of the agent's eyes and rushed at him for emphasis. "Put it on the desk, hot-shot. Now! Do it!"

The agent stopped, his weapon aimed almost at Slaughter's midsection. He just stood there, only another two feet to go for a kill zone on Slaughter's body. It was obvious he didn't want to concede the loss.

Slaughter cocked the revolver, made that wonderful sound of impending death.

"Shit," cussed the agent. Then he tossed his weapon on the desk.

"Radios, boys. Let's have 'em."

"I've got the only radio," said the lead agent. He used his good arm to unhook it from his belt and set it on the table.

"Thank you, gentlemen. Thank you for your cooperation. Now, throw all your keyrings on the desk and go over there, handcuff yourselves to the radiator."

The agents were slow, but they did it. The young agent rolled his boss around in Slaughter's chair and helped handcuff him. The lead agent looked like he hated him for it.

"That's nice. Now, I'm going to leave your guns and radio over here across the room. You can cry for help and suffer that embarrassment, or you can figure out your own escape. I'm sure you're smart guys; it won't take you long. And I'll be gone, so your job is complete. It's up to you how much more you want your superiors to know."

Slaughter grabbed his briefcase, double-checked to make sure Phong's portfolio was still in it, and left, glad that no one had been seriously hurt. It took less than two minutes for him to clear the building.

He drove several blocks away, stopped at a pay phone, looked up a number and dialed. He hated to spend the time, but he needed the insurance. He'd locked the other set of Phong's photos in the State Department vault so that they'd be safe. But now they were out of reach, at least to him.

On the third ring a young man's voice answered the phone, his smart-ass attitude overriding the canned greeting. "Instant PhotoMan. How can I help you?"

"Can you make copies from photographs?"

Again, the voice came back full of youthful cockiness. "Sure. Do it all the time. No problem."

"Can you do it while I wait?"

"Yup. It'll take about thirty minutes."

"That's fine."

"Bring 'em on, then. I'll be here. I'm slow right now, and there aren't any jobs ahead of you. You know where we're at?"

"I do. I'll be there in half an hour."

Slaughter hung up and ran back to his car.

* * * * *

Cortez had watched as Slaughter ran away from the State Department building. He'd just gotten there; hadn't been waiting long. He dropped in several cars behind Slaughter's car, getting things ready. Cortez's man, Alvarez, picked up the tail in a black Chrysler.

Cortez's phone rang.

"Yes."

"This is Mills."

"Yes, Mr. Mills. What can I do for you today?"

"I need you to wait. Don't do anything yet. Slaughter called Phong just before he left. I don't know what he's done, but I may need him to undo it. Don't do your job yet. Understand?"

"I have my orders, Mills."

"Well, I just changed them!"

Cortez smiled, slid a CD into the player. "You can't. Not without convincing me that it's necessary or getting Duncan to rescind them."

Mills raised his voice. Cortez listened closely, waiting for him to cross the line. "Listen, Cortez, Slaughter has a bunch of classified information with him. I just found out that Phong gave him a large stack of files and photos. We need to get that back or destroy it."

"I can take care of that."

"Cortez, you will wait for further instructions!"

That was as far as Cortez would allow Mills to go. He was at the line. "Sorry, Mills. You will need to contact Mr. Duncan. I take my orders from him. And Mills?"

"Yes?"

"You should be more polite on the phone. I think it would be a good idea. Better for your health." He turned off the phone.

Screw Mills and his disrespectful tone of voice. Cortez was ready to take Slaughter down now, and he wanted to take Slaughter down now. He wouldn't let Mills ruin his plan. It was too perfect, a plan he'd been waiting to use on someone for months. He would only use one man. An expendable man. Cortez would keep all the credit. It would be done and over with. Slaughter would disappear. If he had some evidence with him, it would disappear, too. Cortez would have proven his worth to Duncan again.

Cortez loved being valued like this, respected by Duncan and the others. He'd sought respect all his life, but it had eluded him for the same period of time. Even in the gangs back in Mexico

City, where he'd done his very bloodiest work, they had never really respected him. They'd feared him, sure, and that had felt pretty good. Fear is a hard thing for a small man to instill. But he never got respect; it had passed him over entirely.

Yes, sir, Slaughter would be a career-enhancing ticket to punch, even if he hated to do it. Slaughter was different from most of the jobs he'd been given. He sparked something inside Cortez that he'd never known before. Maybe it was admiration. Maybe just curiosity. But something, certainly, that set him apart from the typical victim. Cortez had watched him walk to the car, watched the confident tilt of Slaughter's head, even as his face radiated concern.

"Should I do it now?" Alvarez sounded anxious over the radio, in a hurry to end it.

Cortez held up his two-way radio, thinking about the plan once more. Alvarez was ready, his vehicle filled with explosives. He had already called home to his family in the slums of Mexico City and said his good-byes. Told them of the great riches they would get after his death. Listened to them beg – plead with him not to do it. Come home, instead, they'd said. Work with us in the fields. Please, please don't leave us.

Cortez looked at his own face in the mirror, picked some food out of his teeth. He admired Alvarez's devotion to his family, actually felt a little bad that they would never get the money. "Wait until he approaches the intersection, Alvarez. You need to hit him hard to get a good detonation. Make it look like a bad traffic accident where the gas tanks exploded."

Alvarez's peasant accent increased as the moment of impact approached. Fear replaced his desire to sound American, chased away his dream of fitting in. It would never happen now. "Bueno. I will do that, of course, Mr. Cortez."

Cortez was half a block behind Alvarez, still thinking that it was a shame to kill Slaughter. A tough man, a man of principles. A man who'd suffered, much like Cortez himself had suffered in the Mexican prisons. A man who, like himself, had survived. Been sent down a hard road, a path of conflict, and excelled. Cortez felt bound, somehow, to him. Connected. Didn't enjoy the idea of destroying him. It was quite a new experience for him.

He keyed the mike. "Are you ready, Alvarez?"

Alvarez was crying now, painful sobs distorting his transmission. "Yes, Mr. Cortez."

Cortez lifted in his seat, watched the black car accelerating toward Slaughter's Maxima. He pulled to the curb to watch the fireball and avoid the falling debris.

"Ram him! Now! Hit him hard!"

Alvarez did not answer back. The front of the black Chrysler jumped up, blasted at Slaughter's car.

12

Slaughter rushed for the Instant PhotoMan. The street was crowded; all of the traffic was moving slow. He tried to jink his way in front of the gold Volvo beside him, make a little extra headway. But the woman didn't see him, almost hit him, slammed on the brakes. Fortunately, the car behind him had kept good distance, which left him room to swerve back into his own lane. He looked over as the Volvo slid by, the child's car seat lurching forward. He watched, like a worried parent, as the woman's baby tried to fly out of it. But the straps held. The woman looked over at him, smiled with relief, wiped her hand across her forehead.

He slowed down, decided he wasn't in *that* big of a hurry. He glanced in the mirror as he stopped for the red light, still tagging along behind a slow-moving dump truck. The car behind him, a Chrysler, suddenly jumped up in acceleration. What the hell was he doing?

Slaughter searched for an escape, started breaking the traffic down into segments, timing each segment as it came through the intersection, still watching the Chrysler. He worked out a quick, desperate plan – all the while hoping the other driver would wake up and realize he needed to stop. Maybe the man was having trouble seeing him, a small car in the shadow of a big truck.

The Chrysler had no room left to stop or even slow down. Slaughter nosed up, locked his steering wheel hard left. The hood of his car barely squeezed underneath the bed of the dump truck, but as soon as it did he stomped the gas, shot into the oncoming lane and angled toward the cross street, swerving around several honking, skidding cars and a dozen pedestrians.

He was still crossing the intersection when it happened. He looked back, saw the Chrysler try to follow him, try to veer around the dump truck, too. But the Chrysler clipped the corner of the truck.

There was a huge rush of air that hurt Slaughter's eardrums, as if a huge, noisy vacuum had sucked up the world's air in half a second. And then came a monstrous explosion. Slaughter kept driving, dodging traffic, but looking back to see what in the world had happened.

A rolling fireball burst from the Chrysler, roared to the storefronts, then climbed up the buildings toward the sky. The Chrysler disappeared, disintegrated into a million pieces that pinged against the metal of Slaughter's car. The gold Volvo went with it. Several other cars, too.

The dump truck flipped over and landed upside down, setting off two more explosions. Thousands of windows shattered. The rear end of Slaughter's car was lifted up, and the blasts' concussion pushed him sideways.

Slaughter held the wheel and battled for control as the apocalypse rained down. Three seconds had passed. Maybe four. But he couldn't believe the war-scene around him. Newspaper boxes and bus stop panels were blowing along the street. Cars that hadn't been at ground zero crashed into each other. Pedestrians were cut apart by shrapnel. Some of them crumbled to the sidewalks in crimson heaps. Others went hysterical, looping around in bleeding circles.

There was too much damage, nothing he could do except call emergency services. He snatched his phone off the seat and stomped the gas, accelerated away from the crash, weaving around the stopped cars like they were pylons, trying to miss the people who had climbed out of their cars to see what had happened around the corner.

*   *   *   *   *

Cortez nosed away from the curb a half minute after the explosion, fought his way through the debris while it was still raining down on the street. He'd been three hundred yards away when the dump truck's tanks exploded. First one, then the other, sending two more fireballs scorching the buildings as they chased Alvarez's blast toward the sun. The street scene was beautiful, like a surrealist's painting. Cortez wanted to remember it clearly so he could appreciate it when he had more time.

He backed up fast, then slammed on the brakes and whipped the wheel hard to the left. The front end of his car skidded one hundred and eighty degrees around. Cortez hauled ass down the street. He hit a pedestrian who was running to help the victims, but it didn't seem to matter. In the midst of all this devastation, who would even notice one more casualty.

He wheeled a hard right at the next corner, and then another. Slid to a stop in the middle of the next intersection, the direction Slaughter had headed. He looked for Slaughter's Maxima. Didn't see it. Looked some more. Got out, the center of attention now as the shocked crowd shifted their silent gapes in his direction.

Slaughter was gone, nowhere to be seen. Cortez took a few steps, looked long and carefully in all directions. Looked again.

Then he started smiling. By the time he climbed back into his car he was laughing.

"Okay, Amigo," he said as he put his car in gear. "You're one lucky son of a bitch, Slaughter." He shook his head, still smiling. "One lucky son of a bitch," he said again.

He drove from the scene, a flamenco CD in the player with the volume turned up very loud.

* * * * *

Slaughter was constantly looking out the back window now, keeping his eyes moving along the street. He was expecting them now. The games had officially begun. The explosion was just the beginning and he knew it.

The Instant PhotoMan was on a quiet street. But hell, every street was quiet compared to the one he'd just left. It was a basic law of relativity. He spent an anxious twenty minutes parked in the shadows, watching the store. He wanted to wait longer, be even more careful. But the clock was ticking – twenty minutes were all he could spare. He trotted across the street and entered the photography shop as the only other customer left. It was small, but neat, with about fifteen feet of retail space, then a counter that cleanly divided the space into two parts.

"Hello," Slaughter said, suddenly wishing he had checked the mirror for shrapnel cuts on his face. "I called earlier about making copies from a picture."

The kid fit the voice on the phone. Cocky. Arrogant. He was tall and skinny, maybe nineteen. Curly red hair grew wild on his head, and acne migrated across his face. A girl's high school ring hung around his neck on a cheap silver chain.

He looked at Slaughter like his time was too valuable to waste. "You're right, you did. Got the pictures?"

"Yes, I do. Here." Slaughter opened his briefcase and handed them over without hesitation, very casually. It was hard to do. But the pictures, on their own merit, were already too powerful. Any significance he added by stalling could have sent the kid to the police. His guts were jumping. There were a thousand other things he should be doing. But right now, the most important thing for him to do was stay calm in front of this young man.

The kid sucked in his breath when he looked at the first picture, looked up at Slaughter after viewing each one. He shuffled through them, then set them face down on the counter. He looked suspiciously at Slaughter. "Where'd you get these?"

Slaughter looked at the pictures, as if he might have brought the wrong ones or something. "Why? What's wrong?"

The kid laced his arms together. "I didn't say anything was wrong. I asked where you got these pictures."

"The archives at the Library of Congress."

The kid stepped back, started adjusting the camera's lens, cropping the sides to fit the first photo. "Oh? These are real old then?"

"Why, yes. I suppose they are." Slaughter smiled, offered an admiring look at the kid's handiwork, dug his hands into his pockets.

"Right." The kid shook his head, snapped the first photo, slipped another prisoner's face under the glass.

"You don't think they're old?"

The kid grabbed a magnifying glass, scrutinized one of the photos before sliding it under the glass.

"Naah. The process used on 'em is new, an accelerated chemical that's been developed overseas. The paper size is foreign, too, and didn't even exist until a few years ago."

Slaughter raced ahead for an answer. "Well, I suppose that makes sense. After all, they are recent copies. Only the originals were old."

The kid looked up from his work. "The originals weren't *very* old. A year or two, max."

"I'll be damned. How can you be so sure?"

He pointed carelessly at a piece of a picture's background, something behind the P.O.W. "Check this out, mister. See that soldier's arm there?"

Slaughter stared at the spot. "Is that an arm?"

"Yes. It's an arm. I checked it with a magnifying glass. It's got a digital compass watch on the wrist, and those watches haven't made history yet."

Slaughter studied the kid, said nothing.

Another photo, another grisly face under the glass. The kid looked up as he clicked the camera. "Who are these guys anyway? They look like shit."

"They are political prisoners."

"They're P.O.W.s, man. Anybody can see that." The kid snapped another photo without looking away from Slaughter. "Old ones, too. Judging from their age and pajama clothing, I'd say from the Vietnam war. That about on the mark?"

Slaughter started to answer, make up something reasonable. But the kid cut him short, walked to the door of the small shop and locked it. "I don't imagine you want any more strangers seeing these, do you?"

Slaughter remained silent.

"You know, I've never actually seen these kinds of photos before. Where'd you really get 'em? You a reporter or something?"

Slaughter watched the kid move around the store. "No."

"These guys still alive?"

Slaughter didn't answer.

"I'll take that as a yes. You trying to help them?"

Slaughter still believed he was better off silent. The kid could draw his own conclusions; Slaughter would not validate them.

"These copies gonna help somehow?" The kid snapped the last shot, took the film out of the fixed camera. He looked at

141

Slaughter, shook his head slowly at the missing answer. "You watch the door, man," he said over his shoulder. "Be cool if anyone comes up."

"Can I watch you work?"

The kid turned around, easily, liked he'd expected the question. "Why? You want to make sure I don't print a bunch of copies for me and my buddies?"

Slaughter didn't answer. He checked his watch, made it significant.

"All right. Sure, I guess. Come on back."

Slaughter followed him, watched the kid move through the red-lit darkroom, admired his skill. He seemed like a good kid. A smart kid. He made two perfect sets of copies that seemed better than the originals. When they finished, Slaughter pulled out his wallet.

"Naah, don't bother. It's on the house. These guys get out, you have 'em autograph one of my photos and send it to me."

Slaughter put his wallet away, held out his hand. "Can you keep this quiet until then?"

The kid shook Slaughter's hand. Smiled. It was the first time Slaughter had noticed the braces on his teeth. "Even longer," the kid said. "All the time you need. Good luck, man."

"Thanks."

Slaughter checked the street from the camera shop and nothing seemed to have changed. He stepped out of the shop and headed toward the corner, stuffing one set of the photographs into a mailer. Traffic was light. He was doing okay.

He dropped a set of copies into the mailbox, addressed to Laura's office. Then he crossed over to his car and locked another set in his trunk. Put the originals back in his briefcase. He was feeling a little better now, ready to get back to work.

Slaughter twisted into his seat and drove away, wove in and out of lanes, kept his head searching while he worked his cellular phone. A man answered the phone at Laura's office; a strangely familiar voice that surprised him. He couldn't quite identify it.

"This is Jacob Slaughter for Ms. Warden."

"Just a minute." His call wasn't placed on hold; the phone seemed to have been handed over to Laura.

"Yes, this is Laura Warden."

"Hi, it's me. I need your opinion about something."

"Yes. What can I do for you, sir?"

A shiver sliced up his back. "Huh? Laura, who's the guy who answered the phone?"

"No. I won't have any time available until next week."

"Jeez, Laura. What's going on? I'm coming over. Just be careful until I get there."

"No, I'm sorry, but you can't come to my office until next week. I'm . . . well, much too busy."

"Damn, Laura, I don't know what you're doing, but you're scaring the hell out of me. Listen, I have to see you, make sure you're all right. Can you take the hall that connects your office to the next building?"

"Are you talking about next Wednesday or next Thursday?"

"I'm talking about right now! Go to the side street exit. Wait inside with the guard until I get there. Ten minutes."

"Okay. That will be fine. Good-bye."

Slaughter hung up, shot around a corner of the small business district, yelled "shit" three times, tromped on the gas and rocketed his car into an alley between two bars. Paper and dust swirled up in a storm behind him, as if his was the first car ever to pass through here. The alley was narrow and dangerous, a tube easily corked at both ends by police, or assassins. But it was a short cut to the highway, a short cut to Laura. The risk was nothing.

He reached the interstate ramp and stomped harder on the accelerator. The Maxima's engine responded quickly. He was going fast now, much faster than the other traffic, starting to stand out too much. With Mills against him, a routine traffic stop could easily cost Wooten his life and keep Slaughter from helping Laura.

He started throttling down as he approached the overpasses where troopers could be waiting, then accelerating at the straight, flat sections of I-95 where he might be able to see them. Blasted down the H.O.V. lane, swerving in and out of traffic.

He didn't want to make Laura wait for him. He slid through the exit and made three quick turns, which brought him to the building next to hers. He pulled up and she jumped in. They were off before her door closed, the road stripes turning into a blur and the force pushing him back a little. He roared back up the ramp and headed down I-95 in the direction of Richmond. It was as good a direction as any. He just needed time to talk.

She wanted to speak, he could see that. An unusual look for her. She wanted to ask some questions, try to get some answers. Who wouldn't? But she did not.

"What was all that about? Why were you so strange on the phone."

The look vanished as she turned to look out the window. "I don't want to talk about it."

"You don't want to talk about it? You scared the shit out of me! I thought you were in serious trouble."

"I had a patient, Jacob. I was right in the middle of a session and it was going badly. I was having a little trouble concentrating."

He looked over at her. Checked the road ahead. Looked at her again. "You're going to stick to that story?"

"Yes. And honestly, Jacob, it's none of your damn business."

"Whoa, hold on, Laura. What's gotten in to you?"

She shifted around in her seat, the skirt of her suit riding up her leg a little, catching Slaughter's attention. Even with everything else going on, her leg was a serious distraction. He thought it was an amazing phenomenon, would have expected it to be impossible.

144

"I'll tell you what's gotten into me, Jacob. Walter called me an hour ago. He said you'd quit your job, walked out. Stolen something from the State Department in the process. Is that right?"

"Mills called you? Wasn't *that* nice of him."

"Was he telling me the truth or not?"

Slaughter rose up, tried to look over the car in front of him for a break in traffic. "He was close, although his version is a little different than mine."

She put her fingers on her forehead. "That's terrific, Jacob. Just terrific. So what do you expect me to say. Hooray for you? Well, I'm not in a hooray kind of mood."

"Hey, Laura, I'm sorry, but – "

"Damn you, Jacob, I am so angry! You're back on your crusade to save Wooten, and you don't care if it destroys us. You've lost your job over it. What's going to happen next?"

"I'm not sure. But I won't let it destroy us. It's just – "

"It *will* destroy us, Jacob, it will! Can't you see what will happen? Ninety percent of my patients come through government referrals. I'll be forced to choose between you and my career. Walter was very clear about that. I don't want to think about the consequences if I don't help you, but if I do, I'm sure it'll destroy my practice. I've worked so hard, Jacob. It's not right for you to put me in this position."

Slaughter found a hole, accelerated into it, then changed lanes again. "I have to fight for Chuck Wooten, Laura. You know why. Christ, you're the only person in the entire world who knows why! So don't ask me to back off."

She shifted even more, completely sideways in the seat, her eyes demanding that he look at her. "Back off, Jacob. Please. You could get killed over this."

"Why do you say that? Did you hear about the explosion downtown?"

She looked a little confused. "Yes, of course I did. It's been all over the news. What does that have to do with you? The F.B.I. is calling it a terrorist bombing."

"That wasn't a terrorist's bomb, at least not by my standards. Terrorists usually blow up innocent targets, terrify a nation by making its citizens feel vulnerable."

"Isn't that what happened? Didn't a car bomb destroy a big part of a block? Didn't –"

"I think that was all incidental. Maybe it was done to look that way, I don't know. But this bomb, Laura, this was an assassin's bomb."

She waited, her lips tight together.

"I was the target. The car that exploded was coming right for me. It even tried to follow me when I turned out of its path, blew up right behind me. Laura, I'm not sure what to do next to help Wooten, but I want to do it fast. I may not have much time."

"You say that so casually, Jacob. So you realize they will kill you over this!"

He looked at her eyes, wanted more of what she knew. "They?"

The anger in her voice jumped up two notches. "Yes, they! Whoever just blew the city apart. They!"

She huffed around in her seat, sat there staring out the front windshield. Nothing was said for a couple of miles, until she unfolded her arms, reached her left hand over and touched his leg.

"Please, Jacob, just let Walter handle it? Or go ask for your job back and work for Wooten on the inside?"

He guarded the tone of his voice. "Listen, Laura, Cuthbert and Tanner and Mills are up to their ears in some kind of cover-up. I think I know what it is."

She pulled her hand back. "A cover-up, Jacob? Isn't that a little dramatic?"

"Dramatic? Sure, it's dramatic. Does that mean it's not happening? No. And I'm pretty sure what they're involved in is criminal."

"Oh, I see, Jacob. Not just a cover-up of something embarrassing. Now it's a *criminal* cover-up."

He didn't know her, had never heard her like this. "Why are you doing this, Laura? Why are you so skeptical?"

"Because you sound paranoid, Jacob. Delusional. Just listen to yourself. P.O.W.s are still alive in Vietnam, the heads of our Government are conspiring against them, someone's blowing the city apart trying to kill you."

"Hey, it's not paranoia if they really *are* out to get you."

"Doesn't matter. Either way you come out a loser. You're either losing your mind over this or you're running the risk of dying over it. It's just not worth it, Jacob. It can't be worth it. Wooten helped you, sure, but that was decades ago. You can't carry that cross forever. He'd never expect you to sacrifice like this."

Slaughter kept driving, hid behind the silence while he thought through what she'd said. He loved Laura and, more importantly, he trusted her. He never took her advice lightly. Her vision was better than his. Clearer. Unhampered by emotional freight. But this time she was wrong. He turned to her, caught her attention and spoke low, almost in a monotone.

"I know three things, Laura, that are not open to dispute. One, Chuck Wooten saved my life. Two, he is still alive in a Vietnamese prisoner-of-war camp. Three, I'm going to get him out or die trying. If you won't help me, fine. I'll take you back now."

He rolled down an off-ramp, U-turned under I-95, headed back toward Washington. There was an agonizing silence between them for several miles. He heard her breathing, listened as it slowed down, little by little.

Then Laura touched his sleeve. He eased into the slower traffic lane.

"If you can't go to work, Jacob, how are you going to help Wooten?"

"That's what I wanted to talk to you about, why I wanted your opinion. I was thinking about going public."

He turned, wanted to see her reaction. Nothing else would need to be said, he'd know it all from her look. Good idea or bad idea.

She stared out the windshield for a long time. A minute, maybe.

"I've got a friend who's the news director at the NBC affiliate here in Washington. He seems like a solid guy. I could call him for you."

He checked the mirror. There weren't any cars jockeying for position back there. He stuck his head out of the window and searched the sky, looked for airplanes or helicopters that might be following him. He saw nothing suspicious. No one had kept up with him. They were safe

"Thanks, but I can call the networks on my own, Laura. You don't have to help. I'll take you back to work now, if you think you're safe there. There's no reason to get you involved any further. Sorry I've gotten you in this deep."

Laura squeezed his hand and picked up his phone. "I'll call him for you, Jacob. I don't know how much more I can do, though."

He pulled the phone away, put it in his lap. "Thank you. Really. But I'd prefer that you didn't. Someone's already tried to kill me. You should stay the hell away from me or you'll be in danger, too. It was stupid of me to come to you; I wouldn't have done it if I hadn't thought you were in trouble when I called."

She smiled. "Who knows? Maybe I am in danger. Doesn't matter anymore. Give me the phone."

"Only if you're ready to stay with me until this is over. I don't want anything to happen to you."

"What? You're not seriously suggesting that we hide out, are you?"

He laughed a little, saw her smile. It sounded funny when she said it, as if they were Badlands outlaws heading for Hole in the Wall. "No. Of course not. We're not going to hide out. We're just going to check into a motel for a day or so. Take a break from our regular patterns until this thing shakes out. We won't be hiding, just playing it safe. That's all."

Her smile grew until she was laughing. "It sure sounds like hiding to me."

He didn't answer. She kept staring at the cellular phone like she'd never seen one before. After another minute, he caressed her fingers, then handed it back to her.

* * * * *

Cortez had had no trouble finding Slaughter's car again, maybe thirty minutes after Alvarez had blown a big piece of D.C. asphalt into tiny pieces. Men like Slaughter were always easy to find because they coveted familiar routines. They either stayed close to home or close to work, with rare exceptions. Those were Cortez's two choices. They were easy choices. Slaughter was too smart to go home, so Cortez would find his victim near the State Department. It was as easy as that.

He had found the car an hour ago, just as Slaughter hurried out of the photo shop with the large envelope in his hand, went to the corner and dropped it in the mailbox. He didn't have to guess what Slaughter had done; the sign on the building told the whole story. It had created a dilemma for him – should he let Slaughter go so he could check out the store or follow him first and take him down?

Maybe Slaughter had left the originals behind, planning to come back later and pick up more copies or enlargements. Maybe he had told the store's employee what he was doing. Maybe the employee had called the cops and reported it.

It had been a difficult decision, a hard choice that had demanded an immediate answer when Slaughter climbed into his car and pulled into traffic.

Cortez had let Slaughter go, knowing he would be easy to find later. He was that predictable. Right now Cortez was more worried about the pictures, the precious evidence Mills was so worried about. If Mills was worried, Duncan would be worried. He would wait a little while longer, see if Slaughter, or the cops, showed up. If not, he would get back anything Slaughter had left behind.

While he waited, he called Luis at home, knew he would be there waiting for the call. Cortez hated to share any of the glory for this kill, but he would rather share it than fail. Besides, he would only allow Luis to catch Slaughter. Killing him was an honor Cortez had reserved for himself.

Luis' big voice answered the phone on the first ring. "Yes."

"As it turns out, Luis, I do need your help. Call my company for an update on the situation, then get going. Find him. Get him. But I want to talk to him first. Do you understand me? I want to talk to him first."

Luis answered in a slow, rumbling eruption. "Yes."

Cortez hung up. He checked his look in the rearview mirror, then got out of the car and went to the trunk. He picked up two small bottles of chemicals and slid them into separate pockets of his jacket, then walked over to the store. Entered, looked around. There weren't any customers in the store, just a blemish-faced teenager behind the counter.

"Hey," said the kid, friendly enough, but a little too snappy. "Help you?"

Cortez smiled, flashed those pretty teeth, saw them draw the kid's attention away from his own acne scars. "Good afternoon."

The kid started losing ground immediately. Cortez's empty gaze and slow movements were dissolving the kid's cockiness, just like they were supposed to do. Damn, Cortez truly did love the power of intimidation.

"Sir? Can I help you?"

Cortez put his hands in his pockets, slowly. Watched the kid follow his hands with a mesmerized looked. "I was supposed to meet a friend of mine here. But obviously I've arrived first, so I guess I'll have to wait."

The kid fiddled with the cash register. "What's he look like? Maybe he's already been here."

Cortez stepped up to the counter and leaned on it, pushed himself pretty far over it. The kid backed up a half step. "Maybe so. He's six or seven inches taller than me but not heavy. Blue eyes. Brown hair with some gray in it. Sort of good looking. Have you seen him?"

Now he'd find out if the kid would tell the truth. The truth might earn him a few minutes. The kid's life would last as long as it took to tell what Slaughter had done. A lie would be disrespectful. Jeering. Almost the same as laughing at him. He hated thinking about it, felt himself getting enraged at the idea of this punk laughing at him – Angelo Cortez. Who did this kid think he was? How dare he laugh at him. He deserved much more respect than that.

The kid looked sincere, gently touched an acne sore on his cheek. "Sorry, mister. No one like that's been in here –"

Cortez drew his gun in a fast, smooth action that riveted the kid's attention, shut him up and kept him staring. Cortez had the hammer back, the barrel aimed at a blemish on the kid's face. Cortez knew the shame of facial disfigurement, knew how hard it was to keep your hands from picking at the scabs.

"Let me take care of that for you, boy."

The kid didn't flinch. He didn't look scared and didn't look away. Not, at least, until the pistol fired and the muffled blast tossed at his head a little piece of lead traveling faster than sound. It shattered the young man's cheekbone, blew his face away.

Cortez holstered his pistol, ducked under the counter and stepped over the kid, went into the darkroom. He searched it thoroughly but found nothing. On his way out he stopped, rolled the kid's head with his polished boot until the boy's dead eyes looked up. "Was a bad idea to laugh at me, sonny-boy."

Then he moved his foot and the head rolled back into a sticky puddle. Cortez strolled out of the shop.

The first small bottle was potassium permanganate. It shattered against the inside wall of the mailbox with a muffled pop. Cortez glanced around again, saw no one paying attention as he fumbled for the other bottle.

The second vial was pure glycerin, a common ingredient of household products. It shattered too, and Cortez strolled away. He would be out of the neighborhood before the two chemicals had sufficient time to transmute themselves into a combustible mixture that would ignite spontaneously.

13

Slaughter had agreed to the NBC news director's agenda. It was his television station and, therefore, his rules. The Chancellery Restaurant at eight o'clock p.m. Too public for Slaughter's taste, but a risk he would take. He got there early, waited five minutes for a table, and had been sitting for about ten minutes.

The Chancellery was an old restaurant but still nice, still known as a good place for casual dining. Tonight it was busy, crowded. Most of the diners wore suits and discussed politics, the kind of people who would head back to their offices and work another few hours after finishing their dinner.

Slaughter tried to concentrate on what he would say, but it was hard. He was tired, in both his mind and body. His stomach hurt. His eyes ached, battled their lids, tried to stay open. He hadn't really slept since seeing Wooten, and the restless nights were finally catching up with him. Fatigue was becoming his enemy, too.

At one time, not too long ago, his entire life had been like this. His nightmare would make his sleep terrible or, more likely, not allow him to sleep at all. Then, his body would crap out and he would collapse for several hours. Helpless. Defenseless.

He hated remembering what it had been like – what it would be like again. It was worse than the torture in prison, those six or seven terrifying hours when he would have no option of escape, no chance to shake himself awake and get out of bed. No way to run away from Chuck Wooten.

Laura had conquered that nightmare about the same time he had brought Wooten's body back. But now his life would be that way again. It made him think of suicide, just for a second. Just as long as it took to remember that Chuck Wooten was still alive and waiting. Just as long as it took to remember his commitment.

He ordered more coffee. It would make him jumpy, but hopefully it would keep him awake as he silently recited Laura's description of the newsman, waiting in the back booth for someone who matched it. 5'10". Brown hair. Late thirties. A precise dresser, whatever she'd meant by that.

The exact man she'd described walked in the restaurant's front door and scanned the crowd until he saw Slaughter. He smiled as he headed back to him, but then Slaughter saw his hand slip into his coat.

Slaughter suddenly saw nothing but the disappearing hand. He flashed back thirty years, prepared himself for an attack, jumped up and walked quickly into the man, subtly grabbed his wrist and coaxed it from under the coat. He smiled at the few customers who'd noticed while putting pressure on the wrist's weak angle.

"Hey," said the man, low, and a little shaky. The pain put some peculiar music in his voice. "What the hell are you doing?"

Slaughter led him to the table. "What's in your pocket?"

"What? Damn, let go of me. You think I'm going to hurt you or something?"

"Not now I don't."

"Never planned on it. Let go."

Slaughter let him go and sat down at the table. The man sat down, too.

"Hey, I'm not much for this Vietnam Vet bullshit, okay? I was getting my business card. It wasn't a reason to go fugazi on me." He twisted, faced the table while he smoothed the sleeve of his linen sport coat. "Jeez."

Slaughter stared at him, watched every move he made. "Sorry. I'm just a little jumpy."

"Yeah? Well right now I'm a little short on patience. Laura said you had a big story for me. I'm listening. Let's get to it."

"I'm sorry if I hurt you," Slaughter said. Then he waited.

The man had three choices: insist that Slaughter hadn't hurt him, insist that he had, or act like it was forgotten. Whichever way it went, Slaughter would know exactly what kind of man he was dealing with.

The newsman picked at the cuff of his shirt, adjusted the reveal to about a half inch. "Yeah, well, no big deal. Maybe I should have expected it. No harm done, all right. You want to start over?" He stretched his hand across the table. "Christopher Friedman's my name. I already know yours, Mr. Slaughter."

Slaughter shook Friedman's hand.

"How long have you been in the news bureau, Mr. Friedman?"

"Ten years. Call me Christopher."

Slaughter poured some more coffee down his throat. "That's a pretty long time, Christopher."

"Worse. They're kind of like dog years when you work in network news. Makes it count for about sixty, maybe more."

"I suppose. What'd you do before that? Which branch of the service?"

Friedman smiled, transmitted a little respect for Slaughter's perceptiveness. "Air Force. I was a silo man out in the great

155

midwest. Is this an interview? 'Cause if it is, it's going in the wrong direction."

The waitress came, but Friedman waved her off.

"I didn't intend for you to interview me. I just want to make an announcement, use your television network to say something."

Friedman grinned and rolled his eyes in a tight, small circle. "We're not exactly a local access station, Slaughter. We're NBC News. Kind of a big forum for making an announcement. You know what I mean, Jake. Can I call you Jake?"

Slaughter shrugged.

"Why not the newspapers, Jake?"

"Because it would take too much time, Chris. Besides, lots of people don't read them."

Friedman picked a cracker out of the basket, slathered it with butter. "You've got that right. So, what's your beef? What's so important that you want everyone in America to hear it?"

"I want to tell them that, if President Simons does the right thing, twenty-three live P.O.W.s from the Vietnam War will be home within the month."

Friedman's fingers crumbled the cracker. The shattered bits fell onto his linen sport coat and stuck there. "Huh?" His eyes searched around the room then came back to Slaughter. He leaned forward, whispered. "What the hell are you talking about?"

Slaughter leaned over the table, too. Matched the volume of Friedman's voice. "There are still American prisoners there. I have proof. Simons can get them home in less than thirty days. It will be easy."

Friedman jerked back, started to say something loud. But he caught himself, looked around, leaned back over the table. Kept it quiet. "Get out, man. You're talking about Vietnam, Jake. Even if prisoners *were* left behind there, wouldn't they have all died from old age by now?"

"No. Their ages range from forty-eight to sixty-two."

Friedman's face went back to cynical, the look of a man who'd heard it all; had heard most of it twice. He dusted the crumbs off his jacket and reached for another cracker.

"Okay, Jake, what's the catch? Why are you telling me this? Why do you want to tell the whole damn world? Aren't you sworn to secrecy over there at State, the hand in the flame kind of loyalty?"

Slaughter watched him with the cracker. He was dainty, almost prissy. Slaughter had never seen a man handle a knife with such a flourish. "Yes, we are. But something's gone wrong. I'm not going to make any specific accusations, but my loyalty is absolutely clear. It's to the prisoners. I want them out. You can help."

Friedman tilted his head back, almost laughed. Probably would have if he hadn't had a mouth full of cracker. He swallowed, then chuckled, like he'd just caught the joke, embarrassed that it had taken him so long. "That's right." He wagged a finger at Slaughter. "That's right, I remember now. You were a P.O.W. yourself once."

He buttered another cracker, then stood to leave, holding the cracker between two fingers. "Listen, Jake, I respect the sacrifice you made over there, I really do. But your story is tainted by your own experiences. I can't air it; it'd be prejudicial. Maybe you could try one of the talk shows. Maybe Geraldo's show."

Slaughter set a large envelope on the table. "Take a look."

Friedman glanced down at the envelope as he popped the cracker. He looked at Slaughter, then slowly picked the package up with both hands. He tapped the edge of the envelope on the table, stared at it, rotated it around with his fingers, tapped it on the table again.

"I can tell this is classified stuff, Jake. I know you shouldn't be showing it to me."

"I think I should."

"You know it could kill your career if I open it."

"I know. It doesn't matter."

157

Friedman fiddled with the envelope while their eyes locked up. Finally, he snapped it open and reached inside. "What the hell, man. It's your neck."

"Keep them low, please."

Friedman lowered the envelope, looked disinterested. He slid out the bundle. The top photo was Captain Charles Wooten.

"Oh, shit!" Friedman sucked in his breath, quick and loud as if he'd been shot. Some of the diners twisted around to see what had happened, but Friedman sat down instantly, hid the photos in his lap before anyone saw them. He looked up at Slaughter, slid all the photos back into the envelope and shoved it back across the table, couldn't seem to get rid of it fast enough.

"There's more," Slaughter said. "I've got dossiers, records. Proof."

Friedman protested with his hands. "I don't need to see any more. Maybe I'm too young to have fought in the war, but I've been around long enough. You don't have to point me at the sun just to prove that it's daytime. When do you want to go on?"

"Tonight. As soon as possible."

"You've got it. Come right over to the studio, be there no later than nine o'clock. We'll prerecord it. You'll be the lead at ten. I'll keep the slot open. We'll broadcast a trailer of the interview every ten minutes until newstime. We'll put it out on our radio station, too. Get you a big audience. You comfortable with that?"

"Yes."

Friedman stood up and started to walk away. "This will be great, Jake. See you then."

"It's Jacob."

Friedman turned and grinned again, a very feminine look. "Okay, then. It's Jacob." Then he hurried out of the restaurant.

Slaughter waited ten minutes before he moved. He paid the waitress, and when a table of ten rose to leave he fell in behind them. Slaughter was at the end of the group, walking in their direction, searching for a cab to take him out of town. Back to the hotel where he'd left Laura.

The sidewalks were about half-full of people, most of them in a hurry. Going home, probably. Some were tourists, walking and pointing and taking pictures, their cameras and suntan lotion never more than a fanny-pack away. The lingering sunlight still made everyone feel safe, but it wouldn't last much longer. The stores would close soon, the sidewalks would thin out, and police cars would begin their domination of the streets.

Someone out there wanted him dead. Whoever it was had already killed several people in the last attempt, blown them up, or burned them, or cut them down with flying shards of sheet metal and steel. He felt terrible for the victims, for the young mother and the baby in the gold Volvo. Hated the person who'd killed them.

But at least he knew they were after him. It would be easier to survive, knowing he was a target. He turned around and checked his back, then scanned the sidewalk across the street. Then the rooftops. The doorways. Automobiles that might be slowing down. Up ahead. Repeated the process, twenty seconds to a cycle. No different than walking patrol in Indian country. A land of unseen enemies. All of it hostile. But he knew the rules, knew how to deal with it. Knew how to live through it. Knew the mantra.

Expect trouble. Expect it everywhere, anywhere. Be ready to go savage when it hits, do the unspeakable acts of violence. Do them without thinking. Maybe then you might survive.

The guilt and the shame could be dealt with later.

After less than a block he caught the man following him. Cuban, or maybe Mexican. Big and round-chested. His waist and hips were peculiarly small, giving him an appearance not unlike an inverted bowling pin. His hair was black and shiny, slicked back off his forehead. His face was big but not fat. Too hard looking to hide fat. Slaughter looked back twice, and the man was watching him each time. The big man looked like he was walking on tiptoes, his head rocking back and forth over the heads of the crowd.

Slaughter walked into a drugstore, went to the magazine rack, waited a couple of minutes before he walked out. The man was waiting, leaning against the metal pole of a street sign. The pole was bending from his weight. Slaughter walked off in the opposite direction and turned a corner. The walls of a tall building hid him. He stopped and turned, waited for the man to come around the edge of the building. He would grab the big man when he rounded the corner, take him down to the sidewalk and try to get his questions answered without getting killed.

But the man did not come. He waited. Other people rounded the corner and bumped into him, looked annoyed. But no big man. A minute passed.

Could it be possible that the man knew Slaughter had stopped? The big Mexican had only been a few paces behind him, but for some reason he hadn't turned the corner. Slaughter stepped to the edge of the bricks, nosed out to look down the street and find out what had happened. Maybe he'd been mistaken. Maybe the Mexican was a store security guard who'd been chasing a shoplifter. Or an office worker looking for his ride home.

Slaughter started twisting his head around the building, hoping some other pedestrian wouldn't come from the other direction and crash into his face. The sidewalk he had just left was starting to come into view, but he couldn't see the street sign yet. Didn't know if it was still bending. So far, no sign of the Mexican.

Suddenly, a big, brown hand surprised the hell out of him, had him by the throat before he knew what was happening. The hand was right there, waiting for him, and snatched his neck just as Slaughter nosed out, almost lifted him off the ground. The giant hand dragged Slaughter around the corner and hauled him right into the big man's face. Slaughter saw the earphone, knew there must be others.

"You're coming with me," the big man said. "Don't make trouble."

Most of the pedestrians panicked, rushed away, cleared the street for a hundred feet in both directions. A few stayed and gawked. Slaughter tried to scream for help but couldn't make a sound. No one volunteered to help or even looked like they were thinking about it.

Slaughter dangled in the man's grip, struggled to breathe as the tips of his toes glided toward the curb. A limousine roared up and braked hard. It slid to a stop and a rear door flew open. The big man started pushing Slaughter into the car. The driver of the limousine jumped out to help. It had only taken ten or fifteen seconds.

"Come on, Luis," the driver shouted. "Let's get out of here."

Luis lowered Slaughter's feet to the ground and pushed his head toward the rear seat. Slaughter's feet planted on the concrete. Now he could do something with this big gorilla.

He bent over until he could see Luis's big feet behind him, then wiggled over to the right side of Luis's bulky body and hooked his left foot behind Luis's massive right leg. He forced his head back out of the car and drove himself upward with his right leg. He pushed hard against the giant chest, arched his back to help throw Luis off balance, then smashed the back of his head against Luis's nose.

The grip slipped from his throat as Luis starting spinning his arms, falling backward, shouting in angry Spanish. Slaughter jabbed his elbow into Luis's face, over and over as they separated. Luis fell all the way to the ground, laid there for a few seconds as if he was considering the best way to get his huge body vertical again. Slaughter turned, headed toward the growing crowd. He had run two seconds, maybe less, before the Mexican driver jumped onto his back. The driver was much smaller but still the sudden thrust of weight buckled Slaughter's knees. They were going down. Slaughter strained to rotate his head away from the ground, managed to get his body pointing skyward. The other man's head hit first, absorbed all the impact as it smacked the curb. Slaughter heard the noise it made, like the crack of a bat. The man didn't move after that.

Slaughter jumped up and turned back to the big man, Luis. He was rising, speed building in his huge body, anger swelling his eyes. Slaughter took five steps toward Luis, who had just flicked a knee up to support himself. Slaughter snap-kicked his foot at Luis's face. Luis grabbed for Slaughter's leg but missed, caught Slaughter's shoe squarely in the mouth. Luis rocked over backward. Slaughter kicked him several more times, harder and harder and harder. Luis caged his head behind those enormous hands as Slaughter kept kicking at his eyes, starting to do some serious damage. A thick, fast-flowing stream of blood ran from Luis' nose and joined several smaller streams from his mouth and right eye. Together they formed a river of blood that ran down Luis' face and onto the sidewalk, toward the gutter.

Sirens were singing their way down the block – wailing and screaming their way through the traffic. Relief – that was his first thought. Let the police come and tell him who these guys were. And where they worked. And what the hell was going on.

But then he thought it through. He would be stuck here, possibly for hours, while they sorted through the details looking for a believable story. He might even be detained until the situation was worked out. And then there was the issue of his photos, the ones he still had with him, the ones the police would see, and probably seize, if he was arrested.

No, his best option was to get away. It had to be. He turned and checked the two men. The driver wasn't moving, and Luis' movements were all triggered by pain. Nothing threatening. He grabbed his attaché out of the gutter and started to run, looked at the limousine as he passed, saw the keys, jumped in and squealed away.

He only drove it a dozen blocks or so. The police would be broadcasting a description of the stolen car soon, so he slid into an empty space, gave the car a quick check before he left it.

Sirens were spreading out behind him, like hyenas encircling their prey. Not much longer before they got here. A quick shuffle through the glove compartment, but there was nothing there except tissue. No registration. He snatched open the console compartment, but nothing. Over the visor? Wait, here was something. A business card, Mr. Duncan, Dynet Industries, written on one side. There was a long list of international telephone numbers on the other side. He pocketed it and slid out of the car, walked with the crowd as they crossed the street.

Four blocks later he entered the lobby of the Downtown Sheraton, went straight to the pay phones.

"Dynet Industries. How may I direct your call?"

Slaughter faced away from the wall, watched the lobby closely. "Mr. Duncan, please."

The female operator sounded like an air traffic controller. Flat. Vapid. "I'm sorry, there is no one here by that name."

"You must be mistaken. Check again."

"No," she said, leaving no doubt about her self-confidence. "I don't have to check again. There is no one here by that name."

"I was told to call him here. He gave me his card, told me to call him here. This is regarding a matter that is very important to him. If you're not going to put me through, I want your name, because I'm not going to take the blame for this breakdown."

There was a pause, the kind of silence he expected to hear if security was about to be breached, the few seconds it takes to make that decision.

"Hold on a minute, sir."

Slaughter waited for Duncan. It didn't take long.

"This is Duncan. Who - the - hell - *is* - this?"

Slaughter flinched at the voice, at its odd familiarity. He almost hung up, fidgeted with the phone, ready to get rid of it but not quite able to let go. Then Chuck Wooten shuffled through his mind, all broken and bleeding and dying. But still hoping. Still faithful. Slaughter's mouth went into involuntary action. "I'm the man who's going to bring the P.O.W.s home. You won't stop me, you shit."

Nothing. Not a sound or a breath for a half minute, maybe more. A very long time in silence. Then, "What did you say?"

"You heard me. I'm going to bring the P.O.W.s home."

Duncan's voice was so calm it was eerie. "You're a fool, Slaughter."

"And you're a son-of-a-bitch. Makes 'being a fool' sound like high praise."

"Until you're a dead fool. Then you'll just be one more piece of unreported American history. Nothing more."

"That won't happen. I'm bringing them home."

"I sincerely doubt it."

"Bet on it."

*   *   *   *   *

Duncan slammed down the phone, felt like he wanted to choke the life out of someone. He hauled his fat ass out of his chair like a breaching whale, plodded across his richly decorated office and flung open the meeting room door. He caught himself before he said anything, though. Reminded himself of who he was about to talk to. Remembered to calm down before he said something that might get him hurt. "Mr. Cortez."

Cortez was sitting in a chair reading People magazine, calmly, as if this was a dentist's waiting room. He marked the page with his finger, flipped it closed over a picture of Madonna, glanced up casually. "Yes, Mr. Duncan."

164

"Mr. Cortez, I've just had a call from Slaughter. He's ready to bet that those P.O.W. bastards are coming home. Damn it, I can't have that man loose, running around the city saying shit like this. You understand that, don't you?"

Cortez was smiling at him now, those damned teeth always his first response. "I'm sorry about that, Mr. Duncan. Honestly, I expected that problem to be over with. I was distracted by that business at the photo shop, trying to recover Slaughter's evidence. But I have put two very good men on Slaughter. My best men. I told them not to worry about anything – the police or federal agents. Just get Slaughter and bring him to me. Frankly, I expect to hear from them any moment now."

"Well, they must have failed because he was just on the telephone trying to piss me off. You're going to have to do it yourself, Cortez. I know it'll be hard to do alone, but no one else seems capable. Damn, is this guy really that hard to stop?"

Cortez stood up, dropped the magazine on the huge mahogany table, took a second look at the cover. "No," he said. "He is not that hard to stop. But he does have the luck running with him. And luck is much better than skill."

Duncan was exhausted. The pressure was on him to kill Slaughter. Tanner was screaming at him. His clients were screaming at him. And his ulcers were screaming at him. But he couldn't just bark orders at Cortez, no sir. He had to ease into it, get Cortez moving on his own or risk some pretty serious consequences. Begging was not too far out of the question.

"I need some luck myself, Cortez. You can provide it. Will you do it? Please."

Cortez slid on his flashy sport coat, adjusted his shirt sleeve, and straightened his gaudy cufflinks. Then he headed to the door. "I'll take care of it right now. Don't worry about it again."

Duncan walked to the door with him. "Thank you, Mr. Cortez. Thanks very much. You have no idea how much I appreciate it."

Cortez left. Duncan closed the door and turned around, fell back against it.

"What an asshole," he said in a low voice.

14

Slaughter stood by the pay phones, wanting to call this Duncan character back and promise to kick the shit out of him when this was over. He knew it would be a pointless, juvenile waste of time; he also knew it would make him feel so much better.

He read the business card again, tried to spot a pattern in the phone numbers of the foreign offices. If he'd had more time, and enough change, he would have called some of them, tried to trick some information out of whoever answered the phones. But he didn't want to use his own calling card. Maybe he'd buy a prepaid phone card after the interview, do some dialing and smiling then.

But whatever Dynet's business was, it didn't frighten him. Duncan could never frighten him, either. Neither could the two Mexicans he'd just fought with or the people who had sent the Chrysler into the back of the dump truck. Tanner, Mills, Cuthbert – none of them could frighten him, either. He was too sure of himself where fear was concerned, would not be bothered by the minor risk of death.

But failure, now that was another story. Deserting Chuck Wooten again, consigning the rest of his shitty life to that torturous existence, that was the thing he could not even think about. It scared the hell out of him to face it again. He had been wrong to quit once before, when that body was identified as Wooten's. It shamed him now. He would never fail him again.

He made a quick lap through the Sheraton's lobby, just to make sure everything seemed normal. Guests were checking in, and out, and several were reading or waiting in the large upholstered chairs. No one seemed interested in him, and no one looked out of place.

He went back to the phones and called Christopher Friedman. His secretary said he was just making his way back from their meeting and, if Slaughter would wait for him to get to his office, she would connect him. It only took about fifteen seconds, but it felt like five minutes.

"Yes, Jacob, what is it?"

"How safe is it at your studio, Christopher?"

"Safe, sure. Very safe." He laughed. "Hell, we've got locks on the doors and everything. Why?"

"Some men attacked me after I left the restaurant. I'm guessing they don't like what I'm doing, and want to stop me."

"You guess? You're not sure?"

Slaughter shook his head, stopped when his eyes locked onto someone new in the lobby. "We didn't really get a chance to talk. Maybe next time we'll have some coffee first, get to know each other a little better."

Friedman laughed again. "Funny. Okay, you got me, Jacob. What happened, really?"

"I was jumped by a Mexican tag-team in a black limo. What part didn't you understand?"

Friedman kept laughing, like he didn't have time for this, but enjoyed it too much to stop. "You've got to be kidding! So was I! But mine brought some girls with them. We talked, went on a tour of the White House – "

"Sure, it sounds funny now. But I wasn't laughing ten minutes ago."

Friedman turned serious on a dime. "Wait a minute, Jacob. Is this for real? You were actually attacked?"

Slaughter pulled the phone away and looked to see where it might be broken. "Yes, I'm serious. I'm not in much of a mood for kidding."

"Damn. Sorry. But wild stories of limo-driving Mexicans grabbing pedestrians off the streets of Washington . . . well, you've got to admit. It sounds like a joke."

"It sure didn't feel like a joke."

"So . . . what? What does that do to our plan?"

"Nothing. I'm all right, I just want you to expect trouble. It's following me around now, and I don't want to catch you unprepared."

"Not to worry, Jacob. Just make sure you get here. We're all set up and ready. You can breeze in, do your bit, and split before anyone figures out what your doing. I'll have NBC's security men covering the building"

"Are they armed?"

"You kidding? Television stations are prime targets for terrorists and wackos. They see us as the power, the voice for their propaganda, the tool to convert the masses. Yes, Jacob, our guards are armed."

"Good. See you in fifteen minutes. Nine o'clock."

"I can send a car to get you. Where are you?"

"I'll be careful. You be ready." Slaughter hung up and walked through the lobby. He stopped at the doors and looked out on the street. Even though a slight trace of sunlight still reigned the sky overhead, it was completely dark on the sidewalk. There was no way to tell if someone was waiting for him. He stepped through the doors and turned right. Then he stopped, five feet from the Sheraton's doors and leaned up against the wall, waited to see if anyone followed him.

A man and his wife came out right away, laughing, and headed in the other direction. Then no one. A minute passed. Thirty seconds more would be enough.

Time. Slaughter turned to walk away. But just then the doors were shoved open so loud it made him spin around, crouching, dropping his attaché. Two men in suits, both of them about thirty years old, charged out of the Sheraton and ran right toward Slaughter.

Slaughter braced to make his stand, knew he would have to use their weight and momentum against them, trip-throw them past him and then attack. He spread his stance, raised his opened hands to a fighting position, lowered his center of gravity.

The two men stopped like cartoon characters might, screeching and back-pedaling like crazy. Their faces looked terrified and their bodies relayed their panic – hands and arms up, head back farther than their shoulders, their balance shot to hell. Their chest and stomachs and faces – all kill zones – were wide open. Easy targets. It was obvious they weren't professionals.

"What do you want? What do you want?" The man on the street side was reaching for his wallet, squeezing out some pinched words. "Money? Here, I've got some money. Just don't hurt us. Please."

Slaughter grabbed his attaché and ran away, noticed the cab the men had been running for. The police were everywhere at night, and they would be here soon. If these men weren't a threat to him, he had no time for them. He ran to the corner, planning to walk again the second he rounded it. Just before he turned it, one of the men yelled a loud threat at him. Wasn't that always the way?

Friedman met Slaughter in NBC's lobby, cleared him through security, then led him to a small room, about twelve by fifteen. It was right off the main studio, and one entire wall of the room was glass. The main studio was busy with technicians preparing for the eleven o'clock broadcast. The news anchors were sipping coffee and working on the set. Two armed, uniformed guards stood outside the room, on either side of the glass. No one paid any attention to him.

There was a reporter in the room. An attractive young woman with red hair, wearing a pea-green suit. She was sitting in one of the two chairs and rose when Friedman opened the door. "Hi," she said. "I'm Jennifer." She held out her hand.

Slaughter shook it as he took inventory. The only other person in the room was a cameraman, all the way over on the other side, tall and skinny and wearing a ball cap, golf shirt, and jeans. He was kneeling on the floor and adjusting his equipment.. He stuck his head out from behind his eyepiece and nodded when Slaughter looked in his direction.

"Jacob," Friedman cut in, breaking the handshake with his words. "That's Chuck over there. He and Jennifer are the only ones here who know what this is about, and I only told them a few minutes ago, here in this room. I haven't let them talk to anyone since they were told."

Slaughter looked at both of them again. It felt strange that they knew his secret. He liked the feeling and hated it at the same time. "Thanks. Are we ready? I'd like to get going."

Chuck, the cameraman, hoisted his big camera onto his shoulder and aimed it at Slaughter. Without looking, he traced his fingers across the control board and made small adjustments for about ten seconds. "Okay, I'm ready," he said. "Jennifer, give me a voice."

"This is Jennifer Bowles, with NBC News, Washington. Tonight – "

"That's good, I got it. Mr. Slaughter?"

Jennifer sat down, looked at Slaughter's seat until he did the same. "Just say your name, Mr. Slaughter. What you do, where you're from, things like that. Use your normal voice."

Slaughter knew he was blushing, tried not to squirm. "Hello, I'm – "

"Got it," Chuck yelped. "Ready and waiting."

Jennifer smiled, acted confident that this would be easy if he would just relax. "Ready, Mr. Slaughter?"

He reached into his attaché and pulled out Phong's photos, set them on his lap. "Yes. Let's do it."

The camera rolled and Jennifer took control. She was very professional, asking questions that were natural lead-ins to what Slaughter wanted to say. She established his credentials early, gave the listener every reason to believe what he was about to tell them. He was impressed by her skill, by how easy she made this for him. She could have been a stateswoman.

He said it all, too, took about five minutes doing it. Told the world everything. American servicemen were still being held as prisoners in Vietnam. They would be released if Vietnam was granted a Most Favored Nation trade status – something that should be done anyway. Only a presidential signature was keeping these brave, forgotten men from their families. The United States government had everything to gain by granting Vietnam's request, so there were no good reasons those men wouldn't be coming home very soon. But, Slaughter said, it wasn't working out that way. Something had gone wrong.

"Mr. Slaughter," Jennifer asked, "although you have not made any specific charges against President Simons or his cabinet, it sounds as if you suspect some serious impropriety on their part. Do you have any proof, something that would substantiate your claim that those men are still there?"

Slaughter looked down at Phong's portfolio on his lap. Showing the pictures was something he had to think about again. So far, he'd just said words, and they had been pretty powerful. He had described the condition of the prisoners, and they had made Jennifer squirm. Just the words. The pictures were much worse, maybe too much for the general public.

But then he thought, hell, why not? Why not use everything he had, all the tools at his disposal? This was his one chance, his one opportunity to sway public opinion, get Americans to put pressure on the White House.

He rifled through them without showing them. He'd already planned, if he showed any photos, to show Wooten's first. He was the senior officer there, and his friend. He wanted his photo to become a symbol.

But he changed his mind, right then and there, with the camera rolling. Wooten *was* the senior officer, and that was precisely why he wouldn't show his photo first. As gruesome as it was, as bad as Wooten had been tortured, he had been given special treatment because of his seniority. Never wanted it, Slaughter was sure. Probably fought like hell against it. But he would have had no choice. They'd kept Wooten healthy so they could parade him out.

Slaughter dug through them until he came to one of the worst photographs, suddenly flipped it up so that Jennifer and Chuck could see it.

Chuck's voice burst out from his stomach, as if he'd been punched. His camera wobbled around on his shoulder. Jennifer squeezed her eyes closed and turned away, put her hand to her mouth as her cheeks swelled out.

Their reaction angered Slaughter. The anger wasn't directed at Chuck and Jennifer, certainly, but at the decades of errors and omissions that had allowed those men to suffer for so long. He stood up and walked toward the camera, the photo in front of him, the rest of them in his other hand. Chuck was struggling to keep him in focus, but Slaughter didn't slow down. He was losing control, getting a good glimpse of what it would be like to lose his mind. He began to rage. Couldn't stop himself.

"You want to see proof? Huh? I'll show you proof. Here, how's this?" He flipped to the next photo. "And this." Then another. "And this! Are you watching this, Tanner? Damn you!" Then another, and another, until he got to the last one. Wooten's.

"And this is Captain Charles Wooten, Tanner. No more bullshit, all right? Get these men home!"

He stopped, inches from the camera. The room was completely quiet. Chuck was on the floor, focused up at

Slaughter, looking like he might cry. Slaughter turned, saw that Jennifer had left the room. He had no idea when. The large window to the studio had a hundred faces pressed against it, all silent and sad. He saw his face on a bank of monitors in the studio. He picked up his things, walked to the door and opened it. The studio was silent, too. He could hear quiet shuffling as the crowd cleared a path for him, allowed him to move through them.

As he neared the exit, someone started to clap. It wasn't a clap of happiness or joy. Maybe it was a show of respect or praise. A few more joined in, then others. By the time Slaughter touched the door handle, the applause was too loud for him to stand. He had done nothing to deserve it.

He slipped away without talking to anyone, unsure about what he'd done and uncomfortable with the guns that NBC's security men were carrying. He had stepped into the glare of the camera's lights for this interview, was anxious to slip back into obscurity again.

It took more than an hour for Slaughter to get back to the small hotel room he had taken for the night. He checked and double-checked his back, would not chance anyone following him to Laura. When he walked in, she was sitting on the bed, glued to the television.

"Hurry, Jacob, they've been broadcasting your interview for almost an hour, preempted their regular schedule for it. Every station has picked it up. Christopher must have sold it to the news pool, 'cause it's absolutely everywhere."

He sat down beside her. "How does it sound? Convincing?"

"Yes! Hairs stood up on my neck when you held up those poor men's pictures. Of course, that's after I calmed my stomach down. The networks say they're being swamped with phone calls. A reporter at the White House says a protest is already building in Lafayette Park."

"Oh, shit, that reminds me. I've got to call Sarah Wooten. I wanted to tell her myself. I hate that she might hear it from the television."

"Too late for that. I'm sure she's heard by now."

"I still want to call her." He turned to the phone. Laura flipped through the channels."

"Jacob, come back here. Listen to this!"

He turned back to the television.

"Ladies and Gentlemen, CNN has just learned that Jacob Slaughter, the foreign service officer who made the unprecedented allegations we've been broadcasting, has just written and sold a book, his second, which is a novel about P.O.W.s left behind in Southeast Asia. CNN has obtained a portion of the finished manuscript from the publisher and has learned that the plot of Slaughter's book is identically parallel to the interview he gave to NBC.

"CNN has also learned that Slaughter, a former P.O.W. himself, has told coworkers at the State Department of several plans to capitalize on his experiences in a Vietnamese prison. Furthermore, Secretary of Defense Tanner has just confirmed that old file photos of Captain Wooten and the other prisoners Slaughter identified had recently been stolen from the Defense Department's records of confirmed dead P.O.W.s.

"In light of this investigation, CNN will cease broadcasting the original interview with Jacob Slaughter because of the high probability that it is fraudulent."

When the reporter shifted to other news, Slaughter switched stations. The same story was showing up on all of them. Secretary of State Mills came on the air, too, telling how much Slaughter had liked to talk, even brag, about his prison days.

Slaughter watched helplessly as his efforts turned into scandal. The reporters were getting meaner, their reports more slanted. For Slaughter, it was like watching a large sailboat slowly capsizing or a plane flying into the ground from high altitude. It had that same desperate drama of slow-moving doom.

Slaughter felt ashamed, embarrassed. He wished he'd never gone on the air, would have done anything to avoid the attention. He had always been uncomfortable in the spotlight.

But then, Chuck Wooten climbed back into his vision, and he was ready to do it all over again.

* * * * *

The corporate meeting room was full by ten-fifteen p.m.. Vice-President Cuthbert was on the video-conference television, observing and conversing through his electronic connection. Noise and smoke and angry tones filled the room and shrank it. Men huddled around in small groups, some of them drinking liquor from the bar, all of them looking unhappy. Duncan was nervous, had not wanted to call this emergency session. But he'd had to do it, had to earn back their confidence, say something they wanted to hear.

He stood up and waited for everyone's attention, but few of the executives noticed. The ones who did seemed to glance over at him, then turn their backs. This was the first time Duncan had felt such hostility from his clients.

Almost five minutes passed. Duncan kept swiveling his large body, using it to catch everyone's eye. But they ignored him, and the grumbling continued. Finally, Vice-President Cuthbert's disembodied head harrummphed the meeting to order.

"Gentlemen," Duncan began, "you have all seen Slaughter's interview. Most of you have seen the rebuttal story that is following it. Any comments?"

He thought it might go back to chaos, everyone yelling at once. But it didn't. These men understood order, understood that problems, even problems this serious, were simply situations that required a little more effort. Nothing more. They had the money, the organization, and the power. There was nothing they couldn't overcome.

176

A man rose, about halfway down the long table. He was over fifty, maybe even sixty. His glasses were thick over his bright, green eyes. His hair grew long where it grew at all. He was the only man there in a sport coat.

Duncan was glad to see someone stand. It deflected the attention from him. "Yes, sir," Duncan said. "I'm sorry, but I'm afraid I don't know your name."

The man's voice was relaxed, no trace of jitters. "My name is Henry Thomas. I am the president of Crawford Books. We're the company that released the excerpts from Slaughter's manuscript. This is my first meeting with you gentlemen, although I have been working with this organization for years. Vice-President Cuthbert has asked me to give an update on our efforts against Slaughter."

"Please, Mr. Thomas, go ahead."

"Thank you. Well, as of one hour ago my company has distributed fifty-seven copies of the manuscript excerpts. Requests are still coming in from all over the world, and we will continue to fill them."

There was a splatter of polite applause.

"That was pretty quick work, Mr. Thomas. Where in the world did you get that manuscript, anyway?"

Thomas looked down and spoke to the tabletop. "Well, as you know, we only released a small portion. Just a few thousand words, pages that would do the most harm. We said we were holding back on the rest. I argued that the publication rights would be worthless if we released any more of it. Actually, I could have sold the entire manuscript for a fortune, if it existed."

"Smart," said Duncan. "And where did you get those pages? They were absolutely terrific."

Thomas adjusted his glasses. "I wrote them. It only took a couple of hours, going as fast as I could. Frankly, I didn't really know I had it in me anymore. But then, the material pretty much wrote itself. I told the networks it hadn't been edited yet,

177

because it's not really ready for publication. I guess it wasn't too bad, though."

Everyone laughed, even the vice-president, his amplified voice louder than the others. Thomas blushed as he sat down. The businessman on one side of him shook his hand; the man on his other side slapped him on the back.

"Good job, Mr. Thomas," Duncan said. "Very good job. Now, who else?"

A bookish-looking man jumped up, unsmiling, like he'd been waiting for Thomas to finish with his silliness so he could have his turn. He had a thin face, long and drawn down toward a sharp chin. His hands were exceptionally small. The tiny bones and muscles were clearly outlined as they shifted around under his skin.

"Yes, sir, Mr. Neumann."

Neumann ran the largest credit reporting agency in America and therefore maintained a tight squeeze on the testicles of commerce. He had the remains of a German accent, maybe only a generation or two removed from its motherland. But Duncan could not be sure, had never been able to uncover any records on Neumann.

Neumann adjusted the wire frame of his glasses, then swept his right hand through the air in a flourish. "I have personally eliminated Jacob Slaughter," he said, then waited. He stared at each face in the room, one at a time, and ended up with Duncan. "Maybe he is still alive in some medical sense. I do not know about those things. But I'd challenge anyone to prove it."

The laughter was nervous

Neumann laughed with them. He seemed to enjoy their nervousness, their fears.

"I have removed him from all files. His banks have been notified that his credit history was fraudulent, an embarrassing error of ours that should have been caught earlier. Now he has no record at all, or access to a bank account. His checks will bounce, the lender on his car is repossessing, his utilities are being cut off. There is no credit report available on him anywhere, since all the other agencies subscribe to our data in order to update their own files. He cannot even use his calling card. In almost every sense of the word, he no longer exists."

Neumann sat down. Duncan looked around the room, saw the others shuddering. He shuddered a little, too. "Good work, Mr. Neumann. Who else?"

Vice-President Cuthbert cleared his throat in a deeply presidential way. Everyone turned to the monitor.

"Gentlemen," Cuthbert began, "this combined effort is, as usual, tremendous. America's businesses, blending their talents with America's government to fight against a common foe. For our part, let me promise the following: Slaughter's passport will be canceled and the Department of Justice will file federal charges against him for a variety of crimes. Both of those things will be done immediately and will have a profound effect on Slaughter. However, these actions may not be severe enough or quick enough. Mr. Duncan, please continue. I have to go to another meeting." The screen suddenly went to fuzz.

Duncan walked to the monitor and switched it off, scanned the conference room full of executives. They were men he had worked with for decades, mostly. Men who understood the relationship that business *really* needed to have with government. Men whose loyalty was based, if for no other reason, on a generous income stream.

"Gentlemen," he said, "I know what you expect of us here at Dynet. And I want to reassure you that we are the best in this business. The services we offer extend far beyond the coordination of your collective interests. We are, in the final analysis, facilitators of all the things you cannot accomplish on your own. So, we will eliminate Jacob Slaughter from our society." He nodded to Neumann. "As you have already done on paper. It will be easy. It may even have been accomplished already."

*　*　*　*　*

At ten-thirty p.m., Slaughter sat on the bed with Laura and watched Vice-President Cuthbert make a live, unscheduled, television speech. In it, Cuthbert detailed Slaughter's allegations, then gave a convincing rebuttal of each one. He closed by offering his deepest apologies to the American people, especially to the families of the twenty-three deceased heroes Slaughter had specifically named. Cuthbert expressed deep sorrow and grief for the intense pain they must be feeling now that Slaughter's allegations had been proven false.

Slaughter scanned the dial after Cuthbert's short speech. All the major networks had carried it and were following it up with a similar apology from the networks themselves. Christopher Friedman was doing the groveling at NBC.

Slaughter hit the television, missed the on-off button, smashed at it again. Then he dialed the number he'd gotten from directory assistance and listened to the phone ringing.

"Hello," said the voice at the other end. It was the same voice he'd heard challenging Mills at the secretary of state's press conference. The same voice he had listened to and admired when he'd worked for the P.O.W./M.I.A. national organization.

"Mrs. Kinsey?"

"Yes."

"This is Jacob, Mrs. Kinsey. Jacob Slaughter. Please don't hang up on me."

The line buzzed with the hum of low-voltage electricity. He waited. He respected her too much to push her.

Finally, Mrs. Kinsey spoke. "Why are you doing this, Jacob? Why can't you just leave us alone?"

He felt so sad, so sick, he almost had nothing to say. "Mrs. Kinsey, you must believe me. Your husband is still alive over there. I need your organization's help to get him out. The government has been lying to you for years, decades. You know they have. We've seen it too many times. Please, don't start believing them now."

Mrs. Kinsey was ice-cold. He'd never heard her voice like this, even when she'd battled with Mills at the press conference. "Yes, Jacob, you're right. The United States government has lied to me before. I have been scammed several times over these many years. But mostly by people like you. I absolutely will not stand for it again."

"But your husband, Mrs. Kinsey. I have photos. You've seen them."

This troubled her, he could tell. She started to say something, probably ask a question about her husband. Who wouldn't want to ask? Who wouldn't want to say, "Let me see them up close. Hold them in my own hands. Please."

But when she spoke again it was final, the sound of defeat so loud that he wanted to quit himself.

"My husband is dead, Jacob. I've just seen all of the evidence, things that the government had no choice but to withhold from me until now. I guess I should thank you for that, for putting them under enough pressure to make them tell me everything."

"No, Mrs. Kinsey. No! They haven't told you everything. Just let me meet with you. Let me talk to you."

He heard her choking on pain, remembered her on television, backing away from Mills, searching for her chair with a wandering hand, trying to catch herself before she fell.

"Good-bye, Jacob. Please, don't ever call here again."

She hung up.

* * * * *

Walter Mills rushed across Kinsey's small country kitchen, ready to catch her if she fell. Mrs. Kinsey's grown son stepped in front of him and cut him off. But she sat down unassisted, crumpled into the antique oak chair and started crying.

Her son turned to Mills. He was about thirty years old. Tall and good-looking. His handsome face was disillusioned and angry, but very much under control.

Mills waited for the words he expected to hear. Harsh, hateful words that would ask why it had taken so long for America to tell them the truth, why they'd been allowed to suffer so terribly while they'd hoped in vain for his father's return. Mills braced for them, tried to come up with a good answer.

But the questions didn't come. The young man stepped around him and walked silently toward the door. He was still holding the photo of his dead father's body, the face twisted and shriveled by time. It was the proof they had sought for so long, had begged Mills for on a dozen other occasions. It was a believable picture of his father, dead. Kinsey's son opened the door and held it for Mills.

"Good-bye," he said.

Mills held his hand out. The young man looked at it, then turned back to the kitchen, watched his mother sobbing in there.

Mills withdrew his hand and left.

15

Slaughter eased the phone down, slowly hung it up. But he kept staring at it, wanting to call Mrs. Kinsey back, trying to think of some other words that might work on her. But none came to mind. He doubted, really, if any existed. She was not going to help him. She had been very clear.

He shifted around on the bed, turned to talk to Laura, hoped she might have a suggestion. But she stood up just as he turned, started pacing the floor of the motel room. Her hand was pinching her lower lip in that nervous habit of hers. She went back and forth across the small room, one hand across her stomach, the other at her lip. He watched her for several minutes. Never said a word.

Finally, she stopped in front of him. "Jacob, can I see those pictures again? The ones of the prisoners?"

He kept watching her, trying to figure out what was going on as he picked up the photos and handed them to her. She walked around the bed, sat down with her back to him.

*   *   *   *   *

She held the photos in her hand, but she didn't want to look at them. She kept thinking of heartbroken mothers in city morgues, terrified as the coroner pulled back the sheet for an identification of their sons' bodies. She'd understood the emotional shock of those women since medical school. Was actually feeling it now, for the first time.

Maybe just holding the pictures would be enough. Just hold onto them, hold them tight with her eyes closed. She could remember what her victims looked like, knew the cast of their faces as well as she did Jacob's. She didn't really have to do this to herself.

But she also knew it would not work out that way. It wasn't in her nature to take the easy road, had never been her way. No matter how she tried to trick herself into believing that she hadn't contributed to those poor men's deaths, she would not allow herself to believe it. It was a lie, and she would confess it. At least to herself.

She needed to be alone. Jacob kept glancing at her, trying to act like he was just looking around. She knew how much he needed help, could see it in his eyes, clearly. And for some reason, the more she realized what he needed, the less inclined she was to help him. She was, on some level, starting to resent him. How could he do this to her? How could he do this to their relationship? Hadn't everything been going pretty well for them up until now? Why did he have to make this such an issue? She wanted to grab him by the shoulders and scream at him: Damn you, Jacob, you're going to destroy us over this! Is that what you want? Are you willing to pay that price?

She slid off the bed and went out on the balcony. The summer night was cloudy but warm, the day's remaining heat and the city's hot emissions accenting each other. A light breeze sent the smells and sounds of Washington across the Potomac: wet garbage, exhausts, food, sirens, radios. The signature of a big city. Her city. The place where she had always wanted to practice psychiatry. The throbbing heart of the nation.

But standing on the balcony, her senses received an overdose of this near-lethal mixture and she wanted to be back home in Seattle. Go back about three decades to that wonderful time when her father and mother were spoiling her with love, if such a thing was possible. Crawl up onto her daddy's strong lap, look down at her own little knees and tell him she had done something very, very wrong. Something she was really sorry for now, but she had done it all the same and now she didn't know how to fix it. Listen carefully to her daddy's advice. He would know what to do. He would help her make it right.

She sat down in a patio chair and pulled her knees up to her chin, pressed the stack of pictures flat against her breastbone, kept her eyes on the sky. She knew there were twenty-three of them, photos of twenty-three men who were going to be left behind, again. Twenty-three courageous American men who'd answered their country's call back in the sixties and early seventies, only to find the phone line out of order when they'd tried to call back for help.

She liked the number, twenty-three. It was about right to balance the scale. Actually, she had helped hundreds of Vietnam Vets. No, thousands. But she remembered very few. Jacob, of course. And some others. But the rest had been sent back out into the world. Cured. Or at least as close to being cured as the definition could be stretched. She'd tried to forget them and go on to the next patient.

But the ones who had known something, the ones who had some knowledge that could embarrass the government, those patients had been a completely different story. There had been about twenty of them, a few more, maybe. By some wicked twist of fate, they had learned too much over there. A whole lot more than the government could live with. They had come home with absolute knowledge that American prisoners had been left behind.

Her job was to get them talking, have them tell her the extent of what they knew. Then she would pass it along to Walter Mills. He or someone else in power made the decisions, based on her clinical recommendation. Those soldiers always disappeared. It was pretty simple. The government had no other choice, Mills would say, than to transfer them to another facility where they and their secret would be safer. Where they could be debriefed while they received excellent care.

Laura had tried to get rid of Abbey, her attacker, that way. After telling Mills what he'd done to her, she'd lied about what he had seen in Vietnam, sure that it would get him transferred. But instead she found him hanging from the black pipes in her ward, dangling several feet off the ground with no chair around, close to the spot where Edgar Jennings had been suffocated. She had almost fainted when she'd found his body during her early rounds. But she didn't. She'd walked over and sat on Edgar's old bed, studied the corpse as it twisted from the sprinkler pipe.

After Abbey's death she confronted Mills, demanded to know exactly where the other men she'd reported had been sent. It took several hours of arguing and pleading before Mills broke down and told her the truth. They were all gone, he'd said. Like Abbey. The government hadn't really had a choice. The men were too much of a threat to America.

From that second forward, she never reported another soldier's sighting of P.O.W.s to Mills.

Now, Jacob was in trouble, was becoming a big problem to some dangerous people. People who would not hesitate to destroy him, or her, or anyone who threatened them. And Jacob was definitely a threat. She would be, too, if she helped him. It would end her career. Maybe her life.

She had to wonder, forced herself to ask the question: Was he worth it? Did she really love him that much, enough to destroy herself? Was anyone worth that price?

* * * * *

Slaughter was talking on the phone when she came back in. He watched her, started bending over the phone table, trying to hang up.

"Yes, Sarah. No, I don't care what Cuthbert said when he called, you were right all along. Your father *is* still alive, honey. And we're going to bring him home. I promise. But we're going to need help. Lots of it. Go to the national organization and convince them I'm telling the truth, get them to pressure President Simons. Yes. It's very exciting. But they're not home yet. All right. You're welcome. I'm happy, too. Good-bye."

Slaughter hung up, didn't move as Laura picked up the business card he had shown her earlier. She fidgeted with it in her slender fingers. Looked at it a long, long time. Then she looked at Slaughter, her eyes wandering all across his face. She did that for a minute. Then another. Finally, a smile creased her lips, the same relenting smile she would give him whenever he talked her into something. She looked up and breathed deep, stared hard at nothing, exhaled.

She had her arms crossed over her stomach, the photos pressed against her T-shirt. Her weight was on her left leg, her right foot tapping the floor in a rapid beat.

"Jacob, I think I can help you find out something about this company, Dynet."

187

Slaughter moved slowly, knew the road was laced with mines. "Well, I could sure use it," he said. "There are no records of them in any source I've checked. They're not – "

She interrupted him with a flick of her hand. "There wouldn't be, Jacob. The nature of their business mandates that they stay hard to find."

He started to say "What?" but caught the words just before they escaped. He waited, like he had lots of time. It was killing him.

"Jacob, I'm not really sure I can help you because the information I have is confidential. Privileged. But let's just say that one of my patients worked for Dynet. He told me a lot about what they do. It's just that, well, I can't tell you what he said. I know how important this is, Jacob, I really do. But I'm bound, absolutely, by my ethics. And by my obligation to my patient. Do you understand?"

Slaughter stepped around her and started to pace. Took the photos she held out to him and paced some more. What to say? What to use? Logic? Yelling? Pleading?

"Laura, I understand obligation, believe me I do. But isn't getting twenty-three Americans prisoners home a hell of a lot more important than some rote pledge you might have taken at graduation?"

Laura climbed onto the bed. Crossed her legs, leaned back, watched him.

He sat down, too, decided to try arguing with her. But she moved away and picked up the telephone. Dialed. It was an easy number. Automatic. Her office. "Janice? Hi, this is Laura. Pull the file on patient G-457, please. I need his home phone number."

Laura was quiet. Listening. Waiting. Then she reached for the pad and wrote something down. "Thanks, I've got it. And Janice, roll my calls over to the answering service and go home early. I'll have the day shift catch up on your filing."

She hung up, dialed again.

"Hello," she said. "This is Doctor Warner. Can I . . . do you mind speaking with me for a few minutes?"

Slaughter wondered what the man was saying. Whatever it was, it took more than a minute and caused Laura'a head to nod twice. She glanced back at him, as if to see if he was losing patience.

"Dynet," she finally said. "Would you be willing to tell a friend of mine some of the things you've told me about them?"

It was a blunt question, the kind that only had two decent answers and forced the person to make a decision. Yes or no. But as he watched, he saw that the patient was coming up with some other options. Laura listened some more, then began to offer some assurances. Slaughter repeated the promises he heard her make. He intended to honor them, just as if he'd made them himself.

"Good," she finally said. "How about twenty minutes? Yes, that will be great. I really appreciate it, more than you know. Please come see me next week, okay? I'd like to spend a few sessions with you, off the clock, just to see how you're doing."

The man said something that made her laugh, and the laugh rinsed some of the strain from her face. "Sure," she said. "I just bet you would."

She hung up and lowered her head onto Slaughter's shoulder. "His name is Kelly. He'll meet you at O'Shea's Bar, in Arlington. He's medium height and kind of big, said he'll be wearing a camel hair sport coat. He looks like a guy who used to run a lot, used to stay in real good shape. You'll have to look hard to see it, though. He'll meet you there at eleven o'clock. Chances are he'll be drunker than anyone else there."

"Aren't you coming?"

She shook her head, threw the hair out of her wet eyes. "No. I don't care to see him go through this again."

Slaughter held her. Thanked her. Did it all very gently. He wanted to stay there long enough to convince her of the value of her actions. Wanted to stay so bad he hurt. But he was almost a half-hour away from Arlington, and he had no idea where O'Shea's was. He backed away, left her to deal with her own feelings. He was sure she had timed the meeting so it would work out like this.

He stepped carefully out of the motel room. The night was dark. The air was thick and wet, yet the street still looked dry. Slaughter walked from the motel, nearly six blocks to the street where he had left his car. He stopped in the shadows and checked it out from a distance.

The car looked fine. He'd hoped it would be. The taxi rides were feeling more and more dangerous. Lots of things could happen, and he would not have control. He preferred his own car. Earlier, he had stopped at a long-term lot and stolen a plate from a Buick parked several cars deep. He'd put it on, believed it might do the trick.

Then he saw him. The big Mexican with the skinny ass – Luis – stepped out of a coffee shop with two Styrofoam cups. Luis headed down the street and stopped at a brown Dodge, crawled into the driver's side, the injuries from earlier making him flinch and twitch. His car was on the opposite side of the street from Slaughter's, at a spot where he would be able to see Slaughter get in but too far away to run up to Slaughter on foot. He guessed that Luis planned to follow him for a while, get out of the area where he might have already been observed by someone. Then he would probably do anything he was capable of doing.

Slaughter started to turn and go back the way he had come, catch a cab to Arlington. But there were answers in that Dodge. Even if he didn't exactly know what the questions were, he could guess that the big Mexican worked for Dynet Industries. He would go over there and force some answers out of him, use some of the torture techniques the Vietnamese had taught him. See how well that big bastard held up.

But would the man at O'Shea's wait? Where could he do the most good for Wooten? He thought about Laura and her contribution to his life. More accurately, he thought about her gift of his life.

He would follow her plan. It was probably best. Odds were that the man at O'Shea's would have more knowledge than the Mexican. He would probably be more cooperative, too.

Slaughter backed around the corner and went down the block. He found a cab from a company he hadn't used before, climbed in, and asked to go to O'Shea's.

16

O'Shea's, as the name suggested, was an Irish bar, originally owned by an old man who had retired and left his sons the business. There were several newspaper clippings hanging in-between the outer and inner doors, and Slaughter glanced at them as he entered. Several of the articles included pictures of the retired owner seated on a bar stool and waving a pint of stout at the camera.

It was a little after eleven o'clock when Slaughter stepped inside. It was a small place, with a thick, wood bar running the length of the left side and tables everywhere else except the rear, where a regulation pool table stood, unused. There were about thirty people in the place, smoking pipes and drinking beer and chattering away in their wonderful Irish brogue. They looked up when he entered, seemed to make some sort of judgment about him, then returned to their conversations. The old man from the newspaper articles sat at the front end of the bar, with what looked like the very same pint of stout in his hand.

There was only one man in the place with a camel hair coat. He looked like a high school basketball coach, or an actor long out of work. Good looking in a faded fashion and still plenty fit. You could see that at one time the guy's body had been a top priority for him. But not anymore.

The man had two empties in front of him and a finger circling for more. The bartender caught the signal and ambled over, stuck a finger into each of the glasses and clinked them together in his left hand.

"And whatever he's having," the man said, tilting his head in Slaughter's direction.

Slaughter was stunned. He hadn't even seen the guy look up when he entered. No, that's wasn't it exactly. The fact was, the guy *hadn't* looked up. But from where he sat, angled toward the pool table with his back toward the door, the man had picked Slaughter out with some kind of uncanny peripheral vision.

The bartender's head turned in a lazy arc and his eyes settled on Slaughter. "What'll it be, buddy?"

"Scotch, rocks," Slaughter said, as he walked to an empty stool beside the man, all the while comparing his own clothes, hair, and shoes to everyone else's, trying to figure out how the man had made him.

Slaughter sat down, nodded as the bartender dealt out a cheap paper coaster with an elaborate coat of arms stamped on it. When the bartender left, Slaughter swiveled to stare at the side of the man's head. Then he twisted back toward the entrance, still wondering how the man had picked him out. "Neat trick."

The man shrugged, his big shoulders rolling up and forward. "No trick to it. You stick out."

Slaughter checked himself again. Half the people here were dressed just like him.

"I'm Jacob Slaughter." He held out his hand.

The man glanced at it as the bartender came back. He took a hard hit from the drink as it passed from the bartender's hand to his, then eased the glass down and rotated his body around. "Yup. Nice to meet you. I'm Kelly. Here, have a drink."

Slaughter's glass was just hitting the bar. He picked it up quickly and collided into Kelly's. "To the wind at your back."

Kelly nodded, drank it all.

"I saw you on TV, Slaughter, talking about those prisoners. Now why'd you want to go and stir up that hornet's nest?" His finger went up, the bartender stepped into view and refilled his glass, almost left the bottle. Their long years of teamwork played out as Slaughter watched.

"Because it's the right thing," Slaughter said. "And, because I have an obligation I'm anxious to fulfill."

Kelly picked up his cigarettes, tapped one out, fiddled with it. Slaughter noticed that the ashtray was clean. The cigarette's filter was wet, right out of the pack.

"You mind if I smoke, Slaughter?"

"No."

Kelly studied the cigarette like it was a complex equation he needed to solve. He rolled it around, looked at it from every possible angle. "You smoke?"

"No," Slaughter said.

"Never?"

"No."

Kelly snorted. "Smart." He took another drink.

"I never had the chance, really. My folks would have busted my butt, and that sort of stayed with me for a few years after I left home. By the time it sunk in that they couldn't stop me, well, let's just say cigarettes were in short supply.

"You mean the Vietnamese wouldn't give you any?"

The question shook Slaughter, his history thrown at him by a stranger. Television had bared it all: his service record, his background, all the information he had tried to leave behind. It was the world's knowledge now, and it made him squirm.

"No, not exactly. They would give them to you. You just had to be willing to pay the price. That's all."

Kelly drank again. One sentence; one drink. Easy math.

"Price was too high, I guess?"

Slaughter drank, too. He couldn't remember the last time he'd finished a drink so quickly. "Yes. The price was too high. At least for me it was." He took a drink from the fresh refill, washed some of the acid from his mouth, the memory of those few prisoners who had passed the time easily with good food and plenty of privileges. "Some men smoked in there."

Kelly lifted the cigarette to his mouth, sucked down the unlit aroma, then stuffed the white tube back into the pack. "I'm sure they did."

Slaughter watched Kelly's ceremony with the cigarette, wondered how long it had been going on.

"Six years," Kelly said, as if to answer the silent question.

Slaughter felt himself blush, suddenly worried that Kelly could read minds, too. "What?"

"Six years I worked over there. Even saw those prisoners a time or two."

Slaughter could barely hold back the avalanche of questions. But he managed, waited for Kelly to say more, not sure how long he could hold the questions in.

Kelly rattled his ice, his finger went up again, the bartender came over and refilled. When he left, Slaughter moved into it a little, being careful not to sound judgmental.

"Well, whatever brought you in contact with them must be old news, I guess. Except to the twenty-three men still there."

"Yes," Kelly said. "Real old news."

This was taking too long. Slaughter was getting frustrated, had to get things moving, had to find out what Kelly knew, then get back to some of the other work that needed to be done. "Look, Mr. Kelly, Laura told me nothing about you, but she did indicate that you might be willing to help. I found this card in the car of a man who attacked me earlier today. Do you recognize this name?" He held up Duncan's card.

Kelly didn't look at it. He was too busy studying the liquor, swirling it around with the ice before it vanished down his throat. "That would be Duncan's card. Right?"

Slaughter turned the card and read it for the hundredth time. "Yes. It is. How in the world did you know that? You know him?"

Kelly signaled for another. When the bartender came back, Slaughter slipped his hand over the top of his glass. Kelly cut his eyes over to see it.

"Sure, I know Duncan. He's the only one at Dynet that's smart enough to run a piece of that business, but stupid enough to put his name on a card. A big ego thing, I think."

"And what kind of business is that, Kelly? What does Dynet do?" Slaughter asked the question boldly, without waffling. But it hadn't been easy. Questions like that were death. With stakes this high, no one could ask them without getting a little rattled. The trick, of course, was not to show it.

Kelly looked at him for the first time, eye-wrestled with Slaughter for a minute. "Didn't you check them out on your computer at work?"

"No, I didn't. I was out of time before I learned of Dynet, have been under the gun since I left."

Kelly chuckled, deep and boozy, like he understood exactly what that felt like. Running out of time and running for your life. Trying to do both things at once. He seemed to find it funny, but he didn't laugh. "You should have checked, Slaughter. They would have lit up your computer like nothing you've ever seen before."

"Really?"

Kelly's voice was turning into a drawl, an old veteran dazzling the new recruit with glorious war stories. "Hell, yes. Over the years, dozens of investigators at Justice have opened cases on Dynet. All kinds of charges. Zillions of hours spent on them by F.B.I. agents. D.E.A. guys have been after them, too."

"They sound like organized crime, then."

"Can't prove that," Kelly said. "At least, no one has proven it yet. Every case against them – and there have been hundreds – has been shut down without prosecution. The agents, hell, they just keep trying to do what's right. They find enough reasonable suspicion to open a case and gather the evidence. But Dynet always manages to avoid a trial. Not by plea bargaining, either."

"That sounds like it would be impossible."

"Sure it does. I'd say it *was* impossible if I hadn't witnessed it for so many years. I don't know how they do it, but they get some strings pulled, some agents are reassigned, and the cases get closed. The whole process is pretty impressive, really."

"Mr. Kelly, can I ask you what your part was in all of those activities?"

The finger, the bartender, the refill. A gulp. "Okay, Hot-Shot, I'll tell you. But only because Laura asked me to. Don't get confused about my intentions. Understand?"

"I understand."

"Good." Another deep gulp of booze, followed by a long, low hiss between his teeth.

"I was a civilian advisor in Vietnam, Slaughter. Like everybody else back then, I worked for the C.I.A., helping them get money and drugs flowing so that South Vietnam could finance their war effort. It was a giant industry, I tell you." He started to drink, held off, put the glass back on the bar.

"But hell, everyone already knows that. Anyway, after the war, our government had to get out of that messy sort of business. So Dynet came along and privatized all our activities. It was where they got their start, and they've just been growing larger and larger every since."

"What are they doing now? Surely that operation would have died out by now."

Kelly looked around the room. He was careful about it, almost unnoticeable. It was interesting that the alcohol hadn't eroded his instincts. "Oh, sure, you're right. Hell, it would be childish, now, to do the things we were doing back then. But the guys at Dynet were smart. Very smart. Our old operation gave them access, even intimacy, with major, global players on all sides. So they redefined and expanded their role. Phased out the drugs and cash, and built up strong alliances with companies that wanted to sell cars, soft drinks, and cigarettes. Legitimate businesses that needed illegitimate work done to insure their success. A company – and that's really what Dynet is – a company that's willing to quash competition. Bribe or murder people who impede their client's goals. They will even incite small wars if their governing board of clients believes there is enough benefit to it."

"Mr. Kelly, if they've been doing this for all these years but there's never been any prosecution, doesn't it seem likely that they're still tied to the government?"

Kelly's head tilted back, his eyes seemed to focus on the ceiling as if it was a self-test for drunkenness. He apparently passed, raised the finger for the bartender.

"Naah, not really. Not Dynet. But the *businesses*, their *clients*, now there's your connection. You've got to remember that American industry is the giant engine that keeps this country moving. Can you even imagine where we'd be, as a nation, without our great businesses? Those companies give a whole lot of people their paychecks, and those paychecks drive America's economy. Those huge corporations also produce the weaponry that keeps this country safe, and the communication networks that keep us in touch with the rest of the world. Without them, we'd lose our ability to defend ourselves, our stock market would weaken, and the dollar would go right down the shitter."

Slaughter raised his glass and smiled. "You sound like an economist."

"Hell, I'm no damned economist. Don't take John Kenneth Galbraith to understand something as simple as this: Strong businesses are America's greatest defense against attack."

"I didn't mean to offend you, Mr. Kelly. Sorry. It makes sense."

Kelly was getting drunk now. Slaughter could guess that a bad temper would come along for the ride.

"You damned right it makes sense! Okay? So, now, you tell me, college boy. Let's say you're the President of the United States and a company – Dynet, for instance – comes to you representing the demands of a private association of business leaders from the largest corporations in America. Do you: A, immediately throw him out of your office; B, listen to him, then throw him out of your office; or C, do whatever the hell he tells you to do because without his help your political career has the life expectancy of a fruit fly?"

Slaughter didn't want to answer.

Kelly pressed the attack. "Well, smart guy, what do you do? I'm waiting."

"I listen," Slaughter said. "And, I guess, I cooperate as much as I can."

Kelly started to roar. The bartender looked at the old owner for a signal.

"You do a hell of a lot more than that if you want to survive. You do *exactly* what you're told. Boy, I don't give a shit how high up the ladder you are! When they say to kiss up, buddy, you pucker!" Kelly spun around on his stool, his eyes stalking Slaughter like they were looking for surrender.

Slaughter knew he should give it, say the words that would show Kelly they were the same kinds of men, agree with the man for agreement's sake. But he couldn't do it. It was too big a stretch. "No. I'm sorry, Kelly. I wouldn't."

Kelly's anger bubbled over and he went into motion, his legs swinging toward the floor, his hands moving up. Slaughter jumped away from his stool, getting as ready as he could without returning the challenge. Kelly's feet hit the floor and his ankle turned. He crashed down on his back.

He didn't try to get up right away. He just laid there, unmoving. Stayed down there on the stained hardwood with a look of drunken embarrassment blooming onto his face. Then he rolled over onto his knees and drooped his head against the floor.

A minute passed, but Slaughter didn't offer to help. He didn't want to pile more shame on the man. He would wait as long as it took. Kelly finally propped himself up with one hand, his head down and shaking, his body completely vulnerable. Slaughter squatted down in front of him.

"Are you all right, Mr. Kelly?"

Kelly looked up, surprised Slaughter with the tears in his eyes. He grabbed Slaughter's wrist, held it so tightly there was no possibility of getting away. "You'll never get those poor bastards out, you know. I wish to God I could help you, would die to undo some of what I've done to them. But you won't make it. Don't you understand? The government doesn't want 'em back. Nobody does."

17

Slaughter threw a fifty on the bar. The bartender didn't move. Looking bored, he continued to lean against the back counter. He'd seen it all before, maybe too many times.

Kelly started getting up and Slaughter helped him, as much as was necessary. They shuffled out the door while everyone else watched. Slaughter stayed close to Kelly, just in case he needed support.

The muzzle flashed the second they hit the sidewalk, brilliant in the dark night but still soundless as the lightburst beat the explosive noise to Slaughter's senses. He shoved Kelly, hard, tried to push him to the ground. Slaughter wasn't really sure who was the target, but it was instinctive for him to divide the kill zone in half. His hand was on Kelly's upper arm, pushing on him to go down. Then the charge of current electrified Kelly and threw Slaughter clear.

It was as if Kelly had been struck by a god. A miracle, nothing less. The drunken, ambling Irishman was pure juice now. His instincts, probably so deeply insulated that alcohol could never reach them, demonized his body and sent him flying, angled between Slaughter and the pistol.

Slaughter was dropping to the ground, straight ahead and face first, the way he'd been trained, the way that would allow him to continue firing back. Except he had nothing to fire. No weapon with which to defend himself. But it didn't really matter, Kelly's flight was so impressive that Slaughter found himself slowing his own descent, watching the brilliant performance.

Kelly was shielding him now, still airborne, blocking Slaughter's view as the bullet struck Kelly in the chest and rammed him backward. But Kelly hit the ground on his feet. He rocked a little on impact, then gave a quick glance to make sure he was in front of Slaughter. A human shield. He made his command, strangely calm, but very forceful. "Run, Slaughter! Damn you, run! Get out of here!"

But Slaughter didn't run. He couldn't run. He would not leave Kelly alone. He would never, ever leave another man behind. He charged at the gunman, going around Kelly's human barrier. Then the second shot lit up the night. Then another, and another. Kelly's body absorbed each of them while making jerky progress toward the gunman, blocking Slaughter off as they both rushed in the shooter's direction. Another bullet fired, a head shot that finally stopped Kelly less than a foot from the gunman. The noise was distinct and ugly in Slaughter's right ear, a hard crack followed by a thick sludging sound.

Slaughter was almost on the gunman as he swung his pistol toward him. But Slaughter was quick. He grabbed the barrel with a sweep of his left hand and jammed his little finger in front of the cocked hammer. The hammer snapped down on his finger, but the pistol didn't fire. Slaughter cranked the barrel around, twisted the end of it back toward the shooter. Wrenched it out of the man's grip. Aimed it at the center of the man's ugly face and started to shoot.

The man stood there, unarmed, proper and dignified, his face badly pitted with scars, his black eyes boring down on

Slaughter, looking for something that, somehow, Slaughter understood intuitively. Then the man smiled – a beautiful smile that erased away his ugliness.

A crowd of men streamed out of O'Shea's and skidded to a stop. Slaughter stood by Kelly's body, wondering what they thought had happened. Worried that some of them might think he'd killed Kelly. But he didn't look back at them, kept the pistol's front sight in sharp focus on the dark little man.

The man was beaten, clearly. Slaughter had him. If he could just pull the trigger.

The trigger tension was impossible to overcome. Slaughter kept sending the signals to his finger – harder, pull harder. But the trigger wouldn't budge. He pulled harder, or at least tried to, but still the trigger didn't move. He was doing his best, using all his strength. But the trigger was strong. Too strong.

The ugly little man with the wonderful smile turned from Slaughter and the crowd, started to walk away.

A devil festered up from Slaughter's stomach, clouded Slaughter's personal vow with hate and pain – gave him plenty of reasons why he should kill this man. The devil had a maniacal voice that spewed out of Slaughter's mouth, hissing and growling as the tip of Slaughter's finger struggled, once more, to pull back on the trigger. "You hold it right there!"

The man slowed down. He stopped. Turned. He raised his left hand a little, then scraped some dirt from under a nail with his right.

"You won't shoot me, Mr. Slaughter. You know you won't. You don't have it in you any longer. You've come too far to slide back into that seething pit. And, my friend, we both know it. Don't we?"

The small Mexican looked up at the sky, took in and savored a deep breath of warm air, then smiled and gave Slaughter his back.

Slaughter stretched his arm out, aimed right at the center of the man's skull. Squeezed harder on the trigger. Felt it began to move. Braced for the recoil. "Stop!"

The front sight started to wobble and his hand began to shake. Slaughter tried to glue Vu Van Vinh's face onto the back of the small Mexican's head, give himself the extra ingredient he needed to shatter the man's pumpkin, violate his vow.

Kelly's body went into convulsions on the ground. A leg jumped out at an awkward angle. Slaughter held his aim as he knelt down and felt for a pulse that didn't exist. Some men in the crowd were talking about chasing after the Mexican, but none of them sounded serious.

Sirens were heading his way, only a couple of blocks away. The shooter stopped at the corner, cocked an ear toward them, then turned back to Slaughter.

"Goodnight, Mr. Slaughter. Have a pleasant evening. We will meet again soon."

The man disappeared behind the building, the sound of his steps picking up a rapid tempo.

Slaughter stuffed the gun in his belt and ran after the fading footsteps.

* * * * *

Walter Mills sat on a couch in the Oval Office, sipping another glass of brandy with President Simons and listening to him retell his favorite stories of life in the White House. They were alone in this historic room. Just him and Simons, two men of history, not yet immortalized in text.

Their time in the spotlight would end soon. Another few months and Simons would be gone. Mills would go with him. Cuthbert, probably, would sit at the desk where Simons was propping his feet. But Mills didn't really care. Eight years was enough time for anyone to sit at that famous desk, or across from it.

Kennedy had sat in this office and faced down Khrushchev during the Cuban Missile Crisis. Johnson had bombed the hell out of Vietnam, and started his own Great Society. Nixon had opened trade with China, and hired men like Gordon Liddy. Simons . . . well, Mills knew that he and Simons would leave their own legacy. The scribes just hadn't finished writing it down yet. Mills sat there, drinking and praying they would never find out the truth.

Alex Simons was only forty-nine years old. He was young for a president and could pass for forty. His dark hair, strong-looking face, and muscular build made him look more like a running back than a president. He moved quickly and decisively, his dark blue eyes always flashing around, taking in everything, missing nothing.

They had been friends for twenty years – long, long before politics had encroached on their relationship. But seven years ago, Simons had entered the national arena. As so often happens, his election and his survival required the placement of trusted friends in key positions. Mills had been the Director of Veteran Affairs for the last administration, so he had already learned the keys to political survival in D.C. Simons appointed him secretary of state based on that experience and their friendship. Mills had worked hard to prove himself as a negotiator, felt worthy of the job.

Mills kept up the easy dialogue, listening to Simons relax. It was a rare pleasure for his good friend. A pleasure for Mills, too, seeing Simons' handsome face break into that impish, lovable grin. He grin was genuine, probably his biggest asset during the campaign. People loved him because they immediately felt comfortable with him, even if their meeting was via the television. He had that wonderful, charismatic attraction about him.

Mills refilled both glasses from a decanter on the table, walked one of them over to Simons and handed it to him. He held his own glass out until Simons tapped it. The clink of expensive crystal tinkled through the room.

Mills took a sip, waited until Simons had done the same. Then he spoke over his shoulder as he walked back to the couch. "Alex, I'd like to ask you something."

Simons wasn't drunk, or even close to it. But he was mellow, and his guard was down. "Sure, Walter. Go ahead, what is it?"

"How much does the stuff we do bother you?"

Simons swirled the brandy in his glass. "What do you mean? What stuff?"

"You know what I mean. The unusual things we do, the things that require us to operate outside of the system, violate the Constitution."

Simons sat up in his leather chair, but the question didn't seem to interest him now that he'd heard it. He waved it off, propped his feet on Kennedy's desk. "What are you talking about, 'operating outside of the system'? Hell, Walter, we are the system."

Mills faced Simons. "You know what I mean, Alex."

Simons produced his grin. "No, Walter, I don't think I do. In fact, I don't think you do, either. We really *are* the system of government in this country. You, me, the rest of the Cabinet, the Senators and Congressmen, and the leaders of industry. We're it."

"That's my point exactly. Where does the Constitution mention 'leaders of industry'?"

Simons didn't answer right away. He took a hard pull from his brandy, watching Mills closely, back on alert status. Mills was straining the seams of their friendship for the first time, having no idea where it would rip to shreds.

But he knew that Simons recognized the dilemma they were in. It had been a dilemma for every president since Nixon. No one had told any of them how things really worked in the White House until they'd taken the oath and met the outgoing administration's keeper of secrets. The presidency was a big, unholy mystery, something you learned about when you got here. Not one second before.

Simons climbed up out of the chair. "Come on, Walter. I grant you it's not the way things were intended. But it *is* the way things turned out. The Founding Fathers intended our government to be evolutionary, and that's what we've done. We've evolved. Of course, most people don't realize it because they can't shake their minds out of high school government books. But the system taught in those marvelous, outdated books is dead. Only the ghost survives, haunting all those wonderful old buildings here, and propping up the disabled carcass of the electoral process. But the real work – the system that really keeps this country strong and moving – is done by people like us."

"No," Mills said. "Not like us."

Simons turned the volume up, a measured increase, not too forceful. "Yes, Walter! *Exactly* like us. Together, we all decide what's best for this country. And then we do it. Efficiently. There's not a lot of wasted effort or oversight. No long-winded debates on the cable channel. No letters from constituents telling you what a jackass you are for your stand on their pet peeve. I don't see a problem with that, Walter. It's for the best. I know you understand that. So, why are you so worried?"

Mills didn't want to argue with Simons. He had never liked conflict. Peace, that was his foremost goal for every occasion. Keep everything in balance, make everything work out. Never stir up the mud, never challenge anyone directly. Peace was more precious than any slogan-powered ideology. He was sure of that. It had absolutely nothing to do with his size, or strength, or the fact that violence had never been an option to him.

"I'm sorry, Alex. I didn't mean to offend you. I know you're doing your best. But – "

Simons walked over and poured both of their glasses full. "Hell, Walter, you don't need to explain. I know what's bothering you. I know what's eating at your guts. It was seeing that picture, wasn't it?"

"Pardon me?"

"Seeing that P.O.W., Wooten. Seeing a fresh photo of an American still in prison over there, a current reminder that they're still there. That got to you, didn't it?"

"No, not really. It's just that I – "

"You can be straight with me, Walter. I try like hell to avoid that kind of pain, too. But there's nothing wrong with being compassionate. Hell, I'm the most compassionate man alive. It had to bother you when Slaughter stuck that photo in your face. I know, because it sure as shit bothers me every time I look at it."

Mills started to take a drink. He looked into the glass for a moment, then changed his mind and set it down. "I think I've lost it, Alex. I don't feel good about what we're doing anymore. I want to resign. I want out. Don't want to wait until the end of this term."

Simons didn't look worried or angry. He smiled. Walked to his desk and picked up a picture. Rubbed his fingers along the frame. "Look here, Walter. See this photo of you and me with the Mid-East leaders? Remember brokering that peace accord?"

Mills nodded.

"You stopped a war, Walter. Saved men's lives." Simons set the photo down, hung his butt on the edge of the desk. "And remember the great work you did last year in Amsterdam?"

Mills married a smile to his nod.

"I'm glad you do, because those were both extremely powerful negotiations. Millions of people, if they would take the time to learn anything, would be thanking you for your work there. But whether the average America realizes it or not, you're efforts have helped keep them safe and prosperous. Isn't that what they all want?

Mills didn't answer. Knew he wouldn't have to.

"Sure it is, Walter. We try like hell to do our very best, do what will work in this great country's best interest. The trick, of course, is figuring out what that is. Like this deal with the P.O.W.s – hell, I don't know what's right. I seriously doubt that anyone does. But I've been dealt this hand, and I don't have any choice but to play it out. I'll do the best that I can with it, keep a sharp eye on the past and a sharper eye on the future. Try to do something I can be proud of. And I need to be able to count on good advice from people I trust. People like you, Walter. So you need to tell me now if you're really going to resign? I need to know if I'm going to have to do this job without the benefit of your help."

The phone rang, but Simons didn't answer it. Mills knew he would wait for his answer. Stay or go. Decide.

The phone continued to ring. Mills looked at it, then looked at his friend. Simons acted like he couldn't hear it.

Finally Mills rose, waved his hands in surrender. "Okay, okay, you win. I'll stay. But let's get this Wooten fiasco cleaned up as soon as possible."

"I'll stoke the fire, Walter, because I know how important it is to you."

Simons grinned again, like he'd done all his life, a winner who consoled the loser with an immediate concession.

"Thanks, Alex."

Mills ambled out the door while Simons lunged for the phone.

* * * * *

It was almost midnight, and Slaughter was having trouble getting back to his hotel. He had taken two cabs and walked some of the way, waiting in the dark shadows as others passed by him. There were large stains of Kelly's blood on his clothes, making him look like trouble. So he took it slow. Careful.

It had rained a half hour ago, then stopped, leaving the air heavy, damp, and hard to breathe. Car lights ricocheted off the wet, shiny street.

He stopped often, checked his tail every half block, then moved, stopped again, repeated the procedure. Over and over until he was sure he would arrive safely, with no one following him. He would not lead anyone to Laura, would not put her life in danger, too.

He kept the handgun he'd taken from the little Mexican, tried to relearn his love of small arms. The hard rubber grips were large. An excellent fit. He wondered why such a little man had selected such large, combat grips.

Slaughter's hand felt natural with the pistol in it. The blue metal frame fit with a machinist's precision. This was a tool he was proficient with, had used many times before with amazing, deadly accuracy. But those things had happened a long time ago, and he didn't like remembering them. There was nothing good back there in the past.

People had died for no good reason. His guys. Their guys. Hell, it was ridiculous to pretend that it mattered. They were all human beings, precious lives with mothers and fathers and loving children who'd been shot, blown up, disemboweled, and tortured because of conflicting ideologies. The whole endeavor had been stupid, and he was embarrassed by the foolishness of it. Ashamed of what he had done. He would never involve himself in killing again, would never again let the devil of destruction rule him. Absolutely not. He knew exactly what the price was, and he would not pay it. He would rather die first.

But even as he reaffirmed that vow, he knew there were more times coming when he would have to prove it. And that worried him. He kept thinking about the moment he'd taken the vow, the day of his own release from Vietnam, the instant when the plane's tires had slipped away from Asian soil. He remembered the men he had done time with, started counting them, using the names they'd given each other. Rabbit. Mole. Popper. Gun-Shy. A dozen others. He remembered them all, every last one of them. Remembered their faces, their voices, their hometowns, their religions. Knew the names of their kids and the number of days of each one's confinement. Knew more than he wanted to remember.

Damn, he should have done something different, even though he still wasn't sure what. Maybe he should have ignored Wooten's orders. Could the end result have been any worse? Of course not. But he had done exactly what Wooten ordered; he had kept quiet. He had barely been able to live with it before. If he failed now, and let Wooten die, Slaughter would kill himself. There were no other options. The haunting would kill him anyway, and he'd already learned that a quick bullet was better than torture.

He squeezed the handgun, then stuck it in his belt near the small of his back. It put pressure on the sore spot where the V.C. bullet had shattered the bones near his spine on the day of his capture. He was still surprised he'd survived the shooting, wondered what his chances of survival were now. Wondered if he would be the next person to put a bullet into his body.

When he finally walked into the motel room, Laura was coming out of the bathroom, wrapped in a large hotel towel. He startled her, but her face quickly went to relief. She started toward him, impulsively, but stopped, stepped back a couple of feet. She stared at the dark stains of blood on his clothes and shoes.

"What happened, Jacob?"

211

He looked at the stains, too. His first time to see them in the light. "I met with Kelly. Someone shot at us as we left the bar. Kelly protected me, saved my life."

Laura eased backward, toward the bed. Her searching arm reminded him of Mrs. Kinsey at Mills' press conference. "Is Kelly dead?"

"Yes."

She sat down, never took her eyes off Kelly's blood. "Did he tell you anything before he died?"

"Yes."

She looked at him with flat, empty eyes. "Good. I'm glad he helped you before they managed to kill him."

"What? Laura, what are you saying? He was shot protecting me. It was an instinctive thing, I think. It was me they wanted."

Her eyes stayed distant. A polite smile bent her lips. "Oh, I know. They would have shot you after they shot him. But if you hadn't been there, they would have shot him anyway."

Slaughter felt like they were on moving sidewalks, going in opposite directions. The distance between them seemed to increase, even as they both remained still.

She sat there, silent, her eyes traveling a thousand miles away.

He closed the gap between them, stood in front of her. He smoothed her wet hair with his fingers and spoke gently. "Laura, what are you talking about? How do you know this?"

She jerked her focus away from some other world and looked up at him. "What? Oh, I'm sorry, Jacob. What did you ask?"

"How do you know this?"

She glanced away, as if the other world was just over in the corner. "I can't tell you, Jacob. I shouldn't have told you about Kelly, either. I'll be in trouble for putting you two together."

He stood there, trying to ease his questions out. "Laura, what are you talking about. Who will you be in trouble with?"

Laura stood up without pushing off with her hands. She glided slowly across the room as if she was a specter in a dream. Then she turned. She smiled. She started back toward him.

Somehow, he felt a little frightened of her. Her steps were slow, but her face wore the mask of relief, the unburdened freshness that draws Catholics to the confessional. He glanced down, saw Kelly's blood on his shoes, then looked up at this smiling woman. He couldn't put the two of them together. He retreated three steps.

"Laura, what's going on?"

She stepped, again, then again. Like a bride coming down the aisle. Then she was against him, her arms rising, slipping around his neck. "Hold me, Jacob. Hold me tight. Hold me for the rest of my life. Will you do that?"

He cupped his hand behind her head, pulled it close against his chest. She shuddered, deep inside her body. Then she shuddered again. He felt the spasms in her chest, as if something was fighting its way out.

Then her tears erupted. They flushed through her like he never imagined possible. Her body twitched and jerked, as if a demon was being exorcised from her soul.

She cried and cried, and he cried too, not knowing any reason for it except that the woman he loved was in terrible pain and he couldn't do anything to help.

* * * * *

The Southern drawl was pure irritation to Cortez. The stupidity of Tanner's folksy dialect made Cortez proud of even the simplest elements of his background, the parts that would normally shame him – the history of his own great race and the rich color of his native tongue. They were things he knew he should value more but didn't. But he kept quiet and listened to this high-powered rube talk stupid Southern to him.

Tanner's power was vast, and – despite his foolish dialect – his intelligence was legendary. Cortez tried to keep that in mind, continued trying to ignore the accent, just as he had done for so many years.

"You want to tell me what you're doing here, Cortez?" Tanner accented his name at the end, buzzed the last letter much too long, stretched it into two ridiculous syllables.

"I killed Kelly after he met with Slaughter. I killed the kid at the photo shop, too. There are no loose ends yet. I thought you should know that."

Tanner's heavy head flopped sideways. His meaty right eyebrow lifted. "That's good, Cortez. Kelly was on the list, was getting soft and guilt-ridden. Since Laura put him and Slaughter together, it's good that you did it when you did, a little ahead of schedule."

"I know. He's dead now."

"Fine, Cortez. That's fine. Anything else?"

Cortez tilted his head back, kept it high and proud, looked squarely at Tanner. "I didn't succeed in killing Slaughter."

Tanner's eyes snapped down to a squint. "Again? You telling me you got Kelly, but missed Slaughter? This guy's making you look sort of foolish here, Cortez. What's your excuse this time, boy?"

The mushroom cloud rolled skyward as atomic energy surged through the lower portions of Cortez's brain, down where the amygdala was ready – anxious – to pour high-test gasoline on his neural fire. He swung his arms up and put his legs in motion. Nobody talked to him like this. Nobody. He'd shown respect; he deserved it back. Tanner would die for this!

He sprung toward Tanner, made six quick leaps before the secretary of defense drew a large frame revolver from his desk and pinpointed it on Cortez's chest.

Tanner didn't even stand up, just sat there in his chair with his fat fingers hanging onto the revolver. "I know what you're thinking, boy. But you gotta remember that as far as I'm concerned you ain't nothing but a prickly little Mexican with a small man complex. And I tell you the truth, I'm damn sick of you coming to me with bad news and your hot-shit attitude. Now, I might be willing to put up with your crap if you were doing your job, boy. But you ain't. So here's the deal." Tanner started swinging the revolver back and forth across Cortez's chest, carelessly, like he was talking with it.

"I suggest you get your little-bitty butt out there tonight, right now, and kill Slaughter. You see, I've had no choice but to send some other men after him. Some very good men. If they have to do your job for you, I'm going to send your sorry ass back to the slums of Mexico. You got that? Boy?"

Cortez's lip was quivering. He was a snake, ready to strike, but he held himself back by the thinnest thread of common sense. "I need to talk to Duncan first."

Tanner stopped the revolver's wandering, nailed it to the center of Cortez's skinny chest. "Now, now, Cortez. Don't shit me, boy. You do what I say, you take my orders from now on. You comprende that?"

Cortez battled with his lip, managed to curl it into a smile that he knew came off as a sneer. "Yes, Mr. Tanner. I will take care of Slaughter right now."

*　*　*　*　*

Tanner kept holding the revolver, aiming it at the slammed door. Damn, he had enjoyed that. It took the edge off all the times he had taken crap from people while climbing this hill. Times when he had been absolutely one-hundred percent right but still caught the shit that rolled down. Oh, sure, maybe he had been a little less refined in the way he'd presented his opinions, certainly a little less physically appealing in his heavy human suit and balding head than the people above him. An out-of-his-league team player from the backwaters of Mobile, using bluster as a curtain to hide behind.

But he *had* climbed the hill. Now, as secretary of defense, he didn't have to feel like the red-headed stepchild anymore, even if it didn't make him feel any better about himself. After all, he did have the power. Yes, sir, he really did. He had made it, by God, all the way to Cabinet level. He wasn't sure how, really. He knew he wasn't any Einstein. He couldn't articulate like most of the power people in D.C., either. Everything he said came out with that silly Southern twang. But he had made it in spite of all that.

Maybe he was just lucky. Or maybe he had managed to fool them all, even President Simons. He knew why Simons had picked him for this position, but he didn't understand why he'd kept him for two terms. He didn't really want to know, either. He hoped to hell Simons would never figure it out. More importantly, though, Cuthbert was the man who had to remain fooled. He would be the next president. Would there be a Cabinet position for Tanner then? There had to be.

Tanner tried to stop worrying about it, savored the way he had made Cortez crawl. He was glad he had kept that revolver in the drawer, decided it would be a pretty good idea to carry it with him for awhile.

But Cortez wasn't really what frightened him. Some day, someone out there would discover that Tanner didn't belong here. He was sure of it now. It had to happen. There was no chance he would be able to fool them forever.

It took almost five minutes to get the call that Cortez had left the building. Tanner had held the revolver the entire time, kept it trained on the door, ready to shoot that little prick if he came flying back in at him.

18

Slaughter couldn't guess what Laura wanted to show him at one o'clock in the morning. But he climbed out of the cab behind her, followed her instructions precisely. She had been much too insistent about what she wanted him to do and not to do. He did not consider deviating from her plan.

He did not turn on the lights of her office. He stayed close behind her and let her lead with the flashlight. He shuffled with her through the maze of office furniture. The persistent lights of D.C., particularly those of the Washington Monument, streamed through the large windows of the office, helped him find his way.

He followed Laura, or more exactly, her silhouette, until they were in her large, private office. She closed the door and locked it, still did not turn on the lights. They crossed the room and she stopped at a side wall. On it was an illuminated keypad. She tapped in a series of numbers, then rested her right hand against the wall, snapped off the flashlight with her left. "Ready?"

He nodded, though he knew she couldn't see it. "Yes. I'm ready."

"Here we go then."

It didn't seem like she pushed very hard at all. But in the darkness, Slaughter heard a click. His hands felt the wall panel crack at the edges, just a little, enough so that he could slip his hand behind it. Laura's hand slid in above his and swung the panel open. She put her hand on his back, gave him a gentle nudge forward.

Slaughter peered into total darkness. He had no idea what was in there or where he was headed. His senses shouted to him that it was very small in there. Dark and confining. His mind rebelled, overpowered his feet and planted them to the floor. He thought about drawing the Mexican's gun, but he couldn't move. He was stuck at the doorway.

Laura must have sensed his panic, transmitted through the hand she kept gently on his back. She stuck the flashlight in his hand and snapped it back on, aimed it into the room. "Sorry," she said.

He followed the light beam. "Yeah. No problem."

When they were both inside, Laura pulled the panel closed and flipped on the fluorescent lights. The windowless room was about eight feet by eight feet, with about ten feet of height. Shelves encroached on all four sides to shrink the floorspace. The shelves were filled with file boxes that seemed to lean over him. A library ladder was attached to a track, and it too ate up some of his space.

Slaughter's phobia pushed him into a corner of the small room. It didn't matter which one, rooms always looked bigger from the corners. From there he could stop measuring the room and take the time he needed to look at the boxes, all labeled by file numbers. "What is all this? Closed client files?"

"Hardly," she said in a worried voice. "Here's the index."

On the shelf nearest the door, at eye level, were four little boxes, miniature metal filing drawers for three-by-five cards. Two boxes were labeled in alphabetical order, and two were cross-referenced by file numbers. It was a primitive filing system.

Slaughter slid open a tray. He skipped over several cards, stopped, looked at some of the names, looked back at Laura. She turned away. He looked some more, picking up speed, going faster and faster. He could not stop. His pain – was it anger or was it agony – was building up. Ugly thoughts about Laura swirled through his brain. They were uncontrollable and made it hard to concentrate.

He pulled several of the files, including his own, out of the boxes and read them. Laura slumped into a corner and said nothing. Slaughter didn't either. He burned up thirty minutes scanning a dozen files. Still, she didn't move. Not once. Not a muscle.

When he couldn't read any more, he slapped the last file closed and paced around the room, four strides to a lap, a step over her legs at one end, and then another lap. Finally, he stopped in front of her, looked down at the top of her head.

"Oh, Laura. How could you have done this?"

She didn't look up, kept her head down and shook it. She pulled her knees up to her chest, wrapped her arms around her legs. "I don't know, Jacob. It all started so innocently, just a small government contract to help get my practice going. I had no idea it would go so far, really. You've got to believe that, Jacob. Once I found out, I stopped. I never told them what you – "

He flipped up his hand and cut her off, turned toward the door while looking at the racks of files, made a quick calculation of how many years it must have taken to do all this work. His stomach hurt and his heart ached. He felt the shelves arc farther over him. "I've got to get out of here." He reached to snap off the light before opening the door.

Laura stood quickly. She wiped tears from her cheeks, trying to keep up with the steady flow. She stopped trying when their eyes met. The tears drained out through her puffy eyes and her lips quivered out her words. "You can't go yet, Jacob. There's one other thing you need to see."

His head flopped forward. He didn't want to see anything else. He knew his limits, knew he'd seen more than he could stand already. "All right. Let's get it over with."

She opened a box and pulled out a large file, thicker than most of the others. It was the only file with red tape across the tab. She handed it to him, sat back down in her spot on the floor.

Slaughter held the file, still closed, trying to concentrate. But it was hard to do here. There were too many things to distract him: the smallness of the room, the horrible files, and the sobbing woman. The woman he loved.

When he did open the file he used caution, as if the words it contained might kill him. The first page riveted him, and he read it several times. The next page as well, and the next, and the next. Twenty minutes later, he set it down and walked out the door. Left Laura alone to cry.

* * * * *

Cortez cruised the late-night streets in his car, feeling the desperation gripping his insides. He checked his phone and radio for the hundredth time, made sure they were both on. Prayed one of them would jump to life and deliver a message about Slaughter. He had plenty of men looking for him now, had given up on keeping the glory for himself. He needed someone to find Slaughter before Tanner's other men did.

Where was he? Where was Slaughter hiding? How come he was so hard to find now? What had changed him, made him less predictable? If he could figure that out, he would be able to find him.

He'd checked every place that had worked before: Slaughter's neighborhood, O'Shea's, the State Department, Laura's office. He'd checked in with Duncan, too, hoping one of Dynet's computers had picked up a lead from a phone call or traffic stop. But nothing. He circled the Lincoln Memorial, parked at the end of the Mall, ran down to check the Vietnam Memorial. He was that desperate, reduced to checking out long shots.

Cortez could feel the time running out. He'd had a good run, all the way to the top of the heap. But it would end suddenly, right here, if he didn't make something happen. Other killers were looking for Slaughter. Tanner had lost faith in his Number One. If those men got to Slaughter first, Tanner and Duncan would be done with him, and Cortez knew it.

It was hard for him to concentrate now. The greater part of his mind stayed focused on the problem at hand – killing Slaughter. But that wasn't enough. He needed all his power, needed to use all his skill to think like his prey, anticipate Slaughter's actions, get there first and take him down.

But as hard as he tried, he couldn't rally the part of himself that had begun to give up. His survival instincts had started considering options, were casting those options in the best possible light.

He would need to know immediately if some other killer got to Slaughter before he did. It would give him a little time, maybe as much as an hour to get a few things ready and leave. There was no place for losers in this profession. If he failed, he would be gone before the others came for him. Already, he was trying not to think about the disgrace of running.

This was not the first time Cortez had faced failure, and therefore he had a plan. There had been other times when the prospect of losing had become possible, even probable, and he had decided then what he would do. But he had always pulled the job off. Never had to put the backup plan into action.

Mexico had always been his first thought. It was his great dream to return. Take his fortune and move back to Mexico City. Live like an exalted king for the rest of his life.

But when he considered it, reality always bit him, reminded him that he could never go back there. The gangs had not forgotten what he'd done to them, and the government had not given up on their desire to prosecute him. And besides, that would be the first place Dynet's men would look.

So Costa Rica had come to mind, with Belize as a second choice. He could insulate himself behind thousands of acres of plantation, live out his life in comfortable exile. It might not be the perfect plan, but he would be alive. In order to be appreciated, some things had to be seen in contrast to the alternatives.

* * * * *

Cuthbert sat in the Admiral's House and brooded in the dark. The vice-presidential mansion was on the grounds of the U.S. Naval Observatory and, like the observatory, was old, shabby, and unfit for someone of his caliber. Hell, Nelson Rockefeller had flatly refused to live here.

But Cuthbert had spent seven and half years here, enduring the hardships of being second best. Soon, though, he would move to the White House. Every morning he would recount the days remaining before he would live where he belonged.

The only room that came close to suiting him was his office. Maybe it was because this room had seen him do such glorious work. Or maybe he felt inspired there, the dirt and crumbling plaster providing the motivation for him to advance beyond it. He guessed it was the latter. That was usually the case. He was never content with what he had. There was always something more that he wanted.

He had been born wealthy. He loved his parents for their money and hated them because of it. Loved them because they'd given him a good start. Hated them because their money took something away from every one of his own accomplishments. Although he never heard anyone say it out loud, he knew what people thought. Everyone – his colleagues in Congress, Simons' Cabinet, his friends, the population as a whole – figured they could have earned a fortune, too, if they'd been given his advantages.

Well, it just wasn't true. Why was he so rich? He could tell them in one sentence. He was a genius, that's why. No one else could have done what he had and accomplish so much so fast. He'd doubled his fortune and still had time to pursue the presidency. He'd been given a little headstart, sure. But it meant nothing. He would have made himself rich and powerful anyway. No one else could have done it. They didn't have the courage. Or the intelligence. Or the self-respect.

That was it in a nutshell. They – all those jealous people who disliked him – didn't respect themselves enough to succeed. To excel, you had to put yourself above everyone else, everything else. There was never any room to consider others, not if you wanted to survive and move forward. If you respected yourself, you could settle for nothing less. It was as simple as that. No lame excuses, no whining about what could have been. No, sir. Get out there and do it, that was his motto. Make it happen. Take care of yourself, because no one else in this world would.

He was ready to do it, now. The quiet time alone had helped him appreciate what needed to be done. This kind of thing came pretty easily to him. If things got ugly, if somehow word of the P.O.W.s got out, Cuthbert would throw President Simons into the breech and shoot him out at the electorate. Let Simons pay the price. It would be self-defense. Cuthbert would have no choice if he wanted to save his own presidency.

He would not let Jacob Slaughter ruin his chance for the White House. Too many other presidents had survived the threat of this exposure. He would not take the fall for the coverup. Hell, he hadn't even been aware of the prisoners before he and Simons were elected. He sure as hell didn't want anything to do with them now, except to keep them hidden where they belonged.

Cuthbert was positive that Tanner understood what needed to be done. He could count on him. That toady little lapdog would do everything necessary to keep this P.O.W. debacle under wraps. After all, Cuthbert held the keys to Tanner's continued success, the power to keep him running with the big dogs, as Tanner himself was fond of saying. Tanner would do whatever Cuthbert needed, use that wicked little Mexican of his to make this problem disappear.

Mills, though, was another story. It was hard to be certain about him. He had the president's ear, much more so than Cuthbert. And that made him dangerous. Cuthbert had to worry that Mills might decide to reveal the existence of the P.O.W.s, decide it would be a good thing, convince Simons to go along with the idea as his presidency wound down. Simons would portray himself as a stand-up guy, righting an old wrong in the face of disastrous political consequences. He would preserve a place for himself in the history books. But Simons' actions could kill Cuthbert's turn at the White House.

Cuthbert had no intention of picking up the tab for Simons' mistake. He would never let Simons do it to him. He had busted his hump for eighteen years to get here. Too many boring terms in Congress. Years of his life spent on campaign trails, shaking filthy hands and eating meals with idiots and smiling beside fat women in print dresses while the Uncle Bobs of America snapped pictures with cheap cameras. He was not going to be denied the presidency now. Not by anyone. He had worked too hard, spent too much time with those detestable voters.

No sir, those prisoners were definitely not coming home. There was no chance of it. It was the best thing for the Party. The best thing for the country. The best thing for him.

19

Slaughter knew most of the story now, or at least enough to understand that there was only one man who could help him. He stopped at the phones in the lobby of Laura's building, dialed directly into the White House, still able to bypass the public switchboard. A presidential secretary answered, her proximity to power sounding in her voice, crisp and polite at two forty-five a.m.

"President Simons' office."

"This is Jacob Slaughter from the State Department. I need to meet with President Simons right away regarding the trade agreement with Vietnam. It's extremely urgent."

The secretary came back with lecture in her voice. "Mr. Slaughter, you should contact the president through the Secretary of State, Mr. Mills. That's the normal – "

"Yes, I know it is. But a situation has arisen that requires President Simons' immediate attention, and Secretary Mills is unavailable. The president needs to be advised or the consequences could have a severe, adverse impact on his record in foreign policy."

That should do it, he thought. Everyone inside the beltway – if not everyone in America – knew how sensitive Simons was about his prowess on the world stage. No staff member would shoulder the responsibility of failing to notify the president of a request put in this way.

"Well . . . just a minute, sir. I believe his chief of staff is still here. I'll transfer you."

"Thank you."

Time to wait. Minutes ticked by. Slaughter checked the pistol, but he wasn't sure why. He'd stopped worrying about being traced, or caught, or killed. Stopped worrying about anything but Charles Wooten, who shuffled through Slaughter's mind in shackles. Wooten's grim ghost raised sad eyes. The question in them had never changed – How much longer?

Slaughter's excuse – his youth – had never worked very well, so he had stopped trying to hide behind it. He knew the truth and accepted it. He was a coward. When the V.C. guards had come that last night to their chamber in Hoa Lo Prison, Slaughter should have done something. Anything. Spit on that little bastard Vinh, or cursed him. Joined Wooten in a show of solidarity. Done whatever would have made the difference. But instead he'd cowered on his filthy mat and shrunk into his cell's infested shadows as that horrible little man hissed at Captain Wooten.

"Our countries have finally reached an agreement," Vinh had said in Vietnamese. "All prisoners are to be released at daybreak."

Slaughter heard the words, and he understood them. He just couldn't believe them. He would be going home. Finally. Thank you, God.

He kept his joy to himself, though, stayed silent in the shadows. Concentrated on what he could learn from the hateful whispers in the adjoining cell.

Vinh's voice bore down hard on Wooten.

"We do not trust your country, Captain. We do not expect your president to honor some parts of this agreement for too many years. So, to ensure his continued compliance, we will require one prisoner from every camp to stay behind. You are the senior officer here, I will let you decide who stays. But it must be someone who has been totally isolated, someone no one but you knows exists. Someone we can say died of diseases some time back if we need to. And, of course, you will need to keep the secret with us or he will die."

Wooten didn't hesitate, not a second. He'd been so damned honorable it was sickening. His voice came up quickly and fluently, so fast that Slaughter, even after replaying the conversation thousands of times, still had difficulty telling exactly where Vinh had stopped talking and Wooten had begun. "I am the leader of these men, Vinh. If someone must stay, it has to be me."

Vinh's demand had frightened Slaughter, but Wooten's offer terrified him. But still he didn't move. He kept silent, already thinking about his trip home. Hot coffee on the plane. A clean uniform if he was lucky. He hoped and prayed Vinh would take Wooten up on his offer. He wanted to go home.

Vinh laughed, a variation of the cackle he would give during an interesting beating. "You cannot stay, Captain Wooten. Jacob Slaughter knows you are here. You two have been isolated in this chamber for too long together. But," he said slowly, as if he wasn't quite sure of himself, "Slaughter can stay. I have no problem with that. Yes. Leave Slaughter behind. I like that even better."

Wooten shifted around on his mat. Slaughter could hear the night chains that bound him clinking.

"No, Vinh. It has to be me. Slaughter will understand that my life will depend on his silence. He's a good soldier, and he will follow orders. I will order him to be silent and he will be. It's me, Vinh, or no one. Those are your choices."

Nothing else was said for a minute. Slaughter crept carefully toward his food hole and listened harder.

Finally, Vinh spoke again. It hurt Slaughter's ears to hear his captor's harsh voice speak complete sentences. For four years he'd only heard Vinh yap out short, terse orders.

"Then it will be you, Captain Wooten."

Slaughter crawled back into the shadows and dreamed of home.

Slaughter'd had the closest friendship of his life with Captain Wooten. Different from any other connection, ever, and completely different from the one he had with Laura. But it was a relationship all the same, with all the same obligations. Trust. Honor. Faith.

And Slaughter had failed in his responsibility to Wooten. Failed miserably. Wooten had held up his end, had made every sacrifice required of him, even when it could have cost him his life. But Slaughter had not. He had left behind the man he'd grown to love, consigned him to a brutalized life while Slaughter lived the pleasures of freedom. It was unpardonable. He could never forgive himself. Mostly because he had faced the truth and knew that, given the chance, he would have left Wooten there again. There was no way he would have ever volunteered to stay behind like Wooten did, no matter how hard he tried to convince himself he would. If he was given another chance today, he would still walk out and leave Wooten behind.

He was that weak. That unfaithful.

It was too painful to think about. Shameful. Cowardly. He would never, ever fail someone like that again. Even if it meant never allowing anyone to count on him.

Slaughter's head was banging and his hands were sweating. Then he heard the telephone click, followed by the voice that sounded just like it did on television.

"Is that you, Slaughter?"

"President Simons?"

Simons sounded pleasant. Relieved, as if he'd been waiting to hear from his young son who'd been out too late. "Why, yes,

Slaughter, this is Simons. I heard you were on the line, thought I'd pick it up and talk to you myself. Sorry about the wait."

"We need to talk, President Simons. Can you meet me right away?"

Simons cleared his throat. "Well, sure, Slaughter. Hell, I guess so. I can't sleep anyway, was just sitting here going over some paperwork. Why don't you come on by?"

Come on by? Is that what he'd heard, as if Simons was getting up a friendly poker game? "I can do that."

"That's great, Slaughter. How about in . . . oh, say, an hour or so? Four o'clock? I know it's the middle of the night, but if that works for you –"

"Four o'clock is fine."

"Good. That's good. I'll leave your name at the gate. See you then."

Slaughter knew this was much too easy. It had to be a trap, a stupid thing to do. "I'll be there."

*　*　*　*　*

Mills parked in Georgetown and walked down the street, thinking how much he would have hated to be president. He would never, ever want the job. Secret Service agents dogged your every movement. There wasn't any freedom. No privacy. You could never even think about going out for a drink or a movie. Too much trouble. Too risky.

But being secretary of state was another matter. It was high enough for Mills, actually much higher than he'd ever believed possible. It was a strange trick of life, a weird benefit of his youth. So small and weak, and therefore so ready to find common ground with others, make allies out of his enemies. Who could have thought his need for peace would lead him into

230

a power seat. A Cabinet position, even better than the presidency. As secretary of state he could still be a part of society. He could go wherever he wanted, do whatever he wanted. Kissinger had proven that. No one cared, really. His free time was his own. He could meet whomever he liked.

And now he would meet Laura Warden. She had called him around midnight and requested the meeting. She had not asked for anything in a long, long time. Years. Not since they'd stopped dating, back when she first starting splitting time between the V.A. and her new private practice. He was happy to meet with her, looked forward to seeing her again.

The long, narrow Georgetown bar still had a decent sized crowd, even though it was almost closing time. He walked in and sat down at a table near the front, wondering if Laura had set up any security for herself. She wouldn't need it, of course, at least not while she was with him. He was sure she knew that.

But he respected her intelligence, and an intelligent person would have security. Too many people were acting out of desperation, and desperate people were unpredictable. He was sure Laura understood that, too. She knew all the players. Surely, she understood what the cost could be.

Yes, he decided, she would have security. Who might they be? Patients? God knows she could recruit an impressive army from those ranks. Maybe people hiding behind her protection who should have been marked for removal but weren't. He knew she'd been hiding men from him for years, knew that drunken Irishman, Kelly, had been allowed to join those ranks. He sat down and waited, ordered a glass of Bordeaux from the young waitress, asked her to bring Laura's when she arrived.

*   *   *   *   *

Laura was at the far end of the bar when Mills came in. She had been there for most of an hour, watching for an advance man who might be sweeping the place, sure that anyone doing that job would have given an accidental signal when he recognized her. Any look – a twitch, a glance that lasted a second too long, a widening of the eyelids – would have alerted her and she would have fled.

But that had not happened. She waited until Mills sat down, then slipped out the back door, into the smells and darkness of the alley. She heard rats scurrying around at the end of the alley, where it smacked into the back of a building. No one was hiding back there or the rats would be silent, cautious. She walked through the alley, all the way to the street. No one suspicious there, either. She came around front, looked along the sidewalk, and checked Mills' car. Then she walked through the front doors of the restaurant and sat down across from him.

Mills didn't stand, just sat there looking at her. But she could read him just fine, even though he was a little better at concealment than most people. It was an occupational advantage. She knew he still loved her, even though he would never say it again. After all these years, he still showed his love through caring eyes and silenced sentences. She understood him as if they were both telepathic.

"Hello, Walter."

He saluted her with his wine glass. "How are you, Laura?"

The waitress came, brought a refill for him and a Pouilly-Fuisse for her.

"I'm okay. Considering. You?"

"The same. Considering everything that's going on. Are things tough for you and Slaughter right now?"

She tilted her glass at him in return. "You know they are."

232

"I figured as much. Do you think you two will get through this?"

"Don't know, really. I doubt it."

He started tracing his fingertip around the rim of his glass. "I'm sorry. You know I didn't plan for this to work out like it has."

"I know. I was foolish to think I could hold onto him. Now, of course, I wish I'd never met him."

"Do you know what he's going to do?"

She animated a big look of surprise. "Don't you? He's going to bring those prisoners of war home."

"Is that a fact?"

She shook her head, straightened her posture. "Yes. A fact. I'm convinced he'll actually do it, too. Unless he gets killed first."

Mills snickered, sipped some wine. "It would be very interesting if he did get them home. Not good, mind you, but interesting."

"You see, that's where we disagree. I think it would be very good. Washington could use a little shaking up. A little revolution would be good for us. "

"If those men come home, Laura, it would cause a big revolution. Nothing little about it. Really, if people ever found out – "

"Even better, Walter. A big revolution would be more fun." She smiled at him as she raised her glass.

"If you expect me to agree with you, you know I won't. Even if I wanted to."

She reached across the table and touched his hand. He watched her closely, didn't take his eyes off her hand.

"And you *do* want to, Walter. You're a good man. You have to be suffering, too. Everyone is."

He kept his eyes on her hand. "It doesn't matter."

"I know that you and I feel the same way, Walter. That's why I wanted to talk with you. Don't you think we can help Jacob?"

He snatched his hand away, leaned back in his seat, looked right at her. "No! Laura, don't misunderstand me. You're right in assuming that I'm on the fence here. I suppose it would be fine with me if Slaughter succeeded. But I'm not going to help him. It would be suicide. You can't either."

She sipped again. "Sorry. Already have."

"What?"

"I told him, Walter. I told him everything. I even showed him the files."

Mills leaned farther away, as if she was infectious. "Oh, Laura, you didn't."

She lifted her head a little higher. "Yes, I did."

"You had no right. You swore to me you'd keep your relationship with Slaughter separate."

"I thought I could. But he's right, Walter. He's so damned right. I can see that now. So can you. Don't you want to do what's right for a change?"

"Hell, *I* don't know what 'right' is! How can you? It's too elusive."

"That's crap, Walter, and we both know it. What's right isn't determined by polls or popular opinion or Cabinet recommendations. Righteousness never changes. Only the motives that produce it change."

"And you're *that* sure Slaughter is doing the right thing, Laura?"

"No. Not really. But I'm that sure we're not."

They glared at each other until Mills' eyes softened and his focus floated down to the table. She knew exactly what it meant, knew she wouldn't be able to count on him.

"So, you won't help him?"

He stood up and turned to leave. "I don't see how I can. I'm sorry. Good-night."

* * * * *

Slaughter wandered around the streets of downtown Washington, waiting for the minutes to drag past until he met with President Simons at four a.m. It was a dark, warm, summer night. Rough, street people – the kind he usually tried to avoid – ruled the sidewalks. He could see them watching him, sizing him up. He saw the questions in their eyes: Could they take him? Was he carrying? Would the risk be worthwhile?

Where was he? What part of downtown had he wandered into? Small, dirty stores, fenced in on the ground floor, lined the streets. Human contents of the tenements spilled out onto the steps and into the gutters. Grown men drank from paper bags as the night eased by them. Others played loud music, or watched for cops, or pushed each other around. How could any of those poor bastards living in the buildings ever get any sleep?

But he really didn't care where he was, only thought about it for a moment, the same fleeting concern that had caused him to check the Mexican's pistol, make sure it was still snug in the small of his back. But he didn't really care about it, either. He was thinking about Wooten, and Laura, and what he had done and what he hadn't done, and finally, what he would not be able to do.

He knew he would lose. Chuck Wooten would not be coming home.

He could talk to President Simons, sure. But Simons must have already struck his deal, and Slaughter had lost. He could feel it now, it made perfect sense. Simons was just meeting him to give him the bad news. And say good-bye, maybe, if he was an honest man. Explain to Slaughter why he had to die and tell him how much he hated to have him killed. But it was necessary. Surely, Simons might say, Slaughter could

235

understand his reasons. There were no choices. Slaughter couldn't be allowed to tell his story to the world a second time.

Slaughter needed power on his side, a world-class expert who could bring people back to the table. He stopped at a sidewalk pay phone, had to roust two night-prowlers away from it. One of them was young, maybe fifteen, and black. He wore his pistol in the front of his pants, for everyone to see. He aimed his belly at Slaughter, as if to scare him.

The other man was black, too. Older, seasoned. Slaughter could see that he'd already proven himself as a warrior, it was apparent by the way he acted. He was a veteran of these streets, had done several tours of duty here. He knew a fight when he saw one, understood that this wasn't the time. The white fool in front of him just needed to make a call. That's all. It wasn't a turf war. He smiled his thick black lips at Slaughter, waved him toward the phone, and stepped away. The kid took one step back. Stood there, waiting, not planning to give away any more ground. Ready to kill, or die, over a pay phone.

Slaughter called Mills' cellular number, turned and stared back at the kid. It was almost funny. There was no privacy here and no protection. But he could say what he wanted and it didn't matter. This inner-city neighborhood was another world and operated under an entirely different set of values. Slaughter's business didn't mean squat to these folks. They just wanted him out.

He heard the ring, turned his back to the kid and listened for Mills' voice.

Mills answered the call with a worn-down hello.

"This is Slaughter."

There was no answer.

"You hear me?"

Another stretch of silence. Then, "Yes, Slaughter. I hear you. How are you?"

"Doesn't matter."

"Okay, then. What do you want?"

"Look, Mills, I've just talked to President Simons. I'm going to meet him at the White House in about an hour. I need him to sign the trade agreement so that the P.O.W.s can come home. Mills, I'm asking you to bring the agreement from the office, follow through with me on the procedures, help me get it done."

"You talked to President Simons?"

"Yes."

"I'd of liked to have been a fly on the wall during that conversation. Did you tell him what Laura told you?"

Slaughter lurched forward, closer to the phone box. "What do you mean? What are you talking about?"

"I spoke with her a little while ago. She told me what she did."

"Liar."

"Come on, Slaughter. You already know she's done work for us. Doesn't it stand to reason that she tells me pretty much everything." Mills chuckled, sadly. "Although sometimes she tells me a little too late."

"Like now?"

"Yes. Like now. She should never have shown you those files. Especially the one –"

"Then you did know! You've always known Wooten was still alive!"

"Don't be ridiculous, Slaughter. Of course I knew. We all did. It's the nation's business. How could we do our jobs if we didn't know."

"How many others knew?"

"Besides me and Simons? Tanner. And Cuthbert. And, of course, the last half-dozen administrations. That's about all. A hundred people, give or take a few."

"You forgot me and Laura."

"Oh, no, Slaughter. I haven't forgotten you. How could I. You're trying to bring it all down on our heads. I haven't forgotten you. And as for Laura, well, she's turned on us, too. You should be happy for that. She's on your side now, using her influence against us."

Slaughter's heart jumped at the sound of her name, at the thought that she might have crossed into his camp. Maybe he hadn't lost her. "Her influence with people like Kelly?"

"Yes. Exactly like Kelly. She knew the strain was breaking him. It was a big mistake for her to put you two together."

"Why are you admitting this to me?"

"To tell you the truth, Slaughter, I'm not really sure anymore. Laura's asked me to help you, says you're the almighty salvation of the nation or some other such nonsense. She respects you a lot, Slaughter. An awful lot."

"Yeah? Well, respect won't get Wooten home."

"No. It won't. Or the others, either."

"So you know about the other prisoners, too."

"Sure, Slaughter. Of course."

"Damn you!"

"I suspect it will."

The kid jostled him in the back, but Slaughter ignored him, stood silent, waiting for Mills to say something that might help save Wooten's life.

"To be honest, Slaughter, I also respect what you're trying to do. Maybe I can help you a little. Not very much, but a little. Understand, though, that I'm making no promises. And my loyalty is with President Simons. I won't ever do anything to hurt him."

"Will you bring the trade agreement to the White House? I'm meeting Simons at four o'clock this morning. Come with me, please."

"That won't do it, Slaughter. Don't you understand yet? He won't bring those prisoners home. He can't. Hell, I'm sure he'd like to, almost as much as I would like to see them come home. But not quite as much, and the difference is too great. I'm on the fence, he's just barely on the other side. But the ground between us is impassable. He could never cross it."

"I think he might."

"You're naive."

"Just give me an answer, Mills. Be a decent human being. Think about those men over there, the decades of sacrifices they've made. What could possibly be worth our abandoning them again?"

The line was silent. Slaughter waited, always the hardest part of negotiation. Finally, Mills' voice cracked. "No. I won't meet Simons with you."

"Come on, Walter."

"No."

"You won't be able to live with this."

"I've been living with it for years."

The kid bumped him again. Slaughter stuck his hand behind his back and waved the kid away. "No, you haven't, Mills. You've lived with some general knowledge that there are prisoners still over there. Just some names in a file. But I know them, Walter. Let me tell you about them, let me put faces on those files, let you know who they really are. For God's sake, Walter, those men had dreams for their lives, plans for children they've missed for decades while they ate roaches and dreamed of food that wasn't still wiggling. For their sake, and for your own, don't turn your back on them again."

"It would be a waste of time, Slaughter. It's over."

"It's not over, damn it! And even if it was, is that an excuse? You have to do what you can, Walter. Then, if you lose, at least you can live with the defeat."

"You're much too idealistic, Slaughter."

"That's not a bad thing."

Some more silence. Even the noisy sounds of this dangerous neighborhood seemed to quiet down.

"All right, Slaughter, I'll meet Simons with you. I'm only going to lay the agreement on his desk, though. You pitch it all you want. I'll give you that opportunity. But if Simons shuts you down, I'm out of it. Are we perfectly clear on that?"

"Yes. I understand. Thanks."

"Keep your eyes open between now and then, Slaughter. You know how dangerous the streets of Washington can be at night."

Slaughter felt himself nodding, turning to heed the warning, locking the black kid in the crosshairs of his eyes. "I do, Walter. I really do. Thanks for reminding me."

"Sure. No problem. See you at the White House, four o'clock."

* * * * *

Cortez was finally going to kill Slaughter. It would finally be over.

The phone call had made his job easy, allowed him to stop searching this big-ass city for Slaughter, gave him time for a quick shower and a change of clothes – his first since yesterday.

He knew where to find Slaughter now. The White House, in a little less than an hour. Let the president meet with Slaughter, hear what he had to say, then kill him when he went out of the gate. Another death in murder city. One of hundreds. Nothing spectacular or unusual about it.

Cortez had plenty of time. There was no point in being early. Hanging around could draw the attention of the Metro Police, or the Secret Service, or the Parks Service, or some other jerk-off agency.

Not, of course, that Cortez worried about any of them. No sir. They were never ready for a man like him, never even came close to being ready. They would stroll up to his car and politely ask for some identification while resting their hands on their guns. He would shoot them in the face while they were being so damned nice.

That's what made America a great place for Cortez. Americans wanted – even demanded – that their cops, on all levels, be considerate. Don't draw until your subject does. Don't shoot until the he does. Don't die until . . . well, that last part was where the system tilted steeply in Cortez's favor. Always had. Probably always would.

He slipped into a black silk shirt and black suit, tied on a dark maroon tie. The suit was one of his favorites because of the way it shone. An expensive suit – showy, impressive. An unusual suit for Washington. Nothing like the rags of his youth, a small kid rolling up the legs of his uncle's hand-me-downs, living a life of taunts and tears until he found the power of violence; learned that his willingness to destroy life could earn him the respect that had quieted those who'd ridiculed him.

He buffed his shoes, then went to the bathroom. His ritual, the last thing before heading out the door. Brush his teeth. He did a good job, smiled at himself. He twisted his head to see the sides of his mouth. He loved those teeth.

20

Slaughter was stuck at the White House security gate, waiting for the guards to check and recheck his suspicious story about a four a.m. meeting with President Simons. He'd stashed the Mexican's pistol along the fence near the far corner of the property, pretty sure that it wouldn't be found in the dark.

He was just about to lose the last of his patience when Mills pulled up and confirmed the meeting. They were both cleared into the compound, and Slaughter rode in Mills' car to the porte cochere entrance.

They followed an aide – a big man with a bouncer's build and skeptical face – through the silent halls. None of them spoke.

The aide knocked gently, then opened the Oval Office door. Slaughter held back, stayed behind him. Mills did the same.

"Mr. President," the aide said, "Secretary of State Walter Mills and Mr. Jacob Slaughter are here to see you, sir."

Slaughter pushed his way around the aide and walked in, heard Mills following. President Simons rose from his chair. The aide closed the door and left.

"Walter," President Simons said, "what an unexpected surprise." Simons' eyes were stuck on Mills, questioning him, even as his lips moved on. "And you must be Jacob Slaughter. It is a pleasure to meet you. Thanks for coming by."

"Hello, Alex," said Mills.

Slaughter said nothing.

Simons walked around the big desk and shook hands with both men. "Please sit down, Mr. Slaughter. Walter, I'm sure you don't need an invitation. Go ahead and take your favorite chair.

"I'll stand," said Slaughter.

Mills didn't move either.

Simons' speech slowed. "Why, sure. Sure. Whatever makes you gentlemen comfortable."

"I didn't come here to be comfortable, Mr. President."

Simons sat down, looking uneasy, not sure of what was happening. Slaughter could see the confusion on his face.

"I know, Mr. Slaughter. You came here to update me on that trade agreement with Vietnam. Well, I can tell you're ready, so we might as well get started."

"Please don't play me for an idiot, Mr. President."

"No, Mr. Slaughter, of course not. Am I out of line here? Maybe I'm not quite clear about why you came. Perhaps – "

Slaughter took a quick step toward Simons. He was surprised that Mills moved with him, as if they were chained together. "I'm here to get those prisoners out of Vietnam. I need the trade agreement signed to do it. It's a fair deal, it's done, and it's ready for your signature. Secretary of State Mills has it with him; he thinks it's a good agreement. So sign it!"

Simons spread his hands wide apart and looked surprised. "No problem, Mr. Slaughter. No problem at all. The entire nation feels that enough time has passed, and they are ready to get on with things over there. Hell, I've got every businessman in America demanding the exact same thing. They've sent stacks and stacks of letters. People in offices all over this country are arguing about who will open the first shopping mall in Hanoi. So there's no problem with what you want me to do. I've already assured the Vietnamese that I'll sign it. It's just a matter of a few days to get everything ready."

Simons cocked his head, narrowed his eyes, steadied them on Slaughter.

"But, as for the issue of P.O.W.s, I was under the impression that Secretary of Defense Tanner had cleared up your confusion about the photo you brought back from Vietnam."

"Don't bullshit me, Simons. And don't pretend there aren't P.O.W.s over there. You've known about them for a full term and a half. How could you possibly leave them there and not even try to bring them home? All those prisoners made the ultimate sacrifice for this country. You owe them your best effort."

Simons glanced at Mills, then came right back to Slaughter. "What the hell are you talking about?"

"Damn you, Simons! You knew they were alive and you left them there." Slaughter's voice cracked as the pain of Wooten's captivity crawled into his throat.

"You're out of your mind, Slaughter."

"Am I? I've seen the proof, Simons. I've read the files. All the files. Even yours."

"What? What file?"

"Your psychiatric file. The long sessions you've needed to keep those P.O.W.s from haunting you while you kept them secret. Damn, how about that, Simons? You're crazy with guilt, just like me. And it hurts, doesn't it. Hurts like hell to know that those men are suffering because you're a coward." Slaughter started moving in, but Mills stepped past him.

"It's no good, Alex. He really does know."

Simons straightened, rose by three inches. His nostrils spread as his eyes shrunk behind the lids. "How did you get your hands on those files?"

"It doesn't matter. We all know the man in the picture *is* Captain Wooten. You've known it all along." He turned, fired a look at Vice-President Cuthbert, oozing in from an adjoining room. "You too, asshole."

Cuthbert stopped, looked like he'd just taken a big bite of lemon. "I'm buzzing for the Secret Service. I do not intend to be – "

Simons' hand went up. He looked at Cuthbert as though he was pissed at the stupid timing of his arrival. "Now there's a terrific idea. Throw Slaughter out, right? Let him do his talking on the street?"

"Any talking he does would land him in a federal penitentiary."

"You honestly think Slaughter cares, Cuthbert? Haven't you learned anything in the last couple of days? Slaughter doesn't give a damn about what happens to him." He turned to Slaughter. "Do you?"

"I don't believe that." Cuthbert marched over to Slaughter and inspected him. "He's spent too much time in prison already. He doesn't want to go back."

Simons ground his teeth. Slaughter could hear them crunching from where he stood.

"Cuthbert," Simons said. "Why don't you just shut up!"

Cuthbert stopped, stood silent. No one in the room spoke. Or moved. Or breathed. Slaughter stared at Simons, felt everyone else staring at him.

Simons suddenly snatched open a desk drawer, pulled out a thick folder, slammed it down on his desk. Slaughter shot a look to Cuthbert, whose eyes were stuck, wide open, on the file.

Cuthbert started stammering. "What . . . what are you doing, Alex?"

"Do you have a better idea? Slaughter knows the worst of it already, knows what's been done up until now. He's a smart man, maybe this will help him understand what's happening and why."

"You can't do this, Alex."

"Is that right, Cuthbert? Why not?"

"You just can't."

Simons covered the file with his hand. Ten seconds later he moved it away. "Watch me."

Cuthbert's face twitched, looked completely unpresidential. "I . . . I – "

"It's okay, Cuthbert, your objection is noted. I'll take the rap for this. Now, get out of the way and sit down. Slaughter, come over here and take a look. I doubt there's anything here you haven't learned already, but if there is, I hope it'll help you understand what's been going on. Maybe then you'll know why our hands are tied so tightly where those poor sons of bitches are concerned."

Slaughter stepped into Cuthbert on his way to the president's desk. The file was about five inches thick and banded with security tape; the initials ARS covered the overlap of the tape.

Simons spun his chair around toward the dark window. He seemed to be concentrating on something outside. "Go ahead, Slaughter, break it open."

Slaughter stalled, took the time to check the faces in the room. Wide-eyed, Cuthbert had shrunk into a chair directly in front of the president's desk. He suddenly looked old – worn out and beaten. But his eyes were firing away at the back of Simon's head.

Mills had migrated to a back wall, leaned against it with his arms across his chest, watching Slaughter with sad eyes. Secretary of Defense Tanner had slipped in – Slaughter hadn't noticed exactly when he'd arrived – and stood in squatty attention behind Cuthbert's chair.

Slaughter snapped apart the security tape, opened the file while everyone watched. Attached to the inside front cover was a photographic evidence packet. He opened it, slid out the photos it contained.

The top photo was Wooten, smeared with the fingerprints of frequent, careless handling. It was dated 1979. Other, more recent, photos of him were clipped behind it. All of them were labeled with the number one.

246

The next several photographs were of Kinsey, all bearing the number two.

Slaughter sifted through the photos. There were sixty-eight men in all, dating back to 1976. Sixty-eight. Twenty-three remained alive.

He looked up, but none of the other men were trying to see the pictures.

Slaughter held onto the photos, didn't bother reading the files. He walked over to Mills, quietly. "Walter, give me the trade agreement."

Mills checked his watch, then looked up. His lids were puffy and shaded his eyes. "I'm sorry, Jacob. I really am. But I'm afraid it's too late to help them. Just like I told you before."

Cuthbert jumped up as though he'd been sitting on a mound of red ants. "Shut up, Mills!"

Slaughter turned toward Cuthbert and zeroed in on him. "Are you still trying to dick with me, Cuthbert? What is it this time? What else have you buried in that diseased conscience of yours?"

Cuthbert started backing away, moving clumsily around the Oval Office. "You're a fool, Slaughter. Don't get into things that you can't possibly understand."

"Cuthbert, I'm bringing Wooten home. You'll have to kill me to stop me, and you haven't got the guts to do that. So stay the hell out of my way!"

Cuthbert was darting from chair to desk to table. "Come on, Slaughter, don't you think we want to bring them home, too? Don't you thing we tried? We have, damn it. We tried for years and years."

"Try some more."

"You don't understand."

"I don't want to understand. I just want them back."

Cuthbert kept dancing around the furniture. "And I'm telling you they won't be coming back. It is absolutely impossible. Will you . . ."

Cuthbert stopped and caught his breath. "Will you just try to understand? This office has worked for two decades to get those men home. Every president since Nixon has known there were still prisoners over there. Each one of them desperately wanted to be the hero who got them out. Hell, it was the Vietnamese themselves who told us about them, provided us with the proof of their existence, promised to release them if we gave them what they wanted. But, time after time, we did exactly what they asked, and they never released any of those men."

"They will this time," Slaughter said. "I'm sure of it. Now's your chance, Cuthbert. Or are you waiting for your own administration?"

"Hell, no, Slaughter. It's nothing like that. But . . . well, what makes you think you can trust them now?"

"I trust them. I trust Lu Kham Phong."

"Okay, Slaughter. Let's work with that. Let's say this Phong character keeps his word and sends the prisoners home. What then?"

"What kind of question is that? They come home, live out the rest of their lives in their homeland without some little prick beating the crap out of them everyday."

"Sure. Okay, I've got a pretty good picture of that scenario. Now, see if you can appreciate the view from where I sit. Remember how the issue of P.O.W.s used to tear at the guts of this country, hamstringing every foreign policy of this nation? You remember that or not?"

"Yes, I remember."

"Good. Well, somewhere along the line this office just decided it would be easier to deny the existence of the P.O.W.s. Stop worrying about them. What the hell, we couldn't get them out anyway, so we pretended they were dead. Some of us went over on fact-finding missions and returned with evidence that the men were impossible to account for, closed the book on them. Hell, you even went with me."

"And then you used me to weaken the P.O.W./M.I.A. lobby."

"That's right. You carried weight with them. Got them off our backs a little." Cuthbert grinned. "Nice work."

Slaughter lurched toward him, but President Simons spun around in his chair. Slaughter could feel Simon's intensity focusing on him, but he forced himself to ignore it, stayed with Cuthbert.

"So, Cuthbert, why did the Vietnamese show Wooten to me when I was over there?"

Cuthbert closed his mouth and looked at Simons. Slaughter turned to face Simons, too.

"Blackmail," Simons said. Then he walked over to Slaughter and stood right smack in front of him. "They're blackmailing us, Slaughter, pure and simple, like we're some dumb husband who got caught with another woman. They tricked us into denying the existence of the P.O.W.s for all those years. We, like a bunch of blind idiots, climbed so far out on that weak limb that now it's bending double. All our testicles are dangling out there."

"So?"

"So, they see our predicament and are threatening to expose the P.O.W.s if we don't give them the trade status they want. They threatened to tell the whole world that we've always known the prisoners were still alive, even though we've been publicly denying it for years. They've got us by the balls, Slaughter, but good. Do you have any idea what would happen if American citizens and our allies found out about this? Any idea at all?

Slaughter stood mute.

"Well, think about it. Every treaty, every statement, every promise made from this office since the mid-70s would be in question. Everything we do from now on would be stained by the unforgivable sacrifice required of those brave men. So, I'm sorry, Slaughter. Really. But this is not just an issue of twenty-three American P.O.W.s. It involves the business of an entire nation and the lives of all American servicemen everywhere. If the world ever finds out that the United States can be blackmailed, every one of our military personnel would be a potential hostage. Just like Wooten."

"Would you get them back if you could?"

"Hell, Slaughter, I would absolutely love to be the one who got them back. It's a precious dream of mine. I'd be a hero. But this hand was dealt long before I took over this office. I cannot, I will not, play it carelessly. It would threaten everything this country stands for. And for what? Twenty-three men? I hate to say it so bluntly, Slaughter, but those men *are* expendable. Always have been. It's no different now than when they hit the battlefields of the sixties. No different than the hundreds of thousands of other expendable soldiers who have died and will die in our future wars. Don't you think we owe them something, Slaughter? Don't you think we have an obligation to the men and women who follow in the giant steps of Chuck Wooten. Don't you think we owe them the dignity of being treated as prisoners, if that's their fate, instead of damned bargaining chips?"

"There must be some way, Simons."

Simons' eyes stopped on Mills for a second, then dropped to his desk. "Well, I sure wish you'd come up with it."

In the distance, Slaughter heard himself say, "I will."

"Just make sure we don't have to go into hiding when you do," Cuthbert snickered, almost laughing. "Don't waste your time on stupid ideas that might make us look bad."

* * * * *

Simons ambled around the Oval Office after Mills and Slaughter left, rolling the last ten minutes around in his head.

The shameful look Mills had given him was still hurting, making him feel worse than he had in a long, long time. He had known Walter for twenty years but had never seen him give anyone such a look before.

No one spoke for several minutes. Then Cuthbert started taking charge. "Tanner, who are you dealing with in Army Special Operations?"

Tanner smiled, but dropped it the instant Simons turned to hear his answer. "Colonel Maddigan."

Now Cuthbert grinned, his keen face getting a sharper edge.

Simons took a deep breath and closed his eyes. "You're both sure it has to be done this way?"

"Absolutely, Alex," Cuthbert said. "If we don't want to lose the White House next election, we have to stop this fiasco right now. You *are* still concerned about our party holding onto the White House, aren't you?"

Simons didn't want to answer, could not have cared less about politics right now. "Well, then, I suppose Maddigan is the right man for the job. How much time will he need?"

Tanner pulled something out of his pocket and read it. "I received this from Colonel Maddigan late last night. He said that after getting your assurance the Vietnamese government was forthcoming with the various locations of the prisoners. Colonel Maddigan has teams of commandos moving into the areas from Thailand. They will be in position soon, have an exact rendezvous time of . . ." Tanner looked at his watch, bit his lip, nodded his head in cadence with his murmured counting of time zones. "Jeez, only about thirty minutes now."

"And they're clear on their orders?" Simons asked.

Tanner looked at Cuthbert. Both of them nodded, but it was Tanner who answered. "They are, sir. They are to locate and remove all evidence of American military or civilian prisoners in Vietnam and preserve that evidence in a secret location."

Simons raised his fist, as though he might hit him. "Damn you, Tanner. Damn you! You know what I'm asking. The prisoners? What's going to happen to the prisoners? At least have the guts to say the words."

Tanner looked like a little boy holding back tears. "They will be removed, sir, along with their effects. Once safely in the hands of Colonel Maddigan, they . . ." Tanner's voice cracked, trailed off into nothing. He hung his head.

Cuthbert stepped up beside him, looking cold and unaffected, wearing the promise of his own administration like a sacred prophesy. "They will be executed, Alex. As we have already discussed, Colonel Maddigan has been informed that we consider those prisoners to be war criminals. His men realize they are dealing with traitors. They have no reservations about their mission."

Simons' chief of staff tapped the door lightly as he entered. "Mr. President. Your car is ready for you."

Simons was wishing this had happened during the last administration. Or during the next one – Cuthbert's. But it was happening on his watch, and he had little choice but to go along. At least it would be an end. Finally. For all of them. It had to end.

"Thank you," he said to his chief of staff. "Give me two minutes."

21

Slaughter shuffled beside Mills through the halls of the White House. The aide had left them alone; the halls were almost empty. Every hundred feet or so they'd pass a uniformed guard, but that was about it. He couldn't hear anyone talking, anywhere.

They didn't talk either. Not a word, all the way to the main exit. Slaughter's head was down, filled with questions, uncertain about the right thing to do.

From a soldier's viewpoint, he was absolutely sure that President Simons was correct. Soldiers, in time of war, *were* expendable. It was not open to debate. If they weren't, war could not exist.

And war did exist. Terrible, savage, torturous acts were continuously committed by brave young men for the sake of their flag, or a phrase, or an idea. And, sadly, some of those same young men would have terrible, savage, torturous acts done to them by other men who were fanatically protecting their flag, or slogan, or national dogma.

Slaughter understood it even better now, recognized that war was a tragedy for everyone concerned: the soldiers, the families, the inhabitants of the war zone, and the nations. The simplicity of that concept, once understood, almost made it possible for him to accept Wooten's fate. Men died in war. It was as simple as that. Some died in skirmishes, some in the cockpit of an exploding fighter plane, and some in prisoner-of-war camps. The time or place didn't really matter.

But was it really the only course for Captain Wooten? And if it was, could Slaughter live with his guilt over it? Slaughter would never get over his nightmares, and how much longer could he survive them? At what point would he be better off dead than living with them? Tomorrow? A year from now?

He looked over at Mills, walking along beside him, keeping back whatever he was feeling, too. Mills did not have the answers Slaughter needed. No one did. If Wooten was to come home, it was up to Slaughter to find a way.

They passed through security and walked outside. An agent followed them across the grounds. The early morning was warm and dark, but it had that sense of beginning about it. The city's noises had finally quieted down. There weren't many sirens wailing. This was the pause between rulers, the cease-fire that allowed the night warriors to slink away with dignity, yielding their ground, temporarily, to the business-suited day shift. It was a truce that both sides honored and understood, but never talked about.

"You want a ride, Slaughter?"

"No." Slaughter answered without thinking. He was staring straight up at the sky. Praying. Begging God for an answer.

When he looked down from the sky he met Mills' eyes. They said what Mills was feeling. It was all over for Wooten. They had tried. There was nothing left to do. Mills held out his hand.

Slaughter didn't shake it. He stood there with his hands dug deep into the pockets of his pants.

254

"I hate to say it, Slaughter, but I told you it wouldn't work. I was sure Simons wouldn't go along. I'm sorry. Really. It would have been great to get those men home. Would have felt wonderful."

"Sure."

"Anyway, you have to feel that you did your best. You really tried, went all the way to the top for those guys."

"Yeah? Well, I feel like shit."

Mills nodded, rocked a little on his heels. "Yes, I'm sure you feel like shit. I don't imagine that part will go away, either. But at least you can look at the face in the mirror and not be ashamed."

"Sure." Slaughter thought the idea over for a second, but he knew the face in the mirror would always be Chuck Wooten's.

Mills extended his hand farther. Slaughter still didn't shake it. He almost did, but then he stopped his hand halfway there and smacked it at the air. "Damn it, Mills, I can't let this end here. I just won't do it!"

"I don't see that you have an option."

"There's always an option. Always something more that can be done."

The uniformed Secret Service agent following them was a negative presence, making it hard for Slaughter to think. He turned to the man and pointed toward the main gate. The agent followed, twenty steps behind them, all the way to it. They cleared the security gate and began to pace in front of the White House

Mills had kept quiet while they cleared the compound. Once outside the gate he stopped, glanced around, then shrugged, tilted his head toward Slaughter. "All right. I'm listening. Skeptical, but listening. The truth, though, is that you don't have much left to work with."

"I've got plenty. You and Phong. And Simons is agreeable if I can come up with a plan. I'll take him at his word, that he'd bring them home if he could." He waited for Mills' reaction.

"He would. Given a decent chance. He won't sully the reputation of his office, though; won't go that far."

Slaughter looked toward the White House, noticed that someone was standing out on the balcony, silhouetted against the bright lights of the Oval Office.

"Simons?"

Mills looked up at the figure and squinted. "No. Probably Cuthbert. The shit. You know, he's the one who's doing the screw job on those guys. He's been handling this issue since the start of Simons' first term. He's always been scared to death it'll ruin his turn as president."

"I could tell that." Slaughter kept staring at the figure. "Yeah, you're right, that's Cuthbert."

They paced the sidewalk in front of the White House, like sentries on duty, all the way to the corner. When they about-faced, Slaughter stagger-stepped and picked up the Mexican's pistol from behind the metal fence. Slaughter's brain hurt and his heart was pounding. He shut his mind down every time Charles Wooten staggered into it, a painful waste of valuable time. He thought about everything he knew, what he had learned, what had been said.

Then Cuthbert's sarcastic last words splintered their way through the middle of his brain.

* * * * *

Cortez was surprised to get the call from Vice-President Cuthbert. Shocked, even. He had expected Tanner to be the one. Or maybe, in a pinch, Mills. But definitely not Cuthbert. He was too cautious. Kept himself too clean.

But it was all the same to Cortez. The message was clear. Slaughter was leaving the White House. Mills had left with him. They'd be out in a few minutes. Wait until they were clear of the gate, then kill Slaughter. Do it immediately, don't let him get away this time.

Cortez wasn't planning to take any chances. He had his car positioned behind the barricades at the end of the street, ready to pick up anyone leaving the White House grounds. His line of sight was clear and unobstructed. He reached over to the passenger seat and picked up the night-vision binoculars, looked all around for cops before lifting them to his eyes.

There was Slaughter, walking slowly down the drive with Mills. Cortez could see them talking. They turned right when they got to the gate, strolling along the sidewalk in front of the White House. Mills was leading Slaughter straight toward him.

Cortez started talking to himself, calming his nerves, stifling the jumps that he never allowed anyone to see. His scars already revealed too much about him; everything else needed to be kept completely hidden.

"Oh, Mr. Slaughter," he murmured, "you have been a hard one. It makes me happy to see you walking like that, watching the ground, ignoring the dangers. I've never seen this side of you, but it will certainly make my job easier. I must remember to congratulate Mills on his fine job of distraction as he leads you into my trap."

He kept watching, kept looking out for cops or federal agents. Slaughter and Mills were still talking. Slaughter was deeply engaged, ignoring everything else. Mills' black limousine followed, a short distance behind them.

Mills was acting a little excited now, something Slaughter had said seemed to please him. The excitement looked contagious, seemed to explode in a back and forth kind of way. Seemed to make Slaughter cautious, too. He was looking around more now, even checked something at the fence near the corner. Apparently Slaughter's excitement and his caution were two emotions that rode together.

Cortez set the binoculars down and got out of his car, started to walk toward Slaughter and Mills, nice and casual. Slaughter had his shoulders turned, had stopped and spun Mills around to discuss something with him. Now, if only Mills would keep up his part, keep his head down and pretend not to notice. If Mills looked up and saw Cortez, there was a decent shot that he'd spoil the trap.

Cortez was closing on Slaughter when the gates to the White House swung open and some agents ran out, looked both ways before the president's motorcade rolled through. Cortez thought it was pretty strange that Simons would put himself so close to the hit but, what the hell, it would give him a chance to show off a little for the commander in chief.

* * * * *

Slaughter was starting to like his idea, even if he had to give Cuthbert part of the credit. It was a simple plan. Most importantly, Mills liked it, was in agreement that it had a decent chance of working. Slaughter stopped on the sidewalk, didn't want to get too far away from the White House while they worked out the bugs.

"Sure," Mills said. "Of course, those families would certainly go along with that sacrifice."

"At least the ones that wanted their men back," Slaughter added. "Some of the women have remarried, though. Have started new lives."

"Then you're right, absolutely. They could never be told. A story would have to be fabricated to satisfy the returning prisoners, keep those men from looking for their wives and families."

"I don't imagine that would be too hard."

258

"Hell, no. It would be easy for Laura to incorporate it into her psychological evaluation and adjustment therapy."

Slaughter grinned. "You know, Walter, this just might work."

"If we can get Simons to go along with it."

"He'll go along. Why wouldn't he. He said he wanted to bring those men home."

"For one thing, Cuthbert would stand in his way. He'd rather . . . well, let's just say he'd rather end it once and for all with no loose strings."

Slaughter shook Mills by his shoulders, suddenly realizing how long he'd been holding Mills in his grip. "Walter, what is it you're not telling me? What's going on?"

Mills looked at Slaughter's hands, then at his face. He look worried, but not angry. "It doesn't matter. We'll either get them back or we won't. Talking about it won't help."

Slaughter slid his hands off Mills' shoulders. "I'm really starting to hate that guy."

"Who doesn't? The thought of Cuthbert as president frightens the wits out of me. But we're going to be saddled with him for awhile, at least four years. I'm hopeful he'll only last one term."

"That's still a long time."

"It won't be for me. I don't plan to stick around Washington. When Simons leaves, I'm going with him. Heading back home to do some fishing. Spend some time with friends before I start a new career."

"You mean after you help me with this?"

Mills smiled, and Slaughter knew it was genuine.

"Sure, Slaughter. We'll do this together. Then I'm taking off. There'll be no place in Washington for me anymore."

Slaughter began to feel proud of the man in front of him, the solid negotiator, slow to anger, seldom combative. Slaughter decided that he was, after all, a decent man. He looked into Mills' eyes, tried to see if Mills caught his gratitude. What he saw in Mills' eyes was wholly unnatural. Demonic.

"Damn, Walter, what's wrong?"

Mills stared straight ahead. Slaughter glanced over his shoulder, in the direction of Mills' gaze. There was only one other person on the sidewalk, a nicely dressed man who looked innocent in the darkness.

"What, Walter? What is it?"

* * * * *

"Damn," Cortez squeezed the words between his teeth. This was exactly what he'd worried about. Mills was going to blow it, unable to hold himself together when the action got up-close and personal. Was he going to run away? Stand there and cry? What?

But who would have expected Mills to be capable of pulling this off anyway? Cortez certainly hadn't; he'd never have cast Mills in the role of Slaughter's escort, the Judas who would lead him to his death. Tanner would have been able to handle the job, sure. Cuthbert, too, although he would never get that involved. But not Mills. Whose brain-dead idea was it to send him?

But it didn't really matter. The darkness concealed Cortez's face. He would be fine. He would just act a little more innocent the next time Slaughter turned around, a little more interested in seeing the White House. Right up to the moment when he would plunge the long knife into Slaughter's body and scramble his insides with it.

There. Slaughter had just turned again. Looked him over pretty carefully, too – as much as possible in the darkness. Still didn't recognize him, only looked confused about something. Begging Mills for some answers. And Mills just staring past

Slaughter, his eyes fixed on Cortez like he was in his own private audience with a god.

Cortez liked seeing the impact of his presence. The great Walter Mills, American Secretary of State, catatonic. Yes, sir, if only the boys from the old neighborhood could see him now. A world leader, fearful of his approach. That would make them respect him. Or at least it would make them leave him alone. He puckered up a little kiss to blow to Mills as he walked straight toward him and Slaughter.

He slowed as the president's motorcade came closer, Simons' limousine and an escort, probably heading for an early morning flight. Cortez was ten feet away from his target now, picking the spot on Slaughter's lower back where he would shove the knife in, angled up to penetrate all the way to the hilt, grinding the handle around a few times before pulling it out. Stirring the razor-sharp blade inside Slaughter's body.

A little slower pace, he decided. That's it, slow down. Let the president's car get close. Let Simons see the handiwork Cortez did for him.

* * * * *

Mills struggled to act natural when he saw Cortez. He focused on the bully's ravaged, little face, tried to box away the panic it set off. But there were years and years of fear stuffed down inside him, and his stomach would not allow more to enter. He fought against himself, tried to get his body into gear, give Slaughter some kind of warning, stop acting like a fool.

But nothing worked. He stood there, frozen, while his fear eased a little, finally allowed itself to be choked down and swallowed along with his self-respect. It was Mills' normal procedure during a confrontation. But this time the mixture of fear and pride hit something en route, touched off a gag reflex that threw it back into his mouth like bile, launched him to some whole new level.

He had never been here before, here in this place with no retreat. He'd been in places where he was beaten, sure, before learning his negotiating skills. And he'd beaten plenty of people, too. Not in the classic sense, of course, but in the way that suited him. He had beaten them with words, won his victories through resourcefulness. But words were useless now. His negotiating skills were not up to this challenge.

For a brief slice of time, he thought about stepping out of the way. That's it, he told himself, just stand aside and let Cortez do his job. Slaughter can deal with it. Or not. And if not, he will die there.

And so what if he did. The whole world was already Mills' problem. He couldn't be worried about every inhabitant of it.

But Mills never really considered doing it. Not for one second. Only thought of it as an option someone else might take. But not him. Not tonight. He knew he was smiling.

"Are you okay, Walter? Damn, you worried me for a minute. I thought you might be having a heart attack."

Mills felt his back straightening. "No, Slaughter, I'm fine, I think. But would you step back there and get my driver to pull up. I think I need to ride."

"Sure, Walter. Just wait right here, okay? Stay calm, I'll be right back."

* * * * *

Slaughter looked over his shoulder, gave the sidewalk another quick check. A couple of early day-shifters were disappearing around a corner at the far end, and the suited man was about to pass them. Nothing wrong. He let go of Mills' arm, stepped back toward the limo, motioned Mills' driver to pull up. Barely heard the words whispered by a stranger – "Thanks, Mills. I got him."

He spun around just as the suited man slid past Mills, three feet away from Slaughter now. He saw the matte-finished knife blade, over a foot long, aimed in his direction. He twisted sideways to make a small target, tried to keep panic under control.

The streetlight splattered the man's ugly face now and Slaughter saw it was the man who'd killed Kelly. He watched him advance like it was ballet. Slow. Deliberate. He heard a car stop behind him. A door opened. Somewhere across the street he heard the click of high heels and a couple giggling.

He was as ready as he could possibly be. But suddenly, something happened to Mills as the ugly man kept moving. Something about Mills' face changed so dramatically that it caught Slaughter's attention, even as the huge knife began slicing toward him.

Mills' scream was deep and resonant, like it had been bottled up somewhere dark and scary for decades. He leaped at the man from behind, clumsy, foolish, and ineffective. But fearless. By God it was genuine fearlessness. Slaughter hadn't seen anything like it since Wooten's actions on his first day in prison.

Mills dove at the man and grabbed him around the neck. Mills' forward momentum spun him all the way around the ugly man, but he held onto that neck like it was a fireman's pole. "Run," Mills shouted. "Go tell Simons your plan!"

But Slaughter didn't run. He made a quick leap and dove toward the fight, knowing he would be too late. He was airborne, flying, watching in slow motion as the ugly man twisted his knife-hand around and flicked the long blade into Mills' belly as he dragged Mills close to him. The ugly man's hand flashed around between them, then Slaughter saw Mills' entrails forcing their way through the huge slit and spilling onto the sidewalk. Mills' eyes bugged out, and his grip slipped from the man's neck. He fell away, sliding off the tip of the blade and crumbling onto the sidewalk.

Slaughter grabbed the bloody knife with his left hand as it came out of Mills' body. He was trying for the handle, but ended up with the razor-sharp blade. It scraped at the flesh and muscle of his hand, carving wild slashes through the air as the ugly little man twisted it around, trying to work it free. Slaughter screamed with pain, then screamed again, and again. Kept screaming. Couldn't stop. Wouldn't let go.

He had the gun, but he didn't go for it – wouldn't break his vow. He wanted to wrestle the man down and beat the crap out him. Hurt him badly, but not kill him. He tightened his grip, pulled hard enough on the knife's blade to drag the man closer to him, saw a brilliant flash of smiling teeth. Their faces collided, the man's short, thick stubble scrubbed at Slaughter's face.

The little man tugged harder on the knife, leaned back and put all his weight into the effort. Slaughter hardened his own grip, tighter, and then tighter until . . . something was terribly wrong. The knife was free, the man had it back, ready to stab him. The man was smiling, beginning to laugh.

Slaughter's brain slowly registered the loss of his fingers, snipped off like kernels by the terrible blade. He raised his left fist, saw the four stumps at the end of his palm, switched to his right hand, tried to concentrate on timing, ignore the throbbing and intercept the steel shank as it slashed again for his vital organs.

The ugly little man swiped twice, but both times Slaughter managed to dance back out of the way. He struggled to peel off his jacket so he could wrap it around his stump, give the useless appendage a purpose, use it to block the blade. But his jacket wouldn't come off fast enough, not with one hand working on it.

The little man spun the knife around in his hand, held it like an ice pick, the blade resting back along his wrist and forearm. He thrust it at Slaughter again, making big, swinging arcs with the blade. He was still smiling, looking relaxed as he began to talk.

"You're a dead man, Slaughter. You know that? Here, let me put you out of your misery. I'll make it fast, you'll be in very little pain. I promise."

Then the little man looked past Slaughter for a second, in the direction where Slaughter had heard a car door. He gave a quick, compact wave.

"Look, Slaughter. President Simons is over there. I've got to stop fooling around with you or he'll get bored and leave."

The man sliced the knife at Slaughter again. It was going to get him this time, the little man was just too quick. Slaughter jumped back so hard his breath was forced from his mouth. He whipped his left arm up to cover his face, blood flying from the missing digits. The blade sliced through his forearm, hit the bone and pushed down on it.

Slaughter was totally defensive. He didn't have time to think about an attack. It was all he could do to react – stay alive a second longer – then react again. But when he'd arched backward that time, the pistol's steel frame dug into his bad vertebrae, the spot where Vu Van Vinh had tortured his bullet wound and almost crippled him. He hated Vinh for the pain. Hated the little man for the same thing.

Then Captain Wooten shuffled into this mind, running in his chains, falling down, struggling back up and then running some more. He was screaming "Kill him, Jacob! Kill him! That's an order, son!"

The little man sliced the length of the blade through Slaughter's forearm, then pulled the knife back and prepared again. Slaughter snatched at his back with his right hand, threw his left stump up for more protection. His right fingers slid around the pistol's handle.

It wasn't even his weapon, yet it was perfect – comfortable and reassuring, like a baseball player's favorite mitt. In an instant he had it up between them, the barrel of the pistol stuck in Cortez's face.

Slaughter fired, automatically, so close to the man that the blast gave him a blood shower. But he squinted to keep the blood out of his eyes, kept aiming at the little man as the blast rocked him back. The man's knife-hand tumbled down to his side, and a glaze quickly spread over his eyes.

Slaughter's took his second shot right away, followed Wooten's orders and did what he had sworn never to do again. The second hollowpoint tore away the entire lower portion of the man's face, all of his mouth and chin, made him too hideous for Slaughter to look at. He turned away, wanted to see if that was really Simons back there on the street.

He was halfway around when he heard the next shot. Only one blast, but so loud he knew he had to be in front of the shooter's muzzle. Then the bullet struck his left shoulder and pushed him back. He stumbled, but he did not fall, stood there looking at the men around the limousine.

Three armed Secret Service Agents stood in front of Simons, but Slaughter could still see the president's face, looking over the agents' heads. One of the agents still trained his sights on Slaughter, his finger riding the trigger.

Slaughter's pistol was low. Both his arms were by his side. "You, too, Simons?" he yelled. "You're this desperate?"

Simons said something to the agents, then looked away. But he didn't keep his back turned, slowly turned again and watched.

Slaughter was going to die here. He knew it as surely as all men did when they took their last breaths. But he was not going down easy.

He tried to raise his pistol, wanted to aim it into the group of blue suits and blast away. But parts of his left shoulder were shattered, making his right arm difficult to move. He only managed to get the pistol up about forty-five degrees. He stood there, trying to stay erect, but leaning farther backward every second. He began to wobble, stumble around like a drunken man.

He kept staring at President Simons. Even as his own body wiggled foolishly, he kept his eyes on Simons. He would make him watch his death. He was ready, waiting for the agent's final shot, almost anxious to end it. Then Simons shuffled around behind the agents, shouting to them, finally breaking through their defensive line and running toward him.

"Put your gun down, Slaughter! Please, lower your weapon."

As far as Slaughter could tell his pistol was already down. It weighed at least a hundred pounds; there was no chance of him raising it. He let it slip from his fingers and clang on the sidewalk.

Suddenly, Slaughter was surrounded by Secret Service agents. He tried to meet them, make some kind of stand. But he couldn't. One of his knees dropped to the ground. Then Simons' face was over him, giving orders to his men, cool and efficient: "Get my ambulance, put a tourniquet above the wrist of that left arm, compress that bullet hole. Move!"

"Mills," Slaughter gasped. "Go help Mills."

Another agent broke into the circle, spoke to President Simons. "Mr. Mills is dead, sir."

Slaughter struggled free of the agents, managed to get both feet back under him. He stumbled over to Mills' body and knelt down, stroked Mills' hair back off his forehead, tried to ignore the pile of intestines hanging out of him.

Mills' eyes were open. But there was no light in them. Nothing. Slaughter looked into them for several seconds, stroking his hair and memorizing Mills' face, wanting to put it right there beside Chuck Wooten's. Once he had it locked in, he wobbled his head around to look at the ugly little Mexican. Confirm his own kill.

Simons walked over to Slaughter, left his Secret Service agents behind.

Slaughter didn't move away from Mills, looked up at Simons from his knees. "You hired that assassin, didn't you?"

Simons glanced around and lowered his voice. It was just between them now. He didn't waffle with the truth. "Yes. He worked for me. I'm very sorry."

Slaughter stayed on his knees, raised his eyes to the sky. A cloud drifted across the moon. "You're sorry? Mills is dead, and you're sorry?"

Simons looked down at Mills. "Mills was my best friend, Slaughter. I had no idea he would act like that."

"What? You mean courageous?"

Simons nodded. "Yes. Courageous. It wasn't exactly his style. It was just supposed to be you, Slaughter. God, I hate to say it, but we had to end this. You weren't giving us any choices."

Slaughter's whole body was throbbing now. A Secret Service agent stepped up, waited until Slaughter was ready, then dropped four fingers into his right hand.

"You're making quite a puddle," he said.

Simons glared at the agent. "Come on, Slaughter. Let's get you to the hospital. See if they can attach those fingers and take care of those other wounds."

Slaughter didn't know what to hold on to: his hand, his shoulder, or his forearm. Then he thought about Wooten and ignored all the injuries.

"No. Listen, Mills and I have a plan to get them out. A plan that will work. Really. It's a good plan."

Simons checked his watch. He stared at it a long, long time. He looked back at the White House, then rubbed his chin. "All right. Let's talk about it. Maybe. . . maybe there's still time to work something out"

Slaughter swayed while he was searched, too worn down to resist The president's private ambulance had arrived almost instantly. One of the doctors covered Mills' face, while the other began to dress Slaughter's wounds.

Slaughter could sense that there wasn't time for him to get medical care. He stuffed his loose fingers into his pocket, held his right hand over his shoulder wound, and dug the remains of his left hand into his stomach. Pushed hard for direct pressure to stop the bleeding.

He climbed into the back of the limousine, alone with Simons. The driver put the car in reverse and roared backward toward the White House gate. Slaughter sat silently with a pocketful of loose fingers and four leaky stumps, wondering how much time Wooten had left.

22

Slaughter was swept into the White House in a surge of Secret Service agents. They propped him up as they chased after President Simons, finally catching him at the Oval Office doors. All of them burst in together.

Tanner was sitting in the president's chair, talking on the phone in a contented voice. Slaughter couldn't see him yet; he was still shrouded by agents. But he recognized that pure-bred Southern accent instantly.

"Yes, sir, Mr. Duncan," Slaughter heard him say. "It's all taken care of. We've got the situation covered over there in Vietnam and, from the gunshots I just heard outside, I'd have to assume . . ."

President Simons took five steps into the room, then spun around and ordered the Secret Service agents to leave. They argued with him all the way out, but Simons pushed them bodily through the door, then closed and double-locked it. As the agents were peeled away, Tanner looked up and saw Slaughter. He lowered the phone from his mouth, but then brought it back up.

"Mr. Duncan," he said, very slowly, as if he was having to invent the words. "Can I call you back in a few minutes? Something weird's going on here."

As soon as they were alone, Simons grabbed a towel from his washroom and tossed it across the room. Slaughter caught it as he collapsed into a chair, watched Simons pace in front of him while he wound the towel around his left forearm and hand. It was difficult to do; he was too lightheaded. He was losing blood, fast. The agent's makeshift tourniquet was not working. Already, a large puddle had formed on the Oval Office rug. He moved his feet to keep his blood off his shoes.

"Hurry up, Slaughter," Simons said. "This is your last chance to save those men. You have very little time!"

Slaughter gave up on the towel, threw it down in the puddle and stood up. His head went empty for a second, and he almost fell. But he didn't, battled his way back to consciousness. "Why? What have you guys done? What's happening to the prisoners?"

"They're running out of time, okay?" Simons checked his watch, the fifth or sixth time since he'd tossed Slaughter the towel. "Now, what was your plan? How was it going to work? Damn it, tell me!"

Slaughter wanted to think it through again. It was really just a skeleton of an idea, still needed to have some flesh hung on it. But Simons was hovering over him with his hands spinning around between them.

He started to speak, but it was too late. Simons was gone, bounding over to Tanner. "Who was that guy you were working with over there? Colonel Maddigan's contact person?"

"You mean Phong?"

"Yes, that's it. Phong. Get him on the phone! There's only a few minutes left, so track him down wherever he is. Use the authority of this office, but find him. Right now. Do it!"

Tanner snatched the phone so fast that it slipped, flew through the air, then banged down on the desk. Tanner chased it, knocking over some pictures. When it was back in his hand he flipped open a notebook and started punching numbers.

Slaughter sat back down, used the time to run through his plan again. Yes, sure it would work, he thought. Why wouldn't it. If they weren't already too late.

"This is Tanner, United States Secretary of Defense, calling on behalf of President Alex Simons. The president wants to speak with Mr. Phong. This is a top priority matter; can you reach Mr. Phong immediately?"

Tanner's mouth swelled into a big, country smile as he turned to Simons and held out the phone. "They're transferring the call, Mr. President. Phong is in his office."

"Great! That's great. Good job, Tanner."

"Thank you, sir."

Simons took the phone and wedged it between his cheek and his shoulder. "Mr. Phong? Mr. Phong?" He looked at Tanner and shrugged.

"Well," Tanner said, "they said he was there. Just hang on a minute."

"Come on, come on, what's going on, where the . . . Hello, Mr. Phong? Yes. This is President Alex Simons of the United States of America. Listen, you've been working closely with Mr. Tanner, have helped coordinate the pickup of some packages by our Army personnel. Is that correct?"

There was some talk from the other end. Simons was not paying attention, that was easy for Slaughter to see. Simons kept his watch in front of his face, his other hand making a useless, frantic motion for Phong to hurry up.

"Yes, yes," Simons said. "I'm sorry to be so rude, Mr. Phong, but I need to know something right away. This is very important. Are the packages still there? Or has our Army already picked them up?"

There was a small door to the Oval Office that moved. Slaughter barely noticed it and totally ignored it. But then Cuthbert came in and Slaughter gave him all his attention. He had some kind of a small frame automatic shaking in his hand. Maybe a .25 caliber. It was hard to tell.

Cuthbert looked worried, or frightened. Lost. His voice rattled, then cracked. It was barely audible when it came out. "Put that phone down, Alex."

Simons glanced up and saw Cuthbert. He ignored him, looked back at his desktop. Then, as if he suddenly realized what he'd seen, he snapped his head back up, stopped talking to Phong, but still held the phone. "What the hell are you doing, Cuthbert?"

Cuthbert looked clumsy with the weapon, like he'd never actually shot a gun before and couldn't guess what to expect from it. But still, he did a good job of looking menacing with it.

"I said, put the phone down. Everything is going perfectly. The P.O.W.s will be dead soon. You don't need to do anything else. Now, hang up."

Simons looked over to Slaughter, and Slaughter knew what he wanted. Could Slaughter help? Did he have anything left to use on Cuthbert? Did he have the power to take Cuthbert's weapon away?

The answer was no. Slaughter had already tried to get up and charge Cuthbert, but he couldn't even get his legs to move. He was barely holding on and didn't even expect to do that much longer. He began to doubt if he could stay alive and out of shock long enough to relay his plan. Something had to happen soon.

Simons understood, it was clear on his face. He nodded, gently, to him. Then Simons turned back to Cuthbert. "There may be a way now, Andrew. It may be possible to bring them back without causing this office problems. Slaughter has a plan. It may not be necessary to kill them."

Cuthbert wagged his little pistol at them. He was getting bolder or, possibly, more frightened. Either way, he seemed more dangerous.

"There's already a workable plan in place," he said. "We all agreed on it. There's no reason to change it now. Put the phone down."

"You realize what you're doing, Cuthbert?"

"I do. I'm holding onto the White House. I'm doing what everyone else is too gutless to do. I'm ending the prisoners of war problem, once and for all."

Simons stared at him, still holding the phone to his chest.

Slaughter was slipping away so fast now he was sure he wouldn't see how this all worked out. He closed his eyes, barely had the strength to listen.

*   *   *   *   *

Tanner had backed away from the big desk soon after Simons took the phone from him. He had stayed close by, though, hoping to get some more praise from Simons. Maybe he would find out what the hell was going on, too. He was close enough to hear both sides of Simons' conversation with Phong.

Then Cuthbert had walked in and he didn't know what to do. The sides were too clearly divided now: Cuthbert versus Simons. He didn't want to make such a definite choice. He would prefer to play the middle ground, shift his loyalty along the lines of power, work for whoever had it at the moment.

But he did decide. He had to. There weren't any options. It was a damn hard choice, too. Sure, Simons was still the president. But Cuthbert was going to hold this office next year. It didn't matter what Cuthbert did tonight, short of killing someone, of course. This whole incident, as wrong as it was, would be swept under the rug. No one outside this room would ever know about it. No one in this room would ever tell. Except maybe Slaughter.

He looked over at Slaughter, tried to see if he was already dead. He looked it, that was for sure, all slumped down in the chair with his eyes closed. God, what a mess. The flesh of his left arm had been blown away. A deep gash split his forearm into two hemispheres. And the hand that dangled at the end of that ravaged arm was draining the last of the man's life out through four little faucets. No, Cuthbert would not have to kill him. He was already dead, or soon would be.

Tanner gave Cuthbert a little grin of allegiance, then shuffled across the room, his head down as he moved over to him. He took up a position behind Cuthbert.

So what if it was the wrong side. Cuthbert would be president soon, and Tanner would have his prestigious job for another four years. If this was the retail price of his position, he would pay it. Loyalty had to be earned. It was a back and forth kind of thing, and he would go this far for his career. Not much farther. But he could stretch to here.

He would just have to learn to live with himself.

*   *   *   *   *

Slaughter *had* to tell them his plan, had to get it out before he died. If he had only known they would get so bogged down here he would have accepted medical aid from the ambulance team. He would be stronger now. More capable.

He went deep inside of himself. His mind wandered around inside his body, looking for the strength he needed. The kind of strength Wooten had shown the day they'd been captured, and on Slaughter's last night with him.

He sat there with his eyes closed and listened to Cuthbert and Simons argue. Back and forth about the damned phone. Hang it up or not. Finally, Simons hung it up. Slaughter fought his eyes open, heard Cuthbert say that it would only be a couple more minutes. No more than five. Then they could all go home. The P.O.W.s would be in Maddigan's hands; it would be impossible to recall the soldiers' orders. The prisoners would die. It would be over.

And then Slaughter felt it, just like he'd seen Wooten struck by it in front of Vu Van Vinh a thousand years ago. That spark of something that said, No, I won't let the fear and the pain control me. If I'm going to die here, I'm going to die proud.

The energy started boiling down inside of him and the bubbles effervesced into his limbs. Gave him power. Gave him strength. He would be able to stand, he was sure. Maybe even walk. Try to go over to Cuthbert and take the gun away. Lay out his plan to the others before it was too late. Ready, set . . .

He jerked his legs up, then planted his feet in the puddle of blood. He propelled himself out of the chair and was almost upright when the gun went off, the bullet whistling past his right ear. His eyes popped open and he saw Cuthbert, maybe ten feet away, aiming the handgun at him with a puzzled look on his face.

Was he hit? He couldn't tell. It didn't matter. He was still on his feet. He stepped, then again. Both steps impossibly difficult.

Then another step, a walking dead man. Closer to Cuthbert. Another step. And then again. He would get there. If he could only get his right arm up, get ready to attack, or fall into him, or whatever he could do with what little energy remained after the trip across the room.

Secret Service agents started yelling and pounding on the door. But the door was bolted and wouldn't open. Cuthbert started to back away from Slaughter. But then he stopped, changed direction, retook the ground he'd just given up. He and Slaughter were close. Cuthbert reached out slowly, pressed the end of the small pistol's barrel against Slaughter's forehead, began squeezing the trigger. Slaughter was sure he would not miss from there. No one could.

Slaughter struggled with his right arm, but it felt empty and would not move. He wobbled there for a second, back and forth, hoping to stay upright. Then he leaned forward and rested the weight of his tired head against the barrel of Cuthbert's handgun. He watched the trigger going back. Saw the fanatical look in Cuthbert's eyes. Kept his own eyes open, watching, not wanting to miss the ending.

The second gun blast was huge – much, much louder than the first one. At the same time, the door to the office crashed open, mixing the noise of splintering wood with the explosion of gunpowder.

Then Slaughter saw Cuthbert falling. His legs had gone boneless, his eyes stared with a curious, puzzled look. As Cuthbert folded to the floor, Tanner stepped up to where Cuthbert had been standing. Tanner had a large-frame revolver in his outstretched hand. It was splattered with human tissue and a heavy red bouquet of spray. He kept it trained on the remains of Cuthbert's empty skull until a Secret Service agent ran up and took it away.

"Get my doctor in here," Simons shouted. "Right this second! You," he said, aiming his long finger at the Secret Service agent who held Tanner. "Let him go! Tanner, get Phong back on the line! Slaughter, I'm going to call this off; I'm going to tell Phong not to release the prisoners. Is that right? Answer me, damn it! Is that right? Are you sure you have a workable plan?"

Slaughter shuffled toward the desk without lifting his feet. Tanner was already there, punching numbers like an efficient bookkeeper. Simons was bent over his desk, his head down and twisted around so he could look up into Slaughter's face, see whatever answer was coming.

"It will work," Slaughter said. "I'm sure. It will work. Don't . . . don't release the prisoners yet. Please."

He propped himself against the desk with his good right arm, waited to hear Simons say the words.

"Mr. Phong? It's President Simons again. You can have your Most Favored Nation status. I swear it by God in heaven. But do not, under any circumstances, do not release those P.O.W.s to the soldiers that are on their way. I repeat, do not release those prisoners to our soldiers until we make other arrangements. Are you absolutely clear on that?"

Slaughter's eyes were closed again. He could not stand any longer. Someone was bandaging his arm, but he had no strength to see who it was, could not feel what they were doing. He dropped to his knees, heard whoever was working on him cuss.

"Great," Simons said. "So you still have the prisoners? That's great. Hold onto them for us. I'll call you back soon. Yes. Don't mention it, Mr. Phong. And thanks. Thank you very, very much."

Slaughter hit the floor when the phone hit the cradle.

23

Slaughter laid on the stretcher, concentrated on the thump-thump-thump of the helicopter's rotor, tried to enjoy his trip to the hospital. His life was slipping away, almost gone. He wanted to savor the last minutes.

A doctor floated over him, working like hell. "Hang on, buddy," he said. "You can do it. Damn you, hang on! We're almost there."

Slaughter had no feelings anymore. Nothing hurt at all. At least, nothing physical. But his heart was aching. He wanted so badly to see Wooten scoop his daughter, Sarah, into his arms and hold her, squeeze his love into her, start making up for some of those lost years.

But even worse, he was sad to leave Laura. He wished he'd had the chance to apologize. Tell her he loved her once more. Thank her for loving him and putting up with his weakness – his fear of another obligation, the reason they'd never married. He closed his eyes, damned himself for his stupidity. For what he was leaving behind.

When President Simon's medical chopper landed, he opened his eyes a little. Laura stood at the edge of the landing pad. He saw her through the window, recognized her instantly, even through the gauzy haze that shrouded everything. She was beautiful as she paced back and forth, pinching her lower lip with her fingers.

She stopped, frozen, while he was pulled out and put on a gurney. Then she burst forward and ran to him, quickly talked her way through the cadre of Secret Service agents that had escorted him.

"Jacob," she sobbed. "Oh, Jacob, I'm so sorry."

She was on the wrong side, his left. He had no fingers with which to touch her. He lost her for a second when the corpsmen shoved his gurney through some doors. He kept watching for her to come back, could barely hear her in the background, arguing with a nurse, using her medical degree and the president's name to force herself onto the staff at Walter Reed Army Hospital. Then she was back beside him.

He suddenly felt stronger for her presence. He wanted to tell her that and thank her for coming. But he couldn't do anything but blink. Could hardly even do that.

"It's all right, Jacob. It's really going to be all right. They've said I can stay with you through the surgeries. I'll be here when you wake up. And you will wake up again, Jacob. I promise."

He was in an operating room now. There were no windows. He could not see anything but a huge light and faces looking down on him. More and more of them were wearing masks now. Someone put a mask on Laura.

She leaned close to him and checked his eyes. First one and then the other. She studied them carefully, then put her mouth beside his ear. "I know, Jacob. I know everything that happened. Everything. Now be quiet, sweetheart. Let the doctors do their job. I'll be with you every second."

His eyes closed against his will. He struggled to keep them open, wanted to keep looking at her soft eyes that were just beginning to stream tears for him. But he couldn't do it. He felt someone cutting off his clothes, but he could not get his eyes open to see that, either. And then, everything traveled far, far away, and disappeared.

The first person he saw was Laura, standing over him, stroking his hair. She smiled when he opened his eyes.

The room was quiet. The hustle of the operating room was gone. The only sound was a muted beeping.

"Hi," she said, caressing his forehead with her tender fingers. "How do you feel?"

His lips wouldn't work, his mouth was too dry. But she was on his right side now, so he wiggled his hand a little and she took it. He touched her palm, noticed how soft her skin was.

"Good news, Jacob. The doctors say you'll probably get some use of your fingers back. Isn't that great. You'll never play the piano, but there's a decent chance you'll be able to handle silverware again."

Slaughter counted himself as being lucky. He would live, and Laura was here. Everything else was incidental.

She couldn't seem to stop smiling. She started to laugh. Then tears paired up with her laughing. She sobbed and laughed for a minute or more, a half-crazy look on her face.

After another minute she managed to stop, looked carefully around the room, then leaned close as she wiped her eyes. "Jacob, can you understand me?"

He raised his eyebrows, then let them fall back down. Kept his eyes as steady as he could.

"Good. Jacob, you need to know two things. Everything else can wait for later. But you have to remember what I tell you. Can you do it?"

He could. He was sure he could, even with the drugs. He lifted his eyebrows again.

She was whispering, almost too close to his ear.

"Walter Mills was killed in a robbery attempt, Jacob. Okay? Have you got that? He was walking alone in front of the White

House and he was mugged. The mugger killed him for his wallet. Are you clear on that?"

He moved his eyes. Up, then down.

"Good. Now this next part won't come out for a few days. They want to give Mills' death some time to settle. But they're going to say that Cuthbert died of a heart attack. They will say he was jogging. Collapsed and died, all very suddenly. Have you got it?"

Some machine that Slaughter was hooked up to began to buzz, and a nurse rushed over to check it. She pushed Laura out of the way. Laura stepped back, her eyes stuck on Slaughter and getting bigger with the increasing distance. She was waiting, standing on her tip-toes now, needing an answer. Waiting for it. Wearing the questions on her face: Had he heard her? Would he remember? Would he go along with the story?

He blinked his eyes. Forced his lips apart and breathed out the word. "Yes."

24

Old B-29 bomber carcasses stood in long, cannibalized formations, tarnished monuments to past wars. Most of the wings were missing. Loose pieces of aircraft aluminum slapped steadily in the harsh desert wind. The haunting sounds were made that much more eerie by the overwhelming silence. Nothing but the metal moved for as far as Slaughter could see, all the way to the horizon – a series of low bluffs that gave the deserted airbase the effect of being in a large bowl.

The hangers of the abandoned airfield outside of Kingman, Arizona, were dilapidated, too – dusty, empty catacombs, more than three acres apiece. Scorpions squared off with the people who dared too close to the corners, challenged the people's movements as Slaughter's guests kicked around the place, looking for some way to kill the day while waiting for the sounds of jet engines.

Eighteen hours came and went, every second of them as slow and protracted as the halting drip of an old faucet. No one was allowed to wander out of the hangar. Anyone dressed in bright clothing was kept far away from the openings.

Small huddles of people waited in silence or spoke to each other in reverent murmurs. Sometimes they would shuffle up to the holes where windows had once been and look out, scan the sky for a minute or so. Then they'd walk away. It was a ritual. Everyone who was allowed took a turn doing it.

Laura stood beside Slaughter, over near a side wall, her arm draped around his waist and carefully avoiding his healing wounds. She'd been silent most of the day. He hadn't spoken much, either. Although they had agreed to forget the bad things they'd said to each other, they were both sure they couldn't. But at least they could bury them. Be like other couples and lock down the hurt and disappointment. Go on from there.

He would be happy to stand there forever. He never wanted her hand to move away.

Their buses were hidden in the next hanger. They had all come under cover of darkness, most of them riding from Twentynine Palms Marine Corps Base in two leased Greyhounds with military drivers. They had left nothing outside of the shabby hangars to indicate that forty-two civilians and a small military contingency had migrated here last night, then spent all day waiting. When darkness fell again, they would leave the same way. But, with a little luck, twenty-three others would be leaving with them.

Slaughter and Laura were the only ones who had arrived by plane, a small military passenger jet. It would hold ten people, enough space for them to be joined by Chuck Wooten and his wife. And, of course, Sarah. In addition to the sack lunches the Marines had provided for everyone, Slaughter had stocked his plane with all the things he thought Chuck Wooten might want, including the three things he knew Wooten loved: orange juice, chocolate bars, and ice-cold beer. He kept dreaming about the celebration, could hardly wait for the prisoners' plane to land. Was it circling somewhere, waiting for darkness? Or was it still crossing the Pacific, an ordinary Air Force transport plane with a crew sworn to secrecy?

Anne Kinsey walked up and smiled at Laura, introduced herself and her son, then asked Slaughter about his hand. She smiled at him, too, and giggled a little when he managed to get the fingers to twitch. There was a sparkle in her eye, as if she knew the whole story. But Slaughter was sure it was impossible. No one would have told what happened that night. Only a handful knew.

And he was glad it had happened, injuries and all. He'd gone over it several times in his mind, honestly believed that if any of the events had failed to happen last week, he and Laura and a bunch of loving family members would not be standing here now, waiting for Wooten and the others.

He did miss Mills, though. He would remember his bravery forever.

The sun was going down, but the desert heat was still drying out their mouths. Most of the drinks – except for the ones they'd saved for the celebration – were gone now, but the hot, thin air continued to blow streams of sand through cracks and old bullet holes. The grainy sand stuck to people's faces and mingled in their eyebrows, but no one seemed to mind.

Kinsey's grown son was the first to hear the plane, right at dusk, when there was still enough natural light for the pilot to make out the runway. Its engines were screaming over the desert wind as it turned onto its final approach. The young man started running for the door but stopped about halfway there and looked at Slaughter. He understood the shake of Slaughter's head, turned and went back to wait with his mother.

Suddenly, the small group of soldiers started banging back the huge hangar doors, making room for the giant aircraft. The crowd of civilians moved back in a receding wave.

The screaming military jet rolled toward them with too much speed, following the quick hand signals of a ground crewman who was running backwards. The big jet barely slowed as it rolled into the hangar. It looked like it might roll right through and come out the other side. All the people had their fingers in their ears, their eyes showing their worry.

The ground crewman backed all the way through the hangar, then stopped suddenly and signaled for the plane to stop. The pilot hit the brakes, hard. The wheels stopped turning, the plane lurched forward. It rocked back and forth several times as it settled down – like a huge, trained bear who didn't like doing tricks.

The soldiers banged the hangar doors closed. The pilot shut down the plane's engines. The hangar was suddenly quiet, except for the steady hum of the auxiliary power unit. Some of the civilians started crying as they strained to see through the plane's windows, trying to beat the flashlights' reflections and catch a ghost's vision.

Then time slowed to baby-steps and nothing seemed to happen. Slaughter became restless, ached for the reunion, hoped that nothing had gone wrong at the release point, or on the flight. He looked around at all the family members, standing on their toes, or sobbing, and he suddenly worried about them, hoped none would be disappointed. No one Stateside really knew for sure how many men were on the plane or which ones they might be. Did all twenty-three survive the trip? There had been no communication from Vietnam or from the cockpit. They would have to wait and see.

It seemed to take forever.

Finally, the plane's rear stairs lowered. A battle-dressed Army colonel walked down them and stopped, looked at none of the people staring at him. Instead, he surveyed the crowd, as if searching for someone in particular. He moved once he spotted Slaughter.

He was a tough-looking soldier. His beret was cocked to the right side of his shaved head, opposite a large, ragged scar that ran the entire length of his face and dribbled down his neck.

He parted the crowd like Moses, marched straight up to Slaughter and snapped to rigid attention. "Good evening, sir. I'm Colonel Maddigan. Are you Slaughter?"

Slaughter straightened in his suit, rose about an inch. "Yes."

Maddigan smiled and reached out his hand. Most of the people behind them were splitting their attention between this conversation and the plane. But none of them said anything. Even the wind seemed to have quieted down.

Maddigan looked at Slaughter's injuries. He grinned, like he could relate to the experience. "Mr. Slaughter, I want you to know how much I respect what you've done. This is a damn fine thing. I'm sure it wasn't easy to accomplish."

Slaughter twisted around a little and gazed at the fuselage, thirty feet away and twenty feet above them. He gave Maddigan his good right hand. "President Simons did it."

The colonel nodded, snorted. "Whatever. I just wanted to thank you personally, sir."

Slaughter wrenched his hand away before Maddigan broke it. "You're welcome."

Maddigan snapped back to attention. He snatched a file from under his left arm and held it out to Slaughter. "Sir, it is my great pleasure to return to you twenty-three of the bravest American fighting men I have ever had the pleasure of meeting. They have all been made aware of the circumstances of their release, sir, and all are committed to the preservation of this sensitive secret."

Slaughter took the file. "Colonel Maddigan, have you thoroughly explained to them that they and their immediate families will be given new identifications? Do they know that their families will be moved, and together they will live under the same restrictions as those in the Witness Protection Program?"

Maddigan smiled again. Only one side of his face moved. "Sir, you could tell them they would have to live the rest of their lives in *this* shit-hole little town and they'd love you for it."

Maddigan blushed. It was an interesting look for him. "Begging your pardon, sir, but you're not *from* this shit-hole little town, are you?"

"No."

"Good." He snapped back to attention, whipped his hand up to a perfect salute. "Mr. Slaughter," he said in a loud, formal voice, as if he were speaking to everyone in the hangar, "request permission to disembark these proud military men, sir!"

Slaughter returned the salute. "Thank you, Colonel Maddigan."

Maddigan's face struggled with a smile. He did a crisp about-face, then marched back to the rear exit stairs of the plane. An enlisted soldier stood at the bottom of the stairs holding a clipboard. Maddigan took the clipboard from the young soldier's hands, turned to face the forty-two civilians in the hangar.

Maddigan cleared his voice, threw out his chest, began in an auditorium voice. "Ladies and gentlemen," he paused. "Wooten, Charles R., Captain, United States Marine Corps."

Slaughter rose onto the tips of his toes, even though he had no trouble seeing over the crowd. He waited in that position, would stay there as long as it took.

First, a pair of feet shuffled down the stairs. Then a thin, frail body came into view. Finally, the specter of Chuck Wooten, looking damned fine in a new uniform, touched American soil for the first time in three decades. He found Slaughter in the crowd before he did anything else, threw a weak salute across the room. He stood at attention and waited until Slaughter returned it. Then he angled off in the direction of a small commotion. Sarah was building momentum, breaking into a run toward the rear of the plane. Mrs. Wooten chased after her.

Wooten did his best to run to them, moving his busted body with sad determination. They collided, and he dug himself into their arms, hugged them so hard his new hat fell off and rolled on the ground. Mrs. Wooten kissed him, stepped back to look him over, then hugged and kissed him again. Sarah turned away from them both, flung her face into her hands and sobbed.

The crowd watch for a minute, then turned their attention back to Maddigan. He shook himself a little, straightened inside his fatigues, cleared a crack out of his voice before he announced, "Kinsey, Robert R., Captain, United States Army."

Kinsey came running down the ramp with a wild-man's whoop. He must have seen his wife from the window because he ran straight to her, lifted her off her feet and spun her around two times. Then he hugged her so tight she gasped, giggling through her tears. It was like he'd never missed a meal, he was that strong. But his face had no meat under the flesh. His eyes were so far back in his head they were completely covered by shadows. Slaughter decided the power was adrenaline, and nothing more.

Kinsey let go of his wife and turned, slowly. Quietly, he studied the grown man who stood too close to be a stranger. He took off his hat and made a small step toward the man. He held out his right hand.

Kinsey's son took the hand and began to shake it. Then suddenly he lunged, let go of the hand and climbed into his father's arms like he was five years old again. And then they were both crying.

Maddigan had stopped to watch, as everyone had. Kinsey and his family began to shuffle away, all of them crying now. Maddigan wiped at his own eyes, then read the third name. "Terrence, William J., Lieutenant, United States Navy."

Another man came down the steps, the prisoner Slaughter had known as Rabbit. He'd been two cells away from Slaughter his first year in prison, a handsome young man with a quick wit.

But no one ran to meet Rabbit. He passed through the crowd as it split apart for him. Everyone stared. Some of the people touched him gently as he walked by them.

Rabbit stopped at the back and turned around, held out his arms, his palms up, as if he would die without a hug. He was crying. His tormented face looked more alone than any face Slaughter could ever remember seeing. Slowly, Rabbit lowered his arms and passed through the crowd again. Walked to the hangar wall and slid down it. Crumbled onto the concrete floor, alone.

Laura slipped away from Slaughter's side and walked over to Rabbit. Slaughter prayed she'd be able to make him understand why his former wife could not be trusted with this secret, that the rest of Rabbit's family was dead. He hoped it wouldn't end up being a terrible problem, was glad Laura was there to help Rabbit get through it.

Everyone turned back to Maddigan, and the clipboard, and the stairs. But Maddigan was still watching Rabbit. Maddigan looked soft now. Compassionate. Hurt.

Slaughter felt bad for the families he hadn't trusted enough to tell, even as he knew it was best. The secret could only go so far.

25

Slaughter was ready for bed before Laura. It had been a long day and a long flight back from Kingman. He climbed into the bed and turned on the television, began watching CNN while waiting for her. He gently touched the remote, giving his left hand some exercise, using his reattached fingers to turn up the volume when President Simons' segment come on.

"Laura, you want to see this?"

She called out from the walk-in closet. "Simons?"

"Yes."

"No. No, thanks, Jacob. I saw it a little earlier."

Slaughter had, too. He wouldn't hear anything new, but he had to listen anyway.

Simons stood at the lectern, smiling, wearing his press-conference face. The podium's presidential seal was already adding quiet significance to whatever he would say.

"Ladies and gentlemen," he began, "I'm very happy to announce that, with the full support of Congress, I have just signed legislation that removes the final trade barriers between the United States and the Socialist Republic of Vietnam. It is exciting to all of us that America's relationship with this former enemy has developed into something so positive. I am convinced that when the final history of our two countries is written, this new relationship will be seen as having a much more significant impact than did the enmity that existed so many years ago. While we are not forgetting the valiant men and women on both sides who fought so bravely in that conflict, I believe that granting Vietnam a Most Favored Nation trading status is a necessary and righteous step along the path of mutual healing."

Simons stopped, looked up and waited for questions. He did not have to wait long.

"President Simons," a reporter called from the front row, "what implications does this trade agreement have on the continuing efforts to account for those military personnel missing in action in Vietnam or held as prisoners of war."

Simons' smile grew bigger. He looked sincere as he leaned against the lectern. "I'm sorry you keep asking the question that has been fully answered hundreds of times before. But, since you have asked, let me repeat what I've said all along. Vietnam has provided thorough and conclusive evidence regarding the missing P.O.W.s and M.I.A.s. There is nothing more they can do. The fact is, every war produces victims. Lots of them. Some of those victims are the men who are never accounted for. But as sad as that is, I believe it is unjust to single out Vietnam and punish them eternally for the unaccounted men of this particular conflict."

Laura stepped into the room, wearing one of his T-shirts. She slid into bed while he snapped off the television.

"Jacob, where is Chuck Wooten going to move with his wife?"

"Arizona. Somewhere around Phoenix. He's hoping the dry heat will be good for his injuries."

She snuggled up beside him. "That sounds nice. It's a long way from Sarah, though, and his grandchildren."

Slaughter sat up straight, used his right hand to smooth the sheets over his legs. "I talked to Sarah at the hangar. She told me she's moving out there, too. She and Benjamin can get jobs in Phoenix, so that she can spend a lot of time catching up with her father. It will be good for her and the kids."

Laura sat up, too. She leaned over and kissed him. "I'm sorry, Jacob. I know how much you'll miss them. Do you think they'll ever come back to visit?"

"Oh, sure. I don't think they'll forget me. Or you, either. Besides, we'll go out there and visit them, too."

"Sure we will. We'll still see them pretty often."

"That's right." He looked around the room. "I will miss them, though."

She scooted under the covers, took his good hand, wove their fingers together. "I know."

Nothing was said for a few minutes. He was thinking about Chuck Wooten. He was a free man again, back on American soil, back in the arms of his family. Back where he belonged.

Slaughter had not failed him. He had made a commitment, and he had kept it. Too many years had passed in the process, but he would forgive himself for that. He had to. The important thing was that someone he loved had counted on him, and he had not let them down. He felt better about himself than he had for decades.

"Laura, I've been thinking."

Her head was on his pillow, her body nuzzled up against him.

"What about?"

He touched her hair. Stroked it. "About us."

"Oh?"

"Yes. I think. . . that is, if it's all right with you, I was thinking. . ."

She sat up, slowly, her eyes wide open and her mouth smiling, just a little. "Yes?"

"Well, you know. We've been together for a long time, and I was wondering if, well . . ."

293

She started to giggle, like a girl being asked out for a first date. But she didn't say anything. Just watched him struggling.

"I guess I'm wondering . . . if you'd marry me?"

She held a hand over her mouth, as though she would break out laughing without it. "You guess? You're not sure you want to marry me?"

He laughed, too. But his was nerves. "No, of course I don't mean that I'm guessing. I mean, Laura, would you please marry me?"

She moved her hand away from her mouth, still smiling and shaking her head with mock doubt. "Gee, I don't know, Jacob. I always figured that when I got married, I'd cut back on my work and start a family pretty quickly. Get a nice brood of kids and a two-story house in Herndon. Things like that. A lot of work, you know. Lots of obligations."

"I know."

"And you're ready for that kind of responsibility?"

It wasn't even a question in his mind. He had no doubt. It was amazing. "Yes. Absolutely. I'm ready."

She sat up on her knees, looked straight into his eyes. "In that case, Mr. Jacob Slaughter, I will marry you."

He pushed himself up with his good arm. Kissed her gently. "Thank you," he said. "Thank you for everything."

She straddled his lap, the hem of her T-shirt rising. "You're welcome." She kissed him back.

Slaughter slid down under the covers, too, feeling great, looking forward to their future together. And looking forward to tonight.

They would make love, and that would be terrific. But tonight, he was anticipating something new and wonderful. Sleep. Chuck Wooten was back home. His specter no longer needed to haunt Slaughter's dreams. Tonight, Jacob Slaughter would sleep alone. He would be beside Laura, of course, holding her as best he could with his crippled body. But his mind would finally be free of the ghost.

It would be wonderful.

According to the United States Senate's 1993 report, the following is a *conservative* listing of names of still unaccounted for U.S. personnel from the Vietnam conflict. Approximately 300 of the 324 names were last known alive in captivity in Vietnam and Laos, out of their aircraft before they crashed, or their names were passed to POWs who later returned.

Acosta-Rosario, Humberto - last known to be alive
Adam, John G. - name mentioned by Soviet correspondent
Adams, Lee Aaron - second hand knowledge provided by returning POW
Algard, Harold L. - possibly captured alive (according to NSA)
Allard, Richard M. - identified by family in Viet Cong film clips
Allinson, David J. - good chute observed
Anderson, Gregory Lee - beeper heard for short period
Anderson, Robert D. - returning POW believes Anderson ejected
Andrews, William R. - voice contact made on ground
Ard, Randolph J. - out of aircraft before crash
Armstrong, John W. - captured, interviewed by Soviet correspondent
Ashlock, Carlos - last known to be alive
Avery, Robert D. - POW according to passed down list
Ayers, Gerald F. - POW reportedly held in cell 5, Hoa Lao prison
Ayers, Richard L. - possibly held in Cu Loc and Zoo prisons
Babula, Robert L. - last known to be alive
Backus, Kenneth F. - believed to eject safely, and alive on ground
Baker, Arthur D. - believed to eject safely, and alive on ground
Balcom, Ralph C. - out of aircraft before crash
Bancroft, William W. - possibly captured, according to NSA
Bannon, Paul W. - possible correlation to live-sighting
Barden, Howard L. - survival possible
Beene, James A. - name heard in prison by returning POW
Begley, Burriss N. - name scratched on floor at Hoa Lo prison
Bennett, William G. - reported as POW on Hanoi radio broadcast
Bodenschatz, John E. - last known to be alive
Bogiages, Christos C. - out of aircraft before crash
Borah, Daniel V. - known captured (NSA). Last known to be alive
Borton, Robert C. - last known to be alive
Bouchard, Michael - possible POW in good health (prison notes)
Bram, Richard C. - last known to be alive. Vietnam named him as a POW
Brandenberg, Dale - believed to have been captured
Brashear, William J. - believed out of aircraft and alive on ground
Brennan, Herbert O. - believed out of aircraft and alive on ground

Breuer, Donald C. - enemy reported their attempt to capture Breuer

Brown, George R. - left alive and unwounded after failed rescue

Brown, Harry W. - last known to be alive

Brown, Robert M. - captured alive

Brownlee, Charles R. - out of aircraft before crash

Brownlee, Robert W. - evaded on ground with RVN Lt.

Brucher, John M. - voice contact made. Last known to be alive

Buckley, Louis - last known to be alive

Buell, Kenneth R. - possibly captured, according to NSA

Bunker, Park G. - out of aircraft before crash

Burnett, Sheldon J. - out of aircraft before crash

Bynum, Neil S. - probably ejected, then captured (NSA)

Carlock, Ralph L. - POW, captured by Pathet Lao forces

Carr, Donald Gene - reported as POW

Carroll, John L. - out of aircraft before crash

Carter, Dennis R. - last known to be alive

Champion, James - observed walking away from crash site in good cond.

Chestnut, Joseph L. - captured. Sighted alive in captivity after the war

Cichon, Walter A. - last known to be alive, probably captured (NSA)

Clark, Richard C. - captured. Name on memorized list of POWs

Clarke, Fred L. - one parachute observed from mid-air collision

Clarke, George W. - hostile captured. Listed as POW. Last known alive

Coady, Robert F. - POW, according to prison hearsay

Cohron, James D. - last know to be alive

Collamore, Allan P. - tap code prison contact made with returning POW

Condit, Douglas C. - believed out of aircraft and alive on the ground

Cook, Dwight W. - identified as POW by Thai returnees

Cook, Kelly F. - believed out of aircraft and alive on the ground

Cornwell, Leroy J. - name reported by returning POW

Cramer, Donald R. - name memorized by POW in Cu-Loc & Zoo prisons

Creed, Barton S. - voice contact on ground, listed as POW

Cressman, Peter R. - believed to have been captured

Crew, James A. - believed out of aircraft and alive on the ground

Cristman, Frederick L. - out of aircraft before crash

Crockett, William J. - possibly captured

Cushman, Clifton E. - reported as prisoner by returning POW

Cuthbert, Bradley G. - seen alive in good chute

Dahill, Douglas E. - last known to be alive

Dale, Charles A. - last known to be alive

Danielson, Benjamin F. - out of aircraft before crash

Davies, Joseph E. - believed alive according to returning POW

Davidson, David A. - captured alive by enemy forces

Davis, Edgar F. - out of aircraft before crash
Debruin, Eugene H. - shown alive in photo
DeLong, Joe L. - listed as POW by DIA
Demmon, David S. - hostile capture, listed as POW, last known to be alive
Dexter, Bennie L. - POW. Capture witnessed. Last known to be alive
Dickson, Edward A. - ejected from aircraft
Dinan, David T. - out of aircraft before crash
Dingwall, John F. - possible POW (SVN). Last known to be alive
Dodge, Edward R. - last known to be alive
Donahue, Morgan - subject of live-sighting reports
Dooley, James E. - POW. Name reportedly seen on prison wall
Duckett, Thomas A. - out of aircraft before crash
Dunlop, Thomas E. - believed out of aircraft and alive on the ground
Dunn, Michael E. - believed out of aircraft and alive on the ground
Edwards, Harry S. - possible POW according to prison hearsay
Egan, James T. - last known to be alive
Eidsmoe, Norman E. - believed out of aircraft and alive on the ground
Elliot, Robert M. - captured. POW according to reliable sources
Ellis, William - last known to be alive
Ellison, John C. - positively identified as POW in picture
Entrican, Danny D. - last known alive and captured
Estocin, Michael J. - captured by enemy, listed as POW
Fallon, Patrick M. - out of aircraft before crash
Finley, Dickie W. - last known to be alive
Fischer, Richard W. - last known to be alive
Fitzgerald, Joseph E. - last known to be alive
Fitzgerald, Paul L. - last known to be alive
Fors, Gary H. - out of aircraft before crash
Foulks, Ralph E. - possible prisoner according to POW returnee
Fowler, Donald R. - last known to be alive
Francisco, San D. - voice contact on ground, listed as POW
Fryer, Bruce C. - out of aircraft before crash
Gage, Robert H. - last known to be alive
Galbraith, Russell D. - out of aircraft before crash
Gallant, Henry J. - last known to be alive
Garcia, Ricardo M. - out of aircraft before crash
Gassman, Fred A. - captured alive by enemy
Gates, James W. - radio contact on ground. Last known to be alive
Gerstel, Donald A. - known captured according to NSA
Glasson, William A. - downed and captured in China
Gould, Frank A. - subject of 1990's live sighting reports from Laos
Grace, James W. - alive, identified by family in Communist prop. film

Graf, John G. - captured by enemy, POW, believed alive in 1973
Green, Frank C. - known captured
Greenleaf, Joseph G. - believed out of aircraft and alive on the ground
Greenwood, Robert R. - believed to be POW at the Zoo prison
Greiling, David S. - captured, name heard in prison system
Groth, Wade L. - last known to be alive
Gunn, Alan W. - last known to be alive
Hamilton, John S. - believed out of aircraft and alive on the ground
Hamilton, Roger D. - last known to be alive
Hamm, James E. - believed out of aircraft and alive on the ground
Hargrove, Olin - last known to be alive
Harris, Jeffrey L. - possibly captured (NSA)
Harris, Reuben, B. - believed downed and captured in China
Harrison, Donald L. - reported as prisoner by returning POW
Hasenback, Paul A. - last known to be alive
Hastings, Steven M. - last known to be alive
Held, John W. - believed out of aircraft and alive on the ground
Helwig, Roger D. - out of aircraft before crash
Hentz, Richard J. - possibly captured alive (NSA)
Herold, Richard W. - out of aircraft before crash
Hesford, Peter D. - believed out of aircraft and alive on the ground
Hess, Frederick W. - out of aircraft before crash
Hestle, Roosevelt - reportedly seen alive at Heartbreak prison
Hicks, Terrin D. - believed captured alive and taken to Dong Hoi
Hodgson, Cecil J. - last known to be alive
Holland, Melvin A. - captured, based on '91 comment by P.L. General
Holley, Tilden - believed to be prisoner at Cu Loc & Zoo by returning POW
Holmes, David H. - out of aircraft before crash. SAR unable to locate pilot
Holmes, Frederick L. - POW believed to have been held at Cu Loc and Zoo
Hrdlicka, David - POW. Voice recording, letter, & signature were released
Huberth, Eric J. - possibly ejected from F4D, then captured
Hunt, Robert W. - last known alive in close proximity to enemy
Hunter, Russell P. - out of aircraft before crash
Huston, Charles G. - left alive and unwounded after failed rescue
Ibanez, Di R. - last known to be alive
Jackson, Paul V. - known captured (NSA)
Jakovac, John A. - last known to be alive
Jeffs, Clive G. - believed out of aircraft and alive on the ground
Jewell, Eugene M. - returning POWs believed Jewell to be a prisoner
Johns, Vernon Z. - captured, POW, last known to be alive
Johnson, Bruce G. - last known to be alive
Johnson, William D. - last known to be alive

Johnston, Steven B. - out of aircraft before crash
Jones, Bobby M. - seen alive in prison by returning POWs
Jordan, Larry M. - downed and captured in China
Kennedy, John W. - known to have been captured (NSA)
Ketchie, Scott D. - out of aircraft before crash
Kiefel, Ernest P. - out of aircraft before crash
Kier, Larry G. - possible POW held in isolation
Knutson, Richard A. - reported as prisoner by returning POW
Koons, Dale F. - POW, reported in good condition at Plantation prison
Kosko, Walter - known to have ejected. ID card seen in prison
Kryszak, Theodore E. - no trace of crew at wreckage site
Kubley, Roy R. - survival possible according to DIA analytical comment
LaFayette, John W. - believed out of aircraft and alive on the ground
Lane, Charles - believed out of aircraft, possibly alive on the ground
Lawrence, Bruce E. - name heard in prison by returning POW
Lee, Leonard M. - believed out of aircraft and alive on the ground
Leeser, Leonard C. - beeper heard for short period
Lemon, Jeffrey C. - possibly captured alive (NSA)
Lerner, Irwin S. - believed out of aircraft and alive on the ground
Lester, Roderick B. - orders given by enemy to capture this pilot
Lewandowski, Leonard - reports of name on radio, and photo in magazine
Lewis, James W. - believed out of aircraft and alive on the ground
Long, John - POW in good cond. at Citadel, Holiday Inn, & Vegas prisons
Lull, Howard B. - POW seen alive, then captured, by returning POWs
Luna, Carter P. - voice contact on ground, believed captured
Lundy, Albro L. - post-capture photo identified by family
Malone, Jimmy M. - last known to be alive
Mamiya, John M. - identified by Thai returnees
Mangino, Thomas A. - last known to be alive
Marik, Charles W. - ejected with good chute
Marker, Michael W. - possibly captured alive (NSA)
Martin, Russell D. - no trace of crew found at wreckage
Massucci, Martin J. - possibly last known to be alive
Matejov, Joseph A. - believed captured (NSA)
Mauterer, Oscar - ejected, alive on the ground, possibly captured
McCarty, James L. - good chute observed
McCleary, George C. - POW positively identified in Christmas photo
McCrary, Jack - radio contact
McDonald, Joseph W. - POW in Ha Lo prison in good condition
McDonald, Kurt C. - believed out of aircraft and alive on the ground
McDonnell, John T. - last known to be alive
McElvain, James R. - name possibly heard on radio broadcast

McGar, Brain K. - last known to be alive
McIntire, Scott W. - out of aircraft before crash. Possible POW (NSA)
McLean, James H. - POW, capture confirmed. Last known alive
McPherson, Everett A. - name believed to be on Cu Loc prisoner list
Mellor, Frederic M. - voice contact, uninjured
Melton, Todd M. - believed captured (NSA)
Milius, Paul L. - out of aircraft before crash
Millner, Michael - last known to be alive
Mims, George I. - believed out of aircraft and alive on the ground
Mitchell, Harry E. - possibly seen
Miyazaki, Ronald K. - survival possible from crash, but no sign
Moreland, James L. - last seen alive and unwounded on the ground
Morgan, James S. - believed out of aircraft and alive on the ground
Morris, George W. - possible voice contact, believed alive on the ground
Morrissey, Robert D. - captured alive. Name on list of POWs (NSA)
Morrow, Larry K. - last known to be alive
Mossman, Harry S. - NSA intercepted enemy orders to capture Mossman
Mullen, William F. - out of aircraft before crash
Mullins, Harold E. - no trace of crew at wreckage site
Mundt, Henry G. - believed out of aircraft and alive on the ground
Netherland, Roger M. - believed out of aircraft and alive on the ground
Newton, Charles V. - last known to be alive
Newton, Donald S. - last known to be alive
Nichols, Hubert - similar name seen on wall at Heartbreak and Zoo prisons
Nidds, Daniel R. - last known to be alive
O'Grady, John F. - ejected and captured
Osborne, Rodney L. - possibly captured alive
Parker, Woodrow W. - POW at Citadel and Country Club prisons
Parsley, Edward M. - reported as possible POW "name familiar"
Paschall, Ronald P. - pulled alive from aircraft
Patterson, James K. - POW, identified by captors to returning prisoners
Pender, Orland J. - possible POW. Name heard by returning prisoner
Perrine, Elton L. - believed out of aircraft and alive on the ground
Perry, Randolph A. - possibly heard on camp radio. Reported by returnees
Peterson, Delbert R. - believed out of aircraft and alive on the ground
Peterson, Mark A. - reported as captured (NSA)
Phillips, Daniel R. - last seen alive and unwounded by returning POW
Phillips, Robert P. - captured, listed as POW
Pierson, William C. - POW, according to prison. Name on prison note
Pike, Dennis S. - out of aircraft before crash
Pittman, Allan D. - out of aircraft before crash
Plassmeyer, Bernard H. - believed out of aircraft and alive on the ground

Platt, Robert L. - last known to be alive
Plumadore, Kenneth L. - last known alive and captured by PAVN forces
Pogreba, Dean A. - believed shot-down and captured in China
Preston, James A. - name heard over Voice of Vietnam or camp radio
Prevedel, Charles F. - last known to be alive
Price, Bunyan D. - seen alive on ground. Captured, listed as POW
Pridemore, Dallas R. - kidnapped from girlfriend's house, listed as POW
Pruett, William D. - beeper heard for short period
Puentes, Manual F. - last seen moving, wounded in ambush
Pugh, Dennis G. - out of aircraft before crash, known captured
Ransbottom, Frederick J. - POW, observed by returning prisoner
Raymond, Paul D. - name heard in prison by returning POW
Reed, James W. - ejected, ordered captured by the enemy
Rehe, Richard R. - observed wounded at NVA interrogation post
Richardson, Dale W. - out of aircraft and alive on the ground, evading
Robertson, John L. - identified by family in post-capture photo
Roe, Jerry L. - last known to be alive
Rose, Luther L. - no trace of crew found at wreckage site
Ross, Joseph S. - name seen on wall at Heartbreak prison
Rowley, Charles S. - positively identified as POW by returning prisoner
Rozo, James Milan - captured, listed as POW, last known to be alive
Russell, Peter J. - last known to be alive
Scharf, Charles J. - last known to be alive
Schmidt, Walter R. - landed alive, listed as POW, last known to be alive
Schultz, Sheldon D. - no sign of crew
Schumann, John R. - POW last known alive working in rice mill
Scull, Gary B. - last known to be alive
Serex, Henry M. - possibly survived as prisoner of war
Seymour, Leo E. - last known to be alive
Shafer, Phillip R. - POW, last known to be alive
Shark, Earl E. - listed as POW by task group in 1975
Shelton, Charles - captured by P.L. forces, voice contact
Shinn, William C. - beeper heard for short period
Shriver, Jerry M. - POW, according to returning prisoner
Sigafoos, Walter H. - possibly captured
Singleton, Daniel L. - returnee had been given name to memorize as POW
Sittner, Ronald N. - believed out of aircraft and alive on the ground
Skinner, Owen G. - out of aircraft before crash
Small, Burt C. - captured, listed as POW
Smith, Harding E. - no trace of crew when wreckage found
Smith, Warren P. - out of aircraft before crash
Soyland, David P. - last known to be alive

Sparks, Donald L. - sent letter as POW. Seen at Hoa Lo, Vegas, Hilton
Sparks, Jon M. - out of aircraft before crash
Spinelli, Domenick A. - subject of post-war live-sighting information
Steen, Martin W. - good chute
Stevens, Larry J. - post-capture photograph positively identified by family
Stewart, Peter J. - post-capture photograph positively identified by family
Stewart, Virgil G. - out of aircraft before crash
Strait, Douglas F. - believed out of aircraft and alive on the ground
Strawn, John T. - possibly captured alive
Strohlein, Madison A. - last known to be alive
Sutton, William C. - beeper heard for short period
Tatum, Lawrence B. - believed out of aircraft and alive on the ground
Taylor, Fred - last known to be alive
Thompson, William J. - POW, according to second hand report of tap code
Tigner, Lee M. - possibly captured
Townsend, Francis W. - last known to be alive. Listed as POW
Trent, Alan R. - possibly captured
Tromp, William L. - captured. Last known to be alive. Listed as POW
Utley, Russel K. - possibly captured
Walker, Bruce C. - alive on the ground. Captured. I.D. in Hanoi museum
Walker, Lloyd F. - survival possible but no sign
Walker, Samuel F. - one parachute observed after mid-air collision
Walton, Lewis C. - captured and moved north by enemy
Warren, Ervin - no trace of crew at wreckage site
Warren, Gray D. - one pilot parachuted and probably captured
Wheeler, Eugene L. - voice contact. Last known to be alive
White, Charles E. - last known to be alive
Wilkins, George H. - identified alive by Thai returnee
Williams, Robert J. - POW. Reportedly seen in Vietnamese magazine
Williamson, James D. - POW
Winters, David M. - last known to be alive
Worth, James F. - last known to be alive
Wood, Don C. - identified in Pathet Lao film
Wood, William C. - out of aircraft before crash
Wright, David I. - possibly captured
Wright, Thomas T. - believed out of aircraft and alive on the ground
Wrobleski, Walter F. - last known to be alive
Zich, Larry A. - POW seen alive in early 1973

---- ---- --- ---- ---- -- ---- ----

"It's over, we can't find them."—*President Richard M. Nixon, referring to prisoners of war on April 11, 1973, eleven weeks after the signing of the Paris Peace Accord*

"It is my studied opinion over the last twelve years that responsible officials within the Executive Branch of the U.S. Government knowingly abandoned U.S. prisoners of war . . . in Southeast Asia. I believe that presidents up through and including George Bush have known that Americans were left alive and, in violation of law, these high officials and certain of their appointed subordinates have continued and perpetrated a cover-up of this reality."—*retired U.S. Army Lt. Colonel James Gritz, former Chief of Congressional Relations, Office of the Secretary of Defense, November 23, 1992*

"Of course Vietnam didn't give a full accounting of prisoners. Now that you have that information, what are you going to do with it, bomb Hanoi?"—*Alexander Haig, former White House Chief of Staff and U.S. Secretary of State*

". . .I think they (P.O.W.s in Southeast Asia) would more appropriately be termed as hostages."—*1995 testimony of Garnett Bell, Negotiator for the Commander, United States Joint Task Force for Full Accounting*

"We can also seize some of these opportunities (for improved relations with Vietnam) to better account for those who remain prisoners of war and missing in action."—*a slip by U.S. Defense Secretary William Cohen, Sept. 19, 1997. Officially, the U.S. Government maintains that it knows of no American servicemen still held as prisoner of war.*

---- ----- ---- -- - -----

Coming next from
Wes DeMott

VAPORS
ISBN 0-9659602-7-7

Vapors is a psychological thriller about America's defense contractors, and the dangerous territory beyond government oversight where secret policy is made. *Vapors* is a story about power, violence, and corruption, and how this savage mixture sucks aerospace engineer Peter Jamison into a deadly fight he does not want and cannot win.

But Jamison is a fool for the love of Melissa Corley, an attorney with The Citizen's Coalition Against Government Waste. When his new enemies snatch her, his addiction to her love turns him vicious—forcing him into the frightening cellar of his soul, the scary place where all humans become capable of terrible acts.

The twists in *Vapors* are exciting, the characters are multi-dimensional, and the ending is shocking. Sterling Watson, whose most recent thriller is *Deadly Sweet* (Pocketbooks), said, "Wes DeMott is in the enviable position of having written a great book with a fantastic ending," and, "*Vapors* captures the constriction and claustrophobia within the FBI, the conformity, paranoia and competition and how all these play out against the possibility that an agent might turn a corner any day and see people shooting at him. *Vapors* has that nailed down, that strange combination of bureaucratic bullshit and violence."

For an advance notice of *Vapors'* publication date, or to contact Wes DeMott for any reason, write him c/o Admiral House Publishing, Client Relations, or E-mail him directly at WDeMott@aol.com